PRAISE FOR
FELICITY HAYES-MCCOY'S NOVELS

'A sparkling, life-affirming novel – sunshine on the page'
Cathy Kelly

'A charming and heart-warming story'
Jenny Colgan

'Page-turning ... curl up and treat yourself
to the perfect escape'
Sinéad Moriarty

'I was utterly charmed – a pitch-perfect delight'
Marian Keyes

'Warm-hearted ... reminiscent of
Maeve Binchy and Roisin Meaney'
Irish Examiner

'Engaging ... sparkling and joyous'
Sunday Times

Felicity Hayes-McCoy, author of the bestselling Finfarran series, was born in Dublin, Ireland. She studied literature at UCD before moving to England in the 1970s to train as an actress. Her work as a writer ranges from TV and radio drama and documentary, to screenplays, music theatre, memoir and children's books. Her Finfarran novels are widely read on both sides of the Atlantic, and in Australia, and have been translated into six languages.

She and her husband, opera director Wilf Judd, live in the West Kerry Gaeltacht and in Bermondsey, London. She blogs about life in both places on her website www.felicityhayesmccoy.co.uk and you can follow her on Twitter @fhayesmccoy and on Facebook at Felicity Hayes-McCoy Author.

ALSO BY FELICITY HAYES-MCCOY

The Finfarran series
The Library at the Edge of the World
Summer at the Garden Café
The Mistletoe Matchmaker
The Month of Borrowed Dreams
The Transatlantic Book Club
The Heart of Summer
The Year of Lost and Found

Non-fiction
The House on an Irish Hillside
Enough is Plenty
A Woven Silence

The
Keepsake
Quilters

Felicity
HAYES-McCOY

HACHETTE
BOOKS
IRELAND

First published in Ireland in 2022 by
HACHETTE BOOKS IRELAND

First published in paperback in 2023

1

Cataloguing in Publication Data is available from the British Library

ISBN 9781529379594

Typeset in Book Antiqua by Bookends Publishing Services, Dublin
Printed and bound in Great Britain by Clays Ltd, Elcograf S.p.A.

Hachette Books Ireland policy is to use papers that are natural, renewable
and recyclable products and made from wood grown in sustainable forests.
The logging and manufacturing processes are expected to conform to the
environmental regulations of the country of origin.

Hachette Books Ireland
8 Castlecourt Centre
Castleknock
Dublin 15, Ireland

A division of Hachette UK Ltd
Carmelite House, 50 Victoria Embankment, London EC4Y 0DZ

www.hachettebooksireland.ie

For Jo

The characters in this novel, their homes and workplaces, exist only in the author's imagination.

The Carson Women

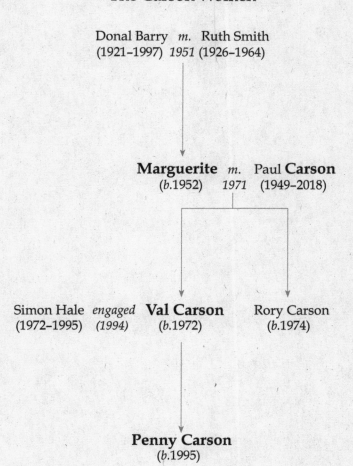

Donal Barry *m.* Ruth Smith
(1921–1997) *1951* (1926–1964)

Marguerite *m.* Paul **Carson**
(*b.*1952) *1971* (1949–2018)

Simon Hale *engaged* **Val Carson**   Rory Carson
(1972–1995) *(1994)* (*b.*1972)   (*b.*1974)

Penny Carson
(*b.*1995)

THE PIECES

THREAD 1

Marguerite

Even the names of fabrics enchanted Marguerite Carson. Chenille, chiffon and cashmere. Dimity, with its intimations of eighteenth-century heroines, and damask, suggestive of eastern bazaars and bowers of exotic roses. Denim defined her youth, when she'd lived in Levi's, but even then, she'd loved vintage textiles, ribbons and lace, and now, more than fifty years later, her mind could still wander happily through a rustling, murmuring alphabet of delights. Georgette, gauzes, crisp starched linen, and pin-tucked muslin. Gossamer-light organza and iridescent shot-silk. Her whole life could be measured out in fabrics, from the hand-embroidered cheesecloth dress she'd made for her wedding, influenced by the heady atmosphere of the Summer of Love, to the dresses she'd sewn for her leggy little daughter, and the dim memory of a 1950s circular taffeta skirt, worn by her mother over net petticoats dipped in sugar water to stiffen them.

Yet the fabric that most brought her mother to mind wasn't taffeta, but tweed. Sensible tweed skirts, redolent of autumn bonfires, worn with gardening boots, a waxed jacket and woollen sweaters. The double thud as wellingtons were eased off on the doorstep, and the smell of grass-stained canvas gauntlets left by the stove to dry. Along with those workaday scents and sounds came a sense-memory, almost beyond conscious recall, which belonged to a drifting state between waking and sleeping. Only by closing her eyes could Marguerite conjure it again – the warmth of her bed, the feeling of deep comfort and perfect safety, and the soft touch of the dark green velvet that bound the edges of the patchwork quilt under which she'd slept as a child.

Chapter One

Marguerite opened the restaurant door and glanced around the interior. The lunchtime rush was over and most of the tables were free. Smiling at the waitress who came to greet her, she indicated a corner by the window. 'There'll be three of us. May we sit here?'

'Of course.' The waitress lifted a chair aside to allow her to wheel her suitcase into the corner. 'Would you like a drink while you're waiting?'

'A coffee. Thank you.'

As the girl went to fetch it, Marguerite sat and looked at her surroundings. This was nothing like the fast-food outlets only a block or two away. Here the tables were laid with crisp linen and polished glasses, and the walls were covered with what appeared to be genuine art-deco tiles. Returning with the coffee, the waitress explained that the restaurant had once been a dairy. 'Back before the First World War. They ladled milk into jugs brought by the customers. And they had carved stamps to put patterns on butter. You can see the design on the menu.'

The charming logo of a cow among grasses and buttercups reminded Marguerite of a length of fabric she'd bought more than forty years ago to make a dress for her daughter. It had been buttercup-yellow poplin with a pattern of daisies and cows. She asked if the original owners' family still ran the restaurant. The girl shook her head. 'No. It's part of a franchise. There's another in Bath, I think, and one in Chelsea.' Not so different, then, thought Marguerite, from all those bustling places a few blocks away. Just differently presented, and none the worse for that. Fast food is fine if you need to eat and run, but this is the perfect setting for a quiet family lunch.

Having lived in London all her married life, she'd had no difficulty in finding the restaurant. It was in a red-brick square behind Bond Street, where white blossom in the central railed garden looked like lace thrown over the trees' dark branches. Five years previously, when she'd been widowed, she'd sold her London house and moved back to her childhood home in Ireland. It was in Wicklow, only a short drive from Dublin, yet London still felt like a natural place for her to go shopping. The spare bedroom in her daughter Val's house was there to welcome her, and a visit improved the chances of seeing her beloved granddaughter Penny, whose job as a TV executive seemed to mean she was seldom free.

That morning, as Marguerite set off for Dublin airport, her garden had been full of golden daffodils growing in drifts under the blossoming fruit trees. Little had changed in the acre of land around the low white villa in the mountains where she'd lived until she married. Her mother had been an enthusiastic gardener and now, thought Marguerite, I'm just the same. If Paul hadn't died, I might have stayed in London. Instead, I potter about the home I grew up in, putting tulips in last year's crocus beds, or cyclamen under the oaks to provide new flashes of crimson, and charmed by the sense of unaltered strength beneath all my superficial changes. No doubt I'll go on enjoying it for the rest of my days, moving colours and shapes but retaining the underlying structure that's bordered my life for as long as I can remember.

The door opened and Val came in, waving when she caught sight of Marguerite. She bent to kiss her cheek and pulled out a chair. 'Sorry I'm late, Mum. Have you been waiting long?'

'You're not late at all. We had a tail-wind.'

'Comfortable flight?'

'Lovely. Smooth as silk and I had a whole row to myself.'

'Penny sent me a text. She's running behind schedule.' Val turned to the waitress, who was hovering in the background. 'I'll have a coffee too, please. We're waiting for my daughter.' No one could have failed to see that Val and Marguerite were related. Each dressed conservatively with touches of style that suggested quiet confidence. Val had inherited her mother's fair hair, clear skin and catlike green eyes and, though Marguerite had grown stiffer with age, both had the same grace of movement.

The waitress smiled. 'That's nice. You, your mum and your daughter being ladies who lunch.'

As the girl disappeared to fetch the coffee, Marguerite considered the unlikely vision her statement had evoked. Camaraderie wasn't a Carson thing. As a family, they were always there for each other, and she and Val knew they could treat each other's homes as their own, but 'ladies who lunch' had conjured up the sort of women who guested on Penny's TV show, over-sharing emotion and quick to give each other relationship advice. Not us at all, thought Marguerite, though it's lovely to sit down together and catch up on all the news – and to be used to eating out again after all the months of Covid restrictions. She turned to Val. 'Why did Penny suggest we meet here, do you know?'

'She sent me a text late yesterday evening. I suppose, if you're planning a short stay, this may be her only chance to spend time with you.'

Marguerite forbore to mention the many visits to London when Penny's diary had been so full that their paths hadn't crossed. She'd gathered that Val didn't see much of her either but, of course, Val had her own work to attend to. She had a full-time job teaching English to foreign students and her evenings were often spent mentoring online, so family occasions tended to be diarised. Marguerite often wished that Val and Penny lived closer to each other, but while Penny's flat was a bike ride from work it was too far from her childhood home in West Hampstead for impromptu visits – even if she'd been the impromptu type, which, emphatically, she wasn't. Twenty-seven-year-old Penny was controlled, efficient and competent, with a flair for team-building and an eye for the kind of quirky soft-news story that made her show one of the highest-rated in morning television.

They'd scarcely had time to taste their coffee before Penny arrived, dressed in jeans and a fashionable oversized sweater. Marguerite smiled in welcome and Val drew out a chair, thinking as she did so that Penny looked pale. Giving them each a peck on the cheek, Penny slung a light backpack and her jacket on the chairback. 'Sorry to keep you. Have you ordered? I'm starving.' She sat down and flipped through the menu. 'They're famous for their duck confit.'

Marguerite was hungry, not having eaten since she'd set out that morning. She chose a salmon dish while Val hesitated between pasta and lamb cutlets. Penny put down her menu decisively. 'I'll have the duck. It comes with sautéed potatoes.'

Val laughed. 'Wasn't that David Faber guy on your show today, then?'

'Faber? No. Why?'

Val turned to Marguerite. 'He's the food guru on Penny's programme. They cook things live on air, and when the show's over, everyone eats it.'

'The crew eats it, not me.' Having caught the waitress's eye, Penny hitched her chair closer to the table. 'You're not exactly an avid fan, Mum, are you? Faber wasn't on today – his slots are Tuesday and Thursday.'

'I watch quite a lot, as it happens. I've even tried that cauliflower dish he did on the programme last week.' Val turned to Marguerite again. 'You roast cauliflower florets and diced squash with garlic, olive oil and caraway seeds, and either blitz it for soup or stir it through rice for a main course.'

'That sounds delicious.'

'It is. I've done it both ways. You should try it. Is he a trained chef, Penny? He's awfully good.'

The waitress, who'd been seating a group at another table, approached, order pad in hand. Val rejected both pasta and cutlets in favour of gnocchi with goat's cheese. She suggested wine but Marguerite laughed. 'If I drink at lunchtime, I'll fall asleep before you get me home! Go ahead, though. You and Penny have some.'

'Let's see if they'll do us a half-carafe.' Val opened the wine list but Penny shook her head. 'Not for me, Mum. I'll have water.'

'Oh, come on, join me. Look, this would go with your duck.' Holding out the list, Val pointed to a Chardonnay.

'I said no. I don't want any wine.' Her vehemence took Val by surprise. Flustered, she put the wine list back in its holder and Penny flushed to the roots of her expertly cut and coloured hair. 'Sorry. It's been a hell of a morning. I'll stick to fizzy water.' She smiled at Marguerite. 'So, what have you been up to, Gran?'

'Oh, you know. Gardening. Committees. I've a party coming up next week, so I thought I'd fly over and buy something to wear.'

'What kind of party?'

'It's not a party, really. Just a meeting of my group.' On moving back to Ireland, Marguerite had joined a group of neighbours who got together occasionally to play cards in each other's houses.

Val had been surprised when she'd heard about it. 'Isn't it rather staid? I mean, I can't see you bidding no trumps with the rector's wife and the doctor's daughter.'

Privately, Marguerite had admitted to herself that the group was dull. It was mostly composed of retired professional people, some of whom she'd known in her youth and had re-encountered on her return to Wicklow. But, unwilling to be disloyal to them, she'd suppressed the thought with a joke. 'I haven't moved into a 1930s novel! We don't play bridge – we're none of us good enough. And I was a doctor's daughter myself, remember, so watch what you say!'

Penny took a piece of rye bread from the basket on the table. 'What kind of outfit do you have in mind, Gran?'

'Your mum imagines I'll go for bias-cut satin with a cowl neckline.'

Penny grinned. 'Does she? Why?'

'She thinks I play bridge with Miss Marple and Hercule Poirot.'

'I never said that!'

Laughing at Val, Marguerite returned Penny's grin. 'Oh, you know me, I'll go through practically every rail in John Lewis's and the chances are that, in the end, I'll settle for a scarf.'

'Gran! You've got millions already.'

'And I love every single one of them.'

Val rapped on the table. 'I absolutely never dissed your cards group.'

'You did, but I forgive you.'

Penny buttered a second piece of bread. 'How long are you staying this time, Gran?'

'A few nights, if I'm not in the way.'

Val threw Marguerite an affectionate glance. 'You're never in the way and you know it. If you're here for a little while, maybe Penny will be free for dinner. I could cook.' They both looked expectantly at Penny, who flushed again. The food arrived before she could speak but, as soon as the waitress left, she squared up her cutlery precisely, and spoke as if she was about to address a meeting. 'Look, you need to know why I wanted us to sit down and have this meal.'

Val was puzzled. 'Was it something in particular? I thought we were just having lunch.'

'Well, of course. We are, and it's nice. I'm sorry I always seem to be busy when you're around, Gran.'

Marguerite shook her head. 'There's no need to apologise. You've a demanding job. It's just lovely to see you whenever you've got time off.'

'Yes, well, I won't have much of that in future.'

'Oh? What's happened? Have you had a promotion?'

Penny made a rueful face and poked at her sautéed potatoes. 'Not a promotion. Kind of the opposite. I'm going to be on leave.'

Val laid down her knife and fork, still puzzled. 'But why?' She frowned, wondering if she'd misunderstood. 'You just said you were going to have less time off.'

Equally puzzled, Marguerite sat with her plate of salmon untouched. Penny looked at their two concerned faces. 'Oh, sod it, this is ridiculous! I might as well just come out with it. I mean I'll be taking parental leave. I'm pregnant.'

Chapter Two

Penny had never been easy to help. At the age of ten she'd announced she was going to be a Wimbledon champion. Though competent at tennis, she'd never shown a particular interest in it and, given the cost of extra lessons, and the complications of getting her to and from them, Val had done nothing, hoping this was just a passing fad. But repression only increased Penny's determination so, eventually, Val had given in and signed her up for the junior branch of a tennis club a few stops away on the Jubilee Line. It didn't take long to become clear that Penny hated it and, as the training got more intense, it was evident that the stress was affecting her health. Yet she still refused even the most diplomatic offers of a bail-out. Instead, she'd held on until the closure of the club's courts for resurfacing had given her a plausible excuse to drop out. The passing years had produced many more examples of her ambition and dogged resolve, qualities that, ultimately, had propelled her upwards in her competitive industry. Yet Val knew that beneath the façade of the powerful TV executive were vestiges of the little girl who could never acknowledge a mistake or accept help.

Now, having shocked her mum and gran into silence, Penny was self-consciously eating duck. Seeing Val preparing to speak, she raised one shoulder defensively. 'You needed to know, so I thought we'd meet and I'd tell you. And now I have, so for God's sake, let's have lunch.'

'But, darling, this is amazing. I mean, I'd no idea.'

'I did a test a few weeks ago. It was positive. My GP's confirmed it. The baby's due early in January.'

Val's jaw dropped. 'A few weeks ago! You never told me.'

'I know. I'm telling you now.'

Seeing Val's hurt expression, Marguerite intervened. 'I suppose you wanted the father to know first, was that it, Penny?'

Penny put a forkful of food into her mouth and said nothing. Aware that this wasn't going too well, Val launched into a speech. 'It really is amazing. How are you feeling? Well, you're obviously fine, you're eating like a horse. No, I'm sorry. What I meant is you're blooming. But it must have been a shock.' She faltered, gulped and, unwisely, kept going. 'Or was it? I didn't even know you were seeing someone. Was it planned?'

'No, it wasn't.'

'Not that it's any of my business ...'

'You're right, it isn't.'

Laying a restraining hand on Val's knee, Marguerite spoke gently to Penny. 'Of course it's your mum's business. She's concerned about you. But you might have chosen somewhere less public to break such important news.'

'Oh, that's where you're focused, is it? On the thought of being overheard?'

'No, not at all. I just said—'

'You know what you *didn't* say, Gran? You didn't say congratulations. You didn't say, "How fantastic, Penny, this is so exciting!"' Penny rounded on Val. 'Ask me who the father is. Go on, Mum, you know you want to.'

This was so childish and unexpected that Val lost her cool. 'Yes, I do. What did you expect? You've just told me I'm going to have a grandchild.'

'And that's all I'm going to tell you.' Penny began to push back her chair. 'Look, I don't need interrogation, or sympathy, or either of you barging in trying to take charge of my life.'

'Darling, don't be silly.' Marguerite bit her lip, wishing she hadn't intervened. Penny was now standing up and reaching for her jacket. Val got up too. 'Look, let's all calm down. Penny, don't leave. You can't go without eating. You're starving, you said so. And no one's interrogating you. Your gran and I are just trying to take in this news.'

Reluctantly, Penny sat down again. Val and Marguerite avoided each other's eyes, unsure of what to say next, and afraid to be the one who spoke first. Penny saw their faces and her jaw tightened. Then, obviously making an effort, she took a deep breath. 'All right, I'm sorry. I'm being a prat. But you can both stop looking as if I'd announced the Apocalypse. I wish you could just be pleased for me.'

She had never spoken of a boyfriend, or shown any sign of having a relationship, and Val's mind filled with lurid visions of one-night stands, spiked drinks, or even date-rape.

Remembering her own advice to keep calm, she resumed her seat, trying to frame the question she felt she must ask. 'We are pleased. Really. If you are.' There was an ominous silence. Val saw Marguerite grip the napkin on her lap. Keeping her voice even, she sought the right words. 'Your gran and I are delighted. Truly. If this is what you want. But, Penny, are you certain? We don't need to know who the father is, not if you don't want to tell us. But does that mean you're going to do this on your own? It's a huge commitment. And you've got your work to think about. I'm not saying a career is more important than a baby, of course I'm not. But you've always been driven by your job. Having a baby is life-changing.'

'You think I don't know that?'

'That's not what I'm suggesting. You're a grown woman and you're not stupid. What I'm trying, and clearly failing, to do, is to ask if you've considered termination. How long is it since you saw your GP?' Out of the corner of her eye, Val saw the napkin crumple in Marguerite's clenched hands.

Penny rose to her feet again, but this time she seemed deadly calm. 'Like you say, Mum, I'm a grown woman, and I'm not the least bit stupid. You've made your position very clear, so now I'll do the same. I haven't considered termination. I'm going to have this baby. And if you're not prepared to welcome your own grandchild, then, believe me, we don't want anything from you. Nothing at all.'

'Penny! That's not what your mother meant.'

'Forget it, Gran. I'll be perfectly fine on my own.'

'Darling, please.' Val tried to prevent Penny from reaching again for her jacket. She was aware of people at a nearby table conscientiously trying to avoid looking round. Penny tweaked her jacket from the chairback and thrust her arms into the sleeves. With a sinking heart, Val recognised the stubborn look on her face. Oh, Lord, she thought. How could I handle things so badly precisely when Penny is going to need all the help she can get? And now, it seemed, there was nothing to be said to retrieve the situation. Penny's eyes held an expression both Val and Marguerite knew only too well. Having taken a stance, she wouldn't back down for anyone, especially if she felt she'd made a mistake.

The waitress was standing behind the bar, frankly engrossed in what was happening. Up to now, they'd all been speaking in intense undertones. Half rising, Val forced a smile and raised her voice. 'I wish you'd stay, but I do understand if you must go back to the office. I'll call you later, love.'

Penny looked at her blankly. Then, realising they'd become a focus of attention, she gave a shrug. 'Okay. Fine. Whatever.' Picking up her backpack, she sketched a wave at Marguerite. 'Goodbye, Gran.'

As the door closed, Val called to the waitress. 'Could you clear this plate, please? My daughter's remembered something important she's left behind at work.' Even to her own ears, it sounded lame but it was the best she could come up with. The waitress removed Penny's plate and Val sat down, realising her legs were shaking. Marguerite leaned over and squeezed her hand, gallantly pitching her own voice so it reached the other table. 'What a shame, and she'd hardly begun her lunch. Never mind. Let's enjoy ours, shall we? I must say this salmon looks delicious.' The sight of her own goat's cheese gnocchi made Val feel slightly sick, and having taken a mouthful, she put down her fork hastily, swallowing hard and pressing her napkin to her lips.

When she lowered it a glass of wine had appeared on the table and the waitress was standing beside her holding another, evidently having decided they needed it. 'Chardonnay. That's what you wanted, wasn't it?' As Val took a grateful gulp, the girl set the second glass by Marguerite's plate and removed herself, registering professional discretion.

For the next twenty minutes they fiddled with salmon and gnocchi, accepted more wine, and attempted to make conversation. The people at the other table soon lost interest in them, and when the waitress brought the bill, she maintained the fiction that nothing awkward had happened. 'Did you enjoy your lunch?'

'Thank you. It was lovely.'

'I'm glad. I hope we'll see you again.'

'I'm sure you will. Thank you.'

'Can I help with your suitcase?'

'Thank you, no, I'm fine. I can manage.'

The waitress held the door for them and they left in good order. Outside on the pavement, Marguerite was stricken by Val's woebegone face. 'I don't suppose Penny's sent a text or anything? You know what she's like – she's usually okay when she simmers down.'

Val checked her phone. There was no text. Though her heart went out to Penny, she felt a spurt of anger. Marguerite had been looking forward to taking a break in London. How wretched to be plunged into a row almost as soon as she'd stepped off the plane. The irritation was followed by a wry glimmer of humour. Whether or not the Carson women were the kind of ladies who lunched, they weren't the kind to make public scenes and need large glasses of wine to revive them, yet here she was with Marguerite, tipsy in a London square at three in the afternoon. She tucked her hand into her mother's arm and hugged it. 'Look, forget Penny, she'll call sooner or later. Just at the moment, you and I need to take this in.'

They had set out for Oxford Circus station when Marguerite stopped in her tracks. 'Oh, my God, I'm going to be a great-grandmother!'

'And I've got to get my head around the thought of being called Granny.'

Marguerite blinked. 'Actually, that's the bit that feels most surreal. Before you arrived at the restaurant, I was thinking about the party dresses I used to make for you when you were little. Shifts and pinafores in cotton, with pretty repeated patterns. It seems like yesterday.' She linked Val more tightly. 'You're absolutely right. We're going to need time to adjust to this. You'd better get me home and sober me up.'

Chapter Three

Bowling along on her bicycle, Penny cursed herself for having indulged in wishful thinking. What on earth had made her think she could just present her news and move on? I've grown too used to setting agendas at work, she thought. Mum and Gran were never going to let me call all the shots on this. Wincing, she reminded herself that keeping cool under pressure was supposed to be one of her strengths. As were clarity and strategic thinking. But to accuse Val and Marguerite of nosiness had been unfair and absurd. And to suggest that they'd want to barge in and take charge of her life was ridiculous. As a family, they'd always been scrupulous about privacy and careful not to invade each other's space. Misjudgement on every level, thought Penny. And here I am, making for home as if my flat is a fortress where I can pull up a drawbridge and hide from what I've done.

Her flat, on the south side of the river, was by Borough Market, where modern apartment blocks jostled little Victorian terraces, and warehouses had been converted to artisan food outlets. The street had an all-pervading aroma of spices and garlic, which meant that not everyone saw it as an attractive place to live. Penny adored it. Ten years ago, when she'd stumbled on it, her job as a runner for a TV production company had paid just enough to rent a bedsit above what had then been a junk shop. Having wandered through the bustling market under the railway arches, she'd noticed a card in the junk shop window with 'Room to Let' written on it in neat, spidery writing. Going inside, she'd found Bill, the elderly owner, scratching a cat under the chin while reading the *Daily Mail*. When she'd explained that she'd seen the card, he'd wheezed and tossed her a key. 'First floor, first on the right. I can't be doing with the stairs.'

The entrance, through a door by the shop front, led to a narrow hall. Directly ahead, and equally narrow, was a steep flight of stairs. She'd let herself in and found the room, which was square and had two sash windows. It was sparsely furnished with the sort of bits and pieces she'd seen in the shop downstairs. The bed looked as if it might have been in an institution, but the mattress was new and still in its sealed plastic cover. There was a small sink in the corner, a work surface beside it, and a two-ring electric hob plugged into the wall. Next door was a bathroom, evidently communal, with a fiercely scrubbed enamel tub, an ancient water heater, and a notice in the same spidery writing, which read, 'Please Leave NO Personal Belongings Here.' The windows in both rooms were thick with dust but everything else was spotlessly clean, and the woodchip paper on the walls had had a recent coat of paint. Returning to the room to let, Penny had sat on a wooden chair and looked around, aware of a bubbling feeling of delight. Her job as a runner was precarious but her feet were on the right ladder and, living here in independence, she could surely build a career. Back in the shop, she'd hardly dared to ask how much the rent was, and when it turned out to be affordable, she knew that nothing could stop her.

Bill and his wife had a council flat a few streets away from the market. Most of his tenants in the rooms above the shop moved on within months but Penny had stayed, renting a larger room and exclusive use of the first-floor bathroom as soon as she'd earned a contract and a rise. Now, approaching her front door, she marvelled at the changes in her surroundings.

Eight years after she'd moved in, Bill had decided to sell off the upper part of his building. Penny's heart had sunk when he'd called her into the shop and dusted a chair for her to sit down on. 'I dare say the wife's right, Pen. She says it's time for a change. She wants me to free up capital so we can swan off on holidays. "Good luck with that," I told her. I can't be arsed with seagulls and I hate foreign food.' Penny had held her breath as he'd continued. 'I'm not getting any younger, though, am I? And the area's gone to the dogs with all this poncy gentrification. No one who comes round here these days wants the kind of gear I shift.' Pushing his cat out of the way, he'd poured tea from the pot he always kept brewing, and offered Penny a Garibaldi biscuit. 'Thing is, Pen, I can't be doing with estate agents. They're wide-boys, the lot of them, with their hair gel and their smartphones. No, I'll tell you what I'll do for you, if you're interested. You've got the makings of a decent flat up there. Knock out the walls on the first floor – open-plan living, my boy tells me they call it. Do the same on the floor above and you've plenty of room for a new internal staircase, a bedroom up top, and a bathroom and storage and that. Re-plumb, rewire, slap on a lick of paint, and Bob's your uncle. What do you reckon?'

Penny's mind had gone into overdrive. In her years of renting from Bill, her career had blossomed. Promoted to a reporter's job, she'd shot and cut material for a weekly news round-up. Then, when a proposal she'd worked on was green-lit by a broadcaster, she'd been given another rise and moved to production. It all felt like flying by the seat of her pants but, at least for the time being, she was solvent. What had followed that conversation was a tribute to her clear-mindedness. A mortgage and a loan for the renovations were arranged in less than a week, and the deal with Bill was done on a drink and a handshake. Then, having found an architect to project-manage the work, she'd stayed with Val for a few months before moving into her finished flat. On her first day there Stanley, Bill's cat, which had grown accustomed to sneaking into her room through a back window, turned up as Penny was eating breakfast. A heady smell of flowers and spices had drifted up from the market, along with cheerful shouts from the stallholders, and Stanley, accepting a crust of toast, had rolled over presenting his black-and-white chin. Tickling him till he purred ecstatically, Penny had looked around happily, feeling splendidly independent and in control of her life.

The lower part of the building was now a successful lifestyle shop run by Bill's son Mark, who had a flat nearby, close to his parents. As Penny wheeled her bike from the street onto the pavement, Mark put his head out of the shop door. 'I just got some new coffee beans from the market. Fancy a natter?'

'Yeah, why not?' Leaving her bike in her hallway, Penny

joined him, and he poured her a coffee that filled the shop with the rich fragrance of Brazilian beans.

'How was your day?'

'Fairly crap.'

'Work?'

'No, that's fine. Well, mad, but that's par for the course. No, it's family crap. I've been out for lunch with my grandmother and my mum.' Penny sat down in an armchair covered with rainbow-striped fabric. 'Is this new? I haven't seen it before.'

'Upcycled vintage. It's newly upholstered. What Bill calls "toshed-up junk".'

Penny grinned. 'How is he?'

'Never better. Still laying down the law and driving Mum mad.'

'Oh, bless him. Give him my love.'

'Sure.' Mark nodded at the chair. 'That'll sell quickly, I reckon. The frame's beautifully made. Late Victorian.'

'It's nice.'

Laughing, he produced a packet of Garibaldis. 'You hate it really.'

'No, I don't.'

'Yes, you do. It would never work in your flat.'

'Well, I can admire it, can't I, even if it's not my style? Anyway, I'm planning some changes up there.'

'I could do you some very opulent gilded mirrors.'

'I wasn't planning on turning it into a brothel.'

'Just on changing your Whisper White walls to White Vanilla?'

'Oh, shut up, Mark, I'm not in the mood.'

'Fair enough.' He sat on the edge of his desk and looked at

her over his coffee cup. 'Want to talk about what happened at lunch?'

'No. Too unedifying. I made a total plank of myself and I'll have to apologise.'

'Okay. Moving swiftly on. Want to catch a film later? We haven't had a night out for ages.'

'No. Sorry, I'm not being awful, I just don't feel up to it. Anyway, I've an early meeting tomorrow.'

'No problem, we'll do it another time.'

Outside, the sun was shining and a woman passed carrying a bunch of scarlet and yellow tulips. Still troubled by what had happened at lunchtime, Penny decided to take a walk by the river. Ever since the confirmation of her pregnancy she'd had the strangest feeling. Dogs strained at leads, teenagers were skateboarding, and couples strolled hand-in-hand along the crowded riverside walk, but everyone she saw seemed untouchable and distant, as if they were in the real world and she was moving in a different dimension. She walked on with her shoulders hunched and found she'd stopped and was leaning on the river parapet, staring across the moving water at the Tower of London. Having eaten no lunch and had a cup of strong coffee, she now felt lightheaded. Her fridge contained only some ageing sushi but, as shopping required more energy than she could summon, it seemed she was going to have to settle for that.

Back in the flat, and finding the sushi was well past its sell-by date, she decided she needed a shower before doing anything else. Halfway up the stairs to her bedroom, cold fear gripped her. It was all very well to announce that she planned to make changes, but how did one baby-proof an open-tread staircase? Or bathe a baby in a walk-in wet room? Or manhandle a buggy up and down a narrow staircase to the street? Desperately, she groped for the mantra that always sustained her at work: focus, regroup and prioritise. None of this needs to be thought through yet, she told herself firmly. All you need to do is take things one step at a time. With an effort, she released her grip on the brushed-steel banister, continued up the stairs and sat on her bed. Briefly, she thought of texting Mark to say she fancied a film after all. It would be a distraction and, afterwards, they might pick up fish and chips. They needn't talk about anything complicated. He had a way of backing off when he sensed you needed space.

She'd first met Mark when, having rented the bedsit, she'd gone into the shop about a kettle. 'You don't have an electric one for sale, do you, Bill? Sorry to be a bother.' Bill had shaken his head. 'No problem, love, if you don't ask, you don't get. I don't do electricals, though. Can't risk the compo claims.'

At that moment, Mark had emerged from behind a bank of shelves, carrying an old-fashioned stove-top kettle. Penny had eyed it doubtfully. 'It's not what I had in mind.'

'Oh, come on! Call it retro. It'll be high-end chic in a few years' time.'

'Seriously?'

'Okay, possibly not. But it'll do the job. Spotlessly clean, sound as a bell, one careful lady owner.' His eyes had had a mischievous glint and Penny had laughed in response. 'How do you know it's had one careful lady owner?'

'I helped Dad clear her flat.'

'You mean the poor woman's dead? That's horrible.'

'Well, it would be if she were but, as it happens, she's hale and hearty.' Setting the kettle on a nest of tables, he'd held out his hand. 'I'm Mark, Bill's son. I help him out now and then. You're the new tenant?'

'Penny. Yes. Nice to meet you.'

'You don't need to feel creepy about the kettle. The woman who owned it retired to Cornwall. She's probably having a cream tea as we speak.'

'Oh. Okay. Well, maybe, then.'

'It's a perfectly good option.'

Later, she'd come back to buy the kettle, having failed to find an affordable alternative. Mark, who'd been on his own in the shop, was matter-of-fact and asked no questions, so she'd relaxed and accepted a mug of tea and a Garibaldi biscuit from a battered tin that was kept under the till. After that, they'd treated each other as neighbours, borrowing the occasional pint of milk and, now and then, seeing a film or having a drink after work. Mark was stocky, dark-haired and dependable, the only son in a family of four daughters who'd all settled down at home close to their parents while he'd flown off to see the world. When he'd met Penny, he'd been in his final year at art college. By the time she'd bought her flat he'd gone to work in a Paris antiques shop, hang out in San Francisco, and do a design course somewhere in Sweden. Then, when Bill had retired and Mark had come home to take over the shop, he and Penny had simply picked up their friendship where they'd left off. But now, having reached for her phone to text him, she hesitated. Everything's different, she thought, and I can't get my head around it. For a long moment, she stared at her screen, longing for someone to talk to. Then she sighed and thrust it back into her pocket, wondering what had become of her tidy, compartmentalised life.

Chapter Four

When Marguerite and Val reached West Hampstead, Val suggested high tea. 'You go up and settle in, and I'll make us an omelette. We could both do with a sit-down and a spot of comfort food.'

Upstairs in the spare bedroom, Marguerite admired the familiar touches that always made her feel welcome. One corner of the duvet had been turned back invitingly and a glass on the bedroom windowsill held a posy of grape hyacinths. After unpacking, and leaving her toothbrush in the bathroom across the landing, she combed her hair and went down to the kitchen, where double doors opened onto the little suburban garden.

They sat at the table with the omelette pan between them, and Val was about to serve when she heard her phone buzz. Seeing her face, Marguerite, who'd held out her plate, looked alarmed. 'What is it?'

'Nothing, it's fine. It's from Penny.' Val transferred half the omelette to the extended plate. 'Eat that while it's hot.'

'What does she say?' Marguerite set the plate down as Val read out the message: *'Sorry I flounced out. Apologise to Gran for me, will you? I'm a bit tired but fine, Mum, don't worry. Busy at work so may not get a chance to call for a bit. Hope Gran has a lovely holiday. I'll be in touch.* She ends with two kisses, so I suppose that's one for each of us.'

'That's it? "I'll be in touch"?'

'And you know she will. You mustn't worry.'

'I do know, of course.' Marguerite accepted garlic bread and applied herself to her omelette. 'This is perfect. Just what was needed to soak up the wine.' Eager not to add to each other's anxiety, they laughed at the lame joke. When the meal was finished Val made tea and they drank it in the sunny garden where an ageing pear tree stood in the centre of the patch of lawn. But the tree, the grass and two earthenware pots of grape hyacinths didn't offer great scope for discussion and, eventually, Val threw a rueful smile at her mother. 'There's not much point in sitting here making chit-chat, pretending we're not both thinking about Pen.'

'Do you really have no idea who the father might be?'

'None. I've never intruded on her relationships.'

'Darling, you said it yourself, she'll be in touch. There's certainly no point in hounding her, we both know that.'

Val stared out at the garden. 'Do you remember the photo I took of her standing under the pear tree? She was six. I'd made her a little calico dress with a high waist and ruffled shoulder-straps. I haven't thought of that dress in years.'

'I don't recall. Was it pink? She went through a pink phase.'

'No. Yellow, with sprigs of forget-me-not. A few years later she'd wear nothing but jeans.'

'Didn't you make her a pair of dungarees at one point?'

'With embroidered stars on the bib and gingham patches on the knees. It didn't go down well.'

'I suppose, by that stage, homemade clothes were embarrassing.'

'They certainly couldn't compete with metallic boob tubes.'

Marguerite laughed. 'I nearly gave up sewing for you when you threw a tantrum about the dress I made for your eighth birthday.'

'Did I? I don't remember.'

'It was broderie anglaise with puff sleeves. You called it babyish. Afterwards, I remade it for your teddy bear.'

'I remember that. Edward. Did he end up in a charity shop?'

'You'd kissed most of the fur off his nose by the time you were too grown-up for him. Far too scruffy even to go to a jumble sale.' Suddenly, Marguerite stopped and frowned. The thought of the bear's bald nose had chimed with an older, deeper memory, recalling the sleep-inducing, rhythmic circles she'd traced on her patchwork quilt when she was a child.

'If she won't talk to us, I hope she has a friend she can confide in.' Val had spoken under her breath and was looking upset again so, determined to keep things light-hearted, Marguerite wrenched her own thoughts back to the present. 'Do you sew at all, these days?'

Val shook her head. 'Not for twenty years. Probably longer. I've still got a ragbag somewhere, and the sewing-machine's in the attic, but cooking's my only claim to domesticity these days – and, living alone, I don't do much of that. Mostly I just come in from work and have baked beans on toast.'

'Darling, that's dreadful!'

'Well, it's not quite true.'

'It can't be. Didn't you say in the restaurant that you'd made something fancy with cauliflower and sesame seeds?'

'Caraway.' Val got to her feet. 'Which reminds me, I have the recipe. You can take it home with you.' Going to a rack, she found a Sunday-newspaper colour supplement. On its back page was a recipe from Penny's TV show under a photo of David Faber seated at a table in a charming kitchen garden. Val held out the magazine. 'If you take the page, I'll chuck the rest. It's mostly celebrity gossip and ads for hearing aids.'

Marguerite looked at the photograph. 'What a lovely setting. Is it his own garden, do you think?'

'That's the impression.'

'Do you watch the show much?'

Val shrugged. 'Occasionally. Rather less frequently than I suggested to Penny over lunch. It's not my thing, but I wouldn't like her to think I don't appreciate her success.'

'Darling, she knows you're proud of her.'

'Does she?' Val sipped tea and stared fixedly at the pear tree. 'Being a single mother isn't easy.'

'I know.'

'No, you don't. Not really. Nor does Penny.' Val bit her lip. 'At least, I hope she doesn't. Because I did my damnedest never to let her see it.' She shot a glance at Marguerite before turning back to the pear tree. 'You know what? I sometimes wonder if the guests on that show of hers are acting. All that emotion isn't normal, is it?'

'You make it sound like *The Jerry Springer Show*.'

'Actually, it's the reverse. Sort of *The Anti-Jerry-Springer Show*. Kissing, and high-fives and people announcing how much they love and support one another. Not Penny at all, but she seems to thrive on it. Perhaps it fills some unacknowledged gap.'

'Look, you're worried about Penny's news. It's life-changing. Nobody knows that better than you, having raised Penny alone. But there's no unacknowledged gap. She knows you love and support her. Don't add to her troubles by inventing one of your own.'

'That's what they used to call it. She's "in trouble".'

Hearing a quiver in Val's voice, Marguerite spoke briskly. 'You're making her sound like a sad Victorian parlour-maid. She's not, she's an independent woman. And I don't think she's crying out for a touchy-feely mum.'

'I can't bear her to think that I don't want to welcome my grandchild.'

'That's not what she thinks.'

'It's what she said at lunch when she walked out.'

'She's apologised. She's admitted she lost her cool.'

'I know. I just don't want to lose her.' Blinking away tears, Val looked across at Marguerite and saw tension in her hands and a strained look in her eyes. She's hating this, thought Val. This isn't our kind of conversation at all, and what's the point of it? Talking won't change a thing. With an effort, she got to her feet and reached for the teapot. 'You're right, of course. I'll make us a fresh pot, shall I?'

Marguerite smiled gratefully. 'Another cup would be lovely.' She watched as Val went into the kitchen to switch on the kettle, and stood up to help her set down the pot when she came back into the garden. Then, side by side, each determined not to upset the other, they talked about cotton and gingham dresses and ruffles and shoulder straps.

Chapter Five

Despite how it had begun, Marguerite's brief stay in London was full of pleasures. The following morning she took a stroll in Holland Park, close to the street where she and Paul had begun their contented marriage. After his death five years previously, she'd found it hard to revisit the neighbourhood. But time had softened the memories evoked by a walk in the park, and subtle changes, such as different shopfronts and new management in their favourite café, allowed her to recall the past while enjoying the present.

Having walked as far as Kensington Church Street, Marguerite caught a bus to Oxford Street and spent a happy hour trying on summer dresses in Selfridges. Then she went to John Lewis's, where she planned to browse and have lunch. There, as she'd anticipated, she found a display of scarves. Among them was a square of fine wool, large enough to use as a shawl and light enough to be twisted and worn round the neck. Its rolled hem was hand-stitched and the abstract pattern in apple green had accents of purple as deep as the colour of old-fashioned pansies. Taking it to a mirror, she tried it on, turning to and fro to see the effect. It draped as elegantly as she'd hoped and, folding it to take to the till, she realised why its colours had attracted her. They reminded her of her first date with Paul.

She'd met him in 1970 at a party in London where, at nineteen, she'd taken a holiday job as an au pair. The frisson she'd felt had been like nothing she'd ever known before. In those days, the Biba store in Kensington was her delight. Most of the clothes were beyond her means, but she loved Biba's earthy palette of olives, rusts and reds, and its signature 'bruised purple'. So, when Paul asked her out, she went there and bought herself new eyeshadow. The little black box with its gilt lettering felt like the height of urban sophistication, and the purple metallic shadow, lavishly smudged round her eyes, had done wonders to boost her confidence.

Not that she'd needed to worry. Paul, who was three years older, was just as smitten as she was. He worked as an accountant for a small firm where his father had worked before him, a scenario familiar to Marguerite whose own dad had begun his career as locum in his father's practice. Perhaps because her love-at-first-sight had been tinged with the safeness of that familiarity, she'd decided to stay in London and marry Paul. It had meant forgoing a plan to study pharmacy in Dublin, so Donal, her dad, hadn't been best pleased. But he'd known that the speed with which she'd abandoned her university place was a measure of her lack of real interest in it and, once he'd met Paul, he'd accepted the engagement, possibly relieved that his daughter's choice of husband bore no resemblance to the stereotype of a swinging Londoner.

Marguerite had been her dad's companion since she was twelve, when her mother had died suddenly, so at first, the thought of moving to London had worried her. But Donal had continued to live and work contentedly in Wicklow and, in the way of small rural communities, the people whose health he cared for had kept as watchful an eye on him as he kept on them. Paul's work had meant he couldn't spend much time in Ireland, but Marguerite had visited each summer, eager for Val and her younger brother Rory to get to know their granddad. And Donal had lived long enough to be introduced to the next generation. One of Marguerite's fondest memories was of Penny in a sagging nappy on a blustery October day staggering across the wildflower meadow behind the Wicklow villa, her pudgy fists clamped around her great-grandfather's thumbs.

Having paid for her scarf, Marguerite took a lift to John Lewis's top-floor restaurant, and carried her lunch onto its glass-railed balcony, which presented a view of the rooftop façades of the buildings across the street. When she sat down, three pigeons descended on whirring wings, not the creamy-beige birds that cooed in the Wicklow woods, but dusty city-dwellers that landed on scaly claws and fought over discarded crumbs at her feet. She drank her latte and ate a sandwich slowly, her thoughts reverting to Val, who'd set out for work looking as if she'd had little sleep.

At the next table, a father and two children were having lunch. Their eyes were glued to their phones while their hands hovered over their plates stabbing forkfuls of salad and transferring them to their mouths. Marguerite watched a pigeon sidle towards them. One child looked up and, catching her eye, pointed at the iridescent feathers around the bird's neck. She was thinking how sad it was that the little boy's father had missed this moment when his sister squealed, 'Grandma!' and, immediately, the family jostled to get the best view of her screen. Their sudden animation was enchanting. Catching a glimpse of a smiling figure returning the children's greetings, Marguerite imagined her own family at a similar session. FaceTime, she thought, or WhatsApp or something. It would be such an obvious thing to do, with Val and Penny here in London, me in Ireland, and Rory with his wife and kids in New Zealand. But the truth is that we know each other far too well to attempt it. Penny would be unavailable, Val would be desperate to make things work, and always putting her foot in it, and Rory is just like his dad and mine, loving, gentle and totally unforthcoming. She had a vision of them all, with rictus smiles, trying and failing to achieve 'quality time'.

At the next table, the family were shrieking with laughter and exchanging extravagant terms of endearment. If we were like that, thought Marguerite, it wouldn't matter that Penny went off in a huff. We'd tell her we love her and laugh it off at our next WhatsApp session and she'd send a funny Gif or something, saying, 'My bad'. Do they still say that, or is it old-fashioned? Not that it matters, because it's not going to happen. Not in our family. When it comes to our emotions, we're inarticulate, and there's no use in trying to be what you're not.

After another half-hour's browsing, Marguerite set out to meet a friend at the V&A. Arriving early, she sat on the steps in the sunshine. Museums and galleries were among her favourite London haunts, as full of surprises and unexplored corners as the city itself. When Val and Rory were growing up, she'd often brought them along. And that was togetherness, she thought defensively, and we all enjoyed it without having to squeal and use superlatives. Paul and I raised our kids in a home in which love was a given, and civilised behaviour implied self-control. I suppose I'd learned self-control in my own childhood, and passed it on because, to me, it went hand in hand with love. And I know Paul's family had the same values, though I can't remember ever discussing them. Perhaps things always get passed down through generations that way, unquestioned because they're never unpicked and examined.

Resting her chin on her knees, she wondered if introspection came with advancing age. She certainly seemed to be doing a lot of it since hearing Penny's news – or, perhaps, since seeing Val's reaction to it. She's frightened, thought Marguerite. Does she really think she might lose Penny? But that's absurd. I must be imagining it. Giving herself a mental shake, she turned her focus to her present surroundings. On either side, feet were clattering up and down the steps, handbags swung, and legs passed, wearing shorts, trousers or skirts, or fanned by summer dresses. Between them, in the distance, Marguerite saw her friend approaching. Standing up, she waved to draw her attention and, glad to leave introspection behind, ran down the steps to greet her.

Chapter Six

Mark passed beneath the railway arches and cut through Borough Market, picking up croissants on the way. Under the glass and cast-iron canopies, stallholders were exchanging banter and, cleared of the previous day's litter and cabbage stalks, the little surrounding streets looked bright and clean in the sunshine. Across the street, Penny emerged from her doorway, wearing sleek cycling gear and carrying Stanley. Dodging a van as he came towards her, Mark called a greeting. 'Morning, Pen. I seem to have gone overboard at the bakery. D'you fancy a croissant?'

Balancing her bike against her hip, Penny held out the cat. 'Thanks, but no thanks. Stanley and I have eaten. He joined me for breakfast. Sorry, can't stop, I've a meeting in twenty minutes.'

Mark lowered his head to search for his keys, so she didn't see his flicker of disappointment. Having fished them out of his pocket, he held out his arms and took Stanley from her. 'Wretched cat. He knows no borders. Cheers then, Penny. Have a good day.' He watched as she shot away, narrowly missing a market cart, and waved as she disappeared around the corner without looking back. Then, with the cat draped over his shoulder, like an exotic furry accessory, he went to pull up the blind and open the shop.

Penny's show aired live from ten till noon, five days a week. This morning she planned to be at the studio for the second hour, though as a rule she took care not to drop by too frequently. Generally, she monitored broadcasts from her screen in the office or from the flat, if she was working at home. But her awareness of the show's minutiae was legendary, and everyone who worked on it understood that, though her style wasn't intrusive, her eyes were always on the ratings. After all, in her late twenties, with newcomers snapping at her heels, she had a hard-won reputation and a position to protect.

She could get to her office in fifteen minutes, on a route that avoided the usual stress of an urban commute. Purple buddleia sprouted from cracks in brick walls and chimneys, and some of the lanes she cut through retained the surface of stone setts that had once been trudged by Charles Dickens. Normally, she loved this bike ride through what felt like an older city. It was a time to focus her thoughts on the day's work. But today the thought of her mum's face kept intruding. The hurt look, the instant attempt to conceal it, and the automatic assumption that this was something that had to be managed and controlled. It's not fair, Penny thought crossly. I know she worries about me, and I know I ought to be grateful, but today's going to be hard enough without having to think about that. I've got to focus because I'm the one who's going to have to manage. This is happening in my world, where I'm the one in control.

The company's office was in Waterloo. Though her room was small, Penny's desk had a panoramic view of Waterloo's soaring office blocks, and of little rows of Victorian terraced housing laid out beneath her, as if on a board game. Having grabbed a quick shower, Penny took a meeting. Afterwards she spent half an hour going through matters arising before descending to the car park to fetch her bike. The studio was a short ride away, on the South Bank, and by the time she got there the second half of the show was in full swing. The first had ended in a five-minute news round-up, followed by a sofa discussion of one of the day's lighter news stories. Often the choice of what to discuss was made on the flip of a coin, seconds before the director cut from an ad-break back to the studio. This was fine by Penny. A combination of brinkmanship with formulaic slots was one of the factors that ensured appeal to a wide demographic, just as the attractiveness of the presenters, Roz and Gail, was a hook to audience members of both sexes and all ages. Attractiveness and dynamism were basic requirements for the show's onscreen talent, from Colette, the stylist who gave fashion tips on Wednesdays, to David Faber with his mop of hair and piercing grey eyes.

The food slot had begun. Standing at the back of the production gallery, Penny studied David's face on the bank of monitors. 'Charming' was a tag frequently used to describe him, though the tabloids generally went with 'strangely sexy'. Five years ago, when his agent had proposed him for the slot, Penny had instantly recognised raw potential. Back then, David had been a thirty-seven-year-old food columnist. He was driven and professional but lacked TV experience, and when his screen tests were seen, someone had said that his image needed a makeover. Penny had flatly rejected the suggestion. There was something about his appearance, some combination of edginess and suburbia, that she knew was perfect for the show. As focus groups consistently validated her instincts, her judgement had been trusted, and time had proved her right. Now, as she watched on the monitor, David looked straight into camera. No words came into Penny's mind to describe him, though professional pride made her seek them again. Then she shrugged. She'd known from the start that what he had was indefinable, and that its very indefinability would be central to his success.

David's Thursday slot, which focused on baking, always included mildly exotic ingredients made fashionable by the supermarkets that bought ad-space around it. The implication was that he devised the recipes at home, drawing inspiration from his kitchen garden. In fact, he disliked gardening, and everything made on the show was rigorously tested by the production company, intent on avoiding insurance claims. Today's offering was buttermilk scones with fig jam and borage flowers. They were baked in real time, leaving space for chat between David and the presenters, and a video insert of sun-dappled borage growing in a London park. Watching it, Penny frowned, anticipating tweets about theft of flowers from public spaces. David was ahead of her. Before a warning could be murmured in his earpiece, he turned to Roz. 'As I always say, you must be certain that flowers and herbs used in cooking haven't been touched by pesticides. So, best to grow your own, or ask in a good supermarket.' Having headed off potential negative comments, he moved on smoothly. 'You saw what I did just now for the jam. It's incredibly simple. Five hundred grams of dried figs and a quarter-cup each of water and brown sugar.'

Roz intervened. 'Oh, come on, there was other stuff too.'

'Just a spot of lemon juice and a little vanilla extract.'

Gail's perfect teeth flashed. 'Don't worry, folks, this is why we make sure you get your favourite recipes in the magazine. So, don't forget to tweet us your votes for David's fig jam, okay? It's a good 'un.' With that box ticked, David went to the oven. Deftly assembling the scones on a board with Roquefort cheese and the jam, he dotted the result with borage flowers and turned it to achieve the best close-up. Off camera, Roz and Gail were already in end-of-show mode, though, aware of Penny's presence in the gallery, they hadn't quite reached for their phones to check the hits on their personal Twitter accounts.

Later, when the crew was wolfing scones, David appeared in the gallery behind Penny. 'Want to try one?' The scattering of little petals echoed the blue veins in the Roquefort, and the warm, floury smell was inviting. Penny crumbled a piece of cheese, dipped it into the sweet, grainy jam and put the bite-sized scone into her mouth. He grinned. 'And there you have it, my Irish Buttermilk Scones with Fig Jam and Borage Flowers.'

He was mocking his own tag-line and she laughed with him, licking the sweet and salty crumbs from her fingers. 'You do know there's nothing Irish about fig jam and borage petals?'

David picked a crumb from her sleeve and winked at her.

'Buttermilk, eggs and flour don't produce a sexy end-shot like that one and, after all, that's what you pay me for.' The exchange was rather more matey than she tended to encourage in employees, so she met his eyes blandly and turned away. Down on the studio floor, she chatted briefly with Gail and Roz and, afterwards, had a quick word with the director. Like the others, he'd checked his phone to see how the show had gone down on social media. Penny, whose phone was set up for more detailed analytics, already knew that the hit-rate was high. A story from the show's first hour, about a bullied child who'd raised thousands for charity, was still being retweeted, and the scones were gaining traction by the minute.

As she cycled out of the studio car park, the thought of Val's concerned face intruded again on Penny's consciousness. Resolutely banishing it, she set out for Waterloo, her mind already grappling with the next thing to be done.

She was back in the office, focused on figures, when her phone buzzed, signalling the arrival of a text. Pulling a face, she told herself that if this was her mum, she ought to take the call. Then she saw the phone's screen and her mouth went dry. At the other side of the room, Lolly, her assistant, was working on timesheets. With a conscious effort, Penny resisted an impulse to look up to see if she'd noticed. Instead, hitting delete, she dropped the phone into her bag. It had taken no more than a second to read the one-line text: *I can be at the flat around 7.15.* There was no signature, and no name had appeared on the display. Which wasn't surprising. David never signed his texts and she'd never linked his name to the number from which he called her phone.

Chapter Seven

David Faber's home would have disappointed his fans and, looking around his living room, he reflected that it wasn't much to his taste either. It was a 1960s townhouse in Blackheath on a road about equidistant from the station and the Heath. Helen, his wife, who'd been born in Blackheath, liked to call it semi-rural living, and resolutely referred to the streets near the station as 'the village'. David found its conscious charm oppressive. The shops and businesses all seemed to be run or patronised by Helen's old school friends, well-dressed and pleasant but, to his mind, insufferably smug. Sometimes, buying courgettes in one shop and sourdough in another, or taking the twins for what Helen called 'a proper romp' on the Heath, he was aware that, as a wholefoodie TV cook he fitted in perfectly, and the realisation made him long to escape.

Two things had reconciled him to living there. The fact that the train to central London took only twenty minutes, and the relief he'd felt on finding that Helen came with a house and no mortgage. She was everything David admired in a woman, and even the sound of her voice could still make him dizzy with desire but, undoubtedly, the house had been a bonus. They'd met five years previously, when he was still married to his first wife, Jennifer, a journalist several years older than he was. Helen was fifteen years his junior and, in contrast to his wife's cynical acceptance of his foibles, had exuded wide-eyed devotion from the start. By then, he and Jennifer had had little in common besides their teenage son, Joe. On discovering David's affair with Helen, she'd ensured he'd emerge from their bruising divorce still paying for Joe's expensive schooling and her own addiction to ski lodges and spas. So, he'd moved in with Helen mentally counting his blessings, while Jennifer had gone her way informing showbiz columnists that, as she and David remained the best of friends, there was nothing for them to write about. That, too, had been a source of relief to David. He'd never been sure whether Jennifer had been livid about the affair or simply bored with their marriage but, with his TV contract coming up for renewal, he'd been acutely conscious of the danger of gossip in *OK!* magazine.

Now he surveyed his living room dispassionately. It wasn't all that bad. Or it hadn't been before the twins had reached the romping stage. When he'd met Helen, she'd worked as a PA for one of her father's friends, and a generous salary had allowed her to furnish the house from Heal's, choosing Farrow & Ball colours and chintzes from *Country Living*. But time had added unlooked-for accretions – a pedal car that the twins had decided to garage under the table, wicker baskets overflowing with miscellaneous toys, and a pair of plastic children's chairs jammed behind the sofa. It seemed to David that bright pink had become the predominant colour, and that a house which was once an acceptable size was shrinking by the minute.

Helen was in the kitchen giving the twins their tea, scolding and entreating by turns and urging Chloë to try one more spoonful. Chloë was a fussy eater. Demetra, known as Demi, had no problem in that direction, but their playschool was showing concern about her socialisation skills. David was pretty certain both girls had become arch-manipulators, but they were Helen's province, not his. She'd given up her job within a month of becoming pregnant and her time was now dedicated to motherhood and turning up on David's arm to celebrity galas and dinners.

There was a scraping sound as a bench was pulled back and the twins were released from the kitchen. They came running in and bounced onto the sofa beside David, faces flushed from the scrubbing they'd just received with a wet flannel, and already dressed in their miniature tartan pyjamas. Chloë leaned on his knee and demanded to know if he'd brought something home from the studio. 'What did you bake?'

'Buttermilk scones and fig jam. You wouldn't like them.'

'Buttermilk? Yuk. What's that?'

'Yukky grown-up stuff. Give me a kiss, it's bedtime.' Her hair smelt sweetly of camomile shampoo. Getting to his feet, David called through to the kitchen. 'Did I say I have a meeting this evening?'

Helen appeared in the doorway, untying the strings of her Cath Kidston apron. 'No, you didn't. Oh, darling! I'd planned a cassoulet.'

Registering regret, he ran a hand through his mop of silver hair. 'I'm sorry, I thought I'd mentioned it.'

'We could eat when you come back.'

'No, you'd be starving. Have yours and I'll heat some when I come in. Or maybe I'll eat with the team after the meeting.'

'What's it about?'

'Oh, long-term planning, seasonal stuff, mostly just admin. Kick-off's at seven.' The extra time would allow him to get to an off-licence. He bent to pick Demi up, thus avoiding Helen's eyes, but with her mind on getting the children to bed, she hadn't really been interested in his answer. Besides, he'd learned from past mistakes. Jennifer had known every detail of his schedule and, consequently, had been in a position to brief her divorce lawyer with disastrous results for David's bank account. So, on marrying Helen, he'd taken pains to tell her his contract required attendance at meetings at odd hours and short notice. At the time he'd had no particular reason for setting up this fiction, beyond a sense that it might turn out to be useful in the future, and certainly would have been helpful in the past. Now he watched Helen apply her mind to dinner.

'I'll do myself a single portion of cassoulet, darling, and, if you're hungry when you come in, I'll defrost another.'

She was a passable cook and he'd always left the family meals to her. It was another thing about his life that his fans might find disappointing but it saved him from what he mentally called the tyranny of catering for a household. Though happy to cater for adult dinner parties, he preferred to allow Helen to deal with Demi's passionate screaming fits and Chloë's demands for ketchup on everything.

Helen's nose wrinkled in concern. 'Darling, you will have time to read them a story before you go out?'

'You bet I will.' David tickled Demi, producing squeaks of delighted laughter. 'Come along, monster, let's brush those teeth!' Helen followed them upstairs with Chloë on her hip. When the kids were tucked in, he sat between their beds and read until they grew drowsy, and bent to kiss them before leaving the room.

In the bathroom and walk-in wardrobe off the satin-striped master bedroom, he showered, selected a clean shirt and shrugged on a jacket, adding a scarf in case the night should be cold. Downstairs, Helen was defrosting her dinner. He came up behind her and, parting the hair on the back of her neck, pressed his lips on her skin. She turned in his arms to kiss him and, for a moment, he wished he hadn't invented the meeting. But it was too late to cancel things now. Besides, he knew that, once out of the house, everything would be different. Striding downhill towards the station, he'd feel alive again, back in the swing and on his way to a place where he was valued not as a father, a breadwinner or a celebrity. Not even just as a highly accomplished lover, though that was a skill he was happy to have acknowledged. Basically, he thought, I'm sick of role-playing. I've done it throughout my professional life and now I'm doing it at home. He was honest enough to acknowledge that this was the outcome of his own choices, yet his spark of desire for his wife changed to irritation. The fact is, he thought,

I'm sick of being stuck on a pedestal. I want to be free to be myself.

He boarded the train feeling upbeat and liberated but, as he sat down, he recalled Jennifer's final words to him in the lawyer's office. 'Okay, that's everything. Goodbye, David.' Picking up her handbag, she'd given him an annoying smile. 'You're free as a bird and, if you had any sense, you'd stay that way. But that's not going to happen, is it? You can't cope with freedom. Let's just hope that next time round you won't foul your own nest.'

Chapter Eight

Penny arrived home from work at six thirty. As she pushed her bike onto the pavement, she saw Mark through the shop window, working at his laptop with the 'Closed' sign on the door. His bent head was almost obscured by a vase of white freesias and another, full of lilies, stood on a table by the till. One of his dad's friends had a flower stall in the market and kept the shop provided with striking blooms that hadn't sold. Occasionally, when Mark declared he hadn't room for all he was given, he left bunches on Penny's doorstep that always made her smile. But now she hunched her shoulders, hoping he wouldn't look up and see her. She hadn't got time to stop and talk, and she wasn't sure she could face him. Her mind was on the evening that lay ahead.

As always, when she entered her flat, she relaxed and felt in control. Evening sunlight streamed through the first-floor windows, casting a lattice of shadows on the stripped, polished floorboards. The room was furnished almost as sparsely as Bill had furnished his bedsits. Having created an open-plan living space that encompassed the whole floor, Penny had installed a sleek kitchen overlooking Stanley's hunting ground in the little back yard and, along with a table and dining chairs, had bought a pair of white leather sofas. A coffee-table in glass and brushed steel had a shelf on which she kept magazines and newspapers. Everything else was stored on one wall in floor-to-ceiling cupboards with white doors. On the other walls, she'd exposed the Victorian brickwork, which had probably been fired in a kiln no more than a mile away. According to her architect, exposed bricks were passé, but the creamy-yellow handmade surface interspersed with soft purples and pinks delighted Penny, who'd briskly told him not to argue. On seeing the result, Bill had been unimpressed. 'If the man who built this terrace intended those bricks to be seen, he wouldn't have forked out money for a plasterer.'

Laughing, Penny had repeated what she'd said to her architect. 'My place, my rules.'

This had produced a loud snort from Bill. 'Talking to you is like talking to my boy Mark. You won't be told, either one of you. I'd be better off saving my breath to cool my porridge.'

Penny showered and, choosing at random, changed into a green, pleated skirt and white cotton T-shirt. She was longing for the glass of wine that usually marked the end of her day, but the doctor had uttered dire warnings about the dangers of alcohol in pregnancy, saying it could provoke untold damage – poor growth, behavioural problems, and 'distinct facial features', including 'a flattened divot, or groove, beneath the nose'. Later, Penny had checked and found you'd have to drink like a fish to inflict a flattened divot, or groove, on your unborn baby, and that a glass of wine at the end of the day before you'd known you were pregnant didn't automatically lead to disaster. Which was just as well, because there hadn't been a 'parental planning period', just the moment of dread when she'd faced the fact that her period was late, googled the stats on IUD failure rates, and decided she'd better cycle to work via the local chemist.

The doorbell rang and, going downstairs, she looked at the screen on the intercom. David was standing in the street below with a bunch of flowers and a bag she knew would contain a cold bottle of Moët. She pressed the button to let him in and, leaving the door to the landing ajar, went to pour a glass of water. When she turned from the fridge he was standing in the doorway, wearing a shirt and jeans under his casual linen jacket, and the scarf she'd bought for his birthday, which was pale grey silk and matched his startling eyes.

Whenever he came into the flat, Penny was struck by his height, perhaps because she was used to seeing him onscreen in close-up, and to looking down from the gallery as he worked on the studio floor. He was an inch or two over six foot and more loose-limbed than he appeared on television. She knew his hands from close-ups too, but mostly from their touch, and the straightness of his bones, the hollows of his ears and the slight tic at the corner of his left eye when he got nervous. That never happened in front of a camera but, here in the flat, she'd seen it whenever he dropped his guard in an argument. His good opinion of himself mattered deeply to David, and she'd watched his mind doing somersaults to prove himself in the right, unaware of the little tic that betrayed his struggle. She'd watched his face while he slept too, his cheek rough and his arm curled around his head on her pillow. She knew his voice in all its shades of caressing, challenge and cajoling. She knew he plucked his eyebrows and dyed his lashes.

When he came towards her smiling, she startled herself by the violence of her reaction. She found herself clinging to him desperately, as if she'd feared he might not arrive. Which was nonsense. He'd never failed to turn up when she expected him, and clinginess had no part in their relationship, which, from the start, she'd never intended to last. I'm out of my depth, she thought miserably. Way out of my depth. I never imagined this could happen. But she'd braced herself for a practical talk on a difficult subject, so she pulled away, trying to regain her cool.

He didn't seem to notice her agitation, because he went to place the flowers in the sink and open the champagne. 'Shall we have a drink while we decide what to order for dinner?' In the months that they'd been lovers, he'd seldom been able to stay the night so, rather than waste time cooking, Penny generally phoned for a takeaway. One of her kitchen drawers was crammed with menus, ranging from the cheap and cheerful chip shop round the corner to expensive restaurants happy to deliver to the area's high-end flats. Already David was rummaging through laminated squares and oblongs, wondering aloud if tonight was a night for steak tartare or an old-fashioned fish supper.

Penny's stomach heaved at the thought of either. 'I'm going to stick to water, thanks, and, look, David, I'm not sure about eating. We need to talk.'

'Do we? Why? And don't be silly, have a glass of this.'

To her annoyance, he'd poured her some champagne. Penny

sat down and took a deep breath. 'Because we do. I've got something I have to say to you.'

'Well, take this and talk to me over the bubbles.'

'Oh, stop it. You sound like a second-rate Lothario.'

He put down her glass and sat beside her on the sofa. 'What's the matter? Time of the month?'

Penny was seized by an impulse to laugh, followed by a conviction that, if she started, she might not be able to stop.

David frowned. 'If I've come at a bad time I'll leave, but you could have sent a text.'

'When have I ever texted you? Don't be stupid.' With an effort, Penny controlled herself. 'Look, I'm sorry. This is coming out all wrong. It's difficult and, if I'm honest, I've wondered if I ought to tell you. But you've a right to know and, anyway, things are going to be different in future. For me and you, I mean. This changes everything.'

He was worried now, setting down his own glass and taking both her hands. 'What are you on about? What's happened?'

'I'm pregnant.'

The colour drained from David's face. He reached automatically for his drink, turning away to down it in a gulp. Penny didn't need to see his face to know what he was thinking. Oh, God, she thought, he's really going to ask me. He doesn't want to, but he won't know how to stop himself. Unable to bear it, she spoke before he turned back to her. 'Yes, it's yours. Who else did you think I might be going to bed with?'

'I didn't. Well, I don't know. I mean, are you certain?'

Penny stood up, determined to stick to the script she'd rehearsed on her way home. 'Yep, perfectly certain. But that needn't bother you, David. I've thought this through. You and I are done. It may be okay for me to have an affair with a married man, but I'm not inflicting a part-time father on a child. Besides, we could never keep it quiet, and you need to think of Helen and the twins.' She could see his mind racing and, beneath his shock and resentment of his dismissal, a hastily suppressed flash of relief. And, really, she thought, who could blame him? Not me.

'But how will you cope?'

'I'll be fine. I mean it, David, we're done. We couldn't have gone on for ever, anyway.'

With more speed than tact, he got to his feet, then hesitated. 'What do you want me to do now? I mean, should I go or stay?'

Had he imagined they were going to sit down to a takeaway? Or nip upstairs for a quick farewell tumble? 'Probably best if you go.'

'Okay. If that's what you want.'

She watched him pick up his scarf and dither before stuffing it into his jacket pocket, as if she might demand he return her gift. I'm not being fair, she thought. He's feeling awkward. He's my employee, and I started this, and it's my damn contraception that's failed. She smiled into his eyes and, to her relief, found her voice behaving properly. 'I'm right, aren't I? You don't want any part of this. We agreed at the start that Helen mustn't be hurt.'

'Look, if you need money ...'

It was said with such reluctance that she barely contained a laugh. 'Oh, David! I make twice your salary. Go away. Go home to your wife.'

But when the door closed behind him, she sank down on her white sofa and pressed rigid hands against her mouth. This was no laughing matter. It had been the decent thing to do, the only course that was fair to his wife and kids. She was glad she'd done it. This wasn't the end of something, though. It was just the beginning. And what on earth was she going to do now?

Chapter Nine

By the weekend, Val had still heard nothing from Penny. After breakfast on Sunday, Marguerite suggested a walk on Hampstead Heath. 'I could do with stretching my legs before my flight home tomorrow. We can take a picnic with us. What do you think?'

They caught a bus to Hampstead and walked up to the Heath, striding against a blustery wind that shook the budding trees and made talking impossible, except in shouted snatches. Outstripping the family groups that confined themselves to paths, they turned off the marked ways to scramble over tree roots and plod on through yielding beech mast. After a while, Val dropped her bag by a fallen tree. 'Shall we stop for a breather?'

Marguerite sat on the tree trunk, raising her face to sunlight filtered through fluttering leaves. 'I wouldn't mind some tea.'

'Not hungry?'

'Not yet. I dare say I will be, though.'

They'd brought a flask, some napkins and a Tupperware

box into which Val had tucked lettuce hearts, tomatoes and two Scotch eggs. She filled the top of the Thermos with tea and they drank from it companionably, sitting side by side on the fallen tree trunk. The earth-clogged roots had reared into the air, leaving a hollow where new shoots, straight as arrows, were already springing from the fallen wood. Marguerite insinuated a thumbnail under a strip of loose bark and gently peeled a sliver from the trunk. A flurry of woodlice scuttled about blindly, seeking to regain the darkness between the bark and the moist pith. Val flicked one from the hem of her jacket. 'Remember we used to call them meelies? Why on earth was that?'

'It's what the gardener called them in Ireland when I was a child. I suppose I picked up the name from him and passed it on to you.'

'I must have passed it to Penny, then. She uses it too.' Blowing on her tea, Val remarked that she'd always wished she'd known her Wicklow grandmother.

Marguerite smiled. 'You look rather like her.'

'No, I don't! I've seen the portrait in Stonehill. She was a stunner.'

Stonehill was the official name of the house in Wicklow, though local people still called it 'Dr Barry's house'. A portrait of Ruth, Marguerite's mother, hung above the fireplace in the drawing room, painted in 1951, the year she and Donal had married. Marguerite had never been able to reconcile her memory of her mother with the slender girl who gazed out from the portrait. Ruth was portrayed as the epitome of 1950s glamour with her hair swept off her face and falling in glossy waves to her shoulders. The withdrawn woman Marguerite had known had had none of that shining vibrancy, and the velvet dress in the painting contradicted her recollection of a mother who wore tweed skirts, hand-knitted sweaters and wellington boots.

Over the years, she'd told herself that this wasn't surprising. You didn't sit for a portrait in your wellies. You wore your best. And artists who painted wives for husbands tended to idealise their subjects, especially in post-war Ireland where commissions weren't easily come by. If this was Ruth portrayed as if seen through Donal's eyes, maybe it could be called a perfect likeness. Besides, thought Marguerite, there are elements in it I do remember. I see them in Val and recognise them in my own face in the mirror: the shape of the cheekbones, and the tilt of the figure's head against the dark background, chosen to contrast with that corn-coloured hair. Accepting Val's offer of the Thermos top, she blew on the tea in her turn. 'I think you're wrong. You do have a look of my mother. So do I, though both of us have my father's eyes and his height. Penny's completely different, physically and temperamentally. She doesn't even take after your dad's side of the family.'

Linking her hands around her knee, Val nodded. 'I know. Penny takes after Simon.'

Simon, Val's fiancé, had died without knowing he was going to be a father. He and three friends had drowned on a jaunt he'd called a rehearsal for his stag night. Though the man from whom they'd hired the boat had insisted he'd tried to warn them about the weather, the coroner's verdict of accidental death had been accompanied by a stern remark about moral responsibility. But Val, sitting in tears at the back of the stuffy room, had known where the real responsibility lay. Young, fit, and full of the assurance that came with their university educations, Simon and his mates would have scoffed at warnings from an elderly Cornishman who made his living by hiring out his boat.

After the inquest, she'd shaken hands with his grey-faced father and seen blame as well as grief in his mother's brimming eyes. Weeks later when she found she was pregnant, she'd known what their reaction was likely to be. The first stunned response had turned to suspicion. Subsequent conversations had made things no better. And, in the end, when a letter from their solicitor had offered financial assistance on the condition that she take a paternity test, Val had refused in outrage and all contact was broken off. By then she'd known her baby was a girl, and had mentally christened her Penny, and the fact that she had her own parents' support had been enough. If Simon's family wanted nothing to do with her, that was fine, because she hated the thought of being shackled to them. I'm not his grieving widow, she'd thought, and I won't share my daughter with people who think I'm a liar. Simon was never close to them and I don't see why I should be. That had been in 1995. Time had lessened her outrage and made her more aware of what might be best for Penny but, by then, it had been too late to heal the rift.

Reaching into the Tupperware box, Val took out the lettuce hearts and a paper twist of salt. Sheltered from the wind by the clump of trees, it was easier to talk. 'I expect it's true that opposites attract. Simon and I really were as different as chalk and cheese. I'm not sure that, if he'd lived, the marriage would have lasted. The good thing is that Penny grew up knowing she was the child of love and commitment, though I've always felt bad that she didn't know her grandparents. Years later, I did try to get back in touch with them. Turned out they'd died in a car crash.' Val flashed a guilty grin at Marguerite. 'Not exactly a lucky family, was it?'

'I'm sorry. I didn't know that.'

'How could you? I never said. It felt surreal and, anyway, they were just a couple of strangers. Not very nice to me and not all that close to Simon. At least, so he told me. Still, grandparents matter, don't they?'

'I can't speak from experience. All four of mine were dead by the time Ruth and Donal married. But I've loved being a granny. So will you when Penny's baby is born.' Val felt a lump rise in her throat and, sensitive to her averted face, Marguerite concentrated on peeling another strip of bark from the tree trunk. They sat in silence for several minutes before she spoke again. 'Truly, you'll love being a granny. And Penny will come around, wait and see.'

Val said nothing. Longing to make things better but feeling she'd nothing valid to offer, Marguerite heard herself repeating what she'd said before. 'It's only a couple of days since she told you her news about the baby. Give her time.'

Val's face twisted. 'But I want to do something to help, and I feel helpless.'

'I expect she'll give you a call next week.'

'But what if she doesn't? I was awake half the night worrying. And, before you say it, I know this is not about me.'

'It is about you.' Marguerite plucked at the green pith beneath the shredded bark. 'It's about all of us, isn't it? That's the point.'

Chapter Ten

It was raining when Marguerite's plane landed in Dublin, but by the time she was in her car the sun was shining. Avoiding the ring road, she drove through the city centre, glad she'd planned her flight to arrive in advance of the rush-hour traffic and could take a route that reminded her of so many homecomings. The early days, when her father had come to pick her up in his Morris Minor Traveller. Later trips, after Donal's retirement in 1985, when Val, then in her early teens, would drag him out for a walk whatever the weather, a stick in his hand and a spaniel at their heels. And later still, when Donal was gone and Penny was growing up, in the years when Stonehill was a holiday home, chilly and slightly forlorn at first but still redolent of past warmth and welcomes.

Though the sale of Marguerite's Holland Park house had yielded enough to modernise Stonehill for her retirement, she'd chosen to keep it almost unchanged. The kitchen, a pantry and a scullery were still in the semi-basement. At ground-floor level, the drawing room, which opened onto a walled garden, took up the whole width of the house at the rear. On either side of the entrance hall were a dining room and Donal's old surgery, with a lavatory and what had been a waiting room at the back. On the first floor, along with a large, utilitarian bathroom, were four bedrooms. Two of these had been called guestrooms in Marguerite's childhood, though she couldn't remember there being many guests.

Nothing about Stonehill was pretentious. It was late Georgian, built for practical use and modest comfort, a white stucco villa with sash windows as neatly disposed as in a child's drawing. Donal's family had lived there for generations, each of which had produced a son who'd become the local doctor. There'd been lawyers and clergymen too, and daughters who'd done charitable work or married the resident magistrate. In those days, Stonehill had offered significant local employment. That had changed by the 1950s when, in Marguerite's childhood, Ruth had kept house with the help of a cheerful woman called Mrs Sinnott, who'd walked up from the village two days a week. By then, the stables to the side of the house had been converted into sheds and a garage, and the poky rooms under the roof, once servants' bedrooms, had become storage spaces for unwanted bits and pieces.

Ahead were the granite gateposts that marked the entrance to the driveway, where the gate stood open, its lower bars hidden by ferns and weeds. Marguerite couldn't remember when she'd last closed it, and the rusted padlock hooked over its bolt probably hadn't been used for fifty years. As she pulled up outside the house the afternoon sun gleamed on unbarred windows. Lifting her case from the boot, she unlocked the porch and went through her front door with no apprehension. She'd never crossed this threshold without a deep rush of pleasure, as if the strength of past generations was waiting to offer comfort and strength.

Carrying her case through the panelled hall, Marguerite went upstairs. When she'd come home for good, she'd decided to use the bedroom that had once been her parents'. It overlooked the wildflower meadow, was larger than the others, and had a dressing room that she could turn into an en-suite. Recarpeted, painted and furnished with a new, well-sprung bed, it was the only room she'd substantially changed, and one in which Donal had made his own changes only a few weeks after Ruth died.

As she placed her case on the bed, Marguerite remembered her twelve-year-old outrage when decorators had stripped the flowered paper from the walls. It had felt as if her mother's presence was being erased from the house, but Mrs Sinnott, who'd been a tower of strength in the bleak days after the funeral, had explained that her daddy felt sad when he saw her mam's things around him, and that making a clean sweep was always the best plan after a death. This kindly, unsentimental logic, and the fact that her mother's portrait still hung above the drawing-room fire, had reconciled Marguerite to Donal's abrupt decision. Later, half apologetically, he'd echoed Mrs Sinnott's explanation. 'We'll never forget Mummy, will we, pet? But we'll just have to pick ourselves up and get on with living.'

Having changed out of the clothes she'd worn on her journey, Marguerite carried her laundry down to the scullery and tossed it into the washer-drier. Then she went up to the drawing room, unlocked the French doors and stepped into the garden. Outside the doors, which were flanked by tall windows, was a gentle slope up to the boundary wall. No doubt this had once been a smooth lawn, but Ruth had decided to seed it with poppies and fuzzy blue cornflowers, had added new wildflowers over the years, and freed repressed plantains and clovers by letting the grass grow long. Enchanted by the hosts of insects and bees this had attracted, Marguerite had gone further, welcoming nettles, thistles and rosebay willowherb, which most of her neighbours, and no doubt all her forebears, would have dismissed as common, intrusive weeds.

Now, leaving the French doors open to air the drawing room, she strolled up the slope and began a leisurely circuit of her garden, keeping one hand on the granite wall, which was warm to the touch and flecked with yellow lichen. Stonehill had never been grand enough for a formal kitchen garden, but the vegetable beds to the side of the house were screened by beech hedges, and there was an orchard with rows of red- and blackcurrant and gooseberry bushes, where blossom had drifted from apple trees and leaves were beginning to spread. Marguerite moved down cool, curving corridors between the wall and the backs of herbaceous borders. Having crossed the drive and completed her circuit, she returned to the house, carrying a handful of flowers she'd picked on the way. There was a jumble of vases by the sink in the old surgery, so she filled one, put the posy in water and left it on the hall table, a touch that made her homecoming complete. Collecting a pot of coffee, a mug and a milk jug from the kitchen, she returned to the drawing room, lit the fire and sank into an armchair.

The portrait of Ruth hung over the mantelpiece. Between the fireplace and the French doors stood a pedestal table and chairs, and against one of the oak-panelled walls was a battered sofa. Displaced by the portrait, a mirrored overmantel hung on one wall above an upright piano, which had a soundboard of pierced fretwork backed with faded pleated silk.

As Marguerite drank her coffee, she considered the image of her mother. The focus of attention was Ruth's hair, bright against the dark background, and a secondary effect of light played on the folds of her velvet dress, which had a fitted bodice with a high revered collar and elbow-length sleeves. Her left hand lay on her knee displaying her diamond engagement ring and wedding band against the green velvet. For the first time, it occurred to Marguerite that the artist's intensely modern treatment suggested the effect her mother must have had on the little rural community she'd married into. An American who'd come to Ireland after the Second World War, Ruth had intended to make a brief stay before travelling on to France and Italy. Instead, she'd met and married Donal who, Marguerite suspected, hadn't been able to believe his luck. No one else in the Barry family had ever brought home such an arresting wife.

Touched by a chill breeze from the garden, Marguerite went to close the French doors and draw the rose-patterned curtains against the dusk. Back at the fireside, she stirred the coals and switched on a lamp on the low table by her armchair. Lamplight falling on the coffee pot provoked a memory of her mother's hands on its green Bakelite handle, and another of herself as a child at the kitchen table, polishing the chrome-faced felt cover that kept the coffee hot. For a moment she lay back in the chair, closing her eyes and allowing the warmth of the fire to reach her bones. Then, with a powerful surge of contentment, she recalled the touch of green velvet, unseen yet deeply comforting in the dark. She had never known the dress in Ruth's portrait, but her whole being knew the fabric of which it had been made. This was the elusive connection that had come to her as she sat in Val's garden in London, and had slipped away before she could pin it down.

She opened her eyes and the past seemed to recede from her like a wave. Fearful of crushing the thought that had just flowered in her mind, Marguerite stood up cautiously. How has it taken so long, she thought, for me to see that the dress in the painting must have been cut up to make an edge for my quilt? She left the room, hardly knowing where she was going, and moved through the house without turning on the lights. The scent of the posy she'd picked in the garden filled the shadowy hallway, and upstairs in one of the attic bedrooms, she found what she sought. It was on the top shelf of a cupboard, where she had put it in 1970, before going to London to take up her job as an au pair. Standing on the same chair she'd used then, she reached for the long cardboard box that had once held a delivery of flowers. Lifting the lid, she turned back layers of yellowed tissue paper, revealing the folded quilt and releasing a strong smell of mothballs. Then she carried it back down to the drawing-room fire.

The quilt was too small for an adult's bed but, throughout her teens, unwilling to lose the connection with her mother, she'd kept it in her room to use as a throw. It was quilted in cream-coloured thread, and its underside was a length of green flannel. On the top, squares of differing fabrics enclosed a central block composed of four pieces of floral satin. Now, over seventy years since it had been quilted, the central block remained perfect. Among the pieces surrounding it, Ruth had included silk and voile alongside brocade and linen. Some of these were worn or had come away from the stitching, exposing the batting between the patchwork top and the flannel back. In one place, at one end, the pile of the velvet edging that bound the three layers together was almost threadbare.

Marguerite smiled. Closing her eyes, she touched the worn green velvet and felt the powerful surge of contentment again. *This was what told me I was loved when I was a child*, she thought. *I'd forgotten until I remembered Val's beloved teddy bear, with its ragbag dress and balding nose where the fur got kissed away.* For a moment she sat motionless, looking up at her mother's portrait. Then, making up her mind, she reached for her phone.

The call was answered at once. 'Hi, Mum. How was your flight?'

'Perfect, I'm here by the fire.'

'And everything's fine?'

'Absolutely. Listen, Val, have you heard from Penny?'

She could tell by the pause that the question was unwelcome, and when Val replied her voice was unnaturally brisk. 'No. Not yet. You said you thought it was best to give her space.'

'I did. It is. I just wondered if she'd been in touch.'

'Well, she hasn't.'

'And you're still worried.'

'Of course I am. I told you. I feel helpless and useless, but there's nothing to be done. I can't beat on her door and try to tell her I'm happy for her. The chances are she wouldn't let me in, and I'd just have made matters worse. So, I suppose I'll have to hold my breath and hope. But, Mum, we've already had this conversation. Why are we having it again?'

'Because while we're waiting for Penny to come to terms with things, we're not going to sit around feeling helpless and useless.'

'But—'

'Don't argue with me, Val. I know I've found the right answer. You and I are going to take on a project.'

THE PATTERNS

THREAD 2

Val

Val's earliest memories of fabric belonged to Marguerite's tie-dye and cheesecloth phase. Bright smocks and shifts run up at home on the kitchen table, and floor-length kaftans in Indian prints bought from Anokhi in South Molton Street. A beaded sash and a pair of slippers with black grosgrain silk uppers embroidered with flowers in gold metallic thread. As a toddler, she'd stolen into her parents' bedroom, taken the slippers to try them on, and was found hopping from foot to foot, enchanted by the sound of leather soles on a wooden floor.

Sumptuous though the kaftans were, Marguerite had worn them on all occasions: striding across Hampstead Heath carrying a picnic basket, marshalling family and luggage on their ferry trips to Ireland, and baking cakes in the house in Holland Park. The predominant scent of Val's childhood was a combination of patchouli and warm frangipane, and the first tragedy she could recall was dropping a splodge of blackcurrant jam on her mum's calico skirt. Marguerite had said it was nothing that couldn't be fixed with a patch, and the following day the laundered skirt had sported a little appliqué bird, cut from a scarf and stitched on in bold contrasting thread.

By the time Val was too grown-up for puffed sleeves and broderie anglaise, Marguerite too had moved on, and the kaftans' sequined panels, quilted cuffs, and crimson trimmings were cut up and used to customise Val's jean jackets. Each had been a work of art and, though she'd never said so, wearing them had made Val feel that she could go anywhere and do anything, lifted by the assurance of her mother's quiet support.

This was the life Val had longed to give Penny. Pregnant and weeping for Simon's death, she'd knitted a shawl for her unborn baby, hooking and twisting anguish and love into the soft yellow web. But there'd been no time to handwash wool in her life as a single mother so, in the end, Penny was wrapped in polyester blankets, flame-retardant and easy to dry overnight.

Eventually things did get easier. She learned to juggle the demands of work, housekeeping and childcare, and found satisfaction in coping alone. She even found time to make frocks for Penny to wear to parties, and the dungarees with stars on the bib and patches on the knees. And later, when Penny rejected these as childish, Val had looked forward to shopping trips with her teenage daughter when Penny would turn to her for fashion advice, and they'd set the world to rights over coffee. But by then Penny, so like Simon in appearance, had begun to show characteristics Val recognised as his. Headstrong and independent, she ignored all advice, however gently given, and took the view that the world was simply there for her to conquer. On good days, Val assured herself that confidence and fearlessness were qualities to be encouraged. With her own choices circumscribed by tragedy, she wanted Penny to be, and have, whatever she set her heart on. But, on other days, remembering that Simon's arrogance had killed him, she was gripped by an unacknowledged dread that she might lose Penny too.

Chapter Eleven

Val sat in the staffroom marking students' assignments and thinking about the conversation she'd had the previous night. 'Slow down, Mum. You've found *what* in the attic?'

'A quilt. Listen. This is important. I hate the thought of you there alone, worrying about Pen.'

'That's sweet of you, but we both know there's nothing to be done.'

'But there is. Listen, darling. You and I can do something together. It came to me as soon as I found the quilt.' Realising there was no point in trying to stop the torrent, Val had given up the attempt. By the time she'd taken in what was suggested, she'd known caution wasn't going to be welcome. Yet what could she say? Marguerite's idea had seemed so arbitrary and ill-conceived that she'd spoken as if addressing one of her students. 'Mum. Hold on a minute. Let's get this clear. You're saying that you and I should make a patchwork quilt?'

'Yes. A cot quilt. For Penny's baby. I'm sitting here by the fire with one my mother made for me.'

'But why?'

'It's something we can create together, the two of us. We'll make it reversible. You'll do one side and I'll work on the other, and when they're done, we can quilt them together.'

'I still don't understand ...'

'A keepsake quilt. Don't you see? I'll take pieces from Ruth's quilt – it's falling apart anyway – and you can use fabrics from Penny's childhood.'

'What?'

'You said you've a ragbag somewhere. Won't there be bits and pieces from the dresses you made for her?'

'But a patchwork quilt? Mandalas and stars and complicated measurements? You know I'm useless at maths, and I'm not a quilter.'

'Trust me, nor was my mother! Her quilt is the simplest piece of work. Square pieces and straight lines. It couldn't be less complicated.'

'Well, but—'

'Val, don't be difficult. I know this is going to work. We'll piece together a patchwork of family memories ...'

'But ...'

'... and all the pieces will combine to welcome the new family member. When Penny comes around – and she will, darling, honestly – she'll know how happy we are for her, and how much we're looking forward to the baby.' It was unusual for Marguerite to be this forceful, so Val was taken aback. Confused, and unsure of her own response to the proposal, she'd temporised. 'Look, this is all a bit sudden. Let me mull it over.'

'Okay, take your time but, truly, I know it's the answer. Call me back when you've had a chance to think.'

Val looked around the staffroom, wishing she had someone to confide in. But saying that she was about to become a granny was likely to provoke unwelcome questions, and trying to fend them off would make her feel worse. And I mustn't discuss Penny, she thought. The tabloids print any snippet of gossip connected to her show. Imagine opening a paper and seeing *Who's the Father? Pregnant Penny's Mum Says She's Worried to Death!*

She abandoned her marking and got up to make a coffee, hoping her response to last night's call hadn't left Marguerite deflated. In her mind's eye, she could see Stonehill, lit by firelight and lamplight with the coffee pot on the table by her mother's low chair. The curtains would have been drawn across the drawing-room doors and windows, and garden flowers would have scented the hall. The thought of the house and of her long-dead granddad, brought a lump to Val's throat. As she switched on the kettle, she recalled childhood visits to Wicklow when, scrambling out of a taxi, she'd run into that welcoming hallway. As a child, she'd been known as 'Granddad's shadow'. Donal had always been at his most animated in her company, striding along identifying birdsong or hunkered down by a stream showing her how to tickle trout.

One summer morning when she was fourteen, they'd taken a walk to the Devil's Glen waterfall, where Donal had sat on a rock and Val had found barley-sugar sweets in her pocket. Accepting one, Donal had patted Rufus, the spaniel, and gestured at their surroundings with his stick. 'All the land hereabouts used to belong to the Synges of Glanmore Castle.'

'John Millington Synge? The playwright?'

'That's the man. Spent his holidays bowling round these roads on a bicycle.' Seeing her reaction, Donal smiled. 'If you find that impressive, I ought to add that your great-granddad frequently picked him up when he fell off. Dusted him down and strapped up his sprained ankles.'

'That's amazing. I've got a holiday essay to write about Synge and Yeats.'

'Yeats the poet or Yeats the artist?'

'William Butler Yeats. I didn't know there were two of them.'

'Jack B. was a painter. William B. was the poet. They were brothers. There were sisters too, who did needlework. I've no insights to offer you on artists, but my dad told me W. B. was a dreadful bore.'

'You mean he knew him?'

'It was more a case of encountering him in the bar of the Shelbourne Hotel. Yeats was holding court one day when my father was reading a newspaper and, apparently, Dad didn't like being disturbed.'

While she waited for the kettle to boil, Val selected a biscuit. It was strange to think that if it hadn't been for that walk to the Devil's Glen she wouldn't be here today marking essays. By working her granddad's anecdotes into her own holiday essay, she'd gained top marks and, spurred on at first by nothing more than unaccustomed attention from a teacher, had developed a genuine interest in reading. That was what took me to Oxford, she thought, and Oxford was where I met Simon.

As Val chose a mug and lifted the steaming kettle, Kate, one of her colleagues, came to join her. 'Is there enough water for another cup?'

'Plenty.'

'Good. I'm dying of thirst. Shall we take them outside?'

Although Val was several years older than Kate, they'd been to the same college and had struck up an easy friendship at work. Sitting on a bench on the strip of paving outside the staffroom, they chatted until, in the midst of a good-humoured rant about the school secretary, Kate stopped suddenly and laughed. 'Who'd have thought that either of us would end up as teachers in Finchley?'

'You had other plans?'

'Didn't we all? I suppose a glittering literary career is everyone's dream if they've chosen to read English.'

Val bit into a biscuit. 'It wasn't mine.'

'No?'

'I thought reading would open my mind and make me go out and do things. But then I got engaged, and he was drowned, and there was a baby ...'

Val's voice tailed off and Kate looked at her shrewdly. 'How's Penny doing?'

'Fine. Madly successful.' Tipping the dregs of her coffee into a flower pot, Val said she ought to get on with her work. Kate nodded. 'Me too. Back to the grindstone.'

Val returned to her table wondering why a teaching job in Finchley should stop you writing. Even if it felt like a bit of a compromise, why not do both? I doubt if Simon could have hacked it, though, she thought wryly. He never settled for compromise and he certainly fitted the stereotype of a man hell-bent on a glittering literary career. He'd proposed in 1994, on the night of their college graduation ball and, though deeply in love, Val hadn't been quite sure how to react. Simon had featured in the unformed dreams she'd just described to Kate, but as a fellow-traveller, not a husband. Yet she'd accepted the ring he'd produced from the pocket of his hired dress suit, and become immersed in plans for a shared future. Like the daughter he didn't live to see, Simon was a force to be reckoned with. It was he who'd decided they should find temporary jobs as teachers. 'We'll take whatever's on offer now and reassess later. Move out of London, or over to Ireland, maybe. Once we're married and solvent, I'll chuck teaching and write my novel. The world will be our oyster, wait and see.'

Within weeks of Val taking her job in Finchley, he'd found the run-down semi in West Hampstead. 'We'll snap it up now before someone else does. If we have a decent deposit, we can easily get a mortgage. I've got ten grand left to me by my godmother. See if you can borrow the same from your folks.' Val's parents had produced the loan and, advised by Paul, she and Simon had made wills in each other's favour. At the time, she'd seen her dad's caveat as just another hoop to be jumped through before getting their mortgage. Simon had bristled, calling it interference, so most of her attention had been on keeping things moving without any fuss.

And all had gone to plan, just as Simon promised. They renovated the house themselves with help from Rory. Simon's parents visited once, on a day up to London, negotiating stepladders and paint pots and looking askance when Val brewed tea on a Primus. For months it had felt like camping out in a DIY shop. And then, with the house completed, it was time to plan the wedding. She'd been looking at fabric samples for her bridesmaid's dress when Simon announced that he and some mates had booked to go sailing. 'You don't think I'm bunking off?'

'From what?'

'Tasting canapés. Ordering marquees.'

'Of course not. Anyway, you're useless at that stuff.'

'But how will you fill the lonely hours without me?'

'Very happily. I'll be checking out bouquets.'

'You ought to have flaming golden tiger lilies. Something to express your inner goddess.'

'Don't be an ass.'

'I'm not. You're my muse. You'll inspire all my novels.'

'I thought you said there was only going to be one.'

'Which, naturally, will turn out to be a best-seller. After which, it'll be one a year, a Booker prize and a villa in the Bahamas.' He'd twisted a strand of her hair around his finger. 'See what I mean? Flaming gold, like a gorgeous tiger lily.'

'I've just used a highlighting kit.'

'Don't spoil the illusion. Tell you what, let's go to bed and you can inspire me some more.'

'Now?'

'Certainly. Live for the moment. We could all be dead and gone by next week.'

The next day he'd set out with his friends, leaning on the car horn and cheering as they drove away. The news of the accident had come when Val and Marguerite were with the florist, and she hadn't been able to bear the heavy scent of lilies since.

One minute I was a student, she thought, with my whole life ahead of me, and the next minute I was a bereaved single mother. As soon as she'd found she was pregnant, she'd rung her best friend from college. 'Come over. I've got news.'

They'd sat in the kitchen, where Val had cried into pizza marinara and Sasha had made consoling noises and tea. 'But I thought you were on the pill?'

'Yeah. Remember when Simon whisked me off on that romantic city break? And I ate something dodgy the night we arrived? Well, apparently, throwing up can affect the pill's efficiency.'

'Wow. Who knew?'

'Not me. I'm going to make damn sure this baby does, though.'

'You're going to have it?'

'Of course. It's all I have left of Simon. I'll cope. People do.'

I hadn't a clue, though, thought Val. I hadn't even realised that, without those wills Dad insisted on, Simon's parents would have been able to claim I'd no right to the house. That narrow escape had been the first financial shock of her bereavement. The second had been the realisation that the only way to avoid the dole or dependence on her parents was to cling to a job that circumscribed her dreams.

On the day of Val's second scan, Sasha rang to say she'd been offered a chance to work abroad. She'd dropped in to say goodbye, bringing a box of chocolates, and they'd eaten them in the little back garden. Val had done her best to be upbeat. 'I can't believe you're off to Vienna! It sounds amazing.'

'Completely amazing. It's only a year's contract, though.'

'But in a castle!'

'It's not a castle, just a town house. Lots of twiddly gilt bits, though. They sent photos. Mind you, they do have a mini castle thing in the countryside.'

'Shut *up*!'

Unspoken between them lay the thought that this was exactly what Val herself had dreamed of. Sacha had tried to play it down. 'It's just being a boring personal assistant.'

'Yes, but to a concert pianist. Think of the people you'll meet! And *Sachertorte* and meringues in Viennese cafés! And concerts, and the Schönbrunn Palace and trips down the Danube.'

'I'll be there to work, you know, not swan around.'

They'd laughed, and Val had tried to conceal the dull lump of misery in her chest. Later she'd wept at the thought of all the doors that were now closed to her, and tried to tell herself that, with a baby on the way, she was lucky to have a roof over her head and be able to pay her bills. As often happens with university friendships, she never saw Sacha again. A couple of postcards had arrived from Vienna, and a card with a bouquet of flowers when Penny was born. But that was all.

Val arrived home from work aware that she needed to call Marguerite, and still unsure of what she was going to say to her. Dumping her unfinished marking in the kitchen, she went upstairs to the little room that had once been Penny's bedroom. Kneeling in front of a run of cupboards, she pulled out numerous files and boxes, and rummaged in a far corner until her hand closed on fabric.

The bulging bag she'd grasped was made of coarse linen. Its drawstring top was caught on some unseen projection but, eventually, she managed to drag it out. It had been an engagement present from one of the neighbours at Stonehill, and the word 'Laundry' was emblazoned across it in scarlet chain stitch. Val remembered laughing about it with Simon, who'd asked if she needed a pair of pince-nez and a handkerchief sachet as well. For years the gift had remained in its wrapping until, one day, when she'd finished making a skirt or a dress for Penny, Val had decided to put it to use as a ragbag.

Now, sitting back on her heels, she shook out its contents. The first to catch her eye was a piece of the pale blue chambray she'd used for the despised dungarees. The fabric had cost rather more than she could afford at the time, and she remembered the note of defence in her voice when Penny had been unimpressed. 'I know it's not denim, darling. I just thought that chambray would be softer and nicer.'

'Dungarees aren't supposed to be nice and soft. They're meant to be workwear. Get real, Mum.'

Beneath the chambray was a piece of rose-coloured glazed cotton. That had been bought for Penny to wear as a bridesmaid at Rory's wedding. Val had made the dress and Marguerite had smocked the yoke, adding little white bullion rosebuds. There were other memories too. A card of the ric-rac used to trim a holland pinafore. Gingham and satin, and a length of chocolate-brown needlecord from which Val had cut a coat for Penny's toy lion. Turning them over, Val found scraps of sky-blue terry-towelling from which she'd made a hooded bathing wrap. They'd taken it on holiday to Ireland, where Penny had emerged from the choppy water, clutched the wrap around her, and gone scampering up the stony beach. Her little sunburned face had looked disconcertingly like Simon's as the hood slipped and the wind blew back her hair.

I know so well how she's feeling now, Val told herself. Having a baby exposes your hidden weaknesses. You're supposed to be the one in charge, but your whole life is spiralling out of control. Picking up the chambray, she laid it beside a scrap of blue gingham and found herself looking about for something to balance the effect. Ten minutes later, she'd achieved a rough assembly of colours, shapes and textures at which she stared intently before bundling them back into the bag. Then, realising her face was wet, she scrubbed at it with a tissue. I ought to ring Stonehill, she thought, but I still don't know what to say. Maybe Mum's right and Penny would love a keepsake quilt. Perhaps, when things are out of control, even an image of order can be helpful. It struck her again that it wasn't like Marguerite to be so insistent. She'd always been energetic, but never assertive.

Getting to her feet, Val found her eyes welling with tears again. Oh, for Heaven's sake! she thought, groping for the tissue. Why on earth should I get weepy over turning out my ragbag and stitching a few pieces of fabric together? I suppose it's because, if we make this quilt, it's going to mean dredging up all sorts of stuff from the past. I'm not sure I can face that. Maybe I'll just say no.

Chapter Twelve

Penny told herself she'd have to take the plunge and encounter David. The sooner a purely professional relationship was restored, the better. On top of that, she had still to work out how and when to let her pregnancy be known at work. She'd already informed her boss and discussed maternity cover, but telling people further down the food chain was a different matter. No one would assume the right to ask who the baby's father was, but many would see this turning point in her personal life as a career opportunity for themselves. So, breaking the news required forethought and strategy.

More than once, she'd reached for her phone, confident that Val could be relied on both for sympathy and discretion and that, if she chose to keep David's name to herself, her mum wouldn't pry. But after each day's work she felt so exhausted that the prospect of actually making a call that had to begin with apologies and explanations defeated her. Numb, adrift, and unable to face her mum or trust her colleagues, she spent her evenings slumped on the sofa in the company of Stanley, who tended to miaow at her window as soon as Mark shut up shop for the night. In the mornings, she watched the show in her office, making notes as it aired and firing off emails afterwards, knowing that, despite her reputation for giving space to directors, this behaviour wasn't sustainable.

Eventually, she pulled herself together and told her assistant she planned to drop by the studio on Thursday. 'Field my calls, Lolly. Okay? You can text me if it's something vital.' This was normal procedure, which didn't require spelling out, and as soon as she'd spoken, Penny wished she hadn't. In the lift down to the office bike store, she reminded herself that the surest way to flag nervousness was to talk too much. Annoyed by her error, she got to her destination hot and bothered, and went to the ladies' loo to splash water on her face. It peered back from the mirror looking blotchy and anxious, and several minutes passed before she could summon her usual air of authority.

She slipped into the gallery during the interview that preceded the news slot. Shamir the director waved, his eyes still on Roz and Gail who were interviewing a father and son writing team who had self-published a book called *Me & Him: The Wages of Sin*. It was Lolly who'd drawn Penny's attention to it and, judging by the interview, it was just as well she had. The authors were dream guests – fluent, witty and, apparently, genuinely modest, they were both strikingly good-looking, and their story ticked all of the show's boxes, from feel-good to edgy. The boy, who couldn't have been more than fifteen, explained to Gail that the book had emerged from a photo project he'd begun at what he called 'a difficult time in my life'. 'I don't really do TikTok and that. It's boring. I mean, I prefer stills to video any day. Actually, if I had my way, I'd only shoot in black-and-white.'

His father interrupted with a laugh. 'Which makes him the nerdy old fogey, not me.'

The boy shrugged. 'Is it nerdy? I just do what I do.' Somehow, his manner avoided any suggestion of humble-bragging and, as Shamir cued a sequence of black-and-white photos, Gail's voice summed up the book's reviews. '"Searingly honest", "a new departure", "a clarion call for intergenerational understanding". I suppose you could say it's a lifestyle book, but it's more than that, isn't it? It's – I don't know – a sort of freeze-frame road movie. Plus, a kind of father-son coming-of-age thing.'

The shot changed to the man smiling fondly at his son. 'I was the one who came of age. Seriously, this guy taught me a lot.'

'Yet it all started because he got himself into a bit of bother.' As Roz spoke, she reached out and positioned a copy of *Me & Him: The Wages of Sin* for the camera. Skimming lightly over the fact that the boy had done time for stealing credit cards, Gail gave him a congratulatory grin. 'And look at you now! Snapped up by a big agency, a deal for your next book, and a knock-on Netflix documentary.'

Everyone laughed on various notes of delight and incredulity, and the boy shrugged again. 'I know! Isn't it mad? I can't believe it. Maybe I'm going to have to learn to love video after all!'

Shamir spoke into his mic. 'Yes! Perfect! Into news and ad-break, clear set and call David, please.'

Steeling herself as the presenters relaxed and the guests were ushered off, Penny waited to see how David would look. Today's recipe was mango and sea buckthorn cheesecake. She watched him walk onto the set, check his worksurface and turn his head for a final touch to his make-up. As the camera operators played with focus, Penny's brain tried to distinguish between what was happening on the bank of monitors and the effect of the tears that suddenly blurred her view. Astonished by them, she stepped out of the light-spill from the desk. This was worse. There was no view of the studio floor from the rear of the dim gallery so, instead of looking down from above at David, she now saw him on the monitors in a series of tight close-ups. His hair, eyes and skin seemed to assault her, and the relief when Shamir turned his attention to cream, eggs and mangos hit with such intensity that it almost made her laugh.

As usual, David's slot went smoothly, and the cheesecake, which he described as 'a no-bake no-brainer', appeared in its final shot looking like something bought in a French pâtisserie. As soon as the show's end-credits rolled, Penny left the gallery, telling herself that the way to deal with her unexpected reaction was to get on with her job and stop being a wimp. When she got down to the studio floor, David was chatting to Mags, the floor manager, and as she threaded her way between the cameras, he came towards her. They met at the end of the worksurface, where the camera crew was already wolfing cheesecake. Before he could speak, she looked him in the eye. 'Good show, Faber. How's Helen? And the twins?'

She'd purposely spoken loudly enough for the others to overhear and, as she'd hoped, Mags came across and chipped in: 'How was their birthday party, David? Did you take pix?' Penny could tell that, in the circumstances, David found the subject awkward, but he took out his phone and began to scroll through party photos. It had been held in the back garden in

Blackheath, where Helen had gone overboard with unicorn piñatas and trestle tables loaded with food stuck with glittery flags. Mags, who had children of her own, made appreciative comments.

One of the camera crew strolled by and asked if David had baked a birthday cake. David flashed a grin. 'Absolutely not! Chloë refused to settle for anything less than Colin the Caterpillar. Helen was outside M&S at dawn.' The hoots of laughter this produced made him scroll on to find another photo.

Right, thought Penny. He's not going to like this next bit but I can't help that. It's the most effective way to create the right image. With a distant, professional smile, as if she'd given David rather more time than he rated, she moved away towards Roz and Gail. After a couple of steps, she called over her shoulder, in a voice she deliberately made patronising, 'Nice show, Faber. Keep up the good work.' And that, she thought, as she kept moving, was perfectly timed and judged. Nothing to see here but the cool, efficient executive dropping by the set to keep the team on its toes.

When Penny got back to the office, Lolly was full of the news that the Twitter response to the father-and-son interview was humungous. Penny dropped her bag on the floor and scrolled through the figures. The specific spike was remarkable and, though the tweets, comments and retweets had peaked while the interview aired, #MeAndHim was continuing to trend. Lolly checked her laptop. 'It's hot on Instagram too.'

Making a brief online search, Penny saw indications that the book was already moving up the charts. As if on cue, there was a rap on the door and a courier arrived with flowers from the authors' agent. They were packed in a stylish black-and-white box, with a card that reproduced one of the book's illustrations. As Lolly placed it on the desk, Penny raised her eyebrows. 'He doesn't miss a trick.' Flipping open the handwritten card, she nodded at the flowers. 'You're the one who spotted the book in the first place. Would you like these?'

A pink flush suffused Lolly's flawless skin. 'Wow. Really? They're beautiful.'

Penny smiled. 'Well, have them. You deserve them.' She was about to say that, without Lolly's nudge, she would have missed a significant trick herself. Then caution kicked in and made her think that her wide-eyed assistant had had enough praise for the moment. There was no reason to doubt Lolly's loyalty, but her own slump in concentration had rattled her and, until she returned to the top of her game, it was wise to watch her back.

Lolly left the office at five thirty, laden with the flowers, but Penny stayed on for several hours, intent on ensuring that nothing else had slipped under her radar. When she reached home, though physically tired, she felt more energised than she had in weeks. The market's gates were chained up and the stalls had been cleared and shuttered, but the surrounding streets were full of people making for restaurants and pubs. Unlocking her front door, she wheeled her bike into the hallway, where she'd had hooks installed to allow her to hang it out of the way. Having lifted the bike into place, she decided she couldn't stand another evening slumped on the sofa, so she went out again, thinking she'd take a walk.

It was a warm night and all the passers-by seemed relaxed and carefree. Stepping off the pavement to avoid the crush, Penny went down Park Street towards the Clink. Then, keeping parallel to the river, she walked to where the *Golden Hinde* loomed anachronistically between high-rise blocks of offices, flats and street-level souvenir shops. It was a full-size reconstruction of Sir Francis Drake's galleon and, like Drake's original, had, in its time, circumnavigated the world.

How weird, thought Penny, to end up confined to a narrow dock in a sprawling city when it was designed to sail the high seas. She sat on a wall outside a crowded café and, leaning back, admired the ship's three soaring masts, two of which were topped by crow's nests. The canvas sails were reefed, revealing the network of rigging, and the black paintwork was relieved by a pattern in crimson and yellow, which encircled the hull and framed the figurehead. Looking up at the gilded hind's head, with its slender neck, large ears and finely carved nostrils, Penny imagined it thrusting through foam-topped waves. When she was ten, Marguerite had brought her here to see it. 'Look, Pen. Think of all the things that came home in the hold. Spices and jewels and exotic feathers and fabrics.'

'What kind of fabrics?'

'Damask. Taffeta. Cloth of gold, maybe.'

'There's cloth made of gold?'

'It's woven from silk yarn with gold wrapped round it.'

'Like Lurex?'

'Well, like lamé. Lurex is a trademark name, and the yarn's plastic-coated.'

'I'm getting a Lurex boob tube. Mum hates it.' Out of the

corner of her eye, she'd seen that Marguerite hadn't liked this and, resenting the unspoken criticism, remarked severely that Sir Francis Drake was a pirate. 'Basically, he stole things for Queen Elizabeth, the one Shakespeare wrote plays for. And he sold slaves. He captured them from the Spaniards.'

'That's true. How do you know?'

'We did Drake in history.' Driven by innate honesty, she'd reluctantly added a rider: 'Drake gave work to escaped slaves too. They sailed with him and were paid. But I bet nobody asked if they'd rather go home to their families. He wasn't a hero, Gran. I bet he stole that cloth of gold.'

Now, with her eyes on the gilded figurehead, Penny imagined herself coming here some day with David's child. An assertive little girl or a boy with David's grey eyes. How did you explain to a child that there are no heroes or villains? That life is full of quicksand and mirages, expedient alliances and unreliable maps? Huddling her sweater around her, Penny thought of the Blackheath party photos. Gifts raining down from the unicorn piñatas. Helen looking frazzled, but lit up with pride and happiness. David's twins holding plates of cake. That's his family, she thought. Those little girls have the prior right to him. So does the lanky teenage boy in the background of the photos, who's already seen his dad mess up one marriage.

Suddenly, it crossed her mind that she'd never thought of David as a chef. She hadn't hired him for his knowledge of food or expertise in the kitchen. They'd seemed peripheral, just as his family had. With her focus on nothing but her job, she'd used him as raw material and created the perfect image for her show. The photos of him picking herbs and fruit in an idyllic garden.

The Instagram videos shot at a rustic table with a background hint of suburban comfort in case it should be required. There'd been a suggestion at the start that the twins might appear, to create the sense of him as a family figure. I was the one who vetoed that, thought Penny. I was the one who spotted that he'd be catnip for female viewers. He couldn't be seen as a husband or a father, because my primary aim was to net an unlimited demographic. Everything was based on figures and cold professional calculation. And then I went and got tangled in my own net.

Reflections of coloured lights were making patterns on the water, turning the muddy Thames into liquid gold scattered with gems. Penny walked past the *Golden Hinde*, then around the heavy bulk of Southwark Cathedral, and cut down to the riverside path, where she leaned her chin on her arms on the stone parapet. A pleasure boat passed, churning foam, and laughing couples crowded the path behind her. It's no use complaining, she thought, and there'll be no one to bail you out. You got yourself into this, and it's up to you to cope with the consequences. There's no data from which to plot your course. You're in uncharted waters. All you can do is try to limit the number of people you hurt.

Chapter Thirteen

In the painful wait before Marguerite got her answer, she carried her phone everywhere lest she'd miss Val's call. When it came, she was in the drawing room, drinking after-dinner coffee, and Val cut directly to the chase. 'Okay, I've had a think, and you're right, Mum. Let's do this. God knows if it'll make any difference to Penny, but it's worth a try, so I'm in.'

'Darling, are you sure?'

'Don't start talking me out of it, now I've made up my mind.'

'I'm not. I'm just glad you think it's a good idea.'

'That's a bit of an overstatement. Look, it clearly matters to you, and Penny might like it. So, let's just say I'm up for it. How are we going to get ourselves organised?'

'Are you sitting there with a notebook?'

Val laughed, and her brisk manner softened. 'How well you know me! But if we're going to do this, we'd better do it right.'

The subsequent weeks were full of texts and emails. Marguerite photographed Ruth's quilt from all possible angles, and images, suggestions and measurements flew to and fro between Stonehill and West Hampstead. Now and again, she'd call Val, who was dealing with end-of-term exams. 'Have you begun going through your ragbag?'

'I told you, I shook everything out when I found it. There's plenty there I can use. And you needn't worry, I have been thinking about it. I just need to get these exam scripts dealt with, then I'll begin in earnest.'

'I'm not badgering you.'

'You are, but never mind. How about you? Have you started?'

'Yes. In a way. I've been sorting fabrics.'

The laugh with which Val greeted this was affectionate. 'Not much further ahead than me, then.'

'It's a process, not a race. Thinking-time and selection are as important as the cutting, piecing and quilting.'

'I've been trying to figure things out. There are so many options. I guess there ought to be some kind of chronological order in the pattern. I was thinking of having the oldest pieces at one end – fabrics from things I made for Penny when she was a baby – and working my way along, so the whole thing will tell a story. The trouble is, though it's logical, I'm not sure it'll make a cohesive pattern. And I can't get the colours to work. What are you doing?'

'Less thinking than you, that's evident! I suppose I'm just looking at what's there, laying things out and moving them round. Observing the stories they tell when they're juxtaposed in different ways. And I'm not badgering, honestly. These things take time, and different people approach them differently.'

'Well, let me take my time, and you take yours.'

Marguerite was relieved. Though Penny had yet to make contact again, Val had seemed more relaxed, so it appeared that the keepsake quilt was already having its effect. Val had mentioned the needlecord she'd found in her ragbag. 'Might it do to edge our quilt? There's a bundle of narrow pieces in the bottom of my bag.'

'Enough for all four sides?'

'Could be. Though lots of joins wouldn't be ideal, especially with corduroy.'

Marguerite had considered this. 'Ruth must have had plenty of velvet to work with. The edging of her quilt has scarcely any joins. Her dress must have had a circular skirt with yards of fabric in it.'

'That much velvet would have cost a fortune. How did she afford it?'

'I've no idea.'

'It can't have been cheap.'

'I suppose not. Look, measure your needlecord when you've got a minute. I should think it's the right weight, and the chocolate-brown colour would work. Light colours tend to get grubby with handling.'

'Okay. How's life over there, otherwise?'

'Fine. Not enough hours for all that wants doing in the garden.'

'Not to mention the mad social round. How's the cards group?'

'Fine. I'm next on the rota to host.'

'Well, I'm glad you're happy and busy.'

'And it's good to hear you sounding cheerful. Speak soon.'

'Okay. But do give me space, Mum. I don't need badgering.'

Though that had been said lightly, Marguerite had resolved to be careful. Many a true word is spoken in jest, she'd told herself. The idea is to relieve Val's stress, not add to it. And Penny's baby's not due till after Christmas. There's plenty of time to get the quilt made before the birth.

June had brought beautiful weather and, with it, a surge of growth, so Marguerite continued to spend much of her time in the garden. She was crossing the hall after an early breakfast when a figure appeared in the porch and waved to her. With a fleeting grin at the memory of security-conscious friends over in London, she opened the inner door and greeted the neighbour who stood there. 'Morning, Caroline. Will you come in?'

'No, thanks. I won't stop. I don't want to disturb you. I was passing and wondered if you needed anything for tonight.' Caroline Blythe was the youngest member of Marguerite's card group, a fresh-faced woman in her fifties who'd joined largely to act as chauffeur to her husband's ageing aunt.

Marguerite shook her head. 'I was up in town yesterday and practically bought my own weight in canapés.'

Caroline smiled brightly. 'Okay. See you later, then. But do give me a shout if there's something you've forgotten. I'm used to making detours to pick up things for Aunt Eve.'

Marguerite smiled back. 'I'm sure I've remembered everything. Thanks, though.' This, she thought, is a downside of ageing. Kind people want to offer you footstools when you still see yourself dancing till dawn. Eve Blythe is a good fifteen years older than I am, and when she goes in for forgetfulness, it's pure affectation. She may be lame and in her eighties, but Eve is sharp as a tack.

As Caroline's car disappeared down the drive, Marguerite stepped out to check the weather. She'd decided that, if the day seemed set fine, she'd get the mower out. By now, a warm wind had dried the dew, so she ran an extension lead through the French doors from a drawing-room socket, and stood planning her first cut through sweet cicely, purple clover, foxtail and lady's smock. In her childhood, the gardener had scythed a meandering path through the grasses and flowers, leading up the gentle slope to where a cast-iron table and bench stood under a willow. In the years after her mother's death and since her own retirement, Marguerite had recreated this effect. The narrow, close-cut path made little difference to pollinators in a garden that offered so much undisturbed growth. Now, with bees and jewel-backed flies humming around her, she switched on the mower and propelled it upwards past a spectacular group of hairy-stemmed thistles. A robin followed her footsteps, inspecting the new-mown sward, while a wren darted out from among the grasses and flew to the willow by the high boundary wall.

As she turned the mower in a series of curves, the sounds of the buzzing insects reminded Marguerite of her childhood fear that they'd fail to escape the gardener's swinging scythe. She'd run to Ruth, who'd been deadheading roses. 'What if he kills them?'

'He won't.'

'But sometimes bees can't fly.'

'That's when they're tired. That's why Mrs Sinnott says to

give them a teaspoon of sugar and water. It's like medicine, to give them strength.'

'Should I get them some now?'

'There's plenty of honey in the flowers to keep them well, Marguerite. They're okay.'

Remembering that reassuring voice, Marguerite's thoughts returned to her mother's quilt. Presumably its pieces had come from dressmaking offcuts or cut-up clothing, though not from the workaday clothes she recalled Ruth wearing. Frowning, she summoned an older, dimmer memory, of net petticoats that had been dipped in a basin of sugar-water, so they'd stiffen when ironed and hold out a calf-length skirt. The scarlet taffeta skirt had had a black poodle appliquéd above the hemline, and the poodle, cut from bouclé, had been curly and soft to touch. So, Ruth had once dressed in the height of fashion. Presumably, thought Marguerite, she just couldn't sustain it. As Val had said, that kind of wardrobe wouldn't have come cheap, and a doctor's wife who spent money like that in 1950s Wicklow would have been called a wastrel, or worse.

Reaching the top of the slope, Marguerite sat down on the bench. The wren's complex liquid call from the willow tree above her was answered by a flutter of wings from the ivy on the wall. The building below looked as foursquare as a dolls' house. At the French doors, a damask curtain moved in the breeze and, at first-floor level, the square windowpanes glinted in the sunlight. The meadow was stippled with tiny flowers, reminding Marguerite of the satin block in Ruth's quilt, and the swirling path she'd just cut produced the effect of couching stitches on green flannel.

Sighing, she wished that Paul had been able to spend more time at Stonehill. When Val and Rory were growing up, he'd managed a week or so in Ireland each summer, but on many occasions when she and the kids had piled into the car and made for the ferry, work had kept him in London. Marguerite had feared he'd be lonely in the Holland Park house, but he'd laughed. 'Far better for the kids to holiday there than loll about here in London. I'll come over and join you when I can.' So, while the rest of the family had walked the hills or piled into Donal's Morris Minor to go swimming, Paul had taken the tube to the office and counted down the days to his annual summer leave. And when he arrived, looking pale and urban, he and Donal would happily spend taciturn hours smoking on the bench at the top of the meadow.

Donal was a catalyst, thought Marguerite, the still centre-point of all our lives. My dad, Paul's friend and Val's confidant. I'm so glad he lived long enough to see Penny. I wish he could be here for Val now. She recalled Val on a summer day, sitting under the willow tree being 'Granddad's shadow', her hair pulled up in a ponytail and her sunburned knees scratched from climbing trees. Forging uphill with the mower, Marguerite had watched the two fair heads bent in conversation and, reaching the top, she'd sat down beside them. That was the year in which Val had begun to shine in her English class, and Donal had sat puffing Maltan ready-rubbed tobacco through many a long lecture on what she was reading at school.

'Granddad, you're not listening!'

'I know a great deal about Keats, as it happens. He was a medic.'

'Only for about ten minutes. Anyway, he was born to be a poet. Imagine messing with blood and guts when your soul was thrilling to the sound of a nightingale! No offence to you, Granddad, but doctors are the opposite of romantic.'

Donal's green eyes had been full of amusement. 'It's teatime. Let's go in, unless you want to stay here communing with nature.'

Energetically, Val had swung her legs down from the bench. 'Bugger nature. If we don't get a move on, Rory will have the lot.' She'd sprinted down the slope and disappeared into the drawing room through the French doors, and Marguerite had followed with her hand through Donal's arm.

That year, when they'd returned to London, Val had insisted she and Marguerite visit the Old Operating Theatre Museum near Guy's Hospital. 'It's in a herb garret above a church. Apothecaries made medicines there, and surgeons did operations. Granddad says Keats would have watched them as a student. Come on, Mum, it should interest you. You were going to be a pharmacist.' Though she loved museums, Marguerite hadn't enjoyed the visit. As soon as she could, she'd gone outside, leaving Val, who'd emerged half an hour later. 'What was the matter? Did you get tired?'

'I just found it oppressive.'

'Did you? Why?'

'I don't know. All that pain and fear and no anaesthetics. And the bit about blood seeping into sawdust. And the thought of poor Keats, who died so dreadfully young.'

'Oh, Mum! The leaflet says they found opium poppies under

the floor when the place was restored, so it's not true to say there were no anaesthetics. And you're being illogical. Keats wouldn't have known he had only a few years to live. Nobody knows how long they've got, do they, so there's no point in worrying.'

Marguerite regretted the loss of that fearless assurance in Val. When Simon died, she'd seemed to become a different person, outwardly calm and efficient but always tensed for another blow. Though everyone had urged her to ask for help, she'd shaken her head. 'Truly. I'm luckier than most. The house is mine and I've got a job. Penny and I will cope.' It appeared that the shock of Simon's death had unnerved her, making her feel that only self-sufficiency was safe, so, not wanting to undermine her efforts to cope with her bereavement, the family had tried not to interfere.

Now Marguerite wondered if that had been wise. Should they have made Val sit down and talk about how she felt? She'd put the question to Donal once, sitting on the bench beneath the willow. 'What do you think about Val, Dad? Is she managing? She's thrown up a sort of shield and I don't know if I ought to try to get past it.' They'd been watching one-year-old Penny stumbling down the wildflower meadow while Val hovered behind, ready to catch her if she fell.

Donal had exhaled a long plume of tobacco smoke. 'It never does to fiddle about with scar tissue. Wounds take their own time to heal. I'd leave her be.'

So, that's what I did, thought Marguerite, and I still don't know if I made the right decision. Val knew that Paul and I were there for her, but I'm sure she was always worried when Penny was young. From the tree above Marguerite's head the wren darted to join its mate in the ivy. Sighing, she closed her eyes and listened to their chirping. Sometimes she'd wondered if Penny's drive to succeed had arisen from being raised by a mum who had always felt insecure.

Chapter Fourteen

Though Marguerite never regretted giving up university in favour of marriage to Paul, she'd always been slightly sorry to have missed out on student life. So, there was huge excitement on the eve of Val's eighteenth birthday when her letter of acceptance to Oxford arrived. They had champagne to celebrate, invited her English teacher to dinner, and Donal sent a cheque from Stonehill with a jokey note saying it had to be spent on fripperies.

At that point in her life, Val was heavily into grunge, so the fripperies mainly consisted of acid-washed jeans and plaid shirts from charity shops. One day a trip to Oxfam yielded a grey chiffon dress, suggestive of *Brideshead Revisited*, which she slashed with scissors and wore with Doc Marten combat boots and opaque black tights. To her annoyance, her dad remarked on a certain similarity to the drooping skirts and vintage sequins her mum had worn in the 1970s. Marguerite laughed. 'I daresay she can ditch the tights if she goes to a college ball.'

Rory was eating Marmite on toast at the kitchen table. He

rolled his eyes. 'Only if she pins the dress together. It looks obscene.'

Val scowled at him. 'You're just jealous.'

'Actually, I'm not into cross-dressing.'

'Grow up, Rory. You wish you were off to Oxford instead of facing a dreary school term. With no prospect after that but an even drearier engineering course.'

Rory took a fifth piece of toast and reached for the butter. 'At least I'm planning to study something useful. As opposed to sitting about, smoking dope and talking Proust.' Pointedly ignoring him, Val swept out, announcing that she'd masses of packing to sort. 'And incidentally, Mum, I won't be going to college balls. They're just for Sloane Rangers and Hooray Henrys.'

There was much sitting about talking Proust in Val's first term, and a certain amount of dope smoked in the process; and as Sasha, with whom she shared a staircase, was the first friend she made, Val's prejudices were soon challenged. Perched on a windowsill above their quad, Sasha rolled eloquent eyes. 'God, Val, keep up, can't you? The Sloane Ranger thing went out with the ark.'

Privately, Val thought Sasha, with her feathered hair, floral skirts and waxed Barbour jacket, was straight out of *The Sloane Ranger Handbook*. The effect was completed by a cut-glass accent and effortless social assurance, but she was also easy-going and entertaining. They hung out together, borrowing teabags, reading each other's essays, and dressing up now and then for a night on the town. Some of their fellow students were as perfectly turned-out as Sasha, but others seemed as dedicated as Val was to grunge and, to her surprise, many looked a good deal grungier. So, grudgingly, she concluded that, as her English teacher had said, Oxford really was a melting-pot. Yet when she met Simon, each sensed in the other a feeling of being out of place.

He was lounging outside with a few friends when she and Sasha emerged from a noisy wine bar. One of his friends, who knew Sasha, suggested they hook up for the rest of the evening. Leaving them to it, Val and Simon drifted away from the others. He wasn't her type. Hardly taller than herself, he was wiry rather than muscular, and had brown hair with blond highlights, cut in a style modelled on Brad Pitt's. Mentally, she approved of his grey marl T-shirt but was less sure about the baggy jeans. Raising his eyebrows, Simon grinned. 'Do I pass the inspection?'

'I wasn't inspecting you.'

'You could've fooled me.'

'I was trying to remember where I've seen you before.'

'At the boring lecture that was so perversely wrong about *Cymbeline*.'

'Did you think so?'

'Utter bollocks. What's your name?'

'Val Carson. Who are you? Some kind of Shakespeare expert?'

'That's me.' He took her by the elbow and turned her away from the light of the wine bar's window. 'You can't believe that the major theme of *Cymbeline* is forgiveness.'

'I assume you're about to tell me that it's not.'

'That it's not. Why it's not. What the major theme actually is.'

'Sounds comprehensive.'

'It'll take hours. We'll need a place where we won't be interrupted.'

Val glanced across and received an unequivocal look from Sasha, who'd evidently been watching and approved. 'Okay. But I need to be up at the crack of dawn, so it can't take hours. Let's say a couple of drinks.'

'Let's hope you're a quick learner.'

'Trust me, I can demolish your theory in half that time.' She removed her elbow from his grasp, waved to Sasha, saying she'd see her later, and led Simon away from the laughing group.

They didn't talk much about *Cymbeline*. Sitting on her denim jacket, which she'd spread on the grass by the river, Val found herself telling him that she felt she didn't fit in. 'Don't get me wrong, I love it here. I've made friends and my tutor's brilliant. I just don't feel I belong.'

'That's not surprising, is it?' Lying beside her, propped on one elbow, he looked up through his curtain of hair. 'You're never going to fit in with the likes of Sasha.'

'Why not?'

'Oh, please!'

'No, seriously. Why not? You're just being an inverted snob.'

'So, you admit that Sasha and you come from different worlds.'

'I don't give a toss about that. She's a friend.'

Simon plucked a handful of grass. 'I didn't say she wasn't.'

'You don't know what world I come from.'

He sat up, pushed back his hair and grinned at her. 'People who move goalposts usually know they're losing an argument.'

'I'm not arguing. You're wrong, that's all.' After a moment, Val scooched her bum off the jacket and lay beside him. 'What world do *you* come from, then?'

'Me? I'm a nice guy from Norfolk. Home's a little village out in the fens, an easy commute from my dad's work. He's in manufacturing. Owns a factory, works his arse off and goes sailing at weekends. I'm the first in the family to make it to uni.'

'Me, too. Well, except for my granddad in Ireland. He's a retired GP.' Val stared up at the cloudless sky, where the stars seemed unnaturally bright. 'What does your dad make?'

'Specialist gloves.'

Thinking he might be joking, Val turned her head sharply and caught a look of amusement. To conceal a blush, she looked back at the stars. 'Specialist gloves, eh? That's a bit niche.'

'Not at all. There are dozens of categories. Anti-vibe. Comfort grip. Aqua. Hard-knuckle. Fingerless. Poly-coated. Want me to go on?'

'Not really.'

'It doesn't make for riveting conversation.' Simon chose a blade of grass and chewed it. 'I bet Sasha's dad does something sexy.'

'He's an investment banker.'

'Well, there you are. Money's always sexy.'

'No, it's not. Take it from me. My dad's an accountant.'

'And the word "sexy" doesn't spring to mind?'

'He's the nicest man in the world but, no, it doesn't.'

Flicking away the blade of grass, Simon leaned on his elbow again, and moved closer. 'Yet it's the first word that came into my head when I saw his beautiful daughter.'

'That's the cheesiest line I've ever heard.'

'You're right. I should have come up with something better.'
He lowered his face and spoke again, just before he kissed her.
'But you know something? I have a feeling you're always going
to leave me lost for words.'

That wasn't true, of course. Simon was never at a loss for
words. Assertiveness was part of his personality. But, for the
first time, Val had found someone of her own age with whom to
talk about books, and where books were concerned, she was just
as assertive. They argued constantly, sitting on park benches or
drifting lazily in a hired rowboat, which Simon handled with
what she thought was impressive skill and assurance. When
she complimented him on it, he just shrugged. 'I grew up sea
sailing. Farting about on a river is a doddle.'

'Shame you can't grasp the simplest fact about James Joyce,
though.'

'You don't get the final word on Joyce just because you're
Irish.'

'Half Irish.'

'Whatever.'

'It's nothing to do with nationality, Simon. And wanting to
write a novel doesn't mean you have God-given insights into
the form.'

Bickering was central to their relationship, as important
as the long hours they spent making love. Unlike many first-
term student affairs, theirs endured. During vacations, they
exchanged letters, becoming increasingly close despite being
apart; and, in term time, friends treated them as an unassailable
couple. Though aware of him as her boyfriend, Val's family had

hardly had a chance to get to know him before the engagement. In the second long vac, he invited her for a weekend in Norfolk. Val was apprehensive. 'Who exactly am I supposed to be?'

'The love of my life, obviously.'

'Isn't it going to be a bit weird? I've never met your parents.'

'That would be the point of the visit.'

'Yes, but a whole weekend's a big deal.'

'We can't just drop in for tea. It takes about a million years on a train.'

'Don't they ever come up to London? We could meet there.'

'Trust me, for my mum and dad, a trip to London's a far bigger deal than you coming down for a weekend.'

Val's brain switched to practicalities. 'So, do we share a room or what?'

'Absolutely not. You'll be in the guestroom. I'll be curled up in my little white bed surrounded by Airfix models.'

'Now that *is* weird. Models of what?'

'Dad's very fond of World War Two Spitfires.'

'So, how come they're in your room?'

'They're mine in name. I got one on every birthday till I left school. Ships too, sometimes. After I was about ten, they stayed in their boxes till Dad put them together.'

'That's really sad.'

'I expect he enjoyed himself.' Simon, who'd been drinking beer, put down his glass. 'Look, you don't have to come if you don't fancy it.'

'No, really, I'd like to.'

'Sure?'

'Absolutely.'

For days afterwards, Val worried about what to pack. At the last minute, she made a panicky dash to M&S, and came away with straight-leg jeans, a vaguely nautical jersey, and a pair of navy-blue deck shoes with very white soles. Simon cracked up when he saw them. 'God, they're so right!'

'Really?'

'Truly. Mum's going to love you.'

'I hope so. M&S charges a lot more than Oxfam.'

His parents turned out to be younger than Val had expected. Their two-storey cottage in a coastal village was furnished much like her own home in Holland Park, and though Simon's room did feature a shelf of Airfix models, it was also crammed with books and a large ghetto-blaster his mum told Val he'd got for his sixteenth birthday. Later, when they went for a walk, she took Simon to task. 'They're perfectly nice people!'

'I never said they weren't.' He put his arm around her. 'My mum likes you.'

'I don't see why she shouldn't.'

'She's decided you're no threat.'

'Stop it, Simon, you talk as if they're characters in a bad novel.'

'It would certainly be a dull one.'

'Don't be horrid.'

It wasn't until she'd accepted his proposal that Val began to see what Simon had meant. His mother took their engagement as something halfway between a betrayal and an affront, and though his father made an effort, he was barely civil. Simon just pulled a face. 'Dad's always assumed I'll come home and take over the business. Oxford was an indulgence to him, a sowing of intellectual wild oats. I told them when I went up that I wasn't interested in the factory. They didn't listen. They never do.'

'Hang on, are you sure you want to walk away from the business?'

'Don't be fatuous.'

'But ought we to get married if they're upset? It's all so sudden, Simon. You even took *me* by surprise.'

'You're confusing two separate issues.'

'I'm just saying it's a lot for them to take in.'

'Look, they've known for ages that I'm not going back to Norfolk, and anyone with an ounce of sense would see I'd be a fool to let you go.'

'But ...'

'Shut up, Val, you're not going to force me into Specialist Gloves.' He pulled her towards him. 'And I haven't spent three years studying only to bury myself in the fens and marry some bouncing female I knew at school.'

'That's the alternative, is it?'

'I said shut up. I adore you. We're soulmates. Made for each other. Go on, try to tell me I'm wrong.'

Val laughed reluctantly. 'You know I can't.'

'So, forget my parents. Forget everything. You and I are going to be married. We'll find a house and plan our life, and live happily ever after. You're never going to regret this. Wait and see.'

The ripped chiffon dress had found its way into Val's West Hampstead ragbag, and was among the bits and pieces she'd shaken onto the bed. Now, after several hours' work on a module she was preparing for her students, she decided to make a proper start on choosing fabrics for the quilt. This time, when she shook out her ragbag's contents, the dress was the first thing to appear. It was sleeveless and had a pleated crossover Empire-line bodice from which the skirt fell in several layers.

Picking it up, Val turned it over, revealing the tarnished mother-of-pearl sequins on the bodice, dotted among the crumpled pleats. She sat down and stared at it, realising that when she'd ripped the top layers of fabric, she'd left the bottom one intact. God, I was young, she thought. So determined to appear louche, yet so careful to preserve a safe, knee-length underdress. Did I know what I was doing? Did Mum notice and smile? Spreading one of the strips of chiffon, she measured its width between her outstretched thumb and little finger, thinking that, with a backing, it might make a central piece in the keepsake quilt. She could tell Penny she'd been wearing it on the night she met Simon. They might laugh together at the thought of her, flamboyant and self-conscious, feeling sophisticated in combat boots and thick black tights.

Chapter Fifteen

Caroline and Eve Blythe were the first arrivals at Marguerite's cards night. She welcomed them in the porch and led the way to the drawing room, explaining that the gathering would be small. 'Jim Foley and Maeve will be here, and Fergus Porter, but there's a summer cold going round, and the rest have cried off. Poor Anne Roche sounded really hoarse on the phone.'

Caroline helped Eve to a fireside chair, speaking over her shoulder to Marguerite. 'I'm sorry to hear Anne's unwell. Should I drop by tomorrow, do you think?'

Eve settled herself into the chair, leaning on her walking stick, and slapped Caroline with her free hand. 'Of course not. We don't all want you fussing about like a mother hen.' This was unfair, considering how demanding Eve was of Caroline, but Marguerite knew better than to interfere. Approaching with a glass of wine, she remarked that at least they'd be evenly matched for cards. Eve sniffed. 'I dare say the half of you would be well pleased if we didn't play at all. As it is, I can see it's going to be gin rummy. God, you'd think someone around here would learn a proper game, like bridge.'

Marguerite smiled. 'We don't all have your head for figures, Eve.' She handed a glass to Caroline. 'We might have a go at whist tonight, though. Let's see what the others think.'

Eve knocked back half her wine in one impatient slug. 'Lord, no! Fergus Porter has never been able to think in more than one dimension. Let's not subject ourselves to an evening of watching him struggle with whist.'

At that moment Jim Foley, the local GP, put his head round the door. Marguerite went and shook hands, and kissed his wife, Maeve. 'It's good to see you. Help yourselves to wine. There are canapés on the table by the piano and, given that there's a cold going round, let me know if it gets chilly, won't you? It's so lovely outside that I couldn't bear to shut the French doors.'

Eve tapped her stick against the mantelpiece. 'Door and windows wide open and a fire lit. That's a thing that wouldn't have happened in my day, I can tell you.'

Maeve Foley laughed. 'It's only a very little fire, Eve, and you're looking very comfortable there beside it.' She bent to smell an arrangement of roses that stood on the piano. 'Are these from your garden?'

Marguerite nodded. 'The petals fall within hours, but I do love them there. They match the silk.' The fabric behind the piano's fretted soundboard had faded to the colour of old parchment, but in the folds there were stripes of its original yellow, which mimicked the golden petals of the roses.

Caroline had sat down opposite Eve, and Marguerite brought them some canapés. As she set down the plate, she remarked that the mushroom tartlets were heavy on garlic. Eve reached out and took one. 'The more garlic the better, as far as I'm concerned.' Popping the tartlet into her mouth, she dabbed her lips with a folded paper napkin. 'When I was a girl, you couldn't find garlic in Dublin. Or anchovies or olives, for that matter. My mother used to bring garlic bulbs from France to plant in a window box.'

'Did you go there on holiday?'

'Quite a lot. She painted, you know, so we went to see the galleries. And my father was a great Francophile.' Eve scooped up another mushroom canapé. The hand in which she held it had tobacco-stained fingers and appeared weighed down by the number of heavy silver rings she wore. Despite her age, she cut a striking figure. A diminutive woman with a nest of white hair, tonight she wore a long tweed skirt, high, laced ankle boots, and an Aran cardigan pinned at the throat by a marble brooch in an angular pewter setting. Holding out her glass to Marguerite, she gestured at the piano. 'I remember roses dropping petals on that piano when I was a girl. Your mother always had them there, and wildflowers in the hall. She was arty. Or she used to turn up at arty gatherings when she was first married. None of the actual artists could hold a candle to her for fashion. I remember my poor mother's friends wearing samples from Neillí Mulcahy's studio and Ruth trumping them all in Fifth Avenue chic.'

Marguerite refilled Eve's glass and pulled up a chair beside her. 'Did you go to the arty gatherings?'

'Oh, I practically grew up in artists' studios. My mother used to paint me. Cheaper than paying a model. Or a childminder, to begin with. And, believe it or not, I made a pretty subject in my teens.'

'And you remember Ruth? You've never said so.'

Eve sniffed impatiently. 'That's because I come here to play cards, not reminisce. Nothing more boring than an old biddy prosing about the past.' Cocking her eye, she looked at Marguerite sharply. 'I hope you're not going to sink into the habit.'

'No, of course not. There's far too much to be dealt with in the present.'

'Good.' Eve reached for her stick. 'Here's Fergus Porter at last. Thank God for small mercies. If we don't start soon, we won't get a hand played this evening.'

The Foleys settled down to play together, and Caroline gamely took on Eve. Marguerite partnered Fergus. As Eve had said, he wasn't much of a player and, being the hostess, she'd felt it unfair to dump him on one of the others. A dim, shambling divorcee, he was making a mess of shuffling the cards and, to avoid adding to his evident embarrassment, Marguerite let her gaze wander to her flower arrangement where a new golden petal had just slipped from its stem. Suddenly, she remembered her mother seated at the piano, her long fingers picking out the notes of a lullaby. Hardly aware of what she was doing, Marguerite closed her eyes, letting the song echo back through the years and merging the bright June evening with the past.

... when you wake
You shall have
All the pretty little horses
Blacks and bays
And dapples and greys
All the pretty little horses
Go to sleep
Don't you cry
Rest your head upon the clover
In your dreams
You shall ride
Whilst your mammy's watching over
Blacks and bays
And dapples and greys
All the pretty little horses ...

It had been a dreary, autumnal day and Marguerite, aged twelve, was suffering from earache. Leaping flames banished the chill of the raindrops that streamed down the windows. Her mother had piled up the sofa cushions and tucked her under the quilt, which she'd carried down from Marguerite's bedroom. Its velvet edge was comforting. There were reflections of the firelight in the fender. When Ruth began to sing, Marguerite struggled upright. '*Mum!* I'm not a baby.'

Ruth took her hands off the keys. 'You used to love this.'

In fact, the song had been soothing so, having made her protest, Marguerite snuggled back under the quilt. For a moment, the only sound in the room came from the crackling flames, then Ruth took up the tune again ... *blacks and bays and dapples and greys whilst your mammy's watching over ...*

Marguerite opened her eyes to see Fergus dithering over the upcard. She wondered when the piano had last been played. Maybe not since the days when Val used to bring Penny to Stonehill for the summer. Or before that, when Rory and Val used to drive the household mad with raucous renditions of Pink Floyd hits. She could remember them, when Val was nine and Rory nearly seven, thumping the keys, bawling about how they didn't need no edu-KAY-shun, and hushing each other with giggles when Donal complained. In Marguerite's own childhood, Ruth had been the only person to play. Her songs were quiet, and often fragmented, and her American accent had been more pronounced when she sang than when she spoke. The shoulders under her hand-knitted jumper had moved more freely too, and her hair, tied at the nape of her neck and wind-tousled, had gleamed like the yellow silk behind the fretted soundboard. I suppose I fell asleep that day when I lay on the couch with earache, thought Marguerite. The velvet was soft against my ear and I must have just drifted off, away from the pain.

Fergus placed an untidy stack of cards in the centre of the table; even gin rummy seemed to feed his sense of inadequacy, and as he turned over the top one, his anxious eyes watched Marguerite like a dog's. Marguerite took the upcard absently, her mind still focused on her mother. How strange, she thought, that the times spent with her that I recall most clearly belong to the border between waking and sleeping. The sound of her voice singing. The rhythmic touch of my own fingers on velvet. The knowledge that, having tucked me in at bedtime, she was somewhere out in the darkness while I slept. At the opposite side of the table, Fergus appeared paralysed by the effort of adding up points, so Marguerite allowed her mind to pursue its own calculation. I was twelve, she thought, when I had my tonsils out and got those earaches. Ruth died in October, on the weekend of my half-term break from school. So, it can't have been more than a week or so after she sang me that lullaby that I came home and they told me she was gone.

October 1964 had been chilly. A stream of patients had arrived at Stonehill, sneezing and grumbling as they sat in Donal's surgery, and saying their rheumatism always got worse around Halloween. The earth under the trees in Ruth's orchard was boggy, and the wildflower meadow, which had had a close cut at the end of the growing season, had lost all its colour and vibrancy.

Marguerite had been half aware that her mother had grown even quieter than usual. But late autumn was always a bad time for Ruth. Without her garden to work in she seemed aimless, a tense figure who spent hours sitting beneath her own portrait, staring into the flickering drawing-room fire. Mrs Sinnott, who by then helped in the house full-time, had told Marguerite that her mother had tablets to make her feel better. 'Your daddy's a great doctor, pet. Don't be troubled about your mam. Isn't she the lucky woman not to have to sit into a car to visit the surgery? And don't we all get a bit pulled down when the nights are long?'

Accustomed to Ruth's silences, Marguerite had accepted this, and Donal had confirmed it when she'd asked him if Ruth was all right. 'It's the time of year, Marguerite. She'll be better when the days get longer.' So, Marguerite's focus had shifted to Halloween parties, and visits to school friends in the half-term break. When she looked back later, she realised it had never occurred to her to question her mother. By then, Ruth wore silence like a shield and, though no one had ever said so, Marguerite had internalised the idea that to trespass on her emotional state was dangerous, as if a word spoken at the wrong moment could break her.

Besides, Ruth had seemed better on the morning of her death. She'd hugged Marguerite and, for the first time in a week, shown interest in how she was going to spend the day. 'How long do you think you're going to be out, honeybunch?'

'I told you, it's Joan's birthday. Her mum's going to drive us all home after tea.'

'Okay. Dress warm as well as pretty, won't you?'

Encouraged by this spark of interest, Marguerite had presented herself to Ruth in her party dress, a long-sleeved A-line shift with a white collar and cuffs. But, by then, Ruth had returned to staring into the drawing-room fire, and had made no comment on being assured that Marguerite intended to wear her warmest coat.

Stonehill was the last drop-off made by Joan's mum after the party. When they pulled up at the house, Mrs Sinnott was on the front steps. For a few bewildering moments, the adults spoke through the car window in low voices, then Marguerite heard Joan's mum's voice sounding flustered and doubtful. 'Should I take her back home with me? Is that the guards' car?'

It was then that Marguerite saw the police car parked at the side of the house. She stumbled out onto the gravel sweep, the goody-bag from the party slipping unnoticed from her lap. Mrs Sinnott came and took her by the shoulders, but she struggled, attempting to break free and run indoors. She was aware of Joan's mum looking helplessly through her car window. Mrs Sinnott hunkered down and, letting go of Marguerite's shoulders, took her face in her hands. 'Hush now. Stop it, Marguerite. Listen and be a good girl.'

'What's happened?'

'We're going to go indoors now, and you'll come down to the kitchen with me, and we'll make a pot of hot tea for your daddy.'

'Where is he? Where's Daddy? Where's my mummy?'

'Your daddy's inside. He's talking to a guard. He'll be glad of a cup of tea, and you and I are going in now to boil the kettle.'

'Why are the guards here?'

'You're not to worry. Your daddy called them. He's a doctor, Marguerite, he has to do everything by the book.'

'But why? What's happened?' She was shaking so much when they got down to the kitchen that Mrs Sinnott told her not to take off her coat. 'You want to keep warm. It's good for shock. We'll put plenty of sugar in the tea too. We could all do with a cup.' Marguerite almost choked on the cup of tea that was handed to her, as syrupy and strong as Turkish coffee. By then she'd grasped that something bad had happened to her mother, and that the guards had come to the house because her father had asked them to. 'Where's Mum?'

'There's an ambulance coming to take her away. Your daddy's seeing to everything.'

'Is she going to hospital? Can I see her? Is she sick?'

Mrs Sinnott sat beside her. ''No, pet. She's not sick. I'm sorry. Your mam is dead. It was an accident.'

The taste of the sweet tea rose up at the back of Marguerite's throat. 'What happened to her?'

'She didn't suffer at all. She wouldn't even have known what happened. She was tired, so she went to bed and took some of the tablets that help her to sleep.'

'But you said she's dead.'

'I know. It was an accident. She must have mistaken the dose. Or maybe she just forgot she'd already taken one. There was no pain or anything, pet, I promise. Your mam just went to sleep and didn't wake up.'

Chapter Sixteen

Penny sat at her desk in the office, watching the show with half an eye on Twitter. Roz was chatting to an ebullient Jamaican woman, whose YouTube channel *It Takes a Village* had become a big hit with expectant mums. Positive responses were already flooding in as Gail summed up. 'So, Deisha, basically what you're saying is that we all need a helping hand?'

Deisha gave her a warm smile. 'It's not rocket science, is it? You just have to remember how people lived before we were all put into little boxes. Look, say you're going to have a baby. It's a big thing. It's scary, especially if it's your first time. I mean, oh, my God, what's happening to me? My body's going crazy. My boobs are expanding, my ankles are swollen, half of the time I can't even remember my own name ...' She flashed a big smile into camera. 'If my husband's watching, don't panic, man, this is hypothetical!' Turning to Roz, she raised one finger. 'No, but seriously – I'm way past childbearing but I remember how it was for me. There was so much intergenerational sharing. Your auntie, your granny, your neighbour, the lady who sold you fish – they all supported you and were part of your pregnancy. And, okay, that can be overwhelming. I mean it does take a village but, on the other hand, too many cooks spoil the broth.' She had an infectious laugh, and Roz joined in. Deisha's finger wagged in good-humoured admonishment. 'Auntie needs to know when to take a step back, but Mum has to learn to reach out.'

A stream of texts and tweets from viewers ran across the bottom of the shot, full of praise for what Deisha was saying. Penny told herself that was fine if you lived surrounded by cosy village characters, eager to give each other a helping hand. Working in TV was more like having to keep afloat in shark-infested waters when everyone around you was focused on survival, and half of them were doing deals with the sharks. And it's just as well, for this baby's sake, that I'm high on the food-chain, she thought. I may have been irresponsible but, with luck, we won't starve. The show's presenters and regular contributors lived with the possibility of being dumped with minimal notice, a state designed to keep them insecure and less demanding. Her own contract was unique. Having doubled the show's ratings and advertising revenue, she'd negotiated a deal that produced an unprecedented degree of job security. Nevertheless, luck was going to be needed. When she'd discussed parental leave with her boss, she'd sensed calculation behind the air-kisses, and known that if her cover turned out to be cheaper and equally dynamic, the company might want to pay her off rather than have her back. Clinging on where she wasn't wanted wouldn't be an option and, as a single mother who'd spent months out of touch with the business, finding a new job at her current salary wouldn't be easy.

As Roz finished commenting on the feedback, Penny told herself she needed to focus and prioritise. Today she was due for her first scan, at St Thomas' Hospital, after which she'd have to work out when to tell her team she was pregnant. In fact, she wasn't sure why she hadn't done so before. *I suppose*, she thought, *I'm plain superstitious. I don't want people crowding round me with congratulations until I've passed this first milestone. Maybe, on some pathetic level, I'm still hoping it's all just a dream.*

She was shocked by the wave of relief she felt when she found that all was well. The sonographer smiled and said she saw no need for further tests at this point. 'Everything's looking good. And you're feeling fine?'

'Perfectly.'

'I haven't managed to get any decent images, I'm afraid. We often don't at this stage, and there's not much to see, anyway.'

'That doesn't matter.'

'I'll do you a printout.'

Well, *that's it*, Penny told herself. *I can't pretend it's a dream any more. It's real.* She took the fuzzy black-and-white printout, shoved it into her laptop, and left the room with her mind in a whirl. When she'd told her mum and gran that she was pregnant, all she'd known for certain was that she wanted to keep the baby. Then she'd had to inform David and, for the sake of his family, end their affair. Since then, she'd hardly seen him, other than on the screen. But now, having had the scan, she wondered if she should tell him about it. After all, this was his baby too.

Outside, she carried her bike down the steps beside Westminster Bridge and began to walk home by the river path. At first, she felt numb but, suddenly, her heart started to thump so hard that she had to stop and lean on the bike's handlebars. What about other milestones in the future? There'd be birthday parties, like the twins' celebration in the garden, and holidays, and parent-teacher meetings, and dental appointments. Would he need to be told about all sorts of stuff like that? But I've thought this through already, she told herself firmly. The decision's made. David is out of my life. It's what we both want. I could see that when I told him. I mustn't get sentimental now, and take the risk of the tabloids somehow picking up the story. Imagine the headlines. *Sexy TV Chef's Exec Prod Has A Bun In The Oven!* The thought was so dreadful and ludicrous that it almost made her laugh and, shakily, she started to walk on.

When she came to a bench, she sat down and stared at the river. There's so much I'll have to do, she thought. If this were a show I was setting up, six months' lead-time wouldn't be half enough. What are the practical problems of having a baby? Logistics? Contingency issues? The skill sets involved? I've got to get a grip on all that. Automatically, her mind began to conjure up spreadsheets and budgets and, back on familiar territory, her tension began to ebb.

On the bench next to hers a woman was nibbling a cupcake and rocking a buggy. All that was visible of the sleeping baby was a wisp of dark hair and the curve of a cheek. The tips of the woman's fingers rested on the buggy's handle, but her attention appeared to be entirely on the cake in her other hand. Catching sight of her, Penny's tension instantly surged back. The river seemed perilous. The path was wide, and the parapet high enough to prevent an accident, yet her heart was thumping again, as if the buggy could be swept away in the tide.

Looking up, and seeing her staring at the baby, the woman gave her a shy, friendly smile. Immediately, the threat seemed to recede and, hoping her panic hadn't been noticed, Penny smiled back. She remembered the guest she'd watched on her own show that morning. Oh God, she thought, it's all very well to be flippant about expanding boobs and swollen ankles. I've read about all that. I can handle it. But why does no one tell you about the blind terror? How come no doctor has ever said that that this thing they announce is the size of an average passion fruit can take over your mind as well as your life?

She had calmed down by the time she'd wheeled her bike past the National Theatre, and felt okay to ride it home. But when she approached Borough Market, where she'd planned to buy something for dinner, she felt overwhelmed by the crowds eating chunks of tortilla, and sourdough rolls with chorizo, or wandering from stall to stall with iced coffees and artisan beers. So, instead she made straight for her flat. That morning, when she'd glanced at Mark's window-display, it had featured metal coffee-tables stencilled with comic-book heroes. Now she saw that it contained nothing but a chaise longue. Mark, who was on the pavement inspecting it, stepped back into the road and collided with her bike. 'Penny! Sorry, are you okay?'

'Fine. I won't sue.'

'So, what do you think?' The chaise had a rolled back, claw-and-ball feet, and a mahogany frame to which its crimson upholstery was fixed with a double row of brass pins. Penny blinked. 'Talk about rococo!'

'I wish. It's Edwardian. Admittedly, with a rococo vibe.'

'Have you had it reupholstered?'

'Nope. All original plush velvet. I think it's smashing. It came out of a house sale and I got it for peanuts.'

'I can't imagine who's going to buy it.'

'Think of it in a Shad Thames New York-style loft.'

'I expect you know your own business best.'

'Even Bill is beginning to say so, and that's absolute proof.' Mark jerked his head towards the shop. 'Fancy a brew? I'll put the kettle on.'

'Well …'

'Oh, come on. I haven't seen you for ages. We'll break out the Garibaldis.'

'Okay. Why not?' Leaving the bike in her hallway, Penny followed him into the shop, deciding that this was a chance to begin sharing her news with the world. Unwittingly, Mark gave her the perfect cue. 'Anything strange occurred since we last had a cuppa?'

'Actually, yes. I'm pregnant.' She braced herself for the first of what she knew would be many such moments.

For an instant Mark's face held an expression she thought

might be disapproval. Then he nodded and asked, 'Tea or coffee?'

'What?'

'Which would you like? I can make either.'

'I just said I'm pregnant.'

'And that's a good thing?'

'Yes. I think so. Yes, it is. I think so.'

'So, I'll put the kettle on, we'll sit down, and you'll tell me all about it.' Seeing her instinctive withdrawal, Mark held up his hands, palm outwards. 'Or not. We'll talk about furniture.' He waited and Penny realised she was thirsty. 'Tea would be nice.'

'Coming up.'

She was still standing by the door when he returned with mugs, biscuits and a milk jug on a tray. 'I've just been to St Thomas' for my first scan.'

'That's a big thing.'

'Apparently everything's fine. They gave me a printout.' She found she'd taken it from her bag and was holding it out to him. 'Not much point, really. There's nothing to see.' And now, dammit, she told herself, he's going to ask about the father's reaction. Or want to know if I've called Mum and Gran.

Mark took the printout from her hand and scrutinised it. 'You should've knocked back several glasses of water.'

'What?'

'Before they did it. If the bladder's distended, the image can come out better.' He grinned. 'Sonograms hold no mysteries for me. I've got four older sisters, remember? Between them, they've got a football team's worth of kids.' He gave back the printout and went to the window. 'Here, just a minute, let me turn this.' Manhandling the chaise longue, he swung it to face into the shop. Penny protested. 'No, don't, you've messed up your display!'

'Bugger that. The back is the most alluring aspect anyway.' It was a riot of carved acanthus leaves, which had stunned Penny with their exuberance. Mark patted the buttoned upholstery. 'Sit down and put your feet up.'

'For Heaven's sake! I don't need cosseting.'

'Who said you did? This is a celebration! No, wait, Garibaldis won't do.' He plunged out of the door, leaving Penny bewildered and wondering what to do if a customer came in while he was gone. No answer occurred to her so, discovering she was tired as well as thirsty, she eased off her shoes, sat down and reached for her tea. The chaise longue's high back curved comfortably, concealing her from passers-by in the street. I was wrong, she thought. That wasn't disapproval, and bless Mark for not asking questions about the father. He's a real friend.

Putting her feet up, she looked at her surroundings. In Bill's day, although the shop had appeared to be chaotic, he'd been able to lay his hand on the smallest item of his stock, producing a chiming clock from a leather hat-box or whipping a tin-opener out of a wardrobe drawer. Now, having been refitted, it was almost unrecognisable, yet Mark's layout conveyed the same suggestion of competent nonchalance. Soon after he'd come home and taken over the business, Penny had invited him to guest on her show. 'You're using craftsmen of your dad's generation as well as designers just out of art school. The story's perfect for my viewers, and the exposure would do you good.'

Mark had shaken his head. 'Thanks, but I don't think so. I hate cameras and I can't do soundbites. I'd feel like a berk.'

At the time, Penny had been miffed. Now, knowing him better, she suspected he'd been right. He was more than capable of explaining the ethos behind his success, but not in a way that could be airily summed up by Roz or Gail. Though shrewd enough to share Bill's view that there was money in junk, Mark had a quality that transcended his business instinct. He could see beyond fashion, damage and dirt to the essence of what had been lovingly made. A perfectly turned piece of wood under layers of scratched varnish. A beautiful darn on a piece of handwoven linen, which, cleaned and framed, could become a work of art. By snapping up things other buyers tended to pass over, he'd created a brand based on sustainability and respect. But, unlike most of the successful creatives Penny had on her show, his principal characteristic was modesty.

The door opened and Mark came in, carrying a couple of plates. 'Right. Budge up.' Penny drew up her feet and he sat on the end of the chaise longue, passing her one of the plates with a flourish. 'There you go. Neapolitan ice-cream.'

'Why?'

'Because, in our family, you can't celebrate without stripy ice-cream. This is from the gelateria so, technically, it might not be Neapolitan. Could be Spumoni. But, hey, everyone's got to move with the times.' He produced a couple of spoons from his pocket, saying he must remember to return them. 'The plates too. I said I'd wash them and drop them round later.'

Penny swallowed a mouthful of cherry and pistachio and chased a dollop of chocolate with her spoon. 'It's delicious.'

'Beats the stuff Dad used to buy when he'd had a win on the horses. That tasted like toothpaste, to be honest. Still, the principle holds. Stripy ice-cream for big occasions has always been the rule.'

As the ice-cream slipped down Penny's throat, she relaxed against the plush velvet upholstery, and stopped feeling that time was her enemy. Mark was right. Obviously, she'd need to get a grip on planning the months ahead but it made sense to acknowledge the milestones she'd pass along the way. When the ice-cream was eaten, she stood up and smiled. 'That was just what I needed.'

'Glad to be of service.' Mark set his own plate on the floor and went to lift a vase of pink peonies from a stand. 'Here, take these upstairs with you. They're way past their sell-by date, which was why Charlie gave them to me, but they're good for a day or so yet.'

'I don't want to deprive you of them.'

'You'll be doing me a favour. Truly. They clash with the chaise.'

Giving up, Penny took the vase. 'Thanks. I was just telling myself that you're a real friend, Mark. I don't know why you're always so good to me even when I'm snarky.'

Up in the flat, she set the vase on the glass coffee-table and sank onto one of her white leather sofas. For a while she relaxed, her eyes on the blowsy, satin-soft petals, and then, with a deep breath, took out her phone. Okay, she told herself, here's the next milestone. First a call to West Hampstead and then one to Stonehill.

Chapter Seventeen

Marguerite took a piece of embroidered cheesecloth from among scraps of appliqué, pieces of drawn-thread work, and sections of inlaid lace. She had just put down her phone after a conversation with Val. 'Isn't it wonderful news? I'm so glad she called us.'

'I told you she'd come round. What did she say?'

'Just that the scan was fine. She was tired, I think. We didn't talk long. I wish I could see her … but you don't need to tell me not to be pushy. I won't.'

'Darling, I never interfere.'

'I know. I'm telling myself, really. She said she was up to her ears at work.'

'Well, I'm glad she called.'

The cheesecloth was part of Marguerite's wedding dress. When she was pregnant with Val, she'd cut up its long, flowing skirt to make maternity smocks, but kept the yoke with its embroidered daisies, which had golden hearts that gleamed like the sun. Now she recalled choosing purple floss to stitch the petals and selecting the shining silk for the flower-heads.

She'd married just after her twentieth birthday, in 1971, and she and Paul had spent the previous Christmas at Stonehill. Though he had been only twenty-three then, his steadiness made him seem older, and Donal's liking for him had grown during the holiday. They'd walked the Wicklow hills in the short, chilly afternoons and spent long, relaxing evenings by the drawing-room fire. And, during Donal's surgery hours, Marguerite had introduced Paul to Dublin, where every pub door opened on groups of friends having hot ports and downing pints of Guinness before rushing to catch a bus home, laden with Christmas shopping.

On Christmas Eve, Paul achieved Donal's final seal of approval. Setting out early after a night of snowfall, they returned with a Norway spruce they'd felled and wrestled into the back of the Morris Minor. Later, Paul told Marguerite that he'd felt like a poacher.

'You don't poach trees.'

'A tree-napper, then.'

Marguerite laughed. 'We get one from that forest each year. The land belongs to a farmer who's an old friend of the family. Incidentally, Dad told me that, for a Londoner, you're a half-decent countryman, so you must have kept a stiff upper lip.'

That afternoon, while Donal was out visiting patients, they tacked up holly and mistletoe, set up the tree in front of the French windows and festooned the sweet-smelling branches with tinsel and baubles.

'Weird to think that, next year, we'll be an old married couple, decorating our own Christmas tree.'

'It won't be as big as this one.'

'Not unless we move the bed out onto the stairs.' They'd planned to begin married life in Paul's London flat, which was close to his office but little more than a bedsit. Hooking a star to a branch, Paul shot her a worried look. 'We'll get something bigger eventually.'

'I know. I'm not complaining.'

'It's decent of your dad to offer to host the wedding.'

'Well, he is the bride's father. And I wouldn't want to be married from anywhere other than Stonehill. Your parents don't mind coming over here, do they? I know they say it's fine, but they're so nice that they'd probably fly to the ends of the earth if we asked them to.'

'They don't mind a bit. What's not to like about a spring wedding in Ireland?'

'I've a feeling your mum will expect me to wear white silk and a long veil.'

'She'll want you to wear whatever you like.'

'Cheesecloth and a headband?'

'Whatever makes you happy.' The look in his eyes was so loving that Marguerite's breath caught at the back of her throat. Unable to trust her voice, she held up a sprig of mistletoe and kissed him gently instead.

When Paul flew home, Marguerite cleaned every inch of the house in preparation for her move to London. Finding her scrubbing, Donal laughed and told her to stop fussing. 'Mrs Sinnott's going to stay on, and I'm fine with my own company. I'll miss you, of course, but you'd have left sooner or later. You wouldn't have stayed here once you'd got your degree.' But, still feeling slightly guilty and eager to leave things as they should be, Marguerite got workmen in to attend to a dripping tap and a rattling window and, determined her bedroom shouldn't become a depressing shrine to her childhood, packed clothes, books and unwanted possessions to give to charity.

At the start of the January sales, she went up to Dublin and joined a queue outside Hickey's fabric shop in Henry Street. As a child, she'd loved dressmaking at school and in the years after Ruth's death it had become her comfort. With Mrs Sinnott's encouragement, she'd worked out how to cut simple paper patterns, and had taught herself to construct new dresses by taking outgrown ones apart. Glad to see her happily occupied, Donal had supplied the cost of the outfits made for special occasions. Everything else had been achieved by saving her pocket money, and finding bargains was a challenge Marguerite had come to enjoy. In Hickey's sale she found the unbleached cheesecloth she wanted, along with skeins of gold embroidery thread and a sumptuous purple floss that would match the Biba headband she'd bought in London. Pleased with her finds, she carried them home in triumph and cut out her dress on the kitchen table.

That evening, she was sitting on the hearthrug embroidering when Donal came into the drawing room. He stirred the fire and sat down opposite her, saying she ought to take care not to strain her eyes.

'I won't. I pulled the lamp round. It's shining straight on my work.'

Rufus, then little more than a pup, had come in with Donal and, wanting petting, thrust his nose into Marguerite's lap. When she pushed him away, exclaiming that he was drooling, Donal clicked his fingers and the dog subsided obediently by the fire.

Donal nodded at the work. 'No harm done?'

'No, it's fine. How was your day?'

'Long, and full of coughs and sneezes. Half of which should never have been brought to the surgery. Every year I tell people to go to bed and drink hot lemon, yet they persist in coming out and spreading their damn winter colds. I suppose that, having spent Christmas cooped up with their families, even a trip to the doctor's makes a break.'

'You say that every year too.'

'I know. I'm becoming a bore.' Donal stretched his legs to the fire, and Rufus transferred his head from the fender to his master's feet. 'Odd to be sitting here on our own when only a few weeks ago you and Paul were putting up the tree.' Glancing down, Donal saw Marguerite's face. 'Don't start fretting again. I won't be lonely when you're gone. It just happens that I like this young man of yours. He's good company.' Donal's eyes softened. 'Your mum would have liked him too, I think.'

It was so unusual for him to raise the subject of her mother that Marguerite was uncertain what to say. She found herself asking what Ruth had worn on her wedding day. 'Was it a white wedding? Did she make her own dress?'

'She didn't go in for dressmaking. She wore a blue suit. A

costume it was called, in those days. It was only six years after the war ended. Not many brides went in for white dresses back then.' Having just booked the village church for her own wedding, Marguerite asked if that was where her parents had been married. Donal nodded. 'It wasn't a big do. The woman who introduced us was your mum's bridesmaid, Nora Blythe. Her husband, Myles, was at school with me. He was my best man.' Lifting his rump from the chair, he took his wallet out of his back pocket. 'Here we are, the four of us, outside the church.'

He held out a small photograph Marguerite hadn't seen before. It was black-and-white, and showed four young people, scarcely older than she was. She didn't recognise the best man or the bridesmaid, but Donal was a callow version of his present self, tall, handsome and self-effacing. Ruth looked as glamorous as she did in the portrait hanging over the fire. Her blue suit had a pencil skirt and a jacket with a peplum, and the pillbox hat on her fair curls had a polka-dot eye-veil.

Donal returned the photo to his wallet, as decisively as if he regretted having taken it out. Choosing her words, Marguerite said it was nice to think she'd be married in the same church. 'Not that Paul and I are religious. It's just a nice feeling, you know?'

Donal threw her a fleeting smile. 'Your mum and I weren't religious either, but the Barrys have always married in that church. More often than not, the incumbent was a relation. One of the bearded pious chaps in those photos in the church hall.'

'Was Mum Church of Ireland?' Immediately she'd spoken, Marguerite shook her head. 'Sorry, that's a stupid question. She was born in Maine, wasn't she?'

'Portland, and she grew up in New York. But I told you, neither of us was at all religious. I'm one of the pills and potions Barrys. The bells and smells gene didn't make it to me.'

Marguerite anchored a purple petal with a golden stitch. 'I thought I was a pills and potions Barry too.'

'I'm not sure I ever believed you wanted to be a pharmacist. Far better to spread your wings and do something less predictable with your life.'

'Like become a wife and mother?'

'It's not the worst of callings.'

Marguerite frowned. On one of her forays into town after Christmas, she'd met a couple of her former school friends, who'd hugged her with excitement outside Bewleys in Westmoreland Street. 'Marguerite Barry! You're in Dublin! What's going on?'

'I'm home for the holidays.' She'd held out her left hand to display her engagement ring. 'It's nearly Marguerite Carson, actually.' The girls had shrieked and insisted she join them for coffee and cherry buns but, though she'd been glad to see them, the experience had been odd. It was plain that, despite her London clothes, haircut and engagement ring, Joan and Emer took the view that she was to be pitied. They were both at university, intent on study and careers, and seemed baffled to find she had no plans beyond marriage.

On the bus home, Marguerite had been plagued by all that hadn't been said aloud. Was it weird, she thought, to settle down at twenty with a gentle accountant who got on well with your dad? Joan was having a turbulent relationship with a second-year who, though brilliant, was in constant danger of being done for drugs. Emer, who'd announced that she'd become a feminist activist, had made up her mind to stay celibate. No one could fight the patriarchy while getting their head around Augustine of Hippo and, anyway, she needed space to find out if she was bi. Beside this maelstrom of drama, aspiration and uncertainty, Marguerite's future had felt mundane. She looked up glumly at Donal. '"Not the worst of callings"? That sounds tame.'

'Marriage can be a complex relationship, and raising a child the most difficult job in the world.' Donal ran his hand down the spaniel's back. 'But just because I like Paul doesn't mean you have to.'

'Don't be daft. I'm in love with him.'

'If he phoned tomorrow and said it was all off, how would you feel?'

'Devastated.'

'And what would you do?'

'I don't know. It's not going to happen, though.'

'How do you know?'

'Because he adores me.'

Donal tugged one of the dog's silky ears. 'I could see that. Make sure you don't hurt him, Marguerite.'

It hardly seemed possible to Marguerite that more than fifty years had passed since that conversation. Each detail of her wedding day was stitched into her memory as precisely as the flowers on the fabric in her hand. Mrs Sinnott's six-year-old granddaughter had been her only bridesmaid, so Paul's mum had assumed the task of helping her to dress. She'd teased tendrils of fair hair from under the Biba headband, and chatted as Marguerite had applied her own smoky gold and purple eyeshadow. Marguerite had observed her in the mirror, thinking how quickly she'd grown attached to this unselfconscious woman who'd welcomed her into her family with open arms. And, as soon as this thought had crossed her mind, she'd felt like a traitor to her own mother. Inevitably, if Ruth had lived to see her married, Marguerite and Donal would have been focused on her state of mind, hoping she'd engage with the celebration and fearing she'd retreat into herself. I can't wish her dead, Marguerite had thought, and I don't. Truly, I don't. But how much worse might her depression have grown with the passing years? What kind of wedding day would this have been if she were still alive? Even if she'd seemed fine, I'd have been worried, because I never knew what was wrong, so I couldn't tell how to make things better when they got bad.

The guests had assembled in the drawing room for a sherry before the church service. Marguerite would never forget the look on Paul's face when she came downstairs in her wedding dress. In his grey suit, white shirt, and the purple tie she'd selected for him, he'd looked less like a London swinger than ever and, pausing on the threshold, she'd had a vision of Joan and Emer shaking their heads. Then he'd met her eyes and held out his hands and, unable to maintain her poise, she'd run towards him, knowing that, whatever the future might hold or what had happened in the past, her marriage to Paul Carson was made in Heaven.

Chapter Eighteen

Val climbed the stairs to the principal's office, knocked on the door and heard him call, 'Come in.' Like the rest of the building, the room was unprepossessing. Sean, the principal, waved her to a chair. 'Sit down. I have something here that may interest you.' A prematurely balding man twenty years younger than she was, he'd arrived a couple of years ago with a reputation for efficiency and the brief of raising the school's profile. He gave Val a smile that, if anything, was deferential and, though she'd had no reason to feel tense, she felt her shoulders relax. Despite her current position as head of the language school's distance learning strategy team, her instinct when summoned to the office unexpectedly was still to assume she might be about to find herself on the dole.

'You've attended a few international conferences for us, haven't you, Val?'

'Not for a good while but, yes, I did a couple. I believe there were concerns about what it cost to send a delegate, though.'

'Yes, I've gathered that, but I don't understand it. You didn't just sit about taking notes. You facilitated sessions, and the papers you published online are still being quoted.'

'I think that, at the time, we were more focused on attracting foreign students based here in London.' The truth was that Sean's predecessor, who'd despised the internet, had never managed to get a grip on distance learning, but it didn't seem politic to mention that.

Sean shook his head. 'Distance learning's a better economic model. We ought to be showcasing your expertise, not spoiling the ship for a ha'porth of tar.' He sat back and raised his eyebrows. 'There's a conference in China early next year. Would you be interested?'

'In attending?'

'They're looking for speakers. I'm sure we could get them to give you a decent slot. After all, you took this school into the field very early. You've a lot to offer.' This was so unexpected that Val struggled to take it in. Though Sean made it sound rather as if he wanted to wheel her out as a kind of dinosaur, he did seem impressed by her record. And that, she thought, makes a refreshing change. She'd built up the school's distance learning programme with very little support, and hadn't been given her current title till Sean had arrived and begun to make structural changes. He was still looking at her with raised eyebrows. 'What do you think?'

'I – it's immensely flattering ...'

'It would mean four or five days in Beijing, a fair bit of preparatory work and, hopefully, something to build on going forward. We might consider whether, in future, you'd be best employed doing less face-to-face teaching. Or none at all.'

'I'll need to think about it.'

'Of course. Take your time. It's early days for submissions. Have a think and, if you're interested, let's discuss it further.'

Slightly dazed, Val found herself back in the corridor. Kate was climbing the stairs. 'Been in to see Sean?'

'He's suggested I might go to a conference.' Val didn't elaborate. Rumours always spread through the staff like wildfire, and she wanted time to consider what Sean had said. Kate leaned against the wall, a pile of books in her arms. 'Lucky you. I wouldn't mind an all-expenses-paid foreign junket.'

'You haven't been to many conferences, have you? It's more like long hours in windowless rooms, strip lighting, snatched food, and information overload.'

'You can always sneak out the back way, though. Play truant.' Shifting her books to her other arm, Kate peered at her wristwatch. 'Oh, God, late again and I've a class waiting.'

Val made her way back down to the staffroom. She'd never imagined anything but jogging on with her usual work until she came to retirement. Now her mind was racing. Though she'd painted a downbeat picture for Kate, the prospect of foreign travel was exciting. And, evidently, Sean was thinking long-term. Could it be that the doors that had slammed when Simon had died and she'd found herself pregnant might be about to edge open again? I have to keep calm, she told herself, and think through the implications. But talk about bad timing! Right now, I'm hardly able to think beyond Penny's next scan.

When she got home, Val decided to ground herself by getting on with her side of the keepsake quilt. She still hadn't progressed much further than grouping colours, weights and textures on a large tray on the guestroom bed. As she stood considering them, her eye fell on a piece of indigo calico with a bright batik design of a couple of elephants trunk to tail. It had begun life as part of the border of one of Marguerite's dresses and been cut out to customise a jacket for Val in her early teens. She remembered the Anokhi dress with its crimson piping and jaunty procession of elephants, and could half recall her regret when she had outgrown the jacket. She'd hated to lose it because she'd loved the two elephants, so Marguerite had removed them before giving the jacket away. Val imagined a central block in which her elephants would be surrounded by squares of plainer fabric. That might work, she thought. Mum described the keepsake quilt as a way of sharing memories, and a piece recycled not once but twice would surely be good for that. Briefly, she held it to her face, remembering the musky scent of patchouli. Then, feeling she hadn't done much but had at least made an effort, she left it on the bed and went to run herself a bath.

The weather had grown muggy in the weeks since Penny's scan and Val had taken to going to Hampstead Heath at weekends, climbing as high as she could in search of fresh air. Today, finding a lone tree, she put her back against it and looked out over the sprawling city. It stretched for miles, pulsating with heat, a stifling mesh of brick, glass, metal, stone, tar and pre-cast concrete.

Somewhere down there, thought Val, Penny is getting on with her life. She's healthy, solvent and successful. Everything I ever wanted for her. And I managed it with no blueprint or pattern. I made it up as we went along and muddled through somehow, and only I knew how close I was to the edge at times. I suppose all mums are the same. We hide our insecurities for fear of passing them on. We even hide them from ourselves. To admit fear would be frightening, and to ask for help would be to accept that we're unable to cope. I wish to hell I could just turn up on Penny's doorstep and hug her. Because now I'm afraid that, in her celebrity TV-world bubble, she feels just as isolated and lonely as I was at her age.

One evening when Penny was three, Marguerite had arrived in West Hampstead half an hour after Val had come home from work. She'd said she just happened to be passing, a fiction that hung in the air as Val crashed about making tea. Penny was hungry and whining. The kitchen sink was full of the morning's breakfast dishes, and when Marguerite turned on the tap, Val had snapped at her. 'Leave those, Mum! I'll get to them later. Just sit down. The tea's nearly made.'

Marguerite had sat down meekly, averting her eyes from the kettle Val had forgotten to switch on. She'd held out her arms to Penny. 'Come and sit on Granny's lap, pet.'

Penny's lower lip had shot out and, anticipating a tantrum, Val had snapped again: 'Ignore her, Mum, she's tired.'

Penny had flung herself onto the floor, kicking. 'I'm *not* tired. *Not*. Shut your fat face, Granny!' Grimly, Val had told herself that she needed to find a new childminder, a problem she'd been aware of for weeks and hadn't been able to face. With an effort, she'd smiled at Marguerite. 'She picks it up from the other kids. Well, one little girl in particular. She's sweet, but her language is dreadful.'

'It doesn't matter.'

'Yes, it does. Penny! Say sorry to Granny!'

'Val, really, it's fine ...'

'No, it isn't. Penny, stand up *now*, say sorry and go to the naughty step.'

As always when challenged, Penny got stubborn. So, the tea was made with water that had barely come to the boil, and drunk in embarrassed haste. As Marguerite left, she'd paused in the hallway. 'I can always look after Pen if you're between childminders. It's so hard to make choices when you're pressured.'

'Yes, well, I obviously made the wrong one, didn't I?'

'Darling, I didn't mean that.'

'I know. I'm sorry. I'm tired and, look, I have to get Penny to bed. Thanks for the offer, but we'll be fine. Really. I'll remember, though. I'll give you a ring if I need to.' She'd shut the door and returned to the kitchen to find Penny, still on the floor, communing with her toy lion. Now there were even more dishes to wash. Exhausted, Val had sunk onto the tiled floor beside Penny, who'd said, with a sweet, confiding smile, that Leo was very hungry. 'You needn't cook for him, though, Mummy. I can do it on my own.' Putting her arm around her daughter, Val had hugged her tightly. We're as bad as each other, she'd thought. She doesn't just take after Simon. I might as well admit that there's plenty of me in her too.

In the years that followed, Val had had boyfriends. Not at first, when life was an endless round of nappies, childcare crises, rushed mornings and tummy-aches in the night, but later, when she felt more in control. Aware that the single mother of an only daughter could easily come to rely on her child for companionship, Val made sure Penny spent time with children her own age, especially when Rory's move to New Zealand deprived her of her cousins. Putting her own social life on hold, she devoted herself to Penny's, signing her up for Guides and ferrying her to after-school clubs. And, anxious though she felt when Penny wasn't under her eye, she'd tried hard not to behave like a clingy mother, and made it a rule not to intrude on her child's private life.

As Penny grew older and Val had more time, she began to re-establish her own contacts, accepting dinner invitations and meeting old friends for coffee. After a while, feeling absurdly nervous, she went on a date. That evening led to another and, by degrees, she drifted into a relationship with a good-looking guy who taught with her at Finchley. But Penny didn't take to him, so the dates tailed off. Other relationships flourished and faded, always low-key and never serious, until a time came when Val decided to let her spare room. The need for a new boiler had blown her budgeting, so unused space was an obvious source of income.

She found a medic on attachment at the Royal Free Hospital who needed a few months' accommodation. Balan Chawla was so soft-spoken and courteous that at first Val worried the room mightn't suit him. The house still tended to be chaotic in the mornings, and ten-year-old Penny was apt to play the Pussycat Dolls at full volume. But Balan assured Val he'd grown up with a large extended family he'd missed since coming to the UK. He'd recently qualified from Madras Medical College and planned to return to Chennai when his time at the Royal Free was up. When

Val showed him around, he said the room was perfect, and that he hoped she wouldn't be troubled by his schedule. 'I may come in late sometimes, or have an early shift.'

'That's no problem. You'll have your own key. There's a table in the room if you need to work.'

'It is perfect. Really.'

'I'll get Penny to keep the music down.'

'That won't be easy if she's anything like my little cousins. Don't worry. I'm a doctor – by the end of a shift I could sleep through an earthquake!'

Though their work commitments meant Val and Balan didn't see much of each other, he settled in quickly and made fast friends with Penny. He was a considerate lodger, scrupulously clearing up in the kitchen, and offering to put out bins and do chores. Occasionally, they'd spend an evening together watching TV, and sometimes he'd cook meals that put the local Indian takeaway to shame.

A month after his arrival, Penny was booked for a week's camping with the Guides. Val kissed her goodbye, thinking this was a chance to do the housework that always eluded her, such as clearing out the clutter under the stairs. She planned to begin that evening but came home to the smell of cooking spices. Hanging her bag on the newel post, she went through to the kitchen and found Balan with three pans on the hob. He gave her his shy smile and said he'd thought he'd make dinner. 'My roster changed, so we could have a night in, if you'd like that.'

It was the first time he'd cooked for her without prior arrangement, but everything smelt delicious, and Val was hungry, so she said yes. It was also the first time they'd eaten together without Penny's presence. The door to the garden was open to the warm evening and, after dinner, Val decided to postpone her housework. She sat back and listened to Balan's description of life in Chennai, and admired photos of temples adorned with carvings and paintwork, streets full of bustle and colour, and golden beaches fringed by trees. 'It's so gorgeous!'

'I miss it. London is a great city but I doubt if I could ever get used to the weather.'

'Do you live by the sea?'

'My parents have a home not far from the beach.'

'Years ago, I had an idea that I'd travel the world. India was high on my list.'

'But you haven't travelled?'

'No. Well, there's Penny ...'

She and Balan had never had such a conversation before, but the relaxing meal and his undemanding presence loosened her tongue and, looking out at the dusky garden, she talked more about the past than she had for years. That night, she slept so deeply she almost missed the sound of her alarm clock, and in the following days, the house-cleaning didn't get done. Instead, she and Balan spent more time together, seeing a film after work, sitting chatting in the garden, and taking turns to cook dinner for each other. Penny was due home on Sunday morning and on Saturday, when Balan was free, Val suggested a walk on Hampstead Heath. 'Have you ever been there?'

'I seem to do nothing but oscillate between the hospital and my bed.'

'Oh, but you ought to see some of the sights while you're here in London. There's a wonderful bird's-eye view from the top of the Heath.'

They took a picnic, caught a bus, and spent the whole day there. At some point, she found Balan was holding her hand. It didn't surprise her. It felt as if they were moving in perfect harmony, instinctively choosing directions as one, and hardly needing to speak to communicate. The chemistry between them was a world away from the sexually charged bickering she'd known with Simon. And of course it is, she told herself. How could it not be? I was another person then. This is different.

When they got home, she led Balan upstairs to her bed. His lovemaking was nothing like Simon's either – though when he twisted a single strand of her hair around his finger Val suddenly felt her heart would break. Balan drew back. 'What is it?'

'Nothing.'

Letting her hair go, he rolled over and stared at the ceiling. 'It is something.'

'Yes, but …'

'I didn't expect this to happen.'

'No. Well, who did?'

He turned his head and his eyes looked into hers. 'I don't have much longer in London.'

Val sat up, holding the duvet tightly around her breasts. 'Look, I didn't expect this either.'

'But you're glad.'

'Yes. Well – yes, but …'

'You could come with me. Why not? You and Penny. You could come with me to Chennai.'

'What? Balan, that's crazy.'

'Why? Why is it crazy? You said you've always wanted to see India.'

'I did. I have. But not this way. I mean, not now. I couldn't.'

'This isn't a proposal.'

'God, no! I mean, I didn't think it was.'

He sat up too, and faced her. 'What I mean is that I'm not saying we should marry. I'm saying I don't know where this might lead us if we give it a chance.'

'But you have to leave.'

'Yes, I do. I've made a commitment to a hospital, and my work is there. But you could come with me.'

Val shook her head violently. 'I've got a job too.'

'You said you hate it.'

'I didn't. I said it bores me and ...'

'... and you feel trapped.'

'I didn't say that. Okay, maybe I did, but I've a daughter to raise, and she comes first.'

'I think I love you.'

'What? Shut up. No.'

'And I think that you might love me.'

'It's practically morning. Penny will be back in a couple of hours.'

'Will you take time and consider it?'

'No.' Val pushed the duvet away, got out of bed and groped for her dressing-gown. 'I can't. She's got friends here. The Guides. She's settled in a school. I can't just uproot her.'

'Would it be so bad to give her a taste of life in another country? You could ask her what she thinks of the idea.'

'No, I couldn't. She's ten years old. I'm not dumping that kind of choice on her. Anyway, I'd have to explain to her about you and me, and I couldn't. I don't know how she'd react.'

'You could find out.'

'No. No, I couldn't. You don't realise how hard it's been, holding things together. I can keep going, but I can't change course. It's too complicated. Too much effort.' Tying a double knot in her dressing-gown belt, Val sat down on the side of the bed. 'You do understand?'

'No, I don't. But I understand that you won't come to Chennai.'

Looking down at London shimmering in the afternoon heat, Val remembered how she'd rolled back into bed, still wrapped in her dressing gown, and spent the rest of the night in Balan's arms. Penny had come home the following day and rushed to her bedroom to put on the Pussycat Dolls. Balan was at work by then, and Val had a splitting headache. Bounding downstairs, Penny had said she was starving. 'What I want is a massive plate of Balan's biryani.'

'There isn't any. You'll have to settle for pork pie and salad.'

'That is so rotten! He knew I was coming back.'

'He's our lodger, Penny. He's not here to cook for us.'

'Well, he might have *thought*. I love his biryani.'

'Leave it, Pen. There's food in the fridge if you're hungry. And turn down that dreadful racket upstairs.'

Disconcertingly, Penny had come around the table and

hugged her. 'You're glad to have me back, though, aren't you, Mum?'

'Go and turn the music down. Of course I'm glad to see you.'

Fighting tears, Val had gone to assemble a plate of food. That night, when Penny was asleep, she'd sat up, waiting for Balan. When he came in, he said he'd arranged to move to a colleague's flat. 'He has a vacant room. I'll pack and be gone tomorrow.'

'No, don't.'

'I'm leaving London soon, anyway. Don't argue, Val. It's better for me to go.'

It had been another instance of life holding out promise and snatching it away. Desolate, she'd watched him go upstairs and into his room. It was empty when she came in from work the next day, and Penny had seemed to accept her explanation that the hospital had required Balan to move onsite. With no one she felt she could talk to about it, Val had buried it deep.

Now, looking down from the high place where she'd sat with Balan, she realised nothing had changed. Her life still revolved around her daughter. It wasn't enough to know Penny was healthy, successful and solvent. The truth was that she'd never stop feeling fearful. She'd never feel safe until she knew Penny had someone trustworthy to love.

Chapter Nineteen

The first time a tabloid called David 'the middle-aged woman's crumpet', he was chuffed. The implication, he'd assured himself, was that viewers saw him as a raffish toy-boy. But now that he'd passed forty, he wasn't so sure. He felt confident on set having just emerged from Makeup, but tended to flinch when he saw himself reflected in shop windows. It was worse at home, where Helen had installed a smoked-glass shower cabinet in the bathroom, and chosen mirrored wardrobe doors. Though David worked out daily, and his height was an advantage, he disliked unexpected glimpses of his unguarded self, especially when naked. So, when a Heal's van arrived in Blackheath, he watched aghast as delivery men unloaded a vast mirror and, having manoeuvred it through the hall, began to unpack it on the living-room floor.

Helen looked up at him anxiously. 'Don't you like it, darling? I thought you would. You said the house had turned into a nursery. That's why I've moved most of the twins' toys up to their bedroom. I wanted this room to have an adult vibe again.'

David watched the efficient removal of the packaging. The mirror was a good seven feet square, had a wide black frame, and looked heavy enough to pull plaster off the wall. 'Are these guys going to hang it? Because I can tell you now, that's going to be one hell of a job.'

'Of course not, darling. You lean it against the wall.'

'You do?'

He hadn't noticed that the majority of the twins' clutter was gone, or seen that she'd repositioned the sofa to free up an entire wall. Having tipped the delivery men, Helen came back and slipped her arm through his. 'What do you think? It's a bit stark now but I wanted to see the effect. Maybe I'll put the armchairs on either side of it.' What David could see was that, from now on, when he sat on his favourite sofa, he'd be facing a full-length reflection of himself.

Helen pulled him across the room and sat on the sofa beside him. 'Like I said, a proper adult vibe.' She wriggled round to lie on his lap and looked up invitingly but, as David instinctively bent to kiss her, his conscious mind intervened, wondering if the mirror's tilt was unflattering. Helen opened her eyes and pouted. 'Sweetheart, what's the matter? Don't you like the frame? It could have been red lacquer but I thought black was sexier. I could return it, though, and get the red.'

'Don't. It's fine.'

'But you don't like it.'

'I do. I think it's much sexier than pink plastic kiddicars.' Resolutely turning his back on the mirror, David hooked one hand behind Helen's knees and, slipping his other arm around her shoulders, tipped her back against the sofa cushions. 'Where are the monsters?'

'Out with my mum.'

'Right. Well, let's test-drive the adult vibe.'

'You said you had a meeting.'

'Not till lunchtime.'

Her skirt slipped up her thigh and, finding his familiar rhythm, David moved his hands to the small of her back. Actually, he told himself, this was fortuitous. What he'd described as a meeting was, in fact, his annual review, so a swift confidence-booster beforehand was just what he required.

Half an hour later, showered, shaved, and wearing what he judged to be an outfit that screamed casual edginess, he strode down the hill to Blackheath station. Ostensibly, his reviews were about tossing around new creative ideas. But, according to Dominic, his agent, their actual purpose was sinister. 'Reviews are a game, David, okay? Don't ever forget it. You'll be sat there with your exec prod, a company boss and a suit sent in by the network. There'll be lots of stuff about rising ratings.'

'That's good, isn't it?'

'And lots more about falling ad revenue.'

'God, is it falling?'

'I said it's a game, David. They'll want you to feel both bought-in and scared of being chucked out.'

'Shit. Why?'

'So you won't let me take any risks when your contract comes up for renewal.'

Dominic had turned out to be right. David had emerged from

his first review with a sense that, though he was valued, he was not indispensable. As a result, he'd called Dominic and urged caution. 'I don't want to push my luck until I'm in a stronger position.'

'I told you this would happen.'

'I'm being strategic.'

'Sure, you are.'

At the time, he'd been receiving bills from Jennifer for their son's orthodontistry, and Helen had wanted to add a conservatory to the Blackheath house. David hadn't mentioned this to his agent, but he'd had a sneaking feeling Dominic knew. At his next review, the suit from the network had pursed his lips. 'I'm not saying the advertising take-up on either side of your slot is disappointing. Or even unexpected at this stage. Let's keep an eye on the figures.' Leaning back in his chair, he'd smiled toothily at David. 'My wife asked me about that chocolate biscuit you made last Thursday. In a teacup or something? In the microwave?'

'A cappuccino cup. It was a muffin.'

'That's the one. She adored it.' Turning to Penny, he'd said he'd talk to the ad sales team. 'We ought to be able to push these figures up.'

When Dominic took David's call afterwards, he'd laughed. 'Ah, yes, the old "keeping an eye on the figures" line. Don't tell me. I know. You want me to be Mr Nice Guy.'

Torn between nervousness and embarrassment, David had said yes. 'I'll be bedded-in by the time we get to the next negotiation. I'd rather we kept our powder dry till then.'

A week later, he'd received a letter stating a change in the terms of his financial arrangement with his agency and, though he'd accepted its contents without objection, he'd known why. Clients who gave Dominic his head in negotiation reaped the reward of their courage if his bullishness paid off. The risk-averse would be required to pay for their cowardice via a hike in Dominic's percentage of their fees.

In the following years, a modest uplift per contract had been established, and Dominic, who'd lost interest in taunting David, informed him of each by email without discussing the deal. Repressing a sense of humiliation, David had augmented his income by taking every celebrity gig on offer, from corporate appearances to judging cake competitions at village fetes, and involved himself in charity work for any cause that would guarantee significant press coverage. By dint of self-advertisement, he'd steadily grown his profile, and middle-aged women continued to watch him in droves. He'd also achieved unforeseen success among twenty-somethings, who'd spontaneously set up *Buns of Steel*, an online fanzine of images taken whenever he turned his back to camera and bent to open the studio oven door.

Half horrified and half delighted, David had watched his celebrity status rocket and seen himself endorsed by social-media influencers. All this being so, he was inclined to unleash Dominic on his upcoming contract. After all, the show's shtick was about reaching the widest possible demographic, and here he was, fanciable by women of all ages. This year, selling himself on these grounds in Penny's presence might be awkward. But, as he took his seat on the train, he reminded himself that, at work, Penny was never less than professional. All he needed to do was to take precisely the same approach.

It had been unlike any affair David had had before. With a keen sense of the value of a mortgage-free existence, he'd taken every precaution he could to protect the security he'd found with Helen. And no one was more aware than he of the vital importance of keeping it from the tabloids. But that first night on Penny's doorstep, clutching his cold bottle of Moët, he'd recognised that, this time, risk was the attraction. A flower stall had been closing as he'd cut through Borough Market and he'd stopped and bought an expensive bunch of roses but, approaching Penny's front door, he'd wondered if this might have been a mistake. None of the usual rules will apply, he'd thought. She's made all the running. I've just been summoned.

By the time he'd climbed the stairs to the flat, he'd abandoned what he thought of as his usual three-point strategy – surprise, seize and seduce – and when Penny opened the door, he was standing on the threshold murmuring, 'Go with the flow.' She'd been wearing a green, pleated skirt with a white top, and was barefoot, something that had flustered him even more. But, after a couple of glasses of champagne, he'd regained his equilibrium and, by the end of the evening, he'd decided that this was the kind of affair he'd always wanted. Despite the bare feet, Penny had retained a certain aloofness. Her flat, with its neutral colours, brushed steel and exposed brickwork, was the antithesis of his suburban home, and the pinnacle of his idea of sophistication. He'd worried she might have exacting standards in the bedroom but, to his amazement, found she was easily satisfied and happy to lie around after sex, eating takeaway Chinese food. And, best of all, each time he'd sneaked off to meet her, he'd been able to cock a mental snook at Dominic, whose conclusion that he was a risk-averse coward had always felt far too close to David's secret assessment of himself.

Not only that but, though Penny's condition was now common knowledge, no one seemed to have the slightest suspicion that he might be the father. What a result, thought David, complacently. Sex without strings and no tears and tantrums at the end. As he left the train at London Bridge, he reflected that Penny's dismissal of him had been a relief in more ways than one. To his shame, he'd always found pregnancy revolting. Jennifer had been sick each morning for three solid months, and had got so large towards the end of her third trimester that he'd found it hard to hide his disgust. Precisely the same thing had happened when Helen was pregnant with the twins and, as in Jennifer's case, he'd resented the time it had taken her body to regain a shape he desired. None of that would trouble him with Penny, he thought triumphantly. This time he was off the hook, scot-free and totally on the up.

When he arrived at the office, Penny was at her desk. Lolly was setting out coffee cups on a table, lining up spoons and handles and placing a paper napkin under each saucer. Normally, office coffees came in polystyrene cups, but china was kept for occasions when the network was represented. Penny gave him a professional smile and said something about the weather as Tony, one of the company bosses, arrived. Penny told Lolly she could go, and ushered them to the sofas that stood on either side of the coffee-table. Inevitably, Tony enquired about David's family. 'All well?'

'Never better.'

'Your kids must have started school?'

'Playschool at the moment. We've got all the rest ahead of us.' Hoping this hadn't made him sound needy, David sat down, relaxed and reached for a coffee. All that was required of him now was to bask in the evidence of the result of his spadework, and receive congratulations on his growing number of fans. Penny's crack about making twice as much money as he did still rankled. This time, when his contract was up for renewal, he'd demand a ratings-related bonus as well as a serious uplift, and maybe then they'd all treat him with more professional respect.

He was leaning back, looking forward to calling Dominic later, when suddenly he was ambushed by self-doubt. Setting down his coffee cup, he struggled to concentrate. When Penny had snubbed him on the set that day in the studio, he'd assumed she was being strategic and admired her professional cool. But might she have meant it? As David floundered, he recalled another of Dominic's warnings. 'Don't try to play games when you're out of your league, David. You'll only make a fool of yourself, and you certainly won't win.'

Penny sat down and flipped open her laptop, looking distant and completely in control. Suddenly David broke out into a cold sweat. What was going through her mind? Was she now as averse to the sight of him as he was to seeing swelling female bodies? She was the one with access to the bosses. Even they were impressed by the growth of his profile: they wouldn't want to piss her off. Was this really the time to rock the boat by demanding more money? Would it give her the perfect excuse to tell the network she wanted him gone?

Chapter Twenty

Still unsure of how to create a coherent design, Val had decided to try a new approach. It was a sunny weekend and, by taking the Tube to Richmond upon Thames, she could walk along the towpath to Orleans House Gallery, where she'd seen there was a quilting exhibition. Richmond was crowded with shoppers, so she cut through backstreets to reach the bridge and cross the river to Twickenham. On the Richmond side, families and tourists were thronging the path, eating ice-creams, but here, in the cool shade of willows, only a few people passed on bikes or strolled by in couples, and the weeds grew lush on the steep embankment that sloped down to the water. What she'd read of the exhibition was intriguing, though she'd heard amusement in Marguerite's voice when she'd mentioned it on the phone.

'What's funny?'

'Nothing at all. I was only thinking it's typical of you to want to research your subject.'

'Years of being a teacher, I suppose.'

'It's a perfectly sensible starting-point, it just wouldn't be mine. I'm either more intuitive than you or much lazier.'

'I couldn't possibly comment!'

'Well, enjoy the exhibition. Take photos. I'm intrigued too.'

As children, Val and Rory had loved this walk along the Twickenham towpath where, in summer, bees droned among marsh woundwort and cow parsley. Penny had loved it too in her schooldays, when she'd come here with Val and Marguerite. It was hard to imagine that this time next year all three of them might be here pushing Penny's baby in a buggy, or that Penny would have time to stroll along eating ice-cream, or to point out swans sailing past followed by grey cygnets. And how much free time will I have by then? Val wondered. The previous night, trying to decide how to respond to Sean's suggestion, she'd imagined having to balance new commitments of her own with the need to be on hand to help with the baby. And that's pretty ironic, she thought wryly. Think of me telling Penny I'm up to my ears in work and can't talk. Not that I've any reason to think she'll need me on standby. It's just that I can't be sure she won't, and I don't really have time to wait and find out. I wish I knew whether the baby's dad will be there to help, but if I ask her, I know she's sure to throw another wobbly.

Orleans House was surrounded by woodland, which Val entered through a gate in the high perimeter wall. The gallery was in a coach house to the rear of an eighteenth-century red-brick octagon building, which was all that remained of the original house. The queue at the exhibition entrance was short. Val joined it behind a middle-aged woman who, like herself, was alone. They exchanged smiles and, once inside, nodded as they parted and, fleetingly, Val thought she seemed nice. She was looking round for a catalogue when an attendant murmured smugly that her focus should be responsive, not cerebral. 'The exhibition is an immersive experience. You can pick up a catalogue on your way out.'

I hate the word 'immersive', Val thought crossly, and I've always resented being told what to focus on. But here I am, so what the hell? I might as well embrace it. If nothing else, it'll make a good story for Mum.

Her first response was to think that, if she was here in search of coherence, she'd definitely come to the wrong place. Though the exhibition was billed as a history of quilting, the curator had taken what could be called a fluid approach. In the entrance, hanging at different heights and sandwiched by sheets of Plexiglas, blocks of patchwork of different sizes turned in a draught. The Plexiglas revealed both sides of the fabrics, some heavily patterned, embroidered or embellished, and others distinguished by nothing more than colour, texture or weight. To reach the first room you had to pass under and through them and, as Val walked in, she felt enveloped, as if she were actually entering a quilt.

The exhibits beyond the suspended blocks could also be viewed from both sides. The first, a quilt made for a double bed, was hung with its underside facing the entrance. This was plain grey flannel on which the quilting was almost invisible. But, walking around it, Val was stunned by an elaborate pattern of swirls and scallops worked in charcoal grey thread on yellow cotton. With nothing else to distract it, her attention was drawn to the stitching, as regular as machine-work but obviously done by hand. This was nothing like what she and Marguerite were attempting. Or perhaps it is in essence, she thought, stepping closer to marvel. This wasn't made as a work of art: you can see it's been used and repaired. It's old and functional but it wasn't just a matter of joining three layers of fabric to provide warmth. Walking around the quilt again, she wondered how long it had taken to create. Months. Maybe years. Maybe, she thought, like our keepsake quilt, it was the work of more than one person. Clearly, it was an act of love and, whether that was love of the work or of the bodies it was made to cover, it radiates an energy you can feel.

Moving on, she found herself facing what had undoubtedly been conceived as artwork. It was a huge machine-quilted panel on which every possible technique had been employed. Appliqué, embroidery, felting and paper combined to produce an abstract design shot through with silver wire that gave the effect of rain falling on multicoloured fields. It was powerful but, to Val's eye, impersonal.

Looking beyond it, she noticed fragments of stitched fabric strung out against a wall. A review she'd read had praised the exhibition's mix of vintage and contemporary quilting so, thinking these fragments might be remnants of older pieces, she went to see. Among them were several that seemed the work of inexperienced hands. Val wondered if they were from samplers worked by children, which, at some point, had been incorporated in quilts. On the smallest piece a daisy was supporting a bee with a stripy body erratically worked in purple wool. Though one of the petals was expertly done, the others straggled. Smiling, Val imagined a mother carefully setting stitches as an example, and sighing over the bee's crooked wings and improbably fat legs. For a long time, she stood there looking at it. It wasn't the sort of thing she'd expected to find at the exhibition, yet the image evoked the deep buzzing of bees in the weeds by the river as effectively as anything ten times more skilled.

There was no set route to follow. She moved to and fro, unaware of where she'd been and where she was going, often stopping and sometimes retracing her steps. A darkened booth in a corner appeared empty, but when she went in, the walls lit up in a whirl of coloured shapes. Apparently, this was a moving mandala, the pattern that had sprung to Val's mind when Marguerite first mentioned the keepsake quilt. Val had a vague memory that mandalas were supposed to represent aspects of the universe. She was pretty sure they had emerged from Buddhist or Hindu ritual, though why they turned up as quilt patterns she didn't know. She stared at the moving shapes for a while, then, sitting on a stool in the centre of the space, found herself thrown off balance. The stool revolved. Mesmerised, Val spun round slowly, knowing she was anchored but feeling the shapes were drawing her in. Then, as if she were hearing him speak, she remembered Simon's voice.

They'd been lying by the river at Oxford, studying for exams.

'Shut up, Simon, I'm trying to concentrate.'

'In that case, what you need is a mandala.'

'I said shut *up*.'

'Seriously. See?' He'd pushed the book he was reading towards her, scattering her notes. '"By mentally entering a mandala and proceeding toward its centre, you're guided through processes –"'

'Just bugger off, will you?'

'"– processes of disintegration and reintegration." That's what mandalas are for. They represent the conscious self's attempts to integrate unconscious material. In other words, they assist concentration.'

The book was a shabby paperback he must have picked up in a charity shop. 'What on earth are you reading that for? You're supposed to be revising.'

'I'll crowbar it in somewhere when it comes to the exams. The trouble with you, my gorgeous muse, is that you've no grasp of strategy. It's unexpected references that get a man a First.'

When she'd sat up and thumped him, he'd rolled across her pages of notes to kiss her, and now, in the midst of whirling shapes and colours, she had a vivid memory of the scent of crushed grass. Bracing her feet against the floor, she stopped the stool revolving and closed her eyes. Circles, squares, octagons, hexagons and diamonds rotated slowly behind her closed eyelids, her mind went blank and when she stood up, she'd no idea how long she'd been sitting there.

Outside the booth, the colours around her seemed more intense, and when Val bent over an appliquéd rose she felt the same sense of envelopment she'd had when she'd walked beneath the hanging patchwork. Wandering on, she found other pieces that stunned, surprised and pleased her, but as she stepped out into the sunny courtyard, she shook her head at an offer of a catalogue. She was carrying impressions that, just then, she felt no desire to break down or analyse.

Picking up a takeaway coffee at the café, she walked round to the front of the octagon looking for somewhere to sit but the only bench was occupied by the woman she'd seen in the queue. Before Val could turn away, the stranger smiled at her. 'Do sit if you'd like to. I'll be off in a minute.'

'I don't want to drive you away.'

'You're not.' The woman held up a cardboard cup. 'I've just finished this, and I ought to get home. It's lovely here, though, isn't it?'

Val sat down and gazed across the lawn to the line of trees that edged the river. 'I like it. Did you enjoy the exhibition? Are you a quilter?'

'No, I'm cack-handed! Actually, the curator is my daughter. That's why I'm here. I came to the opening but that was all bells and whistles. So, I came back.' The woman shot Val a sidelong smile. 'Don't let that inhibit you, though. What did you think of it?'

'I'm not sure. It's certainly immersive.'

The woman's smile broadened. 'That's definitely the word.'

Seeing the twinkle in her eye, Val laughed with her. 'I'm sorry. I didn't mean to be offensive. If I'm honest, the curation put me off to begin with. But I think I was wrong. I came looking for inspiration, and I'm pretty sure that's what I'm leaving with.'

'You're a quilter, then?'

'Absolutely not. I sew a bit, but that's not the same thing, is it? I am making a quilt, though. With my mother. For my daughter.' Val sipped her coffee. 'It's a long story.'

'Sorry, I didn't mean to intrude.'

'You haven't.' Val explained that her daughter was pregnant,

173

and that Marguerite had suggested they make the keepsake quilt. She said nothing about the row, or Penny's circumstances or job, and was careful not to mention her surname. It seemed unlikely that this ordinary, pleasant woman was a tabloid journalist, but she still had no intention of being indiscreet. It was good to talk, though. The woman introduced herself as Jean and, after they'd chatted a while, Val suggested a second coffee. 'If you keep the bench, I'll go up and get them. Do you fancy a flapjack?' When she came back, the conversation turned to Jean's daughter who, according to Jean, had become a high-flier. 'I scarcely see her these days.'

'Tell me about it! I don't see much of Penny. What matters is that they're well and happy, though.'

Jean sighed. 'But how does one know? If something went wrong, I doubt Lynette would confide in me. Apparently, high-fliers aren't supposed to be vulnerable.' Empathising, and feeling she might have given a false impression of her own relationship, Val said Penny didn't go in for confidences either. 'With us, it's a family thing. We don't talk much. I know what you mean about high-fliers, though. Penny's very invested in her work.'

'How lovely that you're going to be a grandmother.'

'Have you any grandkids?'

'Not yet. Lynette's an only child. I try not to make her feel pressured, but I'd love to be a gran.'

Behind them, in a flurry of rose petals, a wedding party emerged from a door in the red-brick octagon building. Jean admired the little bridesmaids' organza dresses. 'Isn't the octagon a charming setting for a wedding ceremony? Those vast arched windows letting in the sunshine and all that gilded plasterwork. No wonder there's a waiting list to hire it.' As the bride and groom posed for photos, their mothers fussed about, arranging her veil and straightening his tie. Jean laughed. 'That's everyone's wedding, isn't it? Archetypal.'

'I never had one. My fiancé died.' Seeing Jean's shocked face, Val went on hastily. 'Don't worry, it was ages ago. Feels like another life. Anyway, I was pregnant with Pen, so I just had to keep going.'

'It can't have been easy.'

'No. But you do what you have to. And I expect you're right about being a gran. When Penny was little, life was a constant series of panics and crises, but this will be different. There'll be time to build a relationship. It won't be long now before we know if it's a boy or a girl.'

'Your quilt sounds lovely.'

'It was my mother's idea. I sort of got roped in. She seems to be flying ahead and I'm stuck, I'm afraid. I can't get the pieces in order and I'm failing to see a pattern. That's why I'm looking for inspiration.' They'd both got to their feet and Val held out her hand. 'Goodbye. It was nice to meet you. Do congratulate Lynette for me. It's a real achievement. I'll keep an eye out for her next exhibition.'

'She's moving to the States, I'm afraid, so there'll be nothing of hers in London for a while.'

'Oh, I'm sorry. You'll miss her.'

'Yes.'

Val watched her walk away, and raised her hand when Jean turned to wave. Disposing of the coffee cups, she made her way back to the riverside, thinking about the swatches of fabric she'd been looking at when Simon told her he and his mates were off on a jaunt to Cornwall. The wedding dress she'd been planning was as traditional as the one she'd just glimpsed on the bride who'd emerged from the octagon. Cream silk with an overskirt, a stiffly boned bodice, and a long-sleeved bolero in fine Brussels lace. She'd hesitated between smooth and figured silk and the shop had given her a book of swatches to take home and think about. After the funeral, she'd moved home and slept in her childhood bedroom while Marguerite and Paul had dealt with phone calls and form-filling, rescinding invitations and cancelling caterers. A few weeks later, when Val went back to West Hampstead, she'd found Marguerite had discreetly removed all evidence of her wedding. The files, the lists, the magazine pages pinned to a corkboard were gone. The gifts she'd left in their wrapping on the guestroom bed had vanished. And the swatches of silk had disappeared, as if her dress, and the whole future life she'd planned with Simon, had been as insubstantial as a dream.

Chapter Twenty-One

Penny was sitting on her bedroom floor when Mark phoned from the shop. 'Hi, Pen. How're things? Are you home?'

'Yeah, I'm upstairs. Things are fine. How're you?'

'Are you free this evening?'

'I'm not really sure.' She'd told Lolly she'd be working from home but had ended up cleaning the bathroom, and was now sorting her shoe collection, so she'd expected to spend the evening playing catch-up. 'Why? What's happening?'

'I'm under instruction to bring you to a party.'

'Oh, Mark, I've got masses of work to get through. Stacks of it.' Penny was shocked to see how much time she'd already wasted. She struggled to her feet and made for the stairs. 'Really. It's a lovely thought, but I couldn't possibly.'

'Don't you want to know who gave the instruction?'

Having reached the living room, Penny sat down and stared at an open spreadsheet. 'I can't come. Honestly, Mark. Thanks, but I'll have to pass.'

'He'll be devastated.'

'Who?'

'Bill.'

'Your *dad*'s inviting me to a party?'

'It's his eightieth. Come on, Penny. It's only a few minutes' walk away, and he really wants you there.'

'So, where's it happening?'

'Round at theirs. Mum's been cooking all morning and Leeann has baked a cake. Two, actually. Whoppers. Half the neighbourhood's dropping in. I said I'd go round when I shut up shop, but it's kicked off already. They started when Leeann's mob got home from school.' Leeann was Mark's eldest sister, so Penny supposed the mob must be her kids. It seemed early for a party to begin but, when she said so, Mark laughed. 'You don't know my family! They'll party from morning till night if they get a chance. And this is a big birthday for Bill, so we're pulling out all the stops. Come on, Penny, he really will be upset if you don't show.'

'I suppose I do count as a neighbour.'

'You count as a friend.'

The budget for the following month swam before Penny's eyes. She dabbed them with her shirtsleeve and, mentally cursing hormones, cleared her throat and said she'd love to come. 'Shall I come down at closing time and walk over with you?'

'Sure. Drop in at five thirty.'

'Oh, but ... I don't have a present for Bill.'

'Mum's banned presents. She says if the flat gets cluttered, he'll want to set up a market stall.'

Penny giggled. 'I bet she's right.'

'It's how he started.'

'Selling off birthday presents?'

'I wouldn't be surprised. Back then, he'd sell you the steam off his porridge.'

'I've got a stash of cards somewhere.'

'He'll like a card. Oops, gotta go, here's a customer. See you later.'

Penny continued to stare at her screen, telling herself she hated hormones. These days, she kept being ambushed by unexpected things. Irrational moments of panic, such as the one she'd had by the river, and the sweat she'd just broken into at the thought of crowded rooms. Weird stuff, like the urge to do housework and how often her hair and nails seemed to need cutting. The housework thing seemed linked to the need to get up in the night to pee. She'd wake at 4 a.m., stumble from her bed to the loo, and suddenly feel she had to clean windows. And, more than once, she'd found herself compulsively tidying at the office. Fortunately, this had happened when no one else was there to notice. Now she started sweating again at the mere thought that she might do something daft in the midst of a meeting. In her cutthroat world, even a hint of weakness could be dangerous, which was why she'd never allowed herself to treat colleagues as confidants. And now, having lost touch with friends she'd known before her job had consumed her life, she had no one with whom it felt safe to talk about what she'd tried to assure herself was ordinary pregnancy stuff. I shouldn't need to, she told herself crossly. Everyone knows pregnancy makes you pee more and produces what the internet calls 'nesting behaviour'. And, actually, my hair looks pretty damn good. But, having built a reputation on hard-nosed pragmatism, it was disconcerting to find herself feeling wimpy. And what if these feelings didn't go away? How will this baby cope, she thought, with a sweaty wimp for a mother? Not just a wimp, either. A Billy No Mates whose brain seems to be turning to mush.

Getting up, she went to look out a card. Lolly regularly picked her up a selection, for colleagues' birthdays and leaving parties. As she flipped through them, Penny worried that none would be suitable, but she found one with just 'Happy Birthday' on it, and wrote a cheerful message inside for Bill. Then, with an hour to spare before she needed to shower and dress, she sat down and got back to work. With the spreadsheet sorted, she worked through a folder of documents needing her signature, the last of which was David's renewed contract.

Penny frowned. Though she'd never allowed their affair to affect her professional treatment of David, it had recently crossed her mind that her life would be easier if she never saw him again. This rogue thought disturbed her. It was what she classed as hormonal – irrational, probably transient, and certainly a betrayal of her high professional standards. I may have been irresponsible in my personal life, she thought, but I do know my duty to the show. David is good for ratings, and that's paramount. Concentrating on the screen, she scrolled through the document, then stopped and went back to the clause headed 'Remuneration'. Once again, the show was getting David remarkably cheap.

This was strange. Each time David's contract had come up for renewal, she'd budgeted for hawkish negotiation, and when

Dominic had asked for no more than a cost-of-living uplift, she'd assumed that David, advised by his agent, was playing a long game. It was a strategy she recognised. But this time she'd been sure David would send Dominic in with all guns blazing. Given his growing celebrity, now would be the perfect time to demand an eye-watering rise, with the threat of taking his talent elsewhere if he was turned down. Instead, Dominic had nodded through the standard opening offer. What was going on?

Unaware that David had convinced himself she wanted him off the show, Penny tried to apply business logic. Plenty of other networked shows would be happy to have David. So surely, from his point of view, a demand for more money wasn't only sensible; it was risk-free. So why *hadn't* he sent Dominic in with all guns blazing? Penny bit her lip. Was it possible that David was focused on something else? Could he have thought that leaving the show would make it likely he'd lose touch with the baby? Might that have been a personal risk he wasn't willing to take? Oh, God, thought Penny, I don't need this. I don't want to sit around analysing David's behaviour. I'm on top of things now – well, as much as I can be, bar the sweats and the mood-swings, as well as the compulsive shoe-sorting. I can't have David messing up my headspace. And now, dammit, she thought, catching sight of the time on her laptop, I've got to go and sing happy birthday to Bill.

Ten minutes later, standing in the shower, she looked at the soapsuds swirling down and around her fast-growing bump. The previous night, when she'd woken and stumbled sticky-eyed to the loo, she'd thought she'd felt a tiny, fizzing movement that might be the baby. But I'm only in my seventeenth week, she'd thought. I could be mistaken. The doctor said to expect movement any time between sixteen and twenty-five weeks. And that first babies can be slow, so I shouldn't get hung up on dates. Now, to her astonished delight, she felt movement again, this time a sort of fluttering, like butterflies in her stomach. Wrapping a towel round her bump, she patted it uncertainly. Way to go, baby, she thought proudly. According to Google you're still only the size of the average pear, but already you're ahead in the ratings.

Having showered, she felt cooler and less wimpy, but still disinclined to go to a huge, jolly party. At least, she thought, Mark will be there to protect me and, if it's crowded, no one will notice if I slip away. Opening her wardrobe, she frowned at a rail of expensive oversized sweaters and linen shirts. They were casual, comfortable and easy to throw on with jeans or cycling leggings, and, paired with looser trousers, had meant that, so far, she'd had no need to shop for maternity wear. But which to choose? There was nothing jolly about this array of cool, neutral colours. In the end, she settled on a white shirt teamed with pale green drawstring-waist trousers, and, in search of something cheerful and celebratory, rooted out a necklace she'd bought in Tate Modern's gift shop. It was a string of chunky, colourful beads made to look like liquorice allsorts, strung on black rubber with a silver clasp. She held it up, felt uncertain, and wondered if Mark would think it appropriate. Oh, for Heaven's sake! she thought crossly. I've always known what I wanted in life, and never questioned my choices, and here I am faffing over a stupid necklace. Fastening it around her neck, she stood back and regarded herself in the mirror. I don't look like myself, she thought. I haven't since all this began. My professional head's all over the place and everything about me seems to be changing. And, even though that fizzing, fluttering feeling is kind of amazing, I wish to hell none of this was happening.

Chapter Twenty-Two

When Penny opened her door, there was a busker on the pavement, vying with the sound of reggae pouring from a nearby pub. As she locked the door behind her, an open-topped car cruised by with Beethoven blasting from its speakers. The driver had his arm around a fair-haired girl in the passenger seat who flashed Penny a smile as they passed. Penny suddenly felt bone-weary. Here was a couple about her own age looking like young love personified, and clearly so happy they wanted to reach out and hug the whole world. I hope they're using birth control, she thought sourly, but the girl's gesture was so intimate that she hadn't the heart to ignore it, and smiled back warmly before going into the shop.

'Am I late?'

'Not at all. Your timing's perfect. Turn the sign on the door, will you? Be with you in a sec.' Mark disappeared and returned moments later, shrugging on a jacket. He was wearing a shirt instead of his usual T-shirt, and stopped in front of a mirror to smooth his dark hair.

Penny grinned. 'Talk about booted and suited!'

Mark laughed. 'I'll lay odds Mum's going to ask why I'm not wearing a tie.'

'Oh, Lord. Do I look okay?'

Mark turned away from the mirror, leaned on the back of a chair, and inspected her. 'You look super.'

'Because I would have worn a dress except none of them fits me now. And I've given up on heels. They're too uncomfortable.'

'I said you look super. You also look perfectly suitable. It's just family, Pen, chill out.'

'The whole family's going to turn up wearing jackets and ties?'

'Of course not. Mum just enjoys nagging. Especially her only son.' Mark took her elbow and propelled her towards the door. 'Don't look so worried. You'll love Sarah. She's a star.' Outside, he hooked his arm through Penny's. 'I haven't bullied you into coming, have I?'

'You may have exerted some moral pressure but, if nothing else, it's flogged me through a huge amount of work!'

Drawing back, and almost colliding with a group of tourists, Mark looked at her anxiously. 'Seriously, are you up for this?'

Penny stepped off the pavement to let the tourists pass. 'Totally up for it. I'm not fragile. Don't fuss.'

'I never fuss over pregnant women. They just get grouchy.'

Penny grinned remorsefully. 'Ain't that the truth! Sorry, I didn't mean to snap. It's nice of you to care.'

They had turned down a street that led away from the market, and now there were fewer passers-by. It had a homely feel, in contrast to the trendiness only a couple of blocks away. Music still floated through open windows, along with laughter and raised voices, but the sounds were less frenetic. Rows of red-brick low-rise flats were interspersed with small public gardens, where children played on slides and see-saws while adults sat chatting or scrolling through their phones. Penny could see that in some of the flats groups of lads were watching football on TV. As she and Mark cut through an estate, a group of women emerged from an entry and waved. Two, who appeared to be about Bill's age, were carrying six-packs of lager. One had a large foil tray covered with clingfilm, and Penny wondered if they were bound for the party. Mark's response to the wave confirmed that they were. He offered to take the tray, but the women shooed him off. 'You want to get a move on. Your mum's called for reinforcements!'

'What's that there?'

'Ham sandwiches. There wasn't room to make them round at yours.'

One of the older women hefted a six-pack. 'And we're bringing our own drinks in case there might be a shortage!'

Penny grabbed Mark's arm. 'Should we have brought a bottle?'

'I dropped some stuff round early this morning. Don't worry. There'll be leftovers parcelled out for a week.' He steered Penny down a street where a group of kids was kicking a ball on the pavement, and people of all ages were gathered around the open door of a ground-floor flat. Music was playing on a laptop balanced on a windowsill, and bunting fluttered from the balconies of the flats above. Older guests had congregated on chairs in the small front garden where Penny could see Bill ensconced with a glass of beer in his hand. The kids dodged out of Mark's way as he ushered Penny through the gate and, seeing her, Bill's face lit up in welcome. 'There's my girl! Glad you could make it.'

'Happy birthday, Bill. Thanks for the invitation.'

'Well, it's not every day a man turns eighty. I told Mark I wanted you here.' Bill waved his glass in Mark's direction. 'And see, boy, what have I always told you? If you don't ask, you don't get.'

He was looking frailer than he'd been when Penny had last seen him, and a lot more mellow than when he'd had the shop. She found the card in her bag and, as Bill opened the envelope, Sarah his wife appeared in the doorway. A short woman in her early seventies, she had Mark's dark hair and eyes and was wearing an apron over a skirt and top. Mark hugged her and Bill introduced Penny. 'Here's the girl without whom you'd never have got me to give up my business, so you say thanks!'

Sarah laughed at Penny's embarrassment. 'Don't mind him, love, he's half-cut already. I let him open his lager far too soon.' Bill waved his glass magisterially. 'Pen was a diamond compared to some of the shysters I had in those rooms. Drink, drugs, the whole nine yards, that's what I had to put up with. But never with her. Paid on the nail, and always kept her nose clean. Best thing I ever did was sell her that flat. Am I right, Mark?'

Everyone turned to look at Penny, and Sarah gave Bill a shove. 'It's far too early in the day to start making speeches. Come in, Penny. We'll find you a drink and get the birthday boy something to soak up that lager.'

With Mark behind her, Penny followed Sarah though the

crowded hallway, and into a kitchen where every surface was covered with trays of food. Mark grinned. 'You do know that Lil and Katie are bringing sandwiches round, Mum?'

'I never asked them to.'

'I bet you demanded them.'

'They can hand them out in the garden, then. Your dad likes a sandwich.' Sarah looked at him critically. 'You might have scrubbed up a bit before you came.'

As Penny suppressed a grin, a young woman joined them, holding a box above her head to avoid the crush in the hall. Mark gave her a hug. 'Hi, Lee. This is Penny from the flat above the shop.' He turned to Penny. 'This is my sister, Leeann.' Sarah seized the box. 'Is that your dad's cake? I thought you said you were making two.'

'I've only got one pair of hands, Mum! Lumo's bringing the other cake round. Hi, Penny, nice to meet you.'

Sarah had taken the lid off the box. 'Has this got walnuts in? 'Cause your dad won't eat nuts.'

'I know. And it has. And the other one hasn't, so stop freaking out. Look, I'm here now, and the others are behind me. Why don't you go outside and sit with Dad?'

'Well, all that food Lumo brought this morning is there on the side, ready for serving, and Mark says Lil and Katie have brought sandwiches, God knows why ...'

'Fine. Me and the girls will sort it.'

'And all the bits I've made are in the oven, ready for heating ...'

'Right. You can tell me later when you want it turned on.'

'Mark brought wine. I don't know who's going to drink it.'

'Mum, get that apron off you and go in the garden.' Edging past Penny, Leeann reclaimed the box and set it on the fridge. Sarah removed her apron and declared that, with all that needed doing, her other daughters could have turned up sooner. Leeann pushed her gently into the hall. 'I told you, they're right behind me. Go and say hello and let me deal with things here.' Her mother left, still protesting, and Leeann sagged against the kitchen sink. 'She's been like that since this morning. God knows what she'll be like at midnight. Open a bottle of wine, Mark. I need a drink!' Taking a glass from a cupboard, she turned to Penny. 'I don't suppose you want one, do you? Can I get you an orange juice or fizzy water?'

'Water would be lovely.'

Mark looked up from the drawer in which he was rummaging for a corkscrew. 'I put some Evian in the fridge this morning, and brought lemons. And I thought you weren't drinking either, Lee.'

His sister gave him a push. 'What are you, the breastfeeding police? Sophie's more than nine weeks old so, unlike Penny, I'm home free. Anyway, it's Dad's eightieth.' Adding a slice of lemon, Leeann handed Penny a glass of Evian water. 'There you go, Penny. Here's to Bill.'

Though the flat was cramped, noisy and hot, Penny felt strangely relaxed. She raised the glass and echoed the toast, remembering what Mark had said about his sisters' mob. 'Are those your kids outside, playing ball?' Leeann accepted a glass of wine, pushed a tray aside and hitched her hip onto the table. 'The tall lad's mine, and the two skinny girls. The rest belong to my younger sisters. I expect there's a few neighbours' kids out there too.' She raised her eyebrows at Penny. 'Is this your first?'

'Yes.'

'You've got it all before you, love.' She lifted her glass to Penny's bump. 'Happy days!'

Mark was leaning against the fridge eating a canapé off a cocktail stick. He offered the tray to Penny. 'Try one. They're delicious. 'Did Lumo make them, Lee?'

'Yep. They have them at the restaurant.'

Though she hadn't felt much like eating all day, Penny took a golden disc, which was caramelised at the edges. 'Is it plantain? Do you mean that Ghanaian restaurant over beyond the market?'

Leeann nodded. 'My husband's the chef there. He's Ghanaian. Well, he was born here, but his mum and dad are from Ghana. He came up with those kelewele bites as starters.' Savouring the roasted plantain, flavoured with ginger, pepper and garlic, Penny recalled herself and David ordering kelewele bites from the fashionable restaurant's takeaway menu. Leeann nodded at her bump again. 'I hope you're okay with them. They're a tad spicy.'

'I'm fine. I've had them before, from the restaurant. They're really good.'

'Lucky you. I survived on Ambrosia Creamed Rice for about a month when I was pregnant with Aaron. The tall kid. He's fourteen. I was about as far gone as you are, and I went right off spicy food. My husband started wondering if the baby was really his!' Leeann spiked another kelewele bite on her cocktail stick and asked if Penny's baby's dad was around.

From anyone else, the question would have raised Penny's hackles but, in the stuffy kitchen, with laughter and music drifting down the hall, she answered the question as casually as it was put. 'No. We're not together. I was raised by a single mum myself. It's not that big a deal.' Turning to put her cocktail stick down on the tray, Penny saw a strange expression cross Mark's face, hastily covered up, as if he didn't want her to notice. Before she had time to think about it, Leeann reached over and offered her another canapé. 'Well, as long as you've got your mum, you're all right, aren't you? Any sisters?'

'No. I'm an only child.'

'See, I don't know how I'd manage without my sisters. Or Mum. We fight like cats sometimes but she's a proper tower of strength.'

Mark, who seemed to have regained his equilibrium, laughed. 'Whereas your poor brother is nothing but a wine waiter.'

'You do have your uses.' Leeann winked at Penny. 'I practised most of my child-rearing skills on Mark.'

'You made a good job of him.'

'Well, thank you. I think so. He's not all bad.' Hearing a kerfuffle in the hallway, Leeann groaned. 'Oh, look at this, no rest for the wicked!' Penny turned and saw Aaron wriggling through the crush of people. He was holding a baby as high as he could, much as Leeann had carried the large cake box. 'Sophie won't shut up, Mum. Bill says he can't hear himself think.'

'All right, give her here. You could have walked her up and down the street.'

'We're having a game.'

'Honestly, kids these days! I was just saying to Penny that, when I was your age, I had to lug your uncle Mark around with me everywhere.'

Aaron threw Mark a cheeky grin. 'These days, kids have rights. We can't be treated like unpaid nannies.' Leeann gave him a good-humoured swipe and took the screaming baby in her arms. 'Go on, then, get back to your game. Has your dad brought the other cake round?'

'He's outside, talking to Bill.'

'Oh, for God's sake! Hold her a minute, Penny. That cake's going to melt if it stays out in the heat.'

Taken off guard, Penny took the baby who, objecting to being treated as if she was in a game of pass-the-parcel, screamed even louder and flailed her fists. Aaron had disappeared back down the hall, with Leeann behind him. Left alone with Mark, Penny turned to him in panic. 'She's going purple, Mark. Is she okay?'

'She's fine. Give her to me, if you like.'

Penny suddenly felt she'd come to a hugely important moment. 'No, hang on. I can do this.' Gingerly, she held the flailing baby against her shoulder and jigged to and fro from foot to foot. The decibel level of squalling reduced, so that, once again, she could hear the music playing at the flat's front window. Mark, who was still eating plantain, watched, poker-faced. Gaining in confidence, Penny tried holding the baby away from her but Sophie responded with a resentful wail.

Hastily, she held the protesting bundle against her shoulder again, moving the upper part of her body in time to the music. It had just changed from Diana Ross to a waltz. A chorus of raucous voices from the front garden joined in with 'I Have A Dream' by ABBA and, to Penny's astonishment, Sophie hiccuped and began to coo. Afraid to stop moving, she continued to sway and the baby turned her head and opened two huge black eyes. The little face was now serene and, with another hiccup, she spewed up a thread of milk.

'Whoops ...' Mark tossed a paper napkin to Penny, who dabbed at the dribble. The baby pursed her lips and blew an enchanting bubble, and the karaoke voices outside rose even louder. Mark put the napkin into the bin. 'That was Mum and Dad's wedding dance. Actually, they had two because they hated each other's choices. "I Have A Dream" was hers.'

'What was Bill's?'

'Chris de Burgh's "Lady In Red".'

'Is red your mum's favourite colour?'

'No, she hates it. It's just that "Lady In Red" is Dad's favourite song. Mum always says the lady in red was the girl she nicked him off. It might even be true. By all accounts, he wasn't the marrying type until Mum pinned him down.'

'So, is this their anniversary too?'

'No, that was weeks ago. Mum belts out "I Have A Dream" every chance she gets. She says we could all be dead in the morning, so why miss out on a chance to celebrate life?'

'That's kind of nice.'

'They're two of a kind, really. See what you want and go for it. I'm the opposite – never certain of when I should make a move.' His eyes were on Penny, who was still swaying to the music and had just discovered Sophie had fallen asleep. As she looked up at Mark to share her triumph, Leeann reappeared, carrying the second cake. 'Here we are, lemon sponge, not a trace of a nut, and Lumo's brought eight candles. Mum says she wants it cut now, so she can take photos.' Startled, Mark looked at the racks of food waiting in the oven. 'What? Before we serve this lot?'

'You know what she's like. I'm not going to argue. Go on, get the ice-cream out and I'll do the plates.' Giving Mark a friendly shove, Leeann squeezed past Penny, who automatically turned her shoulder to protect the baby. All Sophie's weight seemed to be in her chubby bottom, and her little head felt warm. Penny gingerly laid her cheek against the damp, wispy hair and decided that, as the kitchen was hot and Sophie's breathing was even, she probably wasn't about to die of a fever. Moving to the window, where it was cooler, she rocked her gently and watched Leeann put candles on the cake.

Suddenly Penny felt immensely hungry. With a rush of pleasure as intense as when she had calmed the baby, she saw Mark go to the freezer for stripy ice-cream.

Chapter Twenty-Three

Val was only six weeks old when Marguerite first brought her to Stonehill. Paul took a week of his annual leave and they'd driven from London to Holyhead with what felt like half the contents of Mothercare jammed into the boot. No tractor held them up as they thundered across Anglesey, Val slept peacefully for most of the journey and the ferry crossing to Dún Laoghaire was smooth. They arrived in Stonehill to find Donal was with a patient, and were greeted in the hall by Mrs Sinnott who insisted on helping to carry in the luggage. 'It's no bother at all and it's great to see you here. We haven't clapped eyes on you since the wedding.'

Marguerite stood in the hallway amid a growing mound of bags and cases, thinking how strange it was to be there with a baby. The worn, chequered tiles, the dark panelling, and the vase of wildflowers on the console table were unchanged, but this new personality in her arms seemed to re-energise the house and change her relationship to it. Mrs Sinnott beckoned them upstairs and led the way down the landing. 'The doctor said you'd want the double back bedroom. Well, you won't want your own room, will you, Marguerite? It's far too small.' Focused on packing and the baby's needs, Marguerite hadn't asked herself where she and Paul would sleep at Stonehill. As the door opened, she smiled. The embroidered bed linen and faded flowered wallpaper offered a sense of relaxation she hadn't felt since she'd brought Val home from Queen Charlotte's Hospital. 'This is perfect!'

'I slipped a hot bottle in the bed. I know it's summer, and the sheets are aired, but a bottle's always nice.'

'You shouldn't have bothered. I could have made up the bed.'

'After that journey, and with a baby to mind? Don't be ridiculous. Surgery's nearly over. Will you have a cup of tea here and put your feet up till the doctor's free?'

Gently bullied by Paul and Mrs Sinnott, Marguerite took a bath and changed and, with Val beside her in a carry-cot, sat in a Lloyd Loom chair by the bedroom window. As she sipped her tea, she looked down at the wildflower meadow, where lush grasses and flowers grew knee-high. A broad, close-cropped path ran straight as a die from the drawing-room doors to the cast-iron bench and table. Guessing that Donal employed a man who came around with a strimmer, Marguerite felt a pang of regret for the days of the gardener with the scythe. But lots of little things will have changed here, she told herself. Just because I wanted to replicate Mum's idiosyncrasy, it doesn't follow that Dad does too. His associations with the garden go back further than mine. In fact, he must remember a time when Ruth's wildflower meadow was the well-tended lawn he played on as a child.

Val kicked violently in the carry-cot and, still pursuing her train of thought, Marguerite reached down absently to soothe her. I suppose, she thought, everyone wants the surroundings they grew up with to remain forever unchanged. Perhaps that's what makes so many people see childhood through rose-coloured glasses. Permanence suggests security. All the same, clinging to the past can make it impossible to enjoy the present. Better, perhaps, to see everything as part of the stream of time, and to recognise one's own perceptions as just one point of view. She was glad that, before her wedding, she'd cleared out her childhood bedroom. As Mrs Sinnott had said, it was too small for a married couple and a baby. Now was the time to take pleasure in making new memories.

The door opened and Paul came in, carrying Marguerite's bag. 'You left this in the car.'

'Thank you. Did you get some tea?'

He sat on the windowsill and bent to wiggle his fingers at Val. 'I had some in the kitchen with Mrs Sinnott. Your dad put his head round the surgery door to say he'll be free in about half an hour.'

'I can hardly wait for him to see Val. Photos just aren't the same.'

'Mrs Sinnott says he's been wild with excitement.'

Marguerite laughed. 'She's making that up. Dad doesn't do excitement. It's not his style.'

But later, when they were sitting under the willow tree, Donal's delight in Val was evident. Having brought himself up to date on Marguerite's healthcare in a swift series of questions, he took Val, who had just woken up, and held her on his knee. Her eyes, which were still a milky blue, wandered from her mum's face to his, as if making an assessment. Then the corners of her mouth twitched and she broke into a smile. There was a chorus of amazement from Marguerite and Paul. 'She smiled! That's the first time it's happened!'

'Did you see that, Dad? She looked at you and smiled!'

Concealing gratification, Donal said it was probably just wind.

'It wasn't. You know it wasn't, you saw her. Babies can start to smile at six weeks. My health visitor said so.'

As Marguerite spoke, Val's mouth widened again into a gummy smile, and Paul, who hadn't an envious bone in his body, beamed at Donal. 'There you go. First smile for her granddad. She must have been saving it.'

Donal repeated that it was probably nothing more than wind. 'Babies her age rarely respond to a face other than their mother's.' But from that day on, Val was always sunny in his company and the notion of her as 'Granddad's shadow' was born.

The following morning, Donal suggested that he and Paul take off for the Featherbeds. 'They're turf cuttings up in the moorlands. If we take the car up, and bring Rufus, we can stretch our legs on the old military road. It's an easy walk and the views up there are splendid. What d'you say?'

Paul cast an enquiring look at Marguerite, who nodded. 'You did all yesterday's driving so you must need some exercise. Val and I will stay here and have a gossip with Mrs Sinnott.'

When she'd waved them off, she carried the sleeping baby

down to the kitchen, and found Mrs Sinnott listening to *Sunday Miscellany* on the radio. 'Am I interrupting you?'

'Not a bit of it, pet. I only have that old thing on in the background.' Turning off the transistor, Mrs Sinnott pulled out a chair. 'Take the weight off your feet. I'm just throwing together a few scones. I leave them in a Tupperware for the doctor – though, by rights, they should be eaten the day they're made.'

Marguerite sat down and breathed in the smell of baking appreciatively. 'I haven't found buttermilk in London. I use fresh milk and lemon juice but they never taste the same.'

Mrs Sinnott jerked her head at the oven. 'I've my first batch in and, since you're over, I thought I'd best make another.'

'You shouldn't have. I can cater for us while I'm here. You don't have to.'

'Don't worry, I'll be gone by twelve. I've my own house to look after. I just thought you might like these on your first day back.'

Sitting at the table with Val on her lap, Marguerite made a pattern with her finger in the scattered flour. 'I always loved your scones.'

'By all accounts, you don't have much of a kitchen in your flat.'

'It's titchy but I'm used to it now. Anyway, we're moving on in a month or so. We've found a little house in Holland Park.'

'Is that in London?'

'Yes. Near Paul's work.'

'That'll be handy. And I suppose you'll be thinking of a brother or sister for this one soon.'

'Give me a chance! I still can't really take in that I'm a mother.'

Mrs Sinnott flattened her dough and, using the rim of a tumbler, began to produce her second batch of scones. 'There's some women cut out for motherhood, and more that aren't, I'd say you'll do fine.'

'I think I like it.'

'There you are, so. Amn't I right?'

Marguerite looked around at the kitchen's worn Formica surfaces, thinking that when it was installed for Ruth in the 1950s it must have been state-of-the-art. 'I don't remember my mum doing much baking. Or cooking at all.'

'She was a great one for parties when she and the doctor were first married.'

'What kind of parties?'

'Oh, sherry and little bits and pieces she'd pick up in Dublin. Or baked potatoes sometimes. She called that bohemian. They'd all come down to the kitchen, and sit up on the counters eating them, and go out in the garden afterwards and dance till all hours to the gramophone. She'd have me in of an evening now and again, to clean up and wash the dishes.'

'I don't remember.'

'No, well, you wouldn't. That was before you were born. She and the doctor entertained a bit afterwards, but I'd say by the time you started to walk she'd begun to turn in on herself. Went kind of quiet, you know. But, sure, people do. They settle down.'

Marguerite carefully drew Ruth's name in the flour, making the R with a flourish and putting a line underneath. 'D'you think she was cut out for motherhood, Mrs Sinnott?'

'Now that's a leading question!' Mrs Sinnott threw her a sharp look over her glasses. 'We both know your mam wasn't well, pet. Not in the end, anyway. But never doubt that she loved you. I remember her working away at that quilt for you when she was pregnant. Not a notion of how to sew but determined to set every stitch herself.'

'I suppose I've been thinking about her since I had Val.'

'Val's going to look like her, I'd say. Same as yourself. I can see the doctor in her too. Same-shaped eyes. So, how did the hospital treat you over in London?'

'Fine. People were nice. But it's a bit weird going to hospital. I mean, you're having a baby, you're not ill. I thought of having her at home but Paul would have freaked out. Come to think of it, we probably couldn't have fitted a midwife into the bedroom. Maybe I'll hold out for a home birth next time, when we've got space.'

Sliding one baking tray into the oven and removing the other, Mrs Sinnott gave her a broad grin. 'So, there *is* going to be a next time?'

Marguerite laughed. 'Those smell lovely. May I have one while they're hot?'

'You'll ruin your digestion.' Having polished the steam from the oven off her glasses with a tea towel, Mrs Sinnott buttered a scone, turning it neatly in her hand to stop the melting butter dripping onto the floury table.

Marguerite ate it in two bites and reached to wipe her fingers on the towel. Here, she thought, was another difference between her new life in London and all she'd known when growing up in Stonehill. Before she and Paul had married, his mum had gone on a shopping spree for sheets, tea-towels, dishcloths and dusters, saying a bride shouldn't have to cope with the household linen she found in what had been a bachelor's flat. Marguerite had been touched by the gesture, and having everything brand new had been pleasant. But the familiar touch of well-washed Stonehill cotton was nothing like the unyielding texture of those new tea-towels, which, for the first few months, had seemed to move moisture about instead of absorbing it. And the expensive sheets had felt unyielding too. Watching Mrs Sinnott sweep the flour off the table into her hand, Marguerite said how nice it had been to sleep in line-dried bed linen again. 'It smells so much better than things that come out of a drier.'

'Everything kept in that hot press upstairs comes out smelling lovely. My mam used to put a lavender bag in with her sheets and pillowslips. Yours had little sachets of stuff she called sweetgrass. I swear to God, you can smell it in there still.'

'English people don't know what a press is. I mean, they call a hot press an airing cupboard. And scallions spring onions.'

Mrs Sinnott shrugged. 'Each to his own.'

'Where did my mum get sweetgrass in Ireland?'

'She didn't, poor woman. Someone used to post the sachets from the States. I think that tailed off after a while. She settled for what she had in the end, I suppose.'

'Lavender?'

'No, she never took to the lavender. But, like I say, the smell of the sweetgrass seems to hang on in the press.' With the table cleared and the scones in the oven, Mrs Sinnott sat down and, leaning forward, touched Val's hand. 'Isn't she a little dote, though? Your husband says she'd a big smile for her granddad.'

'I know. Her first. He's very good with her.'

'Why wouldn't he be, with all the babies he's brought into the world? And his father and granddad before him. Time was, nobody hereabouts had a child in a hospital.'

It struck Marguerite that she'd no idea where she herself had been born. Shifting Val to the crook of her other arm, she asked if Mrs Sinnott could remember.

'I do, of course. Your mam was booked to go up to a Dublin hospital, but you came early, there was heavy snow, and she ended up here in her bed.'

'Wow. I know I wanted a home birth myself, but that must have been freaky. Was there a panic?'

'Of course not. The doctor never panics. She was lucky, though. There were fierce high snowdrifts. The lines were down and everything. I remember trying to ring my husband from the phone up there in the hall and I couldn't get through.'

'You were here when I was born?'

'I came in twice a week back then. That was one of my days. The snow wasn't too bad in the morning when I walked up from the village. Someone had got a tractor out early and cleared it off the road. But I wasn't here half an hour when the wind came up and brought down a blizzard and, what with that and your mam's pains starting, I wasn't going anywhere.' Seeing that Marguerite was wide-eyed, Mrs Sinnott settled comfortably into her tale. 'Well, it wasn't an easy labour, but she was grand. Mind you, she lost a lot of blood. Afterwards, they had to order a new mattress from Dublin. Odearest, it was, pink with a white design. I think it was Arnotts they got it from. It came down in a van.'

'But tell me about the birth.'

'The doctor had me boiling water to sterilise his instruments. I took up a kettle, and then he wanted towels. I brought in every single one they had in the hot press and, do you know what it is, I'd say he did have a bit of a panic there, just for a minute. He'd cut the cord and handed me the baby and the blood kept coming and, Holy God, if he didn't panic, I did.' Mrs Sinnott laughed reminiscently. 'He wanted another towel and I couldn't shake it out of the pile fast enough, and he let out a roar till I didn't know if I was coming or going. Anyway, he got things sorted and your mam stopped bleeding. And, next thing, he looked around for the baby and, God forgive me, I couldn't think where you'd gone!'

'What? What do you mean?'

'You'd disappeared.' Mrs Sinnott's eyes were mischievous behind her glasses. 'You don't believe me, do you?'

'Well, of course not.'

'It's true, though. We couldn't see hide nor hair of you. There was your dad looking gobsmacked, and your mam with her eyes closed looking like death, and me dumbfounded. And no sign of the baby anywhere. I was literally wringing my hands when the doctor twitched a bath towel off that Lloyd Loom chair beside the bed. And there you were, lying on the cushion. It must have been me who put you there, and threw the towel down over the chair but, to this day, Marguerite, I've no memory of doing either. Isn't that a queer thing? I can tell you I wasn't the better of it for many a long day.'

'Is that the chair that's up in the guestroom now?'

'The one you were sitting in yesterday when I brought you

your cup of tea. I can't recall when it got moved out of your mam and dad's bedroom. I suppose it was when he redecorated the room after she died.'

Later, before Donal and Paul arrived home from their walk, Marguerite carried Val into the drawing room and stood staring at her mother's portrait. With a pang of guilt, she remembered how she'd thought on her wedding morning that Ruth's presence would have made for an anxious, stressful day. Rocking her sleeping baby in her arms, she looked up at the vivid face in the painting. It's still true, she thought sadly. I don't know what changed you from the woman who gave bohemian parties, and danced on the lawn to a gramophone, into the shadowy presence you became. But I do know that, if you'd been here, Dad and I would have been worried about you, and Paul and I wouldn't have had our joyous wedding day. All the same, I wish you could have seen me getting married. And I wish I'd heard that story about my birth from you, instead of Mrs Sinnott. If things had been different, we could have sat down and laughed at it together. I wish it could have been you who brought me tea on my wedding morning. I wish you could walk in from the garden now and meet Val.

Chapter Twenty-Four

The morning after Bill's birthday party, Val called Marguerite. 'I've just had Penny on the phone! She's asked me over to dinner.'

'At her flat?'

'Yes. Tonight.'

Given the long-established understanding that Penny's home existed as an extension of her office, an invitation to eat there was remarkable. Marguerite wondered what had happened to provoke it, but thought this wasn't the time to enquire. 'I know you'll be glad to see her. Give her my love, won't you?'

'Of course. She said to send you hers. Look, I can't talk long. I have a class soon. But how are things otherwise? What are you doing over there?'

'Mostly fighting a losing battle against cleavers and bindweed.'

'Is cleavers what Granddad used to call Sticky Bob? The green stuff that wraps itself round things and has burrs that stick to your clothes?'

'That's it. One of those weeds that strangles everything if you let it get out of hand.'

'How are the card parties?'

'Pretty sparsely populated lately. It's always the same in summer. There's so much to do outdoors when the evenings are long and, anyway, people go off on holiday. We'll be back to full strength in the autumn when it starts to get chilly.'

As if laying down a load, Val released a deep breath. 'It was good to hear Penny's voice.'

'She must be coming up to her second scan.'

'This week, I think. I still can't grasp the idea of being a granny.'

Marguerite hesitated. 'Look, I know it's not foremost in your mind, but don't mention the keepsake quilt to Penny, will you? I'd like it to be a surprise when the baby's born.'

'What? No, I won't. It's been so long since I've seen her there'll be plenty to talk about.' An edge to Val's voice suggested she was feeling slightly anxious as well as pleased. And why not? thought Marguerite. After all, it'll be the first time they've sat down together since that dreadful lunch when Penny stormed out.

Val put her phone down wishing the quilt was the only subject she needed to avoid. I mustn't be pushy, she thought. I have to let her set the pace, and respect her privacy and personal space. Above all, I mustn't ask questions about the father. If she wants to tell me, that's fine but, if she doesn't, it's not my business. This evening's about building bridges. That's the important thing.

As she left the staffroom for her class, part of Val's mind was preoccupied with the question of what she should take with her to Penny's. If going to a friend's for dinner, she'd usually pick up a bottle of wine. But Penny wouldn't be drinking, so perhaps chocolates would be better. Chocolates could always be kept unopened and passed on to someone else. Wine could be handed on too, of course. But if she brought a bottle, Penny might feel she had to open it. And it won't be much fun for her, thought Val, to sit watching as I knock it back. The question revolved in her brain until she got home that evening, and when she opened her wardrobe, she hesitated over what to wear. Eventually she decided on a skirt and shirt worn with heels and a gold chain, which would give a sense of occasion but couldn't be seen as over the top. And none of this nonsense matters in the least, she thought crossly. What matters is that, once tonight's over, we can stop walking on eggshells and go back to how things were.

She'd timed her journey carefully but, unusually, bus and Tube connections dovetailed and she arrived at London Bridge station with twenty minutes to spare. Borough Market had closed for the evening and people were crowding into the pubs. As she circled the market's shuttered stalls, Val's nervousness returned. Determined not to be early, she made herself keep walking and, having gone further than she'd intended, arrived at Penny's street door in a hurry, afraid she'd be late. When she climbed the stairs and Penny appeared on the threshold of the flat, there was an awkward moment in which they both seemed acutely aware of her bump. Then Penny chuckled. 'I know. I'm huge. Come on in, Mum.'

Val hugged her. 'You're not. You look wonderful.'

'Which means huge.' Taking the carrier bag thrust at her,

Penny ushered Val towards a sofa. 'Gosh, you brought chocolates *and* wine.'

'I wasn't sure which you'd prefer. I mean, you won't want a drink ...'

'No, but that doesn't mean you shouldn't have one. Let me get a corkscrew.'

Val sank onto the white leather sofa and leaned back in relief. Obviously, a hurdle had needed to be surmounted, but her secret sense that her daughter might have changed beyond recognition now seemed absurd. Despite the bump, Penny, who was efficiently opening the bottle, looked exactly as she always had – brisk, assured and remarkably energetic for a woman who'd just come home after a full day's work. She was wearing trousers cropped above the ankle, and a flared sweater with a neck that revealed the shoulder straps of a sleeveless T-shirt. The trousers and T-shirt were white and the sweater silvery-grey, and her hair, which she now wore slightly longer, was crimped and had auburn streaks. Val smiled and repeated that she looked wonderful.

'I'm fine.'

'How's work?'

'Pressured as ever. Ratings are up, though, so that's fine too.' Penny joined her on the sofa with the wine and a glass of sparkling water. Kicking off a pair of espadrilles, she took a menu card from the coffee-table. 'I rose to a bowl of olives but it's takeaway for dinner. Is that okay?'

'Perfect.'

'Will posh fish and chips do?'

'I never say no to fish and chips. What makes them posh?'

'Mainly the price. Well, you can have wild halibut or swordfish. Or scallops with black pudding and fish gravy ...'

'No, thanks.'

'I didn't think so. But the beer-battered cod is fab. So's the haddock.'

'That'll do me.'

'Two cod and chips, then. They have mushy peas.'

'Even more perfect.'

'I'll phone in an order. It won't take long to arrive.'

Val watched as Penny hit speed-dial and gave the order without preamble and with the briefest of thanks. In Penny's teens, fish and chips had been a favourite Friday-night meal in West Hampstead, collected from a chippie a couple of streets away and tumbled out of vinegar-soaked paper onto plates that Val had heated while Penny ran round to the shop. As a single working mum, Val had had no time for leisurely baking, and she'd never managed the art of making Balan's delicious curries, but she'd spent long hours at weekends doggedly making freezer meals to recreate the dinners she'd grown up with, redolent of the tastes and smells of Marguerite's kitchen. Penny's school lunches had often consisted of bought pork pies and salads, but her evening meals, though heated from frozen, were made from fresh ingredients with an eye to a balanced diet. And yet, thought Val, my best memories are of those Friday nights of soggy chips, mushy peas, and battered fish that left a greasy slick on the plates and a dodgy smell in the kitchen.

As Penny went to put away the menu, Stanley slipped under the lower half of the window above the sink. She came back with him draped over her shoulder and when she sat down, he settled himself on her knees.

'You've got yourself a cat!'

'No, he's not mine. Stanley answers to no one. He lives downstairs, but he gets bored in the evenings when the shop's closed. I reckon he's got a kind of radar that picks up a signal whenever I order fish.'

'He's a handsome chap.'

Stanley transferred himself to Val's knee, rolled on his back and presented a furry tummy to be scratched. Laughing, Penny stood up. 'I should lay the table.'

'No, sit down. I'll do it.'

'Actually, if you just get plates and cutlery, we can stay here and have it on our laps.'

'That should suit Stanley.'

'Stanley's never demanding. It's one of his most endearing characteristics.'

When the doorbell rang and Penny went to take in the delivery, Val said she'd nip upstairs to the loo before they ate. As usual, the immaculate flat hardly seemed lived in, and the bathroom had nothing on its steel-tiled surfaces but a cake of soap and a folded towel. Having washed her hands, Val couldn't resist a quick peek in the mirrored cabinet above the handbasin. Nothing inside suggested that Penny had a resident man, or even a visiting one, who might keep a toothbrush or a razor in her flat. How awful of me to peek, thought Val remorsefully. It's hardly respecting her personal space.

Tidying her hair, she frowned at herself in the mirror. Behind her indecisiveness about the wine and chocolates had been the question of whether or not she should mention the Beijing conference to Penny. Now she felt it would be better not to. The evidence of the cabinet wasn't conclusive, but if, as it implied, the baby's father wasn't around, Penny would surely need help and support when the baby was born. She mightn't turn to me, thought Val, but I ought to be available if she does. Still, as Sean said, it's early days. He doesn't need a commitment for the time being, so I'm going to enjoy this evening without fretting about next year.

They sat at either end of the sofa, Val cross-legged, Penny with her feet up, and had their fish, chips and mushy peas with pickled gherkins eaten straight from a jar. Stanley lay between them, purring throatily and, now and then, casting a look at their plates. When they'd finished, Penny tipped the scraps into the cardboard box the meal had come in, and he leaped down to eat them, twitching the tip of his black-and-white tail. Val wiped her fingers on a paper napkin. 'Are you excited about your next scan?'

'I guess. It's on Thursday. I suppose knowing if it's a boy or a girl will make things seem more real.'

'Do you know when you plan to take leave?'

'I've said the start of December. My due date's the end of the first week in January.'

Val carefully didn't ask where, and with whom, Penny planned to spend Christmas, but, as if the thought hung in the air, Penny reached out and stroked Stanley with her toes. 'How come we used to spend summers at Stonehill but never went over in winter?'

'After Donal died it wasn't practical. It's fine now your

gran's installed central heating, but when it was just a holiday home, it wasn't easy to heat. Don't you remember how, even in summer, it always took a few days for the house to stop feeling chilly?'

'I guess I didn't notice when I was a child.'

'When Donal was alive, we had a few Christmases there. I remember going up the mountains with him and your uncle Rory to bring home a tree. And your gran and granddad spent Christmas there with Donal before they were married.'

'Was that the first time Donal met Paul?'

'He hadn't been to Ireland before, I know that much. And when Donal took him off to the woods to cut the Christmas tree, Paul was convinced they were poaching. He said so afterwards to Marguerite.'

'Poaching trees?'

'Well, engaged in some bucolic sport that involved putting one over on your neighbours. Paul didn't want to object, in case Donal thought he was wimpy, but he kept expecting a farmer with a gun.'

Penny giggled. 'Poor Granddad. Bucolic sports wouldn't have been his thing.'

'No, bless him, he was a proper Londoner, and law-abiding as they come.'

'I wish I'd met Donal.'

'You did, but you wouldn't remember. I brought you over the year before he died.'

'Really?'

'You'd just begun walking that summer. I remember you staggering down the wildflower meadow hanging on to Donal's thumbs. It was lovely weather. Just like the previous year, when you were born.'

'Poor you, pregnant in summer. I'm gasping if the nights are the least bit hot.'

'How are you otherwise?'

'Fine.' Penny said this briskly, as if regretting an admission of weakness, and Val wished she could find a way of saying she understood. I was exactly the same, she thought, recalling her own defensiveness when she'd been pregnant. Mum must have felt like this whenever I snapped at her and Dad, and said I was fine. It's so hard to let down your guard when you know that, after the moment of respite, you're going to have to resume it. You feel it's better to struggle on, in case the effort of picking up is beyond you. You don't believe that respite could leave you stronger and better equipped. Or perhaps the point is that you can't take the risk of finding out. It just feels too big and too dangerous. I needn't have peeked in the bathroom cabinet, she thought sadly. I can tell that Penny isn't sharing this pregnancy with the father. I recognise that tense insistence on self-sufficiency.

Penny, who'd opened the chocolates, went to make coffee. She spoke over her shoulder. 'Did you take my dad over to meet Donal too?' As they seldom talked about Simon, Val found the question surprising but, concealing her reaction, she said yes. 'We went to Stonehill for a weekend when we'd just come down from Oxford.'

'Did they get on?'

Val remembered that stilted weekend when everything had seemed fine but nothing had gone quite as she'd planned. Simon had been at his cockiest, buoyed up by the knowledge that he'd managed to get a First. She'd got a less impressive degree, but was happy with her tutor's assurance that what had held her back was originality. 'A First would have led to pressure to waste your time here in academia. Far better to take your mind out into the world.' She'd told this to Donal as they'd sat at the top of the meadow, watching Simon throw a ball for Rex, Donal's latest spaniel.

'Your tutor sounds like a sensible woman. I've always thought you've a fine mind, Val. As aware as a visual artist's and as analytical as a research chemist's.'

'I've never wanted to be an artist.'

'That's probably just as well. There are far too many of them already.'

'Simon wants to be a novelist.'

Donal had asked with a poker-face if Simon's degree hadn't led to pressure to waste his time in academia.

'He's not really the academic type.'

'No?'

'I mean, he's not the disciplined type. I mean, he doesn't tend to conform.'

'I've noticed that.'

'Granddad, don't you like him?'

'It makes no odds, does it? I'm not the one who's going to marry him.'

'No, but it does. I want you to like him. Why don't you?'

'I haven't said I don't like him. He's an attractive lad, and he's bright.'

'That's it?'

'No, it's not. He's also deeply in love with you. Anyone can see that. I doubt he'll be an easy partner but he might make a good novelist. He's not without the necessary egotism.'

'But you don't think he'll make a good husband?'

'For Heaven's sake, Val, I'm a country doctor, not a marriage counsellor. I've no idea what makes a good husband. I do know that most men hope that being in love with a woman will make up for anything else she may need and we may lack.'

When they'd had their coffee and chocolates and it came time for Val to go home, Penny insisted on calling a cab, which caused a brief wrangle.

'I'll take the Tube.'

'Don't be silly. It's late.'

'I'll be fine. Really.'

'Look, Granny, I'm making the call, so don't argue'.

Val emitted a peal of laughter. 'Granny! Oh, don't! I can't cope!'

'What will you want to be called? It could always be "Nana".'

'If I have my way, it'll be "Val". Anything else feels dreadfully ageing.'

'You could go for "Grandmama" and feel all Jane Austen.'

'In a dowager's cap, taking snuff?'

'I'd love to see you taking snuff. Would you teach the baby?'

'It'd end up being taken into care. Snuff is pure tobacco.'

Having made the call, Penny selected another chocolate and held up the bottle of wine. 'The cab should be here in five. D'you want another splash?' Val shook her head. She'd already had a glass and a half and was secretly glad to be whisked home instead of having to navigate public transport. 'I've had more than enough. It's been a lovely evening, though. Thank you.'

Penny pushed Stanley, who was trying to lick her fingers. 'Stop it, idiot. Chocolate is poisonous to cats.'

'Surely he knows that instinctively.'

'You'd think, but apparently not. I'm told babies aren't aware of the dangers of staircases either.'

'It's not a problem until they reach the crawling stage.' Greatly daring, Val risked a piece of advice. 'I found that taking one thing at a time made everything less overwhelming.'

She waited to be repressed but, to her surprise, Penny nodded. 'I've kind of worked that one out myself. Thanks, though.'

In the cab, Val glanced at the time before deciding to text Marguerite. It was past eleven, but she had a feeling Marguerite was unlikely to be asleep. Anyway, she thought, if she is she'll most likely have turned off her phone, so she'll see the text when she wakes in the morning. As the sleek car wove its way through jostling London traffic, she typed *Lovely evening. Will call tomorrow* and hit Send. A few minutes later, Marguerite's response appeared on the screen. *In bed after a hot day. Sound of rain on the window. Thanks for your text. Talk soon. Sleep well, darling.*

Chapter Twenty-Five

The following day, when Val was describing their evening to Marguerite, Penny was in the office with Lolly discussing an upcoming guest. Lolly looked up from her long list of notes. 'I checked with the agent. He says she'll probably go ape on air if anyone calls her a national treasure.'

'Make sure that's passed on to Roz and Gail.'

'She won't drink tea, and she wants a bowl of Haribo Star Mix in her dressing room.'

'Well, that's not going to blow the budget.'

Lolly checked her notes. 'He says she does drink crème de menthe, though.'

'At eleven in the morning? That's a wind-up.'

'Really?'

Penny grinned. 'Don't take the risk, though. Tell them to get a bottle in, and stick it somewhere, just in case.'

The national treasure was a theatrical dame who'd come

out of retirement to star in a new Netflix crime series and, unexpectedly, become the chat shows' flavour of the month. Penny would have preferred to book her for any day rather than one when David would be in studio, and any Thursday but this week's, when she was having her scan. But Dame Jane, as she was known, was notoriously hard to pin down, so you took whatever date you could get.

'Okay, Lolly. That's it, I think. She's scheduled for the slot right before Faber's, and I may arrive after she's on air. Don't apologise for me, okay? And don't explain. Meet her car yourself. Say the exec producer has arranged to be in studio to congratulate her when she comes off. Make that sound like a big deal and, with luck, she won't take umbrage if I'm not there at the start. It's a bugger, though. If I didn't have this scan, I'd be sure to be there for the meet and greet.'

Lolly nodded meekly. 'What do I do after I meet the car?'

'Hover. Check that she's happy with everything. And don't leave her side. If she wants anything, have the runner get it. Oh, and she may have someone with her. A personal assistant, or just someone to hold her hand. If so, for God's sake, don't let them run amok.' Lolly looked so alarmed that Penny laughed. 'We don't want last-minute demands for special lighting or a different dressing room. So be young and eager and make her like you. That way, if there's a PA who gets stroppy on her behalf, she'll say she's perfectly happy with what she's got.'

'But what if she doesn't?'

'Use your initiative.' Lolly blinked nervously, making Penny laugh again. 'Don't worry. And, above all, don't panic.

Just stick with her. I'll be there as soon as I can. Anyway, the chances are it'll all go like clockwork.'

Penny's appointment at St Thomas' was for ten fifteen, and Dame Jane was due on air after the show's eleven o'clock ad-break. Intending to make a dash for a cab as soon as she'd had her scan, Penny walked from her flat to the hospital instead of cycling. She took the riverside path and, having a few minutes to spare, paused at Gabriel's Wharf to watch a man drawing in a strip of sand revealed by the low tide. Using a sharp spade, he'd produced a galleon in full sail. Passers-by were leaning over the parapet to throw coins into a box he'd perched on a little sandcastle topped with a flag. Penny found a fifty-pence piece in her pocket and, flicking it into the box, glanced at her watch and walked on.

In the eighth-floor waiting room, she was told that appointments were running late. 'We've had a few in succession in which the baby's position meant the sonographer needed to take a bit longer. We're catching up now, though. You shouldn't have long to wait.' Penny nodded and took out her phone to call Lolly. The receptionist gave a reproving look. 'We do prefer you to keep your phone turned off.'

'Oh, okay. Sorry. Yes. This won't take a minute.' Getting through to Lolly, Penny turned away from the desk. 'Has she arrived?'

'Yep. All good. She's charming. No PA.'

'Right. Well, I may be a bit later than I expected. I should still be there before she comes off, though.'

This was the scan at which she might discover the sex of the baby so, eager to have a chance of a clear image, Penny had remembered what Mark had said and drunk lots of water. Trying to make herself relax, she walked up and down breathing slowly. The clock above the desk moved on to ten twenty-five. And the scan can take up to thirty minutes, she thought, so I'm cutting it fine. The cab to the studio shouldn't take more than twelve minutes max – but I've got to get out of here and catch one, and I reckon I'll need the loo before then. Three more minutes ticked away before a door opened and she heard her name called. As she went towards the dimly lit room, she heard a ping and saw a text from Lolly who, apparently, was getting on like a house on fire with Dame Jane – *she rocks shes live tweeting from the dressing room*. Avoiding the receptionist's eye, Penny sent a hasty reply before turning off her phone – *OK i'll be off radar for 20 at the least*.

The sonographer was a motherly type whose chatty manner explained the backlog in the morning's appointments. Penny listened to her long apology for the delay, agreed that the weather was fine despite the BBC forecast, and decided it wouldn't do any good to say she was in a hurry. She answered the routine questions with most of her mind on the clock, and continued to breathe deeply as the gel was spread on her bump. Even the slight pressure made her aware of her full bladder. Immediately, she went into emergency planning mode. The exit that gave the best chance of catching a passing cab was right next to a Ladies that seldom had a queue. I'll nip in there if I have to, she thought. Better still if I can hang on till I get to the studio.

'I'm going to be quiet now for a bit, while I check up on Baby.'

Penny repressed a desire to say that, in that case, she'd just check her phone. It must be a good ten minutes since this started, she thought, so Dame Jane's in Makeup now. I wonder if she's tweeting from there as well. Her fingers itched to find out and, feeling her tension, the sonographer murmured that there was nothing to worry about. 'I'm getting a lovely clear picture, and everything's looking fine.'

'Good. That's great.'

'I'll just need to do some measurements now, and plot them. Have a think because, after that, if you've got any questions, I'll answer them.'

'No, I'm fine. I mean, I'm fine as long as the baby's okay.'

'I just need to be quiet again for a moment.'

'Yes. Sorry. Yes.'

The sonographer's screen was turned away, so Penny couldn't see the image on it. Several minutes passed before the unhurried voice spoke again. 'When I've got this done, I'll enter everything onto your notes, so we'll have an up-to-date record.'

'But I won't need to be here for that bit, will I?'

'Oh, bless. I expect you're dying to let everyone know your results, aren't you? First-time mothers are all the same. I expect you'll be on your phone as soon as everything's done and dusted.'

'Absolutely. Will it take much longer?'

'It will if we keep gossiping, won't it? Here, would you like a look?'

The screen swung round and Penny found herself looking at her baby. 'Oh, my God!'

'I know. It's miraculous, isn't it? There's the little hand and – can you see? – that's the ribcage.'

As Penny looked at the image, everything else seemed to disappear. She hardly remembered leaving the room with the sticky feeling of the gel lingering on her tummy, and in the waiting room she stood blinking, as if blinded by the change of light. Staring at the printout she'd been given by the sonographer, Penny was overcome by awe. Then her eyes focused on the clock and she rushed into the corridor, fumbling in her bag for her phone. It rang the moment she turned it on, and she heard Lolly's voice.

'Thank God you've picked up.'

'Why? What is it? What's gone wrong?'

'They've just taken the dame down to the set.'

Penny squinted at the time, which was two minutes to eleven. 'Well, that's fine. Ad-break, and she'll be on air in four.' The voice in her ear wobbled. 'Her tweets are trending. She's been firing them off in the dressing room, and in Makeup. Taking selfies with everyone, and talking all the time. So, I didn't get a chance to look at my phone. Then I looked, after they came and took her down to the floor, and, oh, Penny ...'

'Lolly, what's the *matter*?'

'She tweeted that she's going to be making s'mores on air with David.'

'What?'

'Hashtag DameJane, hashtag BunsOfSteel, hashtag Gimme-Smore.'

'You mean, she wants to be on for the last half-hour as well as her own slot? Nobody gets her to stay that long anywhere. It's twelve minutes on the nose and she's gone.'

'The tweet's had about a thousand retweets already.'

'And is Faber doing s'mores today? Hang on, what the hell are s'mores?'

'No, he isn't. They're marshmallow things. He's supposed to be making something else. It's already been trailed online and everything. I don't think anyone up in the gallery's seen what she tweeted. What do I *do*?'

Penny reached the lift and realised that, if she took it, her phone would lose its signal. Don't panic, she told herself. Focus, regroup and prioritise. Making for the stairs, she rapped out a series of instructions. 'Faber must be in Makeup by now. Get down there and put him on the phone. Tell Shamir to stand by to talk to me. Google a recipe for these s'mores.' As she clattered down the first of eight flights of hospital stairs, she could hear Lolly charging down to Makeup. Moments later, she heard David's voice. 'What's going on? What's Lolly talking about?'

'What are you meant to be making today?'

'Carrot and parsnip cake with rose frosting.'

'No, you're not. You're doing s'mores.'

'What? Those marshmallow sandwich things?'

'You know what they are? Thank goodness. Tell Lolly what you'll need for them.'

'Of course I know what they are. The twins live on them. Penny, what's happening? Have you gone mad?'

'Lolly will tell you. Tell her to use the runner. Get off the line. I need to talk to Shamir.' Reaching the fourth landing, Penny leaned against the wall. Shamir's voice, when he called, sounded even more frantic than Lolly's. 'What kind of maniac is this blasted woman? She can't just take over David's slot. I've got everything set up. We've rehearsed parsnip cake. We've trailed it. This can't be happening.'

'Well, it is, so shut up and listen.' Penny had opened Twitter and was stunned to see #GimmeSmores trending in the UK just ahead of #DameJane. 'I've talked to Faber. Lolly's sending a runner for the ingredients for the marshmallow things. You can re-set during the news and the ad-break.'

'There won't be time.'

'There will. You'll have four minutes. Get a grip.'

'I've film to drop into David's slot.'

'So run it. What's the problem?'

'It's about harvesting root vegetables.'

'Damn. Tell Faber he'll have to come up with some kind of link to s'mores.' Penny blinked as #BunsOfSteel leaped ahead on Twitter. 'How's the dame doing at the moment?'

'She's telling a scurrilous story about working with Maggie Smith. No, hang on – she's trying on Roz's earrings. God, now she's rearranging the flowers on the set.'

'See if we can get clips up on social media.' Having caught her breath, Penny continued to run down the stairs. She could hear Shamir calling shots and frantically talking to Lolly, who'd evidently discovered several different recipes for making s'mores.

'I'm a director, Lolly, not a chef, how do I know which to use?'

'You don't have to choose. It's not up to you. I'm just saying that Faber says he'll bake cookies. Basically, s'mores are just chocolate and marshmallow sandwiches made with biscuits. In America, it's Graham Crackers, and that's more authentic ...'

Bursting through the doors from the stairwell into a ground-floor corridor, Penny saw a loo and made for it, raising her voice to a roar. 'Lolly, get back down to Faber and make sure he's got whatever he needs. Tell him he'll have to come up with something to link marshmallows to parsnips. And stop bleating, Shamir. You signed up for live telly. This is the real thing, so ride the wave.'

By the time Penny reached the studio, Lolly was standing in the gallery, staring at the scene below. Roz and Gail, looking poleaxed, were riveted to the sofa, and Dame Jane, a short, fat woman in matronly Crimplene, was lounging on a chair she'd dragged onto the set for herself. Beside her, on a stool, was David, who appeared completely calm. As Shamir cut back from the newsroom, the dame turned to camera and held the eyes of the nation's TV viewers. 'I know you thought I'd gone, but you were mistaken. Because I *really* fancy marshmallows made by a man with buns of steel. Admit it, so do you. I mean, who wouldn't?' Shamir, who'd regained his directorial presence of mind, cut from a close-up of her face to David's reaction, a perfect blend of comic discomfort and indulgent amusement. Everyone in the gallery exhaled in unison and, with a surge of gratitude, Penny watched David's professional magic working, and saw her show's retweets hit an unprecedented high.

After the show, Dame Jane insisted on taking them all out to lunch. 'I know I behaved disgracefully, and everyone coped so well. The least I can do is buy us a bottle of fizz and a bite to eat.' She nudged Penny. 'None of my camping about will have hurt either one of us, dear, I promise, but I dare say I gave you a few interesting moments.' Penny was aching to go home and lie flat on the floor, but she pulled herself together and went along.

They ate in a restaurant overlooking the river and, while the dame was telling more scurrilous stories, Penny stepped onto the balcony, where a row of orange trees stood in large ceramic pots. She heard a footstep and found David beside her, holding a glass of fizzy water. 'Well, that was some morning! You left your drink on the table. Here it is.'

'Thanks.' Penny took the glass. 'You did a brilliant job. Cool as a cucumber.'

'Oh, you know.' David gave her a charming grin. '"If you can keep your head, when all around you ..." Actually, it was a doddle. Like I said, I'm no stranger to s'mores. The twins are addicted to them.'

'The network's going to be pleased.'

'You don't look the better for all the excitement. Are you okay?'

'Yep. Fine.' In fact, Penny had stepped outside because she was feeling dizzy and in need of a breath of fresh air. Taking a gulp of water, she leaned her arms on the balcony rail. 'Sorry I ended up shouting down the phone at you all. I was in St Thomas' Hospital when I heard what was going on.'

'The hospital? Are you okay?'

'Fine. It was just the routine second ultrasound. No big deal. I'm okay. The baby's okay. Everything's hunky-dory.'

'No, but wait. Did they tell you? Is it a boy or a girl? Could they see?'

Penny turned and found David's arms on either side of her, his hands gripping the balcony rail against which her back was pressed. Still feeling slightly dizzy, she steadied herself by leaning against his shoulder.

'You're white as a sheet.'

'It's just all that rushing about.'

'Really?'

'Truly. And, yes, they told me, David. It's a boy!'

Chapter Twenty-Six

The weather in Ireland had grown hot and dry, crisping leaves as they hung on the trees. Marguerite sighed for the wild meadow's drooping knapweed and yarrow and, though she knew time would repair the damage, was sad to watch her grasses bleach. When she walked up the close-cropped path, once green and now shades of burnt orange, she could hear seed pods on either side rattling in the wind. Apples were almost ready to be picked and stored or given to neighbours, and seasonal pruning and tidying took up much of the shortening days.

After a parched week the wind rose bringing heavy cloud and, though she was tired, having spent a long day in the orchard, Marguerite woke at 2 a.m. to the sound of rain. From her bed she could see a curtain flapping, where she'd opened the lower sash of the window a crack before going to bed. Getting up, she opened the window further, and leaned out to enjoy the scent of the wet garden. High above the mountains, a full moon seemed to drift from behind a cloud-bank, flooding the garden in pale, silver light.

Watching the grass shimmer in the wildflower meadow, Marguerite recalled a long-ago night when she'd woken, just as on this one, and opened a window to see her mother standing in the rain. It had been autumn and a harvest moon had turned the bleached grasses to polished silver. Ruth, in a flannel dressing-gown, was standing in the meadow, her hair loose and her face raised to the moon. She'd seemed tranquil. Leaning out of the window, Marguerite had watched her mother's hair grow sleek as it became wetter, and, putting out her tongue, had tasted raindrops running down her own face.

After a while, she'd crept down the landing and put her head around the door to her parents' bedroom. Donal was asleep, lying on his back and breathing gently. The bedclothes on Ruth's side were thrown back and the satin counterpane had slipped to the floor.

That day, Donal had been called out to an accident, and returned late in the evening, looking drained. Marguerite had heard him tell Ruth that a farm-labourer had fallen into a piece of machinery, and that by the time the ambulance had come it was too late to save him. 'He'd been badly mangled when they'd dragged him out of the damn thresher. And they called me too late. If I'd been there sooner it might have made a difference.'

Donal had been sitting by the drawing-room fire, and Ruth had come and laid her hand on his shoulder. 'You did your best. You can't let it trouble you.'

Marguerite had watched from behind the sofa as Donal's body had relaxed and he'd reached up and touched Ruth's face. 'I don't know how I'd manage without you, d'you know that?'

'You'd be fine.'

'No, I wouldn't.'

'Okay, maybe you wouldn't, but I'm here, so don't fret.'

That exhaustion was gone from Donal's face as it lay on the moonlit pillow while, outside in the garden, Ruth stood motionless in the rain. So, leaving her dad sleeping, and her mother in the garden, Marguerite had returned to bed with a sense that nothing needed to be done.

Now, more than sixty years later, she leaned from her window, trying to identify the spot where Ruth had stood that night. But the curves she herself had imposed on the meadow obscured her recall of the landscape as it had been. As she drew back, a gust of wind threw a spatter of rain through the window. The drops fell on the sleeve of her nightdress, making the fabric cling to her arm. Shivering, Marguerite shook her damp sleeve and, pushing down the sash window, turned the brass catch to lock it before going back to bed.

The wet night gave way to a glorious day, and Marguerite set out for the village. She'd shrugged on a sleeveless jerkin and wore rubber-soled boots with a sweater and an old pair of trousers. Beyond her own drive, at the end of which the gate still stood open, the tarmacked road was edged with soggy drifts of leaves. Swinging an empty shopping bag, Marguerite walked steadily, refusing a passing neighbour's offer of a lift. 'Thank you. That's very kind. But I'm enjoying the exercise.' The car, driven by a local farmer, disappeared in the direction of the village, leaving Marguerite to her blustery walk.

Sycamore and oak trees by the roadside showed stark against the bright sky, and occasional gusts of wind shook little torrents of drops from their branches, with the effect of rain falling in fits and starts. Marguerite remembered trying to steer between these occasional showers when she'd ridden her bike down to the village shop in her teens. The area had changed since then, yet so much remained the same. The young farmer who'd offered her a lift was the son of a man who'd been one of Donal's patients, and the girl who now ran the shop was the granddaughter of the woman from whom Marguerite had once bought sweets with her weekly pocket money.

Today, as she emerged from the shop with her groceries, she saw Eve Blythe approaching on a mobility scooter, her ebony walking stick balanced across its handlebars. Eve asked if the shop was crowded and Marguerite shook her head. 'There's a group of walkers buying snacks, but no more than three or four of them. And Maeve Foley's chatting at the counter.'

Eve pulled a face. 'I loathe getting in people's way, staggering about on a stick.'

'You won't.'

'I'd rather wait. Now that we've run into each other, I don't suppose you fancy a glass of Madeira? I like a lunchtime apéritif and it's good to get out of that granny-annex and see human beings.' Eve lived at her nephew's home in a charming purpose-built flat, where Caroline constantly dropped in with offers of help and company. Cocking her eye at Marguerite, she chuckled. 'I suppose you think I'm horrible.'

'No, of course not.'

'If you did, you'd be right. I'm an ungrateful old woman. But Caroline's worthiness always drives me mad.'

'I think you're actually rather fond of her.'

'I do recognise her qualities. It's just that I can't stand saints.'

Laughing, Marguerite said that alcohol before noon didn't suit her. 'I'll come if you won't object to my drinking tea.'

'None of my damn business, and I'll enjoy your company. There's a vacant table for two at Ashton's. Let's whip over and nab it.' Deftly turning her scooter, Eve shot across the road to where tables, separated by flower tubs, stood on either side of the pub's open door. Marguerite joined her, helped her to a chair and went inside to order. When she came out, Eve, who'd been wearing a loose tweed jacket over a sweater and long woollen skirt, had slipped the jacket over her chairback and lit a cigarette. 'Caroline gets all tight-lipped when I smoke. You don't mind, do you?'

'Not for myself, not when we're outdoors.'

'And you've more sense than to lecture someone my age about her health.'

'I'm not really one for lectures, anyway.'

'That's what makes you good company.'

'I sometimes wonder if reticence isn't a form of cowardice.'

Eve sniffed. 'If one's used to Caroline, it's a pleasant change.' She raised her glass and savoured a sip. 'Let's find something to talk about that won't further expose the depths of my ingratitude. Do you know when our card evenings are likely to pick up again?'

'When I spoke to Maeve just now in the shop, she offered to host the next one. She said she'd check Jim's dates and be in touch in the next few weeks.'

'Good. Though I have to say I prefer coming to you at Stonehill.' This surprised Marguerite and, seeing her reaction, Eve smiled. 'I'm not being ungrateful again. I enjoy Maeve and

Jim's evenings. But your drawing room is a wonderful space for a gathering, and I suppose it reminds me of my youth. You won't remember your mother's parties?'

'No. Though Mrs Sinnott talked about them. Ages ago. I think she called them bohemian.'

Eve gave a snort of laughter. 'I'm sure that's exactly the note Ruth intended to strike. Well, they all did. Your mother and mine, back in 1950s Dublin, with their artistic gatherings, and their *Great Gatsby* vibe.' Pulling on her cigarette, she winked at Marguerite. 'That's the word these days, isn't it? "Vibe"?'

'I think I've heard Penny use it. Mind you, it could be passé by now.' Pouring herself a cup of tea, Marguerite asked about Eve's mother. 'She was an artist, wasn't she?'

'She painted. Well enough, I think. I've got some of her stuff at home. She never set the Thames on fire. None of them did, except Justin MacMahon. He was the one who painted your mother's portrait.'

'Really? I've never known the artist's name.'

'MacMahon was the real deal. My mother was small fry in comparison. Nora Blythe. She used her married name professionally. At one point, she was a protégée of Evie Hone. That's why I'm called Eve.'

'How impressive.'

'Mmm. I suspect Evie was just being kind. All that generation of female Irish artists adored her work. And Margaret Clarke's and Mainie Jellett's. They yearned to be terribly modern, which wasn't easy in post-war Dublin. I think, if the truth be told, they wanted to live in the 1920s. Rushing to and fro to France and hanging out in salons.' Eve exhaled a long plume of smoke. 'Most of the men longed to escape to Brittany and be Expressionist. Francophilia was a big thing. Even my father succumbed to garlic and galleries, and he was a very ordinary country vet.'

'So how did your mother meet mine?'

'My father knew yours. They were at school together. Ruth met Nora and, apparently, they got on like a house on fire. My parents were best man and bridesmaid at your parents' wedding.'

Marguerite remembered the black-and-white photo Donal had shown her, taken outside the church on his wedding day. Focused on him and Ruth, she'd hardly had time to notice the best man and bridesmaid. But, looking back, she remembered he'd told her their names, Myles and Nora Blythe. She smiled at Eve. 'You know, I've never taken in that your mother was my mum's bridesmaid. So, did you come to bohemian parties at Stonehill when you were a child? Oh, but of course, you must have! That's why you recall the yellow roses on the piano.'

Eve chuckled. 'Fallen petals. Very arty. I remember saying so loudly and being shushed.'

'What age were you then?'

'Oh, I don't know. Twelve? Maybe younger. Old enough to have a huge crush on Justin MacMahon. But I was precocious as well as obnoxious in those days. I fell madly in love with the curate when I was eight.' Eve sipped her drink and grinned wickedly. 'I attribute my lifelong unmarried state to excess of male company as a girl.'

'Surely the curate wasn't a bohemian.'

'No. But I didn't go to boarding school like my brothers, so a lot of my time was spent getting in other people's way. My mother did a series of sketches in the churchyard. I wandered about annoying the curate.'

'Was that her thing? Sketching?'

'For a while. They all dabbled. Justin was the only one with any focus. He arrived in Dublin determined to paint portraits, and succeeded.'

'Where was he from?'

'Somewhere in the West. He had a country accent. When he came to Dublin, he lived in a tiny room in a house in Harcourt Street. Most of the other men had jobs and did their artistic dabbling on the side. As far as I know, he just starved and painted. Mostly self-taught, but I think he studied a bit with Jack B. Yeats.'

Marguerite wondered aloud if this was why Justin MacMahon had been asked to paint Ruth's portrait. Had an element of patronage or charity been involved? Eve shrugged. 'I've no idea. I mooned about fancying him, but I don't think he ever talked to me. None of them did. I doubt if they even looked at me, other than when I was posing, and then I might as well have been an arrangement of fruit on a stand.' She put down her glass and wiped her mouth with the back of her wrinkled, heavily ringed, hand. 'How's your Penny? Someone told me she's pregnant.'

This question wasn't surprising, as Marguerite had allowed the news to filter out after Penny's scan. 'Yes. It's due after Christmas. It's a boy.'

'Good for her. Not that there aren't more than enough men in the world already.'

Eve was the first person locally to ask after Penny and show no interest in the baby's father. Whether this was tact or Eve's innate self-centredness, it made Marguerite more expansive than she might otherwise have been. 'Val and I have started making a patchwork cot-quilt. My mother made one for me, you know. It's worn, but I still have it.'

Lighting a second cigarette from the butt of the first, Eve squinted upwards at Marguerite. 'Penny's very wedded to her career, isn't she?'

'She's a hard worker.'

'Runs in the family, I suppose. I remember a time when you were all for being a pharmacist. What became of that?'

'Never happened. I was going to find something else over in London but, as my mum died when I was so young, I wanted to be there for Val and Rory when they were growing up.' Marguerite asked if Eve had ever considered a career.

Eve gave a hoot of laughter. 'Oh, I never fancied being a wage-slave. Mostly I sponged off my brothers. Well, they could afford it. After all, they were the ones my parents chose to educate. And now, of course, I'm doing the same thing to my unfortunate nephew. *Plus ça change.*' Inhaling deeply, Eve thrust her cigarette butt into an ashtray. 'You know, I can't imagine your mother quilting. Most unbohemian.'

Marguerite laughed. 'Artistic, though.'

'She wasn't artistic. She found artists glamorous.' Knocking back the last of her Madeira, Eve put her glass down and shook her head. 'Maybe I'm wrong about that, though. Perhaps it was far simpler. Maybe she just threw arty parties for fun.'

It was impossible for Marguerite to recognise her introverted mother in this depiction of a fun-loving bohemian. As she walked slowly home with her groceries, she wondered if

Eve's reminiscences could be relied on. After all, half of her pronouncements appeared to be made largely for effect. But, according to Mrs Sinnott, Ruth herself had used the word 'bohemian' to describe her parties, and Mrs Sinnott had remembered guests spilling out into the garden and dancing till all hours to the gramophone. Though she'd dearly loved to tell a story, Mrs Sinnott had always been a stickler for the truth. So, if Eve's teenage recollections could be confirmed by such a trustworthy witness, perhaps her reminiscences were reliable after all.

Chapter Twenty-Seven

Dame Jane's lunch went on till past 3 p.m. She left in a cab with Lolly whom she'd offered to drop at the office on her way to a Netflix do in Belgravia. Waving them off, Penny told herself she felt as old as the two of them put together.

As she stepped from her own taxi, Mark came out of the shop. 'Talk about a hot-news day!' Penny's first thought was that, somehow, he'd heard the result of her scan. Then, seeing the phone in his hand, she realised what he meant. Mark held it out. 'Leeann was watching your show. She called and said the socials were going crazy. They still are. I've just looked.'

The #DameJane hashtag was still trending and had been joined by #LollyRocks. Evidently, the dame had had her cab take a scenic route to her destination and had stopped to tweet selfies with Lolly in front of several London landmarks, including St Paul's Cathedral and Buckingham Palace. Though clearly wildly excited, Lolly had kept her head. She'd retweeted, tagging the show, the network and Netflix, and invented her own hashtag: #DameJaneFame.

Mark waved a copy of the *Evening Standard*. 'And have you seen this?' The paper had printed one of the selfies, used Lolly's hashtag as a headline and added a screengrab of David flicking a marshmallow into the dame's open mouth.

'No, I hadn't seen it.'

'Well, congratulations! You must be over the moon.'

'I am. It's brilliant. I'd better get upstairs and keep things moving.'

In the cab, Penny had had a vision of telling Mark her baby news over tea and a Garibaldi with her feet up on the crimson chaise longue. The chaise had been moved from the window to a position by the till where it currently showcased a recycled cashmere throw. Penny could see it from where she stood on the pavement and now it seemed to beckon invitingly. But whatever was going on evidently needed monitoring so, sketching a thumbs-up, she made for her door. 'Talk later, Mark, okay? Oh, how have Bill and your mum been since the party?'

'Still eating leftovers. Leeann said to tell you to give her a shout sometime if you fancy a pregnancy natter.'

'That's nice. Thanks. Say I will. See you, Mark. Bye.'

Upstairs, she checked social media, called the office, emailed Shamir, talked to Lolly, responded to queries and congratulations from the network bosses, and gave an upbeat quote for a press release. By the time she was done, her feet were throbbing and needles of pain were digging into her head behind both eyes. About to call Val, she was suddenly overwhelmed by tiredness and, feeling unable to talk, sent a text. *Had the scan. All well. It's a boy! Will be in touch.* Then she flopped onto her bed and fell deeply asleep, vaguely regretting the imagined embraces of the chaise longue and cashmere throw.

Except for a couple of trips to the loo, she slept until morning. When she got up, her headache was gone and she spent the day deluged by calls and emails about Dame Jane, all of which had to be dealt with along with her usual Friday workload. Lolly slipped away repeatedly to take calls and read texts from her mates, but it wasn't till late afternoon that Penny found time to call Val. 'Hi, Mum. I'm at work. Sorry not to talk sooner.'

Val's voice was carefully casual. 'How's everything?'

'Everything's fine.'

'How lovely to know it's a boy, and that all's well.'

'Isn't it? Well, I haven't quite got my head around it. But yes.'

'What did they say at the hospital?'

'Look, I'm really sorry, I can't talk here.'

'No. Don't worry. I'm just glad to hear your voice.'

'I'll be in touch. Can you tell Gran? Say I'll give her a call soon. Everything's kicking off here at work. But I'll get back to you.'

Though the following day was Saturday, there were still masses of emails to be dealt with. Penny worked through them efficiently and, having checked the socials again, closed her laptop and went to lie on the sofa. Among all the kerfuffle since #DameJaneFame began trending she hadn't had time to think about David's reaction to her news. Now she told herself that the concern he'd shown in the restaurant didn't prove anything one way or the other. Any normal person would show concerned interest if they heard a colleague had been in a hospital, and if someone pregnant with their baby had just had a second scan, they'd probably ask about the baby's sex.

Frowning, Penny clasped her hands on her bump. This time the scan had definitely shown a person. It was another milestone. Rooting in her bag for the printout she'd hardly had time to look at, she found herself talking to her baby. Look, I know that, when I was going through his contract, I thought your dad might want to be a part of your life. But don't assume I was right, okay? Because I could've been wrong. He hasn't been in touch since I told him you were a boy, and that was on Thursday, so maybe my theory was way off the mark. Maybe the contract negotiation had nothing to do with you. Maybe he just didn't have the balls to ask for a rise. And if that's so, it's just fine, she assured the baby. You don't need him. The fewer the complications, the better you and I are going to cope.

She stood up and, for a moment, considered sticking the screenshot up on one of her pristine, unadorned walls. But that felt weird. As she hesitated, Stanley snaked in through the window and, winding himself around her ankles, mewed loudly for food. Penny suddenly realised she'd had no breakfast and that it was now past noon. Leaving Stanley purring in a pool of sunlight, she took her purse and went downstairs, intending to grab a sandwich from a stall. Outside, the market was heaving with weekend shoppers and, as Penny hesitated, wondering if she had the strength to plunge into it, she heard someone call her name and, turning, saw Leeann.

'Hi, Pen! How're you doing?'

'Fine. Taking a lunchbreak.'

'Me too. One of my sister's girls has a job at that new café down by the *Golden Hinde*. I said I'd turn up and be supportive. D'you fancy coming along?'

'I don't know. I was just going to bring a takeaway sandwich back up to the flat.'

Leeann laughed and linked Penny companionably. 'Oh, come on. You can't have a lunchbreak without a bit of a walk in the fresh air.' To Penny's surprise, she found herself walking arm in arm towards the river as Leeann explained that her niece had just started in the job. 'It's a nice café. Not a chain. They'll do us a sandwich and, since it's new, it probably won't be crowded.'

Since Penny's last visit, the *Golden Hinde*'s narrow dock had been drained, and scaffolding had been erected around the tall ship. In a cordoned-off corner was a pile of sawn tree trunks and branches, heavy oak chunks with the bark still attached. Men in very clean hi-vis jackets were working on the ship, and a couple of disappointed-looking tourists were standing in front of a notice that read 'CLOSED'. Penny could see where patches of new timber had been used to replace worn and rotten sections of the hull.

As the tourists turned away, grumbling, Leeann rolled her eyes. 'It's not that long since this riverside was crowded with working ships. Now all we've got are cafés and souvenir shops and a replica of a galleon, that's used as a museum.' She steered Penny around the cordon, from which safety-tape fluttered, like ragged bunting. 'Mind you, these lads are doing a proper job. They're real craftsmen, like the guys who work for Mark.' Penny stood for a moment, looking up at the work. Some of the inset patches interrupted the coloured frieze. Others were bright against the black paintwork of the superstructure. Leeann wrinkled her nose. 'Most families round here had someone who worked on the river. My mum's dad was a docker. He wouldn't recognise it now, with all these apartment buildings and those glass towers down at Canary Wharf.'

'My mum's dad was an accountant. Not one of the Canary Wharf glass-tower kind.'

Leeann linked Penny again and they moved on. 'How about your other granddad?'

'I don't know what he did. I never met him.'

'Look, that's the café. There's a window table free.'

Leeann installed Penny at the table with a menu and went up to the counter to say hi to her niece. Looking out of the window at the steel web of scaffolding, Penny remembered her first visit to the *Golden Hinde*. Pointing at the gilded hind's-head figurehead, Marguerite had told her how the ship had got its name. 'It was a way of saying thank you. The sponsor who paid for Drake's voyage had a hind in his coat of arms.'

'What's a coat of arms?'

'A family badge. Knights had them on shields or embroidered on their surcoats, so people would know who they were.'

'Does every family have a coat of arms? Do we?'

'You could design one for us.'

'What do they look like?' Penny recalled her own staccato questions and Marguerite's quiet voice as she explained.

'You draw the shape of a shield and divide it into sections.'

'Draw it on what?'

'Anything. Just a piece of paper, if you like. You put a picture in each section, to represent someone in the family.'

'A picture of what?'

'A picture of something that brings that person to mind.'

It had felt like a challenge so, that evening, Penny had set about it. The basic shapes proved easy and, remembering the garden at Stonehill and the vase of flowers in the hall there, she drew a stylised wreath in a square, to depict Marguerite. Her toy lion, a gift from Paul, had made a suitably heraldic image for her granddad. She'd thought for a while before deciding on a pile of books for Val. Then she'd stared at the empty diamond in the centre of her shield. As she'd sat there, sucking her pencil, Val had come in and asked her what she was doing.

'Nothing.' Hunching her shoulder, Penny had pushed the page under the pad from which she'd torn it. 'Just a thing for school. What's for dinner?'

'I know it's not Friday, but shall we push the boat out and have fish and chips? You run round and get them, and I'll put the peas on.'

Penny had taken her coat of arms with her to the chip shop, balled up and clutched in her fist. Waiting in the queue for her order, she'd torn it up and dropped it into a bin. Now, as she looked at the menu, she recalled the empty diamond, and how she'd sucked her pencil and stared at it. She hadn't wanted to tear up her creation. But what else could I do? she asked herself. All I could think of to put in that space was a picture of a shipwreck. A galleon like the *Golden Hinde*, going down with its pennants streaming and all the treasures of the world in its hold. That's who my dad was. The terrible loss. The guy who drowned. The tragic figure I knew I shouldn't allude to because it might make Mum sad. No one ever said so out loud, but I knew it. So, I knew

I mustn't draw a shipwreck. But there was nothing else to fill that empty space.

'They're doing a sausage sandwich special. Are you up for one?' Leeann put a couple of coffee mugs on the table and, when Penny nodded absently, gave a thumbs-up to her niece. Sitting down, she smiled across at Penny. 'You must be really chuffed about your show's success.'

'What? Oh, the Dame Jane stuff. Yeah, it went down well.'

'You don't sound chuffed.'

'I am, but that's yesterday's story. In TV, you're always focused on the next thing.'

Leeann wrapped her fingers round her coffee mug. 'Showing my ignorance here, but what is it you actually do?'

'Basically, I do whatever it takes to jack up ratings. Which jacks up advertising revenue. It's all about number-crunching and targeting demographics. The trick is to deliver what keeps everyone on board.'

'How?'

'You have to have a nose for it. I do. I always have had.' Penny was about to expand on this when she felt a sudden kick. She blinked and, instinctively, put her hand on her bump. Leeann smiled. 'Have you had your second scan yet?'

'Yep. Everything's fine. It's a boy.'

'Oh, wow! Mark didn't say.'

'I haven't had time to tell him. Well, with everything kicking off at work, I hardly had a minute to text my mum.'

'You texted her?' Leeann sounded shocked.

'Yesterday. We had a quick word on the phone this morning, though.'

'But you got the news on Thursday?' Leeann put down her mug, looking contrite. 'Sorry. It's none of my business. It's just that my mum would hit the roof if me or my sisters didn't go straight round to see her with our results. People are different, though, aren't they? Do you and your mum not get on?'

The question was so unabashed, and Leeann's tone so friendly that Penny didn't take offence. 'No, it's not that. It's just – I didn't have time. My mum understands.' The baby moved again and, surreptitiously, Penny slipped her hand under her shirt to ease her waistband. 'I'm going to have to concentrate on proper maternity clothes. Everything I buy online is the wrong size, or else it looks ghastly, so I keep packing things up and sending them back.'

'I know a couple of places you could try.'

'Websites?'

'Shops. I could take you sometime.'

'You mean go on a shopping trip?'

'If you like. I don't want to be pushy. If you haven't had a chance yet, maybe you'd rather spend time with your mum.'

Penny shook her head. 'Mum and I have never gone in for shopping trips. I'd like it if you were free to come with me, though.'

'Cool. We'll fix a date.'

The sausage sandwiches arrived and Penny was introduced to Leeann's niece. 'This is Pen. She lives upstairs from your uncle Mark. Over your granddad's place.' The girl shot her a smile and went back behind the counter. And that's how she'll see me, thought Penny. Not as the hotshot exec of TV's highest-rating morning show. I'm the woman who lives upstairs from her uncle, over her granddad's old shop. Which is kind of nice. Taking out her phone, Penny pulled up her diary and looked across at Leeann. 'How's next weekend for you?'

'God, I don't know. There's sure to be some Sophie-related emergency, or someone's dog will have eaten someone's homework. I'll give you a call, shall I? Closer to the time.'

Penny put down her phone and reached instead for the mustard. The family stuff had felt too heavy to go into. But, like Mark, Leeann was easy company. I like her, thought Penny, as she bit into her sandwich. And a shopping trip with a friend would be nice.

Chapter Twenty-Eight

Donal died in 1998 at the age of seventy-seven. Only a few months before his death, Marguerite asked Val to come to Stonehill for Halloween. It wasn't easy to persuade her. 'I don't know, Mum. My half-term break is so short, and travelling with Penny would be hellish. She's determined to walk and half the time she falls over. Imagine her on a freezing ferry in October.'

'I'd like you to come.'

'We were there in the summer.'

'Look, I can't explain. It's just that your granddad was looking frail in July. I'd like us all to be under one roof again.'

'Is Dad coming?'

'Yes. It's just for the long weekend. Please, Val. I'll be there to give you a hand with Penny. So will your dad and Rory.'

'Oh, yeah, like Rory will be any use.'

It was so unusual for Marguerite to be assertive that Val eventually gave in and agreed. And, in fact, Rory, who'd just turned twenty, was practical and helpful with Penny. He entertained her in the ferry's lounge, which smelt of toasted sandwiches and other people's damp coats, and insisted she held his hand when he took her for walks on deck. As Penny knew him to be impervious to manipulation, she accepted his restrictions meekly, and diverted her pent-up energy into screaming-matches with seagulls. The crossing was rough and Val was languid and, by the time the ship docked, Marguerite was wondering if the trip had been wise. But at the sight of Donal's spare, upright figure, she ran towards him, knowing, as she'd known on the day she and Paul had married, that this was the right thing to have done.

Stonehill always seemed unchanging, regardless of the season. There was a vase of dried fennel heads on the polished hall table, and lamplight and firelight danced on the walls when they sank into chairs in the panelled drawing room. Val had arrived with a raging headache. Struggling with her packing the previous night, she'd cursed Marguerite and wept angry tears for the quiet break in West Hampstead that she'd been looking forward to. But, sitting on a fireside chair with the teapot on the hearth, she realised she was feeling relaxed for the first time in months. Donal's bony embrace had banished the last of her tension headache and, leaning back as the others chatted, she could hardly imagine why she'd resisted the trip.

Later, Rory carried the tray to the kitchen while Marguerite took Penny upstairs to bed. Val went to sit by Donal, who took her hand and asked, 'How's my girl?'

'I'm okay. Tired.' She wouldn't have admitted this to anyone but Donal, whom you could never fool anyway. He turned her face to the light. 'You're not eating properly, are you?'

'Granddad! Stop diagnosing me! You're retired.'

'That doesn't mean I've lost the use of my eyes.'

'Of course I'm eating.'

'I said eating properly. There's a difference. I'm talking about sitting down, giving yourself breathing-space, and taking time afterwards to digest.'

'You do know I've a toddler and a full-time job?'

'You can't pay proper attention to either if you don't look after yourself.'

Val shrugged. 'I do my best.'

'I know. That's the problem. Women like you can be their own worst enemy. You're a perfectionist, Val. "As aware as a visual artist and as analytical as a research chemist." Remember my saying that?'

'Why bring it up now?'

'Perfectionism and motherhood don't go together. You can't blame yourself whenever your child is difficult.'

'I don't!'

'And there's no point in seeking reasons for everything in life. It's a waste of time and energy. Trust me, I know.'

Rory's return interrupted the conversation, and when Marguerite had sung Penny to sleep, they went down to eat dinner in the kitchen. Mrs Sinnott was dead by then, and Donal catered for himself with the help of a lady who cleaned once a week. He had a beef stew on the hob, had peeled potatoes and had topped and tailed beans. Marguerite completed the cooking as he opened a bottle of wine and, over the meal, they caught up on neighbourhood news.

The local GP's surgery was now in a clinic in the village, but it was evident that, despite his retirement, Dr Barry remained at the centre of the community. His stories were full of references to visits from people who'd dropped in to tell him about a birth, a death or a marriage, to ask for advice, or to chat about the old days. When the first course had been consumed, they moved on to a blackberry and apple crumble, made by one of Donal's neighbours. She'd carried it up from the village in the blue stoneware dish in which she'd baked it, and had left it on the step with a note saying she'd heard the family was coming for Halloween.

Marguerite had found milk in the fridge, and eggs in the larder, along with caster sugar and a vanilla pod, and, savouring custard with her pudding, Val wondered why eggs and milk never tasted so good as they did in Stonehill. After dinner, she and Marguerite went to bed early, leaving Paul, Rory and Donal to finish their wine by the drawing-room fire. Sliding between threadbare sheets faintly scented with sweetgrass, Val was too tired for her usual tally of all she felt she'd done badly or hadn't had time to do. She fell asleep to the sound of rain whirled against her window, and slept through a night of storm without a dream.

The weather continued wild but, leaving Penny with the others, she and Donal managed to slip away for a walk with Rex. They drove to the Devil's Glen and climbed the path to the waterfall, breathing cool, moisture-laden air. Reaching a flat expanse of rock close to the ribbon of water, Val spread out an ancient raincoat she'd taken from the porch at Stonehill. Donal eased himself down to sit beside her, clicking his fingers at Rex, who squeezed between them in a flurry of russet hair and muddy paws. Val raised her voice above the sound of the waterfall. 'It's properly in spate.'

Donal scratched the dog's silky head. 'Almost loud enough to suggest that the devil's back on the rampage. Very appropriate for the time of year.'

Val rested her chin on her knees, wishing she'd thought to bring some barley sugar. 'Mum always made a big thing of Halloween when Rory and I were little. We never dressed up and went from house to house asking for sweets, though. People in London called that American.'

'Well, your mum got it from both sides of the family. Ruth called it trick or treating.'

'What did you call it?'

'When kids turned up round here, it was just "Help the Halloween party".'

'Did you go out in masks?'

'There used to be bonfires in the village. Plenty of apples and nuts and storytelling. Halloween wasn't whimsical or commercial in my day. People round here had a healthy respect for ghosts.'

Val grinned. 'Sounds like that film *The Wicker Man*.'

'That was just generic horror stuff. This was specific, and deeply ingrained. Think of the stories attached to the place names around here. There's this glen, to begin with. The devil's supposed to have blown the roof off a building further up the mountains too. It's said that a crowd of rakes took stones from an entrance to the Otherworld, to build what they called a Hellfire Club, and the devil didn't like it.' Donal laughed. 'People say he objected to the reservoir up at Poulaphouca as well. You can't live hereabouts without a sense that you mightn't want to go walking the roads by night.'

'Poulaphouca means "The Devil's Hole", doesn't it?'

'Devil, or spirit, or ghost. Maybe monster. I remember hearing stories about the *púca* being a shapeshifter. He might be a horse, a goat or a dog, or a hare you'd meet on the road. Or you could play cards with a stranger who looked like an ordinary gentleman and discover he had hoofs, or horns and a tail.'

'At Halloween?'

'Any time. Mind you, Halloween was said to be special. The night when the dead emerge from their graves and the Old Ones are abroad.'

Val put her arm around the spaniel. 'I'm not sure I like that.'

'It's nothing but superstition.' Taking his pipe from his pocket, Donal sheltered a match from the mist that blew from the waterfall. Val frowned, trying to place a connection. 'Poulaphouca comes into James Joyce's *Ulysses*. He personifies the waterfall there as Circe, the daughter of a sea-nymph. The one who turns men into swine and wolves.' Donal winked at her over the bowl of his pipe. 'Now, there's the fruit of an Oxford education.'

Val pulled a wry face. 'Much good it did me! I've practically forgotten all I learned there.'

'In less than five years?'

'It feels like a lifetime. I can hardly remember who I was when I left university.'

'It won't always be this hard, you know. Babies grow up.'

'Other stuff doesn't leave you, though, does it?' Tightening her hold on the dog, Val looked away. 'It's all such a mess. Simon's parents blame me for his death.'

'That's ridiculous.'

'I know. I guess it's their way of coping. But the thing is, Granddad, I blame myself for getting pregnant.'

'That's ridiculous too.'

'Is it? What the hell use is an Oxford degree, if you end up not even knowing how your contraceptive works?'

'Did Simon know?'

'Apparently not. But he's dead, so he doesn't have to deal with the consequences.' Val stared at the waterfall, seeing Simon's body, as she repeatedly did in dreams, turning slowly in green, salty water. 'I miss him like hell, Granddad. Sometimes I think I can feel him so close that I ought to be able to touch him. Like he's beyond an invisible veil. That's what people used to think, didn't they? They believed the veil grew thin at Halloween so the dead return. Girls would look for signs, and use charms to draw lost lovers back to them. They'd brave the churchyard at midnight and wait in the dark for a glimpse or a word. But you know something? I couldn't do that. Not even if I believed in it. The truth is that I couldn't bear to see Simon. I'm too angry with him. I hate that. I hate being angry with Penny's dad. It can't be good for her. But I don't know how to forgive him for going away.'

Donal reached out and gave her an unaccustomed hug. 'The dead don't come back. When they leave us, they're gone for ever. Best not to think about them. It doesn't change a thing.'

That was the last conversation Val had with Donal. The rest of the weekend was spent indoors, where they all sat around, chatting, eating and drinking, and keeping Penny amused. On Halloween night, some neighbours' kids appeared at the door in masks and skeleton costumes, shaking a bag and asking for money and sweets. Determined to take Donal's advice, Val threw herself into family games and chat, and returned to London feeling better for her break. Within weeks, she was back again for her granddad's funeral.

And now, sitting in her kitchen with a piece of squared paper and a pencil, Val found tears in her eyes. Having heard that Penny was having a boy, she'd gone back to her ragbag with a sense that she'd dawdled far too long over the keepsake quilt. Lately, she'd noticed that Marguerite had stopped asking about it in their phone calls. I'm not being fair to her, thought Val. We're supposed to be in this together but the truth is that I was never really engaged by the project, and my interest has waned even more since Penny got back in touch.

Helplessly, she looked down at the sheet of squared paper onto which she'd failed to map a layout. I know what the measurements need to be, she thought, and it isn't complex. All I have to do is bring the separate pieces together to make a harmonious whole. It isn't a lot to ask of me. I just need to concentrate. God alone knows what's become of what Granddad used to call my fine mind. As she focused on the grid of squares, the moving shapes of the mandala she'd seen at the exhibition swam into her mind like fish, accompanied by Simon's teasing voice and her own irritated response.

... mandalas represent the conscious self's attempts to integrate unconscious material ...

Just bugger off, will you, Simon?

... processes of disintegration and reintegration ...

Dropping her pencil, Val thrust her hands into the pile of fabric that, with no coherent layout in mind, she'd already begun to cut up. Blue chambray, yellow towelling and rose-coloured glazed cotton. Broderie anglaise and Lurex, and a piece cut from a nightgown Marguerite had embroidered for her to wear in hospital when Penny was born. Pushing away the pile, Val saw grey chiffon slide across the table and fall like water onto the floor tiles she and Simon had picked out together for their home. As she stared at the grey pool with its tarnished sequins, nearly thirty years of repressed emotion welled up inside her, so forcefully that the effort of containing it made her shake. Then, without thinking, she relaxed and allowed the salt tears to flow while, in her mind's eye, a multicoloured mandala rose and fell like a shoal of spiralling fish.

She had no idea how long it was before she sat down again with her pencil, certain of how she wanted to proceed. Light had faded in the garden by then and, when she'd gone to pick up the dress, she'd switched on the lamp above the table. The scattered pieces of fabric lay on its surface as they'd fallen, linked by nothing more than the fact that they represented the life she'd pieced together after Simon had died. Granddad was right, she thought. The dead you've loved don't return. But that's because, on some unconscious level, they never leave you. I don't know why he didn't tell me that.

For the first time in years, she felt Simon very close to her, standing somewhere just beyond a veil. Okay, Simon, she thought wryly, you buggered off and abandoned me and Penny, but at least you left me that quotation. At the time, we both treated it as unimportant. You'd only bothered to learn it by heart to give you an edge in your finals, and, that day, I was wholly focused on my own train of thought. Anyway, if we'd discussed it we'd have rejected it back then. We believed that conscious effort would give us whatever we wanted or needed. It's taken me until now to see how the conscious needs to integrate with the unconscious, and to recognise how fear and anger can screw that process up. Perhaps if I'd taken up quilting before now, I would have understood sooner. And maybe, if you'd lived, we'd have found it out together. Anyway, I think I've got it now, so thanks.

THE PATCHWORK

THREAD 3

Penny

When Penny was small, the undersides of fabrics fascinated her. The knots and loose threads on the back of a piece of embroidery. The washed-out blur on the wrong side of a length of printed cotton. How woven patterns could appear with their colours and patterns reversed. All these seemed more interesting than bright outer sides and prints that reached all the way to the edge of a roll of fabric without the mysterious narrow band of selvage that refused to fray when picked at by fingernails.

In the 1990s her mum had owned a reversible swing-back jacket that was black on one side and orange on the other. On the day Val brought it home from the shop, Penny spent hours modelling the jacket in front of the wardrobe mirror, turning it inside-out and back again.

'So, which is supposed to be the right side?'

'You can wear it either way.'

'Then why do people talk about the right side of a fabric? They do. I've heard Gran.'

'Some fabrics work that way. Others don't.'

'But why call one wrong?'

'It's the name for the side that's intended to be hidden.'

It made no sense to Penny. Surely the underside of everything was the more interesting. The side that revealed how things were made, and allowed you to see into the mind of the maker. The place where, with luck, mistakes could be concealed or repaired, and different possibilities presented themselves.

Her fascination with what was revealed by what was hidden persisted, along with a delight in how the commonplace could be transformed. Though she seldom wore makeup, she loved its effects – the shape of an eye emphasised by kohl, a nail by varnish, a cheekbone enhanced by touches of shadow and colour. And while, increasingly, her own clothes were chosen for texture and cut, patterns continued to intrigue her. Stripes, florals and geometric shapes. Flocking and felting, and the effect of light falling on slub from different heights and angles. The simplicity of polka dots and the intricacy of paisley.

Most of all, she was drawn to layers and what might be found between them. The smooth, matt, floor-to-ceiling doors that concealed her life's clutter. The lime and horsehair plaster wall that served as a back to the cupboards. And beyond the plaster, hidden until she had summoned it to the surface, the patchwork of creamy-yellow bricks, interspersed with soft pinks and purples, shaped and fired from the earth on which London was built.

Chapter Twenty-Nine

On the morning of Penny's last day at work an envelope addressed to Mark was among the post in her letterbox. Taking it down to the shop, she found Leeann perched on an upcycled rocking-horse. She and Penny had gone shopping more than once since they'd had lunch in the café, and pregnancy chat had begun to blossom into real friendship. As Mark took the letter, Leeann slid off the horse. 'What do you think of Dobbin?'

'Surely he's much too fancy to be called Dobbin?'

'Pegasus, then. Isn't he wonderful?'

The dapple-grey horse on wooden rockers had been enhanced with a pair of butterfly wings. Its sweeping mane and tail were made of long, curled ostrich feathers and the carved head had flared gilded nostrils. Mark grinned at Penny. 'You wouldn't have said he was fancy if you'd seen him in the auction house.'

'Is he an antique?'

'Not as such. He was made by a firm called Collinson. Their early horses are rare – you shouldn't mess with them. This chap's probably from the 1950s, though, so we stripped him back and gave him brand new gesso, paint and varnish. The girl who did him for me works on film sets. The wings and the feathers were her idea. I think they're genius.'

Penny bent to examine the feathers. 'What have they replaced?'

'Horsehair. Rocking horses often go bald. I guess kids swing on their tails and hang onto the manes. Those feathers are the remnants of several 1920s fans. You can pick them up cheap if the sticks are broken, and letting them rot away or get moth-eaten seems such a shame.'

Leeann ran her hand down the horse's back. 'Mark says this will either end up in a terribly posh nursery or a very happening gay bar.'

'"New lease of life", that's our motto. That and "keep an eye on the profit-margin".'

Leeann winked at Penny. 'You should've seen him back in his mudlarking days. He used to go combing the beaches down by the river at low tide.'

'For one summer, when I was ten!'

'He'd come home covered in mud with a box full of bits and pieces, and Mum used to go crazy when he'd clean them in the shower.'

'That's why I stopped. It wasn't worth the aggravation.'

'You stopped because Dad refused to give you any more money for tat.'

'Bill knew exactly what he was doing. He'd take a box of rubbish for 50p and pick out the good stuff. I remember him selling on a Georgian door knob for twenty quid.'

Penny sat down on the chaise longue, which had now acquired a bolster made from an Oriental rug. By rights, she thought, I should be upstairs getting ready for my leaving party, and all I want is to put my feet up and stay here. The party, organised by Lolly, was to be held on the studio floor after the show had gone out. The great and the good from the network and the company would be there and, along with the show's regular talent, former guests had been invited. Several were A-list celebrities, which made it likely that photographers would gather outside. With a desk to clear and her focus on the baby, the party hadn't been high on Penny's radar. Now the thought of it filled her with dread.

Leeann, who was helping Mark move the horse to the window, paused for breath and leaned on its dappled rump. 'If you're free tomorrow, Pen, d'you want to come to Spitalfields Market? We could have lunch.' Immediately, Penny's heart lifted. Feeling tired and knowing she looked unwieldy, she hated the thought of being the focus of photographers' attention. But time spent with Leeann was easy-going and interesting, so she said she'd love to have lunch. Leeann took hold of her end of the rocking horse again. 'Cool. I need to find a birthday present, and my brother-in-law has a street-food truck in the market. We can eat there.'

As Penny left the shop, she looked back to admire Dobbin in his new position. When Mark had taken over, he'd retained the original timber shopfront, which encompassed the window, the shop's entrance and Penny's front door. In Bill's day the window had been crammed with clutter. Now, with discreet lighting inside, and dark green exterior paintwork, the single items

Mark featured were showcased to perfection. Dobbin seemed particularly at home. Framed by the handsome timberwork, and despite the upcycler's quirky additions, he gave the shop the air of an illustration from Dickens, lacking only children in scarves and mittens, noses pressed to the glass.

The leaving party was a cross between a baby shower and a schmooze-fest. Some of the guests seemed excited for Penny but others appeared to have turned up in the hope of finding themselves in a showbiz column the next day. The guy from the company spent most of his time in a corner on his phone, and the struggle through the press at the door had left Penny hot and tired. Leaning against a wall with a glass of water, she saw the large cheerful woman from the young mums' YouTube channel making for her across the studio floor. 'Hi. Remember me?'

'Of course. You're Deisha from *It Takes a Village*. How's everything going?'

'Well, the exposure I got from your show didn't hurt!'

'I'm glad.'

'That's not what matters today, though, is it? How are you? You must be glad to be getting a break from all the pressures of work.'

'I guess so.'

Deisha's eyes narrowed. 'Is this crush too much for you?'

The unlooked-for kindness took Penny aback. 'Not at all. I'm fine. Just a bit hot.' Determined not to appear wimpy, she reverted to *It Takes a Village*, and was impressed to hear Deisha's viewing stats. Deisha shrugged. 'I don't do much to chase figures. I just say stuff I think is important, and people can listen or not. Look, why don't I get us a couple of chairs, if you don't mind me joining you?'

Penny nodded. It was refreshing to sit with someone who didn't keep glancing around for somebody more useful to talk to. So, she sat on the chair Deisha brought for her and continued their conversation about YouTube, noting that David seemed to be actively keeping his distance from her. Which is good, thought Penny. Everything's done and dusted now. We've moved on. Concentrating again on Deisha, she asked about demographics. 'Does your audience extend beyond young mums?'

'You better believe it! Lots of my feedback comes from grandparents. Well, it's not surprising. They're the obvious support network if a mum's out at work.'

'When I was little, I loved going places with my gran. She's amazing with kids.'

'Is she still alive?'

'Absolutely. She lives in Ireland, but she comes over a lot.'

Deisha's eyes crinkled at the corners as she smiled. 'I bet you can't wait for your baby to meet her.'

'I've been so busy I haven't really had time to think about it. You're right, though.' Penny returned Deisha's smile. 'And, evidently, you've guessed I'm going to be a single mum.'

'It wasn't hard. No wedding ring. No mention of the father. No partner dragged along to your leaving do.' Penny laughed and told her it was a fair cop. To her surprise, Deisha leaned over and gave her a one-armed hug. 'None of this is easy, but you'll be good, girl. Now that you're going on leave, your head's likely to explode with all the stuff you haven't had time to think through. But don't panic. You'll be fine. Just go easy and slow and take things one at a time.'

Penny was home again, eating sushi on the sofa, when she recognised the truth of Deisha's warning. For weeks, she'd been suppressing a thought she hadn't been able to face. Now, with no work demands to keep it at bay, it surfaced and, having appeared at the front of her mind, was impossible to ignore.

Thrusting her cucumber maki at Stanley, who sneezed at it in disgust, Penny stood up and began to pace round the room. It was all very well for her to decide that she and David were history, but the fact is, she told herself, this isn't just about us. What will it mean for the baby? I can stonewall everyone else, but I don't want my son to feel he can't ask me questions. And I don't want him to grow up like I did, afraid of saying the wrong thing to his mum. At least my dad was dead and buried. David will be out there, living and breathing. I've relied on the thought that no one at work will ask me about the father. And of course they won't: they don't care enough. Besides, they'd be afraid to antagonise me. But what about family? Mum and Gran and Uncle Rory and the cousins in New Zealand. Do I really intend to hold them at arm's length too?

Having walked too fast, she leaned breathlessly against a wall. The questions seemed to swoop around her, like bats chasing insects. I'm sorry, she told the baby. I'm so sorry. I know I said we'd be fine on our own, but I hadn't thought this through. What am I going to tell you if you ask me who your dad is? Will I make up a story about a passing stranger? Will I say I don't know where he is, though his face will be all around us on magazine stands? Up to now, I've been thinking of you as that little person in the scan. But you're going to grow up and be your own person. You'll have your own life and, most of the time, I won't even know what's going on in your head. And the fact is that, while you're little, I won't be able to manage on my own. I'll have to take all the help I can get, and that means I can't insist that everything's done on my terms. There I was this afternoon, telling Deisha I wanted you to spend time with Gran. Well, how do I expect Gran to cope if you ask her about your father? Is she supposed to lie, or edge away from the subject? And what about Mum? Is she supposed to tell herself that my precious privacy is all-important? More important than you or how you might feel?

Sitting down again, Penny pushed Stanley's nose out of a salmon roll. I still have to think about Helen and David's other kids, she thought. That's the responsible thing to do. I promised myself I wouldn't let them be hurt. But what about my responsibility to my own family? And doesn't this little person inside me come first? Oh, God, I've always been so sure of my own judgement. Now I feel as if I'm completely at sea. Groaning, she leaned back and stared at the bright lights of the city reflected in her darkening window panes. 'Maybe I ought to pick up the phone and call David,' she told Stanley. 'I seem to be pretty useless at thinking this thing through on my own.'

Chapter Thirty

When she opened her eyes the next morning, Penny was still confused. Sitting up, she remembered Deisha's other piece of advice. I've never done easy and slow, she thought, but this time I have to. I need to think before deciding whether or not to ring David, and what I ought to say to him if I do. And there are so many other practical things to get to grips with as well. She'd already created a spreadsheet – baby equipment and clothes to buy, as well as what she'd need at the hospital, dates of appointments, and a list of contacts to print out and stick on the fridge. And there was parenting-skills stuff to be considered. Having never changed a nappy in her life, she'd planned to ask Leeann if she could go round and practise on Sophie.

The thought of Leeann immediately made Penny feel better. Chatting and browsing rails in real shops had been relaxing and, as a result, she'd found several stylish easy-to-wear outfits. One of her favourite buys was a coat in black, white and orange window-pane check. When she'd tried it on, she'd told Leeann it reminded her of a jacket Val used to have. 'It was reversible. Mum wore it for years.'

'Well, this looks great on you. I'd buy it in a heartbeat.'

They'd found black maternity trousers to go with it, and an orange scarf, so when Penny set out to meet Leeann for lunch she felt comfortable, coordinated, and determined. As she walked to the bus stop, she reassured the baby. New outfit, new attitude, she told him. I'm not sure what to do next about your father, but I promise to take things easy and slow.

On the bus, Leeann explained what she was after. 'It's a birthday present for Kit, and she's hell to buy for.' Kit was one of Leeann's two daughters, the girls who'd been kicking a ball in the street on the day of Bill's birthday party. 'Don't get me wrong, she's a great kid, and it's not that she's fussy. She just has principles. I thought I'd find something ethically sourced for her in the market.' They got off the bus at Bishopsgate and walked to Spitalfields. In stylish little independent shops in the streets surrounding the marketplace, crowds of tourists and Londoners were sitting at café tables, or strolling about with street food, enjoying the sights. Under a high Victorian roof, like the one at Borough Market, stallholders sold clothes, accessories, fabrics, paintings and perfumes alongside trucks selling food to be eaten at long, communal tables and benches.

Leeann made for a stall where a tall girl with hair piled up in a 1960s beehive was selling jewellery she'd designed herself. Penny, who'd lingered by a stall stacked with bales of fabric, joined them as the girl lifted a leaf-shaped pendant on a fine chain. 'So, I work with stainless steel, which is one hundred per cent recyclable.'

Leeann explained that Kit was a diehard environmentalist. 'She's organised a Greta Thunberg-style climate-change strike at her school.'

'Good for her.' The girl produced a folded leaflet. 'Most of my steel originates from end-of-life products, and the rest from manufacturing processes. You'll see the percentages here.' Leeann held up the piece and asked Penny what she thought. The delicate oak leaf was cobweb-fine, and the steel had a soft matt glow. Penny said she loved it, but Leeann looked uncertain. 'I suppose I shouldn't buy the first thing I see.' The stallholder offered to put it aside for an hour or so. 'Have a look round and come back if you think this is what she'd like best.'

'Really?'

'Anything for a School Striker. I'll stick it under the counter and you can go have a browse.'

Leeann put her arm through Penny's and eased her through the crowds. They inspected work made of papier-mâché, felt, and fuse wire; old coins and cutlery given new life as bracelets; and broken vintage necklaces recycled as brooches and earrings. Many of the vendors were as young as the girl with the beehive hair-do. Others looked to Penny to be as old as Marguerite. One stallholder said she sourced kimonos and hauris from her home town in Japan. 'They were mostly made in the nineteen twenties and 'thirties. Some are synthetic, these are silk and those over there are hemp.' The hauris were shorter and less elaborate than the kimonos. Leeann took one and held it up. 'This would look good on you, Penny.'

'Yellow silk with embroidered dragons isn't really my thing.'

'Ah, but imagine lying about in it after the baby's born.'

'According to everything I've heard, babies spend their first months throwing up on your shoulder.'

'Which is why God created muslin squares. Oh, look, it's a garment that's seen life.' There was a darn on the sleeve in silk thread that exactly matched the fabric. The careful stitching reminded Penny of Marguerite's skill at repairs and, briefly, she felt an overwhelming longing for her gran. Bending to look at the darned sleeve, she became aware of a pleasant scent of pine. The stallholder spoke behind her. 'The smell comes from the wooden crates we ship them in. We don't use plastic.'

Turning back, Penny smiled. 'I'll take the hauri, please.' The purchase was wrapped in stencilled brown paper and tied with hemp string. As she and Leeann walked on, Penny admired the packaging. 'Isn't it lovely? And the price was so reasonable.'

Leeann grinned and said she wished Kit was with them. 'She could catch you up on the economics of ethical market forces.'

'What age is she?'

'Fifteen going on fifty. But kids grow up quickly, these days, don't they? Kit says it's our fault. We've trashed the planet and left them to deal with the fallout.'

'I suppose that's fair comment.'

'It's a huge thing to take in, though, isn't it? I can't imagine what kind of world there'll be when Sophie grows up. Kit told me the other day that I shouldn't have had kids if I hadn't applied my mind to climate change. Admittedly, she was pissed off because I'd pointed out it was past her bedtime.'

'What did you say?'

'I played the Mum card and told her to get to bed. Then,

because I was feeling guilty, I picked a fight with Lumo. Look, let's have a sit-down. Afterwards, I think I'll go back and get that pendant.'

As they threaded their way between the stalls to a juice bar, Penny tried to see herself, in fifteen years' time, fielding accusations like Kit's from her son. She'd never even thought about the world he was going to inherit. Kids do judge their parents, she thought anxiously. I know I did. And if Kit calls her mum irresponsible simply for having children, what might my child say to me, who got pregnant by mistake?

When they settled at a table with glasses of juice, she asked Leeann if she had any regrets.

'About having kids? Not for a moment. There's no denying what Kit says, though. It shouldn't be up to them to clean up the mess we've made of the world.'

'Proper *Moral Maze* stuff.'

'That's parenting.'

'It must be good to have Lumo to help take the strain.'

Leeann looked at her sympathetically. 'I guess parenting's harder when a baby's dad's not around.' Then, with a sense that this was a subject Penny wasn't inclined to discuss, she steered the conversation back to the yellow silk jacket. 'I didn't badger you into buying it, did I?'

'Of course not. I love it. The colour is stunning. Almost as rich as gold.'

Leeann reached into her bag for her phone, and asked if Penny knew that an ancient Roman burial had been found at Spitalfields. 'Possibly the wife of a fourth-century governor. Married in her mid to late teens. She'd been buried in a silk damask robe and the thread was ninety-seven per cent real, actual gold. I looked it up when my bro-in-law who works here told me about it. Hang on a minute.' Finding the link, she scrolled through a newspaper article. 'Here we go. They don't know her name. Rich grave-goods, including perfume bottles. The silk was from China. Oh, no, poor cow, she may have died in childbirth.' Leeann pulled a face. 'It says she was probably born in Rome and came here with her husband. I wonder if she ever saw her family at home again.'

Penny imagined that nameless woman in gold silk damask, lying for more than a thousand years under layers of earth, brick and stone. 'Does it really say she died in childbirth? I wonder if her baby survived.' Shooting a quick glance at her, Leeann scrolled on, apparently feeling the change of subject had taken them into dangerous waters. She found and read out more cheerful snippets about the area, and Penny nodded, laughed, and offered appropriate questions and comments. But her mind was elsewhere.

As they'd walked from the bus stop to the market, she and Leeann had passed a sculpture of seven steel figures crowded into a small wooden boat. A plaque explained that the boat had carried refugees from Turkey to the Greek islands, and that the sculpture had been installed to reflect Spitalfields's history of sheltering waves of migrants. Some of those migrants were silk-weavers, thought Penny, seventeenth- and eighteenth-century Huguenots from France, fleeing religious persecution. Irish linen-weavers came later, driven out by what school history books call 'economic factors at home'. Those waves were followed by Jews escaping pogroms, and Bangladeshis working long hours to support their families, and now streams of others displaced by climate change and war. Families whose lives had been ripped apart by circumstance to be painfully reassembled in bewildering new homes. So many women must have been pregnant when they made those journeys. And how many more, Penny asked herself, are at sea or trapped in refugee camps as Leeann and I sit here? How do they have the courage to make the choices life forces on them? If they survive, how will they explain them to their kids?

Chapter Thirty-One

Dame Jane's appearance on Penny's show had done wonders for its ratings and, in Dominic's words, David's personal fan base had gone stratospheric. Yet David was feeling hard done by. Responses at home to his trending hashtags hadn't been what he'd hoped. Helen had begun by liking the attention, which had ranged from mainstream to social media and resulted in much excitement at the twins' playschool gate.

Then, weeks after the show had aired, her father had phoned in a strop. Though happy to see his daughter on David's arm at charity fundraisers, he'd been horrified to hear his celebrity son-in-law was trending with the hashtag #FaberFantasies. Helen's assurance that this was all about cake didn't calm him and, after his irate phone call, she'd turned on David. 'He does have a point, darling. It's pretty suggestive. And Dad has a position to uphold.' Unused to anything less than adoration from Helen, and slightly spooked by the thought of what #FaberFantasies might lead to, David had pointed out loftily that her dad imported dental supplies. 'He's not exactly in the public eye.'

'What's that supposed to mean?'

'I mean that he's not a diplomat or, I don't know, the Archbishop of Canterbury. It can't matter to him what people are saying about me.'

'It doesn't.'

'You just said it did.'

'Don't obfuscate. He's thinking of me, David. Your wife. Your family. He's your children's granddad and, frankly, he's showing more concern for their wellbeing than you are.'

'I have literally not the faintest idea what you're talking about.'

'You can't see how this might traumatise Chloë and Demi?'

'What might traumatise them? Your dad posturing on his high horse, or me working my backside off to keep a roof over their heads?' Immediately he'd spoken, David had realised his mistake. The fact that the roof over their heads had been bought and paid for by Helen's father had hung in the air before Helen had stalked off. David had subsequently managed to resolve the quarrel in the bedroom, but the effort it took, and Helen's unaccustomed manner, had left him aggrieved and at odds with the world. So, when Dominic phoned a few days later to say he'd been called by a booker on a celebrity challenge show, David had responded sharply. 'Honestly, Dom, I'm beginning to wonder if you've actually grasped my brand image. I'm on the up, not sliding down the ladder. I don't do game shows and I've no interest in eating worms in the jungle. Vulgar sensationalism isn't my thing.'

In the moment before the response to this, David had almost panicked but, instead of being angry, Dominic had sounded amused. 'First of all, nobody's asked you to eat worms in the jungle. Second, I invented your brand image. And third, I've known some hashtags less vulgar than those you're trending with, but not many. I hear you, though. We'll forget the celebrity challenge. Congratulations on having found your balls.'

Though resentful of his agent's tone, David came away from the conversation feeling empowered. He'd always feared he'd been taken on simply because Dominic had represented Jennifer, who'd been at the height of her career when she and David married. But, clearly, he was now enough of an asset in his own right for Dominic to be willing to put up with hissy-fits. So why should Helen's father imagine he had the right to complain? Okay, the buns-of-steel thing was a bit undignified, but surely it wasn't hard to see that it was a means to an end. It had served its purpose and now, provided Dominic played his cards right, it could quietly be buried in the past.

Dimly aware that tweets could be screen-grabbed and keep turning up for ever, David had bolstered this argument with bluster, mentally dressing down Helen's father in terms he'd never dare to use to his face. It was time, he thought, that the old buffer got real. Dame Jane hadn't been fazed by the hashtag, and what was good enough for a Dame Commander of the Most Excellent Order of the British Empire ought to be good enough for a man whose only claim to fame was that he imported Taiwanese toothpicks to Blackheath.

Now, as he sat on the sofa in his Blackheath living room, the mirror propped against the wall showed David a full-length image of his life. Inevitably, the twins' toys had migrated from their bedroom and re-colonised what Helen had tried to define as a chic adult space. The room had acquired a new lump of bright pink plastic in the form of a kitchen stove complete with toy pots and pans. According to Helen, this was intended to deal with Chloë's food fads by encouraging her to sublimate them in play. So far, it had had no effect beyond strewing the floor with slices of plastic pizza, and producing a jealous tantrum from Demi, who'd screamed until she'd been bought a doll's house of equal value, pinkness and size. Helen had read out an article to David, explaining that the 'Terrible Twos' was an outmoded concept. 'It was always just a catchphrase, darling. These days, child behaviourists are talking about "threenagers".'

'Really?'

'"Ferocious Fours" as well. It's an ongoing thing, and one has to accept that labelling children's conduct is part of the problem. We need to go with the flow.'

The irony of Helen's use of the very expression he'd had in mind when he'd first stood on Penny's doorstep hadn't been lost on David, and the thought of the years ahead weighed on his mind. Looking listlessly at his daughter's doll's house, he found himself thinking of Penny's flat, every part of which he remembered as quintessentially adult. Its glass surfaces, white leather sofas, stripped, polished floorboards and exposed brick. The staircase, with its open treads and brushed-steel banister. The immaculate bathroom empty of rubber duckies, and faintly scented by the Penhaligon soap Penny favoured: musky carnation with a sharp hint of clove. Penny's bedroom was as empty as her living space: white linen, huge feather pillows and a headboard in pale ash. An Eames lounge chair in one corner, and floor-to-ceiling doors concealing a modular wardrobe system that seemed to absorb everything she wore. In Blackheath, Helen left clothes all over the bedroom, a habit that, at first, David had found titillating. These days, he was as likely to trip on a teddy bear as on an item of silky underwear, and the effort of shifting her things off a chair when he wanted to tie his shoelaces was a bore.

Sitting upright and pulling in his stomach, he examined his reflection in Helen's boutique-style mirror, seeing himself as a man in his prime at a crossroads in life. Initially, he'd been reconciled to Penny's dismissal of him, not just because it relieved him of responsibility for the baby but because it lessened his fear of being found out. Not altogether, though, he thought nervously. Not now she was pregnant. Even the thought of what the tabloids could do with the story of a clandestine baby made him sweat. At her leaving party, he'd stayed as far away from Penny as possible, which had meant missing out on being in several photo spreads that had later appeared in high-end magazines. Which was a real pain, he'd told himself indignantly, since he was the one with the trending hashtags and stratospheric fanbase. But now, as if a switch had been flicked, he saw a way forward. What if the need for discretion was simply removed? What if they offered the press the story, instead of hiding it? People like Tom Cruise and Harrison Ford did and, if those weren't exactly obvious comparisons, plenty of names in TV sprang to mind.

Feeling almost dizzy, David struggled to concentrate. He

was on the up. That was clear from Dominic's behaviour on the phone. With better deals and more exposure, he could afford alimony for Helen as well as Jennifer. So why not move on? Staring at himself in the mirror, he remembered his first sight of Demi and Chloë, two blobs on a scan where he'd anticipated one. They were sweet, but he'd never wanted them, he told himself resentfully. A houseful of screaming little girls hadn't been part of the deal.

Raising a son with Penny would be different. Penny would never fill her home with pink plastic, or chintz, or stupid mirrors. She'd never wear Cath Kidston aprons, or freeze portions of casserole, or want him to sign autographs for people she'd known at school. They'd go out to eat or order exotic takeaways. They'd lie about in matching cashmere robes. The baby wouldn't have food fads or tantrums. Obviously, it would need a cot in a corner of the bedroom, but Penny wouldn't put ruffles on it, or leave a changing-mat on the bathroom floor. Probably, there'd be screens – Finnish ones, made of blond wood, or something in steel and parchment – that would banish clutter and serve as a background for magazine photo-shoots.

Running his hand through his mop of hair, David assured himself that, with decent lighting, he could ease his current image into something equally sexy but more dignified. Something that would take him to a whole new level. Compared to Helen, Penny couldn't be called much of a looker, but she scrubbed-up well for awards ceremonies, so she'd be fine on his arm. He wasn't sure he fancied the thought of still being her employee, but the chances were that she wouldn't want to go back to work when she'd had the baby. Women didn't, he told himself complacently.

Helen hadn't anyway, and Jennifer seemed happy to spend her life on skiing holidays at his expense.

Enchanted by possibilities, he stood up and struck a pose, telling himself that, actually, he looked pretty damn good. With Dominic unleashed, he ought to be able to wangle his own series. Totally different from anything ever produced before. He couldn't think what the format might be but, no doubt, Penny would know. Actually, that was the answer. She could become his manager. Or creative consultant. The person who'd find the vehicle that would launch his new career. There was no denying she had skills and contacts he lacked. Which was the point. They'd be a team. A family unit. He could see her now, the baby on her hip and an iPhone in her hand, taking calls from Hollywood on his behalf. She'd look at him adoringly as he strode in from an interview, and he'd whisk her off to lunch in one of his five-star restaurants, each of which would have his name in gold letters over the door. Forgetting to hold his stomach in, David searched for his phone among the litter of plastic cupcakes on the sofa. He'd seen the way out and the way forward. He'd found the answer. All he needed to do was convince Penny that he was right.

Chapter Thirty-Two

With the onset of winter Penny no longer left her kitchen window ajar for Stanley. On a Saturday morning she came downstairs to find him glaring through the glass. Opening the window to let him in, she saw Aaron and Kit in the yard below and, leaning out, called a greeting. Aaron looked up and waved before disappearing into Mark's shed. Later, having eaten and had her coffee, she carried Stanley down to the shop. 'Here you go. He's decided to make me his breakfast-bar of choice.' Mark laughed. 'I bet he's eaten in six other kitchens this morning.' Stanley jumped onto the chaise longue and began washing his whiskers. Scooping him up, Mark carried him towards the back door, followed by Penny, who asked about Leeann's kids. 'It looks like they've got a production line out there. What's going on?'

'They're being entrepreneurs.'

In the yard, a trestle table was ranged with paint pots. On the ground was a pile of twiggy branches and, as Mark and Penny emerged from the shop, Kit was working with secateurs,

Felicity Hayes-McCoy

trimming a branch into a balanced shape. Mark asked her how things were coming along. 'Good. We've done most in white or silver, like we always do. But the next batch is going to be all the colours of the rainbow. Or as many as we've managed to blag from Denzil.'

Mark grinned at Penny. 'Denzil sells builders' supplies under the arches at Vauxhall. He's a mate of Charlie's.' Aaron came out of the shed and picked up the story. 'We get the branches from a mate of Bill's who does landscape gardening. Me and Kit trim them up, paint them and fix them in pots. Charlie sells them at his flower stall as alternative Christmas trees.'

Kit glowered as she began work on another branch. 'Stupid numbers of conifers end up in bins on Boxing Day. Some councils compost them, but it's still pretty silly. These are by-products, and all our paint is water-based. Plus, if you've somewhere to store one, you can reuse it.'

Aaron, who was stirring paint vigorously, looked up and cocked an eye at Penny. 'I can put you down for one, if you want. We do different heights and prices.'

Before Penny could answer, Mark intervened. 'Shut up, you little hustler. Penny's a mate.'

Aaron grinned at him. 'Mate's rates. Obviously.'

'I said drop it. And bear in mind, you and Kit have the use of my shed for your enterprise. Don't push your luck.' Kit asked if Mark still had plans to go to the New Forest and, if so, would he bring back some pine cones. 'You said you were thinking of driving there, and we need some.'

'I'm going today, as it happens. I'll get you some cones if I've time, but I'm making no promises. All right?'

'Okay. As Bill says, if you don't ask, you don't get.'

Mark explained to Penny that he was driving down to view a house clearance. He bent to set down the cat, seemed to come to a decision, and looked up at her. 'Hey, why don't you come along? It's chilly, but the weather's set fine and the New Forest is beautiful. We might find a hotel for tea.'

Aaron pointed out that Mark had said he mightn't have time to gather pine cones. 'And now you're saying you're going to stop for tea?'

Kit gave her brother a shove. 'What part of "Don't push your luck" do you not understand, boy?'

Ignoring the spat, Penny smiled at Mark. 'I'd love an outing.'

'Really? Okay. Great.'

'I definitely won't be bending over to pick up pine cones, though.'

'No problem. I'll do the forest foraging and you can be my auction adviser.'

Penny went back upstairs to fetch a sweater, and was taking one from a wardrobe drawer when her phone rang. Hitching it from her back pocket, she looked at the screen and saw the call was from David. Her jaw sagged and, dropping the sweater, she sat down heavily on her Eames chair. Dear God, she thought, this is not meant to happen. He's not supposed to be calling me while I'm deciding whether or not to call him. But she couldn't sit frozen for ever while the phone shrilled in her hand and her mind did somersaults. So, she took the call and, before she could speak, David's voice sounded urgently in her ear. 'Look, I've got to be quick, but this is important. You and I need to talk.'

'What about?'

'Can we meet? We need to look at the future, Penny. I'm talking family. Things are different now.'

Penny's mind did a triple-loop somersault. He was talking family? Looking to the future? Did this mean her first theory had been right all along?

'Penny? Are you there? Did you hear me?'

'What? Yes.' Penny tightened her grip on the phone. 'Yes, okay. Let's meet. You're right. I'd thought of giving you a call. I can see that things are different ... I mean, in the last few weeks I've wondered ... I mean, since the second scan I've been seeing all sorts of things differently ...'

'You were going to call me?'

'I thought of it. Yes.'

David's voice became decisive. 'Okay. We've got this, Penny. We can do it together. Trust me. We're a team. We'll find a way.'

Aware that Mark was waiting downstairs, Penny asked no more questions. She fixed a date for a meeting, ended the call and, as she picked up her sweater, told herself that this was a responsible step to take. And, actually, it was far better that David had made the running, since she had no plausible reason to call him, now she'd left work. I'm sorry things keep shifting, she told the baby, but I promise they're going to be fine. David and I will meet and come to some sort of arrangement about access. And now I'm going to focus, regroup and prioritise. You and I are off to the New Forest and we're not going to let a phone call interfere with our day out.

Meanwhile, in a Blackheath coffee shop, David was knocking back an espresso. It had all been so much easier than he'd imagined. He and Penny were on the same wavelength. In fact, she'd been way ahead of him. She'd seen that things were different. She'd been going to give him a call. She totally thought they had a future together. It's all actually happening, he thought triumphantly. The stratospheric stats have done the business, and you, David Faber, are moving on, moving out and moving up!

Mark parked the car in the lane by the house and led Penny into the chilly 1930s hallway. Everything from the furniture to the pots and pans in the kitchen was tagged with numbers and either stood about the rooms forlornly or was crammed into cardboard boxes. Mark took Penny's elbow. 'Don't worry. I know what I want to look at and we can ignore the rest.' Upstairs, having inspected a motley collection of wicker hampers and baskets, he made for a stack of bed linen, displayed on a chest of drawers. 'This looked good in the photos online, but let's see.'

After a moment, he moved on to a half-open drawer, which was full of napkins, handkerchiefs and flat boxes of tray cloths. 'This is better. The bed linen's nothing special, but check out the drawn thread work on these. White on white always sells. Mind you, the undyed crash with the blue geometric design would frame well.' Aware that she hadn't even noticed the length of coarse cotton, Penny turned it over and saw he was right. Mark winked at her. 'See, that's the mudlark in me. No stone left unturned.' Having flipped efficiently through the drawer, he piloted Penny downstairs and into the back garden, to consider the contents of a ramshackle greenhouse. 'Bingo! Look at these super terracotta pots. Those deckchairs. And a mangle! That must have come from a previous house. It's Victorian.'

'What on earth would you do with a mangle?'

'Remove the rollers, keep the frame, install a couple of shelves and you've got a side table. People love decorative ironwork. There's lots of options. Whack in some customised storage, and it's a display for your wine collection.'

'Really?'

'Absolutely. Someone will probably outbid me on this. They're getting fashionable. I could do something with the slatted greenhouse shelving, though, and the wicker hampers upstairs and that stuff in the chest of drawers. And I love the collection of lamps in the hallway. There's a couple of non-starters there but if they'd throw in the Bakelite phone, I wouldn't say no.'

Penny laughed. 'You do know you sound exactly like Bill?'

'I'll take that as a compliment. Look, I want to nip back for a word with the auctioneer's rep. There's a sunny corner here and that bench looks solid. You sit down and, when I'm done, we can go for a forest stroll. Or are you hungry? Would you like lunch?'

'No, let's walk, and have tea later. If you don't need to get back?'

'Nope. Bill's minding the shop.'

She sat down, thinking that this was unlike any other time she'd spent with Mark. Usually, they'd have a drink in one of the noisy pubs around Borough Market, or grab a pizza, see a film, and go their separate ways. Today they'd had over an hour in his car, talking non-stop. For the first time, she'd asked if Mark always wanted to take over Bill's shop. Mark's laugh had been rueful. 'Gosh, no. And the timing was dreadful. I'd just found a flat in Rome. Still, Mum was desperate for Dad to retire, and he would have refused if I hadn't been there to step in. You do what you have to, don't you, when it's family? The shop was my granddad's, and he'd started out selling junk off a barrow. Dad would have worked himself to death before he'd let it go.'

Penny had wondered what her own response might be in similar circumstances. I'd probably try throwing money at the problem, she'd thought honestly. And if it came to changing my life, I doubt if I'd do it with Mark's grace and good humour. She'd asked what he'd planned to do in Rome, and he'd chuckled. 'I'd a notion I might end up as an artist. Looking back, I suspect Fate spared me humiliation.'

'So, you wouldn't leave the shop now, even if you could?'

'No chance. I love it. Plus, I'm being educated by Kit.'

'Seriously?'

'Kit's a force to be reckoned with. So are the people who work for me. I'm lucky, I have a great team.' As he'd turned off the motorway, Mark had glanced across at her. 'But you know what that's like. You've built a team too.' She'd nodded, but now she told herself it wasn't the same thing. The idea of learning from the people she worked with hadn't occurred to her, and she knew that if anyone on her team thought they had something to teach her, they were unlikely to say so out loud.

When Mark came back, they drove to Lyndhurst and booked a table for tea. He parked behind the hotel, saying it wasn't far to walk to the forest.

'Good, because I'm slow on my feet, these days.'

'If you need one, we'll find a place for you to sit down.'

The sun was filling the air with the scent of conifers. Mark fell into step beside Penny, adapting his pace to hers. 'How does being on leave feel?'

'Weird, if I'm honest. I still watch the show each morning, but I'm just a viewer now. It's bizarre not to be able to access stats.'

'Maybe you should try going cold turkey.'

'Way too radical!'

Mark laughed. 'I guess you need to keep in touch if you're going to be up to speed when you go back.'

'I'm not sure that I am going back.' It was the first time she'd said this aloud and, true to form, Mark made no comment. Penny wrinkled her nose. 'I should think there's a chance they won't want me.'

'Why? You made the show and it's a huge success.'

'True, but they won't remember that if someone cheaper can keep it rolling.'

'That is so crap.'

'It's television.'

'So, what'll you do?'

'Cope. Now, what about these pine cones?'

Apparently unfazed by this brusque change of subject, Mark indicated a bench by the path. 'Take a seat and I'll forage. Then we'll go and eat cake.'

They returned to the half-timbered, red-brick hotel with a bulging bag of several species of cones, and were shown to a table by a mullioned window. Penny sat down and considered the array of finger sandwiches, scones, jams, cream, macaroons and cake. 'It's just as well that neither of us had lunch.'

'It's not actually obligatory to polish it all off.'

'Well, watch, because I'm about to.'

They chatted with perfect ease, everything was delicious, and the walk had stimulated their appetites. Tipping sugar into her tea as she described the sculpture she'd seen in Spitalfields, Penny folded over the top of the half-empty sachet. Still concentrating on what she was saying, she tucked it into her pocket and found Mark observing her with amusement. 'Waste not, want not?'

Penny blushed. 'Nothing so sensible. I grew up with a mum who was always worried about money. She never said so, but I knew, and I guess I developed pointless little neurotic habits.'

'It's not pointless if you keep the sugar and use it.'

'I don't. I find it in my pockets and throw it away.'

Mark laughed. 'Bill never shut up about money when I was a kid. He had all sorts of rules he'd learned from his dad, the rag-and-bone man. Money in muck, and waste not, want not. Credit cards were anathema. If there wasn't the money to pay for something, you had to knuckle down to work and raise it.'

'Was your granddad really a rag-and-bone man?'

'He was one of the last that went round the estates offering money for old iron. If people had other things to get rid of too, he'd take them and sell them down East Street market.'

Penny fiddled with the half-empty sachet. 'I couldn't wait to make my own money. I didn't want to be a burden to Mum or my grandparents. I think she refused to take money from them, and I felt I ought to be equally independent.'

'Was that the only reason you went into telly?'

'At first. Totally. I knew I could learn the skills and that I had the drive to make it.'

'You're a determined woman. I saw that the day we met, when I sold you a tin kettle.'

'Um. I'm not sure determination is always admirable. It could just amount to acquisitiveness and an urge to dominate.'

Mark raised his eyebrows at her over a smoked-salmon sandwich. 'What were your other reasons for choosing telly?'

'I suppose I found them out as I went along. I've always loved the hidden stories behind the obvious ones. Pictures in sequences tell stories, and what they say depends on how you juxtapose them. I like that. There's something amazing about how vision-mixing makes a story come together.'

'Sounds like you should be making programmes, not being a hotshot exec.'

Penny shrugged. 'Maybe you're right, but that's not where the money is. But, look, I want to know more about rag-and-bone men. Did they really buy and sell bones?' The conversation continued to ramble between the past and the present, and by the second pot of tea, she'd told him that she'd planned a meeting with the baby's father. 'In a week or so, just before Christmas.'

'I didn't know you were in touch. I mean, I thought that was what you told Leeann at Bill's party.'

'I did. And we're not. It's just that we have to organise the future. He rang me. Well, I was going to ring him and he got in first. We both want him to keep in touch. For the baby's sake.' With a feeling that she was babbling, Penny took a macaroon.

Mark appeared to be concentrating on cake. He nodded. 'Of course.'

Penny crunched pistachio and took a sip of tea. There was a pause before she spoke again. 'I meant to say, it's nice of you to offer to store my bike in your shed when I buy the baby a pushchair. There sure as hell won't be room to keep them both in my hallway.'

'No problem. It was Leeann's idea.'

'Well, thank you.'

'Not at all. When the kids' Christmas trees are gone, I'll come in and wheel it round.'

'Thank you.'

Over a third pot of tea, and on the drive back to London, they recaptured the easy intimacy with which the day had begun, and when Penny got out of the car she wondered if she'd imagined that moment when things had grown strangely formal. Mark, who had cursed himself heartily for allowing the moment to happen, said goodbye with a cheerful peck on her cheek. 'I hope you're not tired.'

'Not a bit. It was lovely. Just what I needed.'

When Mark came into the shop, Bill had already closed up and was reading a paper. 'You took your time, didn't you? Any joy at the sale?'

'Couple or three lots I might bid for online. Anything here?'

'Bits and pieces I wouldn't give five bob for. I took a few hundred, though. I've got to admit you're making a go of it, son.' Bill gave him a shrewd glance over his newspaper. 'How was your day otherwise?'

Mark frowned and lifted Stanley off the chaise longue. 'I told you not to let this guy sit on the furniture.'

'Never mind a few cat hairs. Answer the question.'

'I got those pine cones the kids wanted.'

Bill clicked his teeth in disgust. 'For God's sake, spit it out, will you? What's the story with you and Penny?'

Mark gave Bill a level look. 'Back off, Dad. There's nothing to see.'

'I'm not as green as I'm cabbage-looking. Nor's your mum. She's the one who's been asking.'

'Look, Penny's about to have a baby. This is not the time.'

'We're right, though, aren't we? The kids are convinced too, by the way. You fancy her.'

Mark pulled a face. 'It's a lot more than that.'

'Then get in there. This is when they're vulnerable. Put her up a few shelves. Buy flowers.'

'Is that how you got Mum?'

'Your mum hasn't a vulnerable bone in her body. Anyway, she was the one who got me. I'm not complaining, mind, but I hadn't much choice.'

Mark grinned. 'She had a dream.'

'What? Oh, that stupid ABBA song. That was it. She set her sights on me and refused to take no for an answer. It's not a bad tactic. You should try it.' Mark put Stanley out of the back door and returned, saying he'd buy Bill a drink out of his vast takings. Bill sniffed. 'And that's it? End of discussion? What do I tell your mum?'

'Tell her she ought to listen to the words of her own song. I don't go in for strong-arm stuff. Tell her I'll know when the time is right for me.'

Bill shrugged, folded his paper and shoved it into his pocket. 'If you don't ask, you don't get, remember? You just make sure you don't miss your chance, boy. They're few enough and they don't come round too often.'

Chapter Thirty-Three

Like Val, Marguerite was aware that time to work on the keepsake quilt was fast running out. So, when the card group's winter rota appeared in her in-box, she was glad to find she wasn't expected to host again until the new year. By now, her drawing-room table was covered with fabric pieces, and it was easier to drive to play at someone else's house than to have to clear the piles away and reorganise them when her guests were gone.

On her retirement, she'd secretly wondered if, after so long in London, she might find little to do in Wicklow. Instead, she'd slotted back easily into the seasonal round she'd known in her childhood. It was generations since Stonehill had been home to the local rector, but flowers from its garden had always decked the altar at church festivals, and the present incumbent, who also cared for three other dwindling congregations, had expected the tradition to be kept up.

As a child, Marguerite had helped to put lilies on the Easter altar, and bring holly, ivy and hyacinths from Stonehill to the church at Christmas, so it was pleasant to find familiar brass candlesticks still stored in the vestry, and what appeared to be the same sliver of soap in a dish by the sink where vases were filled. Soon, life had become a cheerful round of volunteering in the library, hosting and attending card nights, making trips to Dublin, and helping to organise pensioners' lunches in the village, which left her with few full days to herself.

The next cards night was held in Eve Blythe's flat. When Marguerite arrived, the door was opened by Caroline, who ushered her into the warm, brightly lit living room where curtains were drawn against the night, and Eve, in dark tweed and a gilded belt, was straightening glasses and bottles on a tray. Turning, she pecked Marguerite on the cheek. 'Nice to see someone arrive on time. Caroline will pour you a sherry. Where would you like to sit?'

Marguerite looked round appreciatively. 'What a lovely flat you have!'

Eve took her arm. 'Do sit down. I can't bear it when people hover.' She installed Marguerite in a chair and sat next to her. 'Glad you like the flat. Fair play to my nephew, he gave me exactly what I wanted. A decent-sized room to sit in, with plenty of light, and a kitchen and bedroom that don't take up too much space. I never could cook and I go to my bedroom to sleep, not loll about. There's a sensible crane contraption that means I don't have to put up with Caroline trying to bath me. Not yet, at least.' Accepting a sherry from Caroline, Eve asked where the quails' eggs were.

'In the kitchen.'

'Well, bring them in and, for Heaven's sake, don't forget the celery salt.'

As Caroline gave her a tolerant smile and disappeared into the kitchen, Eve rolled her eyes at Marguerite. 'You see what I have to put up with? I swear she thinks I'm gaga.'

Refusing to rise to this well-worn bait, Marguerite looked around and remarked that Eve owned some interesting paintings. There was a resolutely unsentimental portrait and several unframed abstract works. She asked if any had been done by Eve's mother.

Eve chuckled. 'Most of them. That's her in the portrait, influenced by Evie Hone. The abstracts are her attempts at Mainie Jellett. Actually, I don't think those are bad.'

Marguerite stood up and examined a series of interlocking cubes and spheres, painted in strong colours with bold black outlines. Beyond them there was an arrangement of framed pencil sketches. 'Are these the ones your mother made in the churchyard, while you were annoying the curate?'

'The very ones. You can see how the church's stained-glass windows influenced the abstract. I imagine that's why it's a success. Most of the rest of her work arose from painful attempts to copy things she'd seen in galleries.' Eve waved her glass at another painting. 'That's me in my heyday, by Justin MacMahon.' It was a portrait of a girl leaning on the back of a chair. Her hair and dress were suggested in spare brushstrokes but the detail of the face was precisely rendered. Eve chuckled again. 'He's caught my boredom, anyway.'

'You were beautiful.'

'I know. That's why my mother's friends found me useful as a model. Mind you, I also turned up with no hair and my eyes on my bum. If your technique's rocky, it's good to be able to claim that you're avant-garde. MacMahon was different, though. He could actually paint.'

Marguerite looked at the indifferent eyes and drooping mouth in the portrait. 'I thought you said you were madly in love with him.'

'It had worn off by then. Even as a girl, I could recognise egomania. Not just self-obsession which, God knows, they all had. That young man was mad, bad and dangerous to know.'

'What became of him?'

'I've no idea. He disappeared. Probably lost interest in my poor mother's circle. He wasn't one for gatherings and parties. Mark you, having offered to host tonight's shindig, I've a certain sympathy with that position. Far too much shopping and faff beforehand, and all that drudgery afterwards when everybody's gone.' Marguerite suppressed a smile, aware that Caroline had spent the day in shopping and preparation, and was likely still to be clearing up when Eve had gone to bed. Eve acknowledged her unspoken thought with one of her wicked grins. 'You're right, of course. Oh, Lord, there's the doorbell. What do you think the chances are of a decent game tonight?'

The following day, with Christmas on the horizon, Marguerite decided the time had come to commit to assembling her side of the keepsake quilt. After a morning walk to the village, and a charity fundraising meeting that took up much of the afternoon, she lit a fire in the drawing room before starting her work. As the flames rose on the hearth, she looked up at Ruth's portrait, thinking how differently MacMahon had treated his two subjects. While Eve's hair and dress were hardly suggested, each detail in his portrait of Ruth was rendered with photographic precision. And Ruth's face, the antithesis of Eve's bored indifference, looked preternaturally alive. Perhaps that's it, thought Marguerite. It's not just the dress and the Hollywood hairdo that make her unrecognisable. It's something to do with how this picture is painted. Something I've never been able to pin down.

Getting up, she went to the table, remembering how she'd told Val that thinking-time and selection were as important as cutting, piecing and quilting. Now the time had come to make irrevocable choices, not that they were likely to matter too much to Penny's baby. When I was small, thought Marguerite, I barely noticed the design of Ruth's quilt. I dare say I found the colours and shapes attractive, but its comfort came from touch, not appearance, and the sense of safety it gave me was all about warmth and familiarity. It never occurred to me to wonder about the choices my mum made. And, since she never told me, I'll never know.

Half an hour later, Marguerite had committed to a layout. She'd stuck to simple squares and straight lines and, in juxtaposing pieces, had borne in mind that some of the damage to Ruth's quilt had been caused by the positioning of fabrics of differing weights. Marguerite looked down at the table where embroidered sections from her wedding dress were interspersed with remnants from years of dressmaking done for Val and Penny. These would frame Ruth's central block within the border that would bind the two sides of the keepsake quilt. Just what I wanted, thought Marguerite, happily. It's simple but it's going to work. Each piece will be a chapter in a story told by the patchwork and, when Val's side and mine are quilted together and edged, they'll make a family heirloom.

Next, she needed to take the centrepiece from her mother's

quilt. Before going to fetch it, she added a log to the fire. It was apple wood from a fallen tree in the orchard, and as the heat caught the bark, it threw up a long tongue of flame. Upstairs, as she opened the cupboard where the quilt lay in its box, she wondered if, when she'd completed her layout, she'd find something in the dusky garden to put on the hall table, where purple and yellow winter pansies were starting to droop. Standing on a chair, she lifted the box and blew dust off its lid, revealing the logo of a long-gone florist and a faded image of a sheaf of flowers. The attic was chilly and Marguerite shivered. Carrying the box, she went back to the fire and, using a seam ripper, began to separate the centrepiece from its surrounding patchwork.

Each of the four central satin pieces was a different colourway of a print of floral sprigs on a plain background. Marguerite worked carefully, cutting and removing threads and easing one edge of the first piece of satin away from the piece beside it. To hold the fabric taut on her knee as she ripped through the stitches, she slipped two fingers through the slit she'd created. To her surprise, they encountered a layer of paper between the satin and the batting. Marguerite felt for the edges of the paper, wondering if Ruth had incorporated it in the whole central block. Generally, paper was used in intricate designs that had shapes like hexagons. Why would anyone bother with it when working with simple squares?

It struck Marguerite that hand-sewn quilts turned up in Hollywood films, as a kind of symbol of courage and homely values. Pioneer women had used a technique, called English Paper Piecing, in which complex shapes were basted to paper templates that were often left inside the quilt. Did Ruth, being American, and an inexperienced quilter, think all quilts were made that way? Or did she assume that a central block required it, even though all of her pieces had straight sides? Moving her fingers, Marguerite found that the paper hadn't been basted onto the satin and, when she had cut several more stitches, it slid out easily. As it lay on her lap, she realised she was looking at a letter, written in an untidy hand in blue-black ink. The writing covered the entire sheet of paper, front and back. There were no margins, as if the page had been trimmed to fit behind the satin piece.

My Darling Ruth,

You left me more than an hour ago. I still can't believe you went. You probably think I've gone into a frenzy of painting. That's what you said I'd do, and you've no idea how ludicrous you sounded. I haven't been painting. I've been sitting here, cursing you and drinking Bovril. You haven't a clue about artists or art – or me, if it comes to that – and I couldn't care less that you haven't. I don't want an acolyte cleaning my brushes and telling people I'm brilliant. I don't want your opinion of painting. You've nothing to say that matters. I've told you a hundred times what I want. I want you. I can't do without you. I can't paint, I can't think, I can't breathe, damn you. You're necessary to me. I love you. You love me too. You said you do, so what are you playing at?

I won't believe you're not coming with me. You're necessary to me. We've made our plans. Your marriage was a mistake. I don't see why you can't tell Donal the truth and be done with it. The chances are that you don't understand him either. I'd want the truth if I were him. Any man would.

You kept saying I wasn't listening to you. Well, I was. I don't see why a baby should make a difference. Why can't you see that? I need you. Why else would I have put up with your stupid notions about fidelity? All that guff about not being able to face Donal if you'd slept with me. I listened to that, didn't I? I came up with Paris as the solution. You said yes. We made our decision. Why should the fact that you're pregnant change any of that?

If you want to keep the baby, I won't complain. I don't mind babies. I've told you that. If you have it in Paris, it'll grow up somewhere decent anyway. Why would you want to rear a child in this stupid, benighted country? Or if you can't bear to take it from Donal, come with me now, have it, and send it back to him. Or just don't tell him about it. What he won't know won't hurt him.

I know I shouted. That's why I'm writing this letter. I'm calm now and I'm making my case and you have to listen to me. You keep saying you can't take his child from Donal, and you can't leave it behind, so you have to stay. That's nonsense. You don't love him. If you did, you'd never have promised to come away with me. And if you don't love Donal, why would you want his child? Why would Donal want you, for that matter? He's not stupid. You won't fool him, you're only fooling yourself. You say the proof that you love him is that you can't break his heart. You and I know better. You can't play with fire without being burned, and you're scorched inside now. You're hollow and black and empty. That's what you're taking home to him, Ruth, and that's what'll break his heart. When you're with me there's a flame inside you, living and bright and vital. Without me, you'll just get colder and colder until you lie down and die.

This is your doing, not mine. You chose to play at being a patron and throw stupid parties. You persuaded your husband to pay for a portrait. I'm just the painter who got caught in the middle. You won't do this now. I know you won't. If you give a tuppenny damn for my work, you won't walk away and destroy me. I'll be down at the docks at the North Wall for tonight's sailing. You have your ticket and if you're not there I won't look back any more than you did when you walked out today. I mean it. I'll be there till the ship sails. You'd better come, Ruth. I love your eyes and I love your hair and your stupid, meddling hands, and I love the bones of you.

Justin

Chapter Thirty-Four

Marguerite's first reaction was to let the quilt and the letter fall from her knee. Then, without thinking, she slipped from her chair and crouched by the hissing fire. Though the bark of the apple log was dry, the green pith was exuding bubbles that looked like rows of beadwork. She sat staring at them for a long time, wishing that Rex or Rufus, or any of the Stonehill spaniels, could pad in from the hall and place a fringed paw on her knee.

After a while, she realised she was cold. The garden beyond the French doors was in darkness, and the fire had burned down to little more than a glow. Marguerite stood up stiffly, added more wood, and went to draw the curtains and switch on the lamps. The letter lay on the hearthrug, half under the ripped quilt that had hidden it for more than seventy years. Lifting the quilt, Marguerite wondered about the flowers its box had once contained. They could have been ordered by Donal for Ruth to celebrate my birth, she thought. Perhaps they were. I'll never know. Just as I'll never know if my birth was cause for celebration. Did Donal know about Ruth's affair? Did he suspect it from the start? Might he have begun to wonder as he watched her sink into her deep depression?

Picking up the letter, she sat on the hearthrug again. *You can't play with fire without being burned, and you're scorched inside now. You're hollow and black and empty. That's what you're taking home to him, Ruth, and that's what'll break his heart. When you're with me there's a flame inside you, living and bright and vital. Without me, you'll just get colder and colder until you lie down and die.* That's what he caught in the painting, thought Marguerite. It really does look as if she's lit from within. Poor Mum. The flame must have scorched her beyond hope of recovery, and Dad, who was a doctor, watched her suffer and had no cure.

Though the room was warming, Marguerite still felt chilly. It's shock, she thought. Paul would say I ought to have something to eat. Soup would warm me. But the idea of assembling a meal seemed too complicated, so she switched off the lights, locked up, and went upstairs to bed. Huddled under the duvet, she found her mind racing. Did Ruth tell Donal the truth? Or, having made her choice, did she decide she must keep her secret? If so, thought Marguerite, did she keep the secret till the day she died? She didn't sleep with Justin – that's clear from the letter – but if Dad suspected she'd had an affair, and she never told him about it, how could he have been certain that I was his child?

Turning over to lie on her back, Marguerite recalled Mrs Sinnott's memory of Ruth making her quilt: '... *she was pregnant. Not a notion of how to sew, and she determined to set every stitch herself.*' Why had she put the letter inside it? Was she so much in love with Justin she couldn't bear to destroy it? Did she want me to find it sometime? Did she need me to know that she'd made the choice to stay here with me and Dad? Turning on her side again, Marguerite thought that Eve's assessment of Justin had been right. He was an unashamed egotist and dangerous to know. Had Ruth realised that at the last minute, or had she remained besotted to the end?

Though it seemed to Marguerite that she would lie awake for ever, she drifted into a troubled sleep and woke several hours later, aware that she'd been having a vivid dream. It had taken her back to the moonlit night when she'd leaned out of the window and seen her mother standing in the rain. In the improbable way of dreams, Ruth had seemed both far away and very close. Each individual seed in the meadow grasses had shone like silver, and the pattern on Ruth's dressing-gown had stood out as distinctly as if Marguerite were standing right beside her. Marguerite tried to recall what had come next. The dream-rain had fallen heavily. Donal was lying asleep in the meadow at Ruth's feet. Then they'd all been together in the drawing room and Donal had laid his hand on Ruth's shoulder. *'You did your best. You can't let it trouble you.'*

Ruth had reached up and touched his face. *'I don't know how I'd manage without you, d'you know that?'*

'You'd be fine.'

'No, I wouldn't.'

'Okay, maybe you wouldn't, but I'm here, so don't fret.'

But that's not right, though Marguerite. That's not how it actually happened. That's not what I overheard when I was a child. It was he who told her he didn't know how he'd manage without her, and she who reassured him and said she was there, so he mustn't fret. Already the dream was receding and, feeling parched, Marguerite pushed back her duvet and went to the bathroom for a glass of water. Her mind felt blanketed by exhaustion, and the effort of untangling the wisps from the past was too great. But, just as had happened when, as a child, she'd overheard her parents' conversation, she returned to bed and slept deeply with a sense that nothing more needed to be done.

The following morning, though still tired and shocked, Marguerite decided she mustn't let what she'd discovered distract her from the keepsake quilt. She'd agreed with Val that she'd buy batting to fit between its two sides when they quilted them together, and bring it along with her pieced work when she flew to London for Christmas. So today, she thought, I'll take the train up to Dublin, find the batting, and have lunch somewhere while I'm in town. She drove to Greystones, which was the easiest place to park the car, and caught the Dart to Tara Street station. Walking up the quays and cutting through to the side of Trinity College, she remembered the days when she'd spend her hoarded pocket money in shops like Hickey's in Henry Street, where she'd found the cheesecloth and embroidery silks for her wedding dress. Like so many other shops she'd known, Hickey's was long gone, so she headed for the Cloth Shop in Westbury Mall and found the cotton batting she and Val had decided on.

As she left the mall, where Christmas displays glittered in every window, Marguerite thought of how Ruth must have felt on the day she'd come up to Dublin to tell Justin she was pregnant. Did she take the bus or come by train and walk from the station? Was he expecting her or did she burst in unannounced? Eve had said Justin had lived in a tiny room in a house in Harcourt Street. For a moment, Marguerite was tempted to walk there, but to wander up and down with no idea which house it had been seemed ridiculous. And what would be the point? She had turned away and begun to walk back down Grafton Street when it crossed her mind that she could have lunch in the National Gallery café. While I'm there, she thought, I could find out if any of Justin's work is in the collection. Even if there isn't, there might be information about him. Suddenly, it seemed important to know that he'd gone off to Paris, and hadn't been hanging around in the background of her parents' marriage. Hard as it was to think of Ruth devastated by losing him, it was worse to think that her fluctuating levels of depression could have been linked to a continuing on-off affair.

The gallery's Millennium Wing was built on a site once occupied by eighteenth-century houses. Those that remained on either side were linked by its high atrium where, in a glazed area that had once been a Georgian family's garden, rows of café tables stood on a shining white floor. With a sense that this was another instance of the past being pieced to the present, Marguerite carried her tray to a table facing three storeys of curved eighteenth-century windows and, hardly noticing what she'd ordered, sat down and ate lunch. Afterwards, she approached an information desk, feeling uncertain of what she wanted to say. The guy manning the desk took her faltering enquiry in his stride. 'You can view our whole collection online if you go to our website. Or, just a minute, maybe Sonja can help.' A young woman who'd been passing stopped at the sound of her name. 'Is there something specific you need to know?'

'I'm interested in an artist called Justin MacMahon. He was working in Dublin in the 1950s.'

The woman nodded. 'I'm Sonja Flynn. I'm on the staff here. I've been doing some work on the 1950s. Look, we're in the way, would you like to talk in my room?' Realising that a queue had formed behind her, Marguerite apologised and stepped aside. 'I'm Marguerite Carson. I'm sure you're busy ...'

'Not at all.' Sonja ushered her towards a door and swiped the lock with a keycard. 'Come through. We have very little by MacMahon, and it isn't on display. What's your interest in his work?'

'I have a portrait by him.'

'Really? Wow. I'm glad you came in.'

'Was he significant?'

'He was quite a painter.' Sonja led her into an office and offered her a chair. 'I can pull up what we have on the computer. But tell me about your portrait.'

'It's of my mother. I think she knew a group of Dublin artists at the time. Sort of avant-garde?'

'There were plenty about. The 1950s saw a big post-war surge of international art and culture. Ireland hadn't been bombed to ruins, like much of the rest of Europe, but people had lived with the constant threat of invasion. And, in fact, there was some bombing here in Dublin, and rationing, and a sense of being cut off from the outside world.' As she spoke, Sonja was scrolling through screens. 'So, when the war ended, things opened up and people were eager to travel and build a future based on shared aspirations.' Clicking on an image, she turned her laptop to Marguerite. 'This is all we've got. Studies for a portrait.'

Marguerite looked and saw three images drawn with such intensity that they seemed to leap off the screen. She clasped her hands in her lap to stop them shaking. 'That's my mum.'

'And you've got the finished portrait? That's amazing.'

Carefully keeping her voice level, Marguerite asked if there was background information on Justin MacMahon. 'I gather he moved to France?'

Sonja nodded. 'In 1951. Paris first. Then he lived in Brittany. He didn't come back.' This banished the fear that Justin had stayed in Dublin after all, and continued to be in touch with Ruth. As Marguerite breathed a sigh of relief, Sonja began a new search. 'I don't think he ever got taken on by a gallery. Anyway, he died young. A bit more than ten years after leaving Dublin. Let me check.'

Marguerite's hands tightened again. In her mind she could hear Mrs Sinnott's voice urging her to drink hot, sweet tea. *Your mam is dead. It was an accident. She was tired, so she went to bed and took some of the tablets that help her to sleep. She must have mistaken the dose.* For years, she thought, I've wondered if that was true. Dad and I never said so out loud, but I know we both lived with the thought that it could have been suicide. And if it was, might this be the explanation? Did Ruth find out about Justin's death and decide to follow him? Sonja's voice interrupted her. 'Here it is. Justin MacMahon. Died Rome, 1965. So, fourteen years after he left Dublin.' She looked up from her screen and smiled. 'You know, Mrs Carson, I'd love to see your portrait. Your mother was a striking subject.'

'Yes, yes, she was.' Grasping the carrier bag containing her batting, Marguerite took a deep breath and stood up. 'I'm going away for Christmas, but I'll contact you. Perhaps in the new year. You're very kind. Thank you for taking all this trouble.' She left as soon as she decently could and, once outside, told herself she needed to sit down and think. Crossing the street, she went into the grounds of Trinity College, where she would have studied pharmacy if she hadn't gone to London and met Paul. There was a bench past which streams of students were going into and out of the library.

When she sat down, her relief began to give way to the realisation that she'd never know the whole truth about her mother's death. It might have been suicide, she thought. It could have been an accident. There must have been some kind of investigation about which I knew nothing. No doubt some people gossiped about the fact that she'd been given the sleeping pills by her husband. Anyone who'd ever read an Agatha Christie would recognise the scenario in which the doctor's wife dies in mysterious circumstances. But Donal continued to practise, and the community continued to support him. And, whatever else I'm unsure about, I know he could never have harmed her, just as she couldn't bring herself to hurt him.

Carrying her shopping, Marguerite began to make her way back to the station. There were lights strung on several ships on the river and she knew that, if she crossed it and kept walking, she'd reach the quay on which Justin had waited in vain for Ruth before taking the ship to France. It was such a close call, thought Marguerite. She'd even bought her ticket. If she'd gone with him, my life would have been so different. I might have grown up to think of him as my father. I might never have known Stonehill.

It was late afternoon when she got off the train, drove back to the village, and turned down the road that led to her home. When she got indoors, she noticed she had done nothing about the drooping posy on the console table. Carrying the vase through to Donal's surgery, she lifted out the dead pansies and threw the water into the sink. She was crossing the hall, on her way out to the garden to pick replacements, when Caroline came into the porch and waved. The last thing Marguerite wanted was a chat with a passing neighbour but, knowing she'd been seen, she opened the door. Caroline smiled brightly. 'I can't stop, I'm afraid. I've got a million things to do. I just wanted to give you this. It's from Eve.' She held out a rolled-up magazine. 'It's ancient. Apparently, there's an article in it about something you and she talked about at her cards night. I'm sorry, I've got to dash.' Turning to bustle back to her car, Caroline paused and looked back at Marguerite. 'Are you okay? You look dreadfully tired.'

'I'm fine. I've been up in town. Had a long day.'

'Right. Well, enjoy the magazine. And, look, if you ever need any help, you know where I am. Just call.'

How ungrateful we are, thought Marguerite, as she watched the car disappear down the driveway. I find Caroline just as annoying as Eve does, but the truth is that, as one gets older, one has to accept that one may need help. And where would we all be without Caroline's sort of generous kindness? Leaving the magazine on the hall table, she went outdoors and picked fresh pansies from a patch that was flowering bravely between a curtain of ivy and the orchard wall.

When she'd put them into a vase, she switched on the lamps in the drawing room, then, having lit the fire, sat down with some tea and the magazine. It was rolled up in a rubber band and, when she unfurled it, she found a note from Eve tucked inside. *Thought you might like this. I knew I had it somewhere. Don't bother to return it. It'll only end up in the rubbish. Caroline's dying to have a clean sweep as soon as I pop my clogs. E.B.*

Marguerite looked at the slightly tattered pages on her knee. With a date in the spring of 1950, the in-flight magazine featured tourist destinations in Ireland, and was sprinkled with ads for airlines and maps depicting onward routes from Shannon airport to mainland Europe. One page urged tourists to 'double their vacation enjoyment' by booking TWA 'Circle Trips'. Another, complete with pictures of passengers sipping cocktails on aeroplanes and riding through green mountain ranges on donkeys, suggested that Pan Am travellers should treat an Irish stopover as the gateway to Europe. *Stay a while and discover what this Emerald Gem has to offer!*

Thinking that these were the kind of ads that must have brought Ruth to Ireland, Marguerite flipped idly through the pages and came to an article that made her gasp. Headlined *An American's Enchantment with Dublin's Vibrant Art Scene*, it was illustrated by a photo of Ruth, taken at a party in an artist's studio. She looked very excited and happy, her arm linked in Nora Blythe's, and was surrounded by a laughing group at what seemed to be the opening of an exhibition. It was clear that the text had been written by someone employed at the tourism office:

Miss Ruth Smith, a charming New Yorker en route to visit the Louvre and the Venice Biennale, was delighted to meet a vibrant group of young Irish artists and discover the warm welcome we offer to visitors to our green isle. 'I have no Irish roots but I've always been fascinated by Ireland's culture, and the landscapes I've seen in movies, and, of course, I'd heard of your reputation as Ireland of the Welcomes. What I didn't know was how splendid your art scene is, or what wonderful fashion designers you have these days.' Miss Smith told our reporter that her European trip is the culmination of a lifetime's planning and dreaming. 'I bought a whole new wardrobe of clothes especially for it and, because I was stopping in Ireland, I made sure to include a green velvet dress!' Elegantly dressed when we met her, in a wool coat and skirt and a teal-feather hat, Miss Smith has already made plans to extend her time in Ireland. 'I've made such good friends already, including the artist Nora Blythe whose work is as avant-garde as anything I expect to see in France or Italy.' We're told that, on her way back to New York, Miss Smith plans another stopover in Ireland, and that her new friends have promised her a hearty welcome back to her 'new favourite place in the world'!

Tears pricked Marguerite's eyes. She was so young, she thought. Younger than Penny is now. She'd bought a whole new wardrobe for her dream trip to Europe. It must have felt like a movie. She'd made friends with a group of artists and met a handsome Irish doctor, who lived in a white house among green mountains, like the ones she'd seen in the travel magazines. And when she married him, the dream fell apart and so did she. Poor,

poor Ruth. Poor Donal. How dreadful to see the golden girl he'd fallen so deeply in love with become the sad, introverted woman I remember. I wish he could have talked to me about it – not when I was a child, perhaps, but later on, when Paul and I were married. It wasn't in his nature, though, and perhaps he would have seen it as unethical. He never discussed his patients and I suppose, in the end, that was what Mum had become.

Marguerite looked up at her mother's portrait, thinking that, unattractive though Justin's self-obsession was, he too had been very young, and appeared to have been in Dublin with neither friends nor family to support him. Dad and I were the survivors, she thought. Maybe he was wise to say we just had to pick ourselves up and get on with living. What would have been the point of raking over the coals of their marriage? I don't think the rest of his life was unhappy but, whatever he knew or didn't know, he'd been wounded, and he always said that it didn't do to fiddle about with scar tissue.

Chapter Thirty-Five

Penny sat watching her show, aware that changes had already begun to creep into its format. Tweaks suggested by Gail and Roz, which she'd vetoed before leaving, had been added. Colette's fashion slot had a new place in the hour. And, presumably in response to her #DameJaneFame success, Lolly was being developed as a personality in the programmes' socials, with her own #LollyLoves hashtag. My maternity cover has decided to make her mark, thought Penny, and at her age I guess I'd have been the same. To her surprise, she felt shaken. It had been one thing to sit in her office speculating about this eventuality. It was something else to sit at home and watch it happening, and know that, without her, the caravan had moved on.

On the screen, Roz turned to camera and threw the viewers a knowing wink behind her guest's back. Evidently the show had also moved towards more emphasis on outrageousness, and this way, thought Penny, it's going to lose my broad demographic. On the other hand, it's making it easier for the network to target ad revenue. Not a long-term strategy, but that won't bother the new broom. The show is my baby, not hers. I'm the one who's emotionally invested in its future. She'll see it as a means to an end. The guest, still unaware that he'd been the butt of a joke, walked off to waves from the presenters.

So much for getting A-list names in future, thought Penny, grimly. No publicist will want their clients used as fodder to bolster Roz and Gail's visibility. We'll end up with Z-listers willing to put up with any humiliation for airtime, and that's the surest route to a show being scrapped. Dammit. I left so many warnings and instructions. But it's out of my control now, and there's no point in my obsessing about it. Better do what Mark suggested and stop sitting here watching. Anyway, I need to go and buy something for lunch.

Yesterday, Val had phoned, eager, as always, not to encroach on too much of Penny's time. 'Your gran's coming on the twenty-third and staying till New Year. I wondered if you'll be okay to join us on Christmas Day? Don't worry if you're not sure of your plans yet. You can let me know.'

Penny had felt guilty. More than once, she'd whirled in late to Christmas dinner in West Hampstead, arriving to a meal that was perilously close to drying out in the oven. She couldn't imagine Leeann or her sisters doing that to their mother, or Sarah putting up with it if they'd tried. And how would you feel, she'd asked herself, if you'd put your own life on hold for your baby and ended up with someone who hardly had time to spend with her family? So, she'd hastily invited Val to lunch. 'Come tomorrow, Mum. We can have a natter. And, yes, I'd love to spend Christmas with you and Gran.'

As she turned off the TV, on which Gail and Roz were now pulling funny faces, Penny winced, remembering the diffidence in Val's voice on the phone. She's always prioritised my life over hers, she thought regretfully. Everything was about giving me confidence, and space to develop. And I never really thought about her life at all. There was that year when I went camping with the Girl Guides and came home to find the back bedroom empty, and Balan gone. I liked Balan. I loved his cooking, and how relaxed things were when he was around. But he wasn't vital because, whatever happened, Mum was always there. I didn't question why he left. I could tell Mum missed him, but I never wondered if they might have got close. Perhaps they did. I wish she'd talked about things like that but, of course, she felt she mustn't. I can see that now. I'm going to want to protect my child, not treat him as a confidant. That must be how Mum felt about me. If she was scared or lonely, of course she'd hide it. She and my dad must have made so many plans for their future together, and all her hopes were lost when he was drowned. She didn't want me to grow up thinking that plans could come to nothing. She was desperate to protect me in what she saw as a hostile world. And, okay, maybe there were times when she got the balance wrong, but now I understand how she felt. Maybe today we'll sit down and talk about the future. I could ask her how she organised childcare and stuff when I was little. I could tell her I'm pretty scared, and ask for her advice.

Borough Market was buzzing with shoppers frantically buying for Christmas. Penny crossed the road and joined the crowds milling eagerly round the stalls. The iron pillars supporting the market's roof were wreathed in spruce branches and strings of multicoloured lights. Each stall had its own decorations – ribbons and streamers and paper lanterns, bundles of cinnamon sticks and pheasant feathers, towers of Turkish Delight and glacé fruits.

The air was chilly, so Penny tightened her scarf and turned up her collar. Glimpsed between people's jostling shoulders, she could see Charlie's flower stall where Kit and Aaron's branches stood decked with strings of pine cones. Edging past a queue for spiced cider, she threaded her way through the crowd to a pie stall. The vendor, who was wearing fingerless mittens, blew on his hands when he saw her. 'Hi, Penny. What can I do you? Pork, beef or salmon? Venison, if you feel like splashing out.'

His pies were nothing like the supermarket versions Penny had sometimes had in her school lunchbox. These were hand-raised, glazed, golden rounds of pastry with gloriously crimped edges, a layer of jelly inside, and a chunky, well-seasoned filling of organic meat. 'Pork, I think. Make it a medium one, please.'

'I thought pregnant women weren't supposed to go round eating for two.'

'I'm not. My mum's coming to lunch.'

'Oh, well, that's different.'

'And watch it, or I'll change my mind and ask for a small one.'

'No, you won't. No one can resist a second slice of these.' He wrapped a pie in greaseproof paper and put it into a cardboard box. 'There you go. Hope your mum enjoys it. How're you feeling these days? Everything fine?'

'Absolutely.' In the past, Penny had tended to dash through the market, grabbing something for dinner or breakfast with most of her mind on her work. Stallholders like the pie guy had picked up her name, but she'd seldom paused to chat. Since she'd taken leave from the office she'd had time to feel she was part of a neighbourhood. Stopping now and again to browse, she made her way to a stall in the shadow of Southwark Cathedral. She was standing on tiptoe to eye a basket of watercress, when she felt a tap on her shoulder. Turning, she found a young woman in the queue behind her and, feeling as if she'd been winded, realised it was Helen.

For a moment, Penny could think of nothing at all. Helen smiled at her. 'It is you, isn't it? I don't think we've met since that awards night a few years ago. Oh, sorry – you may not remember me. I'm Helen Faber.'

'Oh, no, yes, er, of course I remember you. What are you doing here?'

Helen looked slightly surprised. 'Shopping. Mainly bits and pieces for Christmas. Presents for people.'

'Oh? Right. Well, it's a great place to shop.'

'I hardly ever get here. It's cool, isn't it?'

'So cool.' As the queue shuffled closer to the stall, Penny marshalled her thoughts. There was no reason to think this meeting was anything but chance, and Helen's pleasure at seeing her seemed perfectly genuine. If I weren't so freaked, I'd feel bad about that, she thought, but right now it's all I can do to make conversation without showing what's going through my mind. Whatever I do, I mustn't panic. I need to chat, buy salad, say, 'Happy Christmas,' and get the hell out of here. And please, God, don't let her mention the baby.

Helen moved to stand beside her and beamed. 'I saw the new

name on the programme credits, and asked David why. He said you were off on parental leave. That's so exciting.'

'Yes. It is. Thank you. Um, how is David?'

'Over the moon since he had his news. Oh, but, of course, you might not know. Do you? I mean, does the company keep in touch while you're off?'

'I'm not sure what you're talking about.'

'Oh, okay, you haven't heard. David's been offered a fabulous job in the States.' Not noticing Penny's startled reaction, Helen rushed on: 'We're flying to LA in the middle of January. It's an incredible deal. They're going to pay all our moving expenses. And it's going to be his own show, broadcast from a gorgeous house they've rented for us to live in. It's huge. There's a pool and a big garden, and they want the twins and me to be in the background while he's on camera, so it's all about family. I don't know if you remember we've two little girls?'

'Yes. Yes, I've seen photos. I mean, David showed photos to the team.'

'Aw. That's sweet. Anyway, Dom, his agent, pitched the format to a US network. You know, it's really down to you, because David's personal profile was built on your show.' Helen laughed. 'Listen to me! I'm just quoting things, as if I know what I'm talking about!' Penny took another step towards the watercress, which was flanked by piles of boxes of tomatoes on the vine. Helen continued, without a scintilla of guile in her shining eyes; 'The twins are so excited!'

'I'm sure they must be.' Wishing the people ahead would get a move on, Penny searched for something to say next. 'I guess it's easy enough to move when they're not yet at school.'

'Well, they'll miss their friends, of course, but they'll make new ones. And the network's paying for us to hire a nanny and bring her along.'

Way to go, Dom, thought Penny. You really must have gone in with all guns blazing. And nobody bothered to pick up the phone and keep me in the loop. It struck her that the upside of this was that no one had thought she'd have a personal interest in David. And the downside, she reflected, is it proves that nobody considers I've any remaining involvement in my own show.

At last, they reached the front of the queue, where the stallholder shrugged when she snatched her bag of watercress from his hand. Penny felt embarrassed. 'Sorry. I'm in a rush. Meeting someone. Thank you.' Turning to Helen, she backed away, smiling. 'It's lovely to see you again. Those tomatoes look fantastic – you should buy some. Have a wonderful time in LA.'

'We will! Congratulations on the baby.'

'What? Yes. Thank you. Happy Christmas.' Penny walked away blindly. After a moment, she realised that, instead of making for home, she had reached the cathedral. Her phone rang as she passed the gate so she went to a bench in the churchyard, put down her parcels, and found a familiar number on the screen. It was David's.

'Hi, Penny. I'm glad I caught you. We need to have a word.'

'We fixed to meet tomorrow. Have you forgotten?'

'No, no, of course not. It's just— Look, I've been thinking this through and I'm wondering if we've made the right choice.'

Penny could almost see the little tic jumping in the corner of David's left eye. He's running around packing, she thought, and he wants to change the date of our meeting. Well, I'm damned if I'm going to make it easy for him. 'Penny? Are you there?' David was sounding less confident now and, as she clenched her jaw, he began to gabble. 'I know what we said. And I do care, Penny. Really. We could be great together, you and me.'

'What?'

'No, hear me out. Marrying Helen was a mistake. I was on the rebound from Jennifer. I was in a bad, bad place. I know that now.'

Penny sat down abruptly on the bench. '*What?* Wait—'

'Listen, please, I've thought it through. I know what we said, but I just can't do it.'

'David, will you shut up a minute? What do you think we said?'

'That you and I could make it together if I divorced Helen. Professionally and personally. A husband-and-wife team. But I can't do it, Penny. Really. I can't desert her. I have to stand by my marriage vows and live with the consequences.' To Penny's profound relief, her work personality reasserted itself. She allowed David's babble to run to a standstill, and waited for him to break the awkward silence. 'Penny? Are you still there?'

'Yes.'

'And you do see, don't you? You know what I'm talking about?'

'Well, I know what you're *not* talking about.'

'I don't understand.'

'Don't you? The LA deal. The gorgeous house. The pool and the garden and Mary Poppins, all conjured up with a click of

Dom's fingers. It's a great format, David. You making s'mores and apple pie, with Helen and the twins in soft focus in the background. A networked show that's all about family.'

'What? That's not even signed off yet. Who have you been talking to? Was it Dom?'

'Did you really think I wouldn't find out, David? Were you hoping it wouldn't be until you'd left the country?'

'No, but, look, don't you see— Wait, Penny, listen to me. I can explain if you'll listen. I was trying to make it easier for you. A clean break. I knew you'd be devastated but, like I said, I can't desert Helen.' David's voice strengthened and Penny could hear him begin to convince himself. 'It's going to be hard for us both, Penny. I do know what I'm doing.'

'Oh, I think we both know exactly what you're doing. You're lying to me, you've lied to Helen, and you're lying to yourself. Dom's got you the big break you've dreamed of, and all you can see or care about are the twinkling lights of LA.'

'I'm not—'

'And here's another thing. I don't know where you got the idea that I would ever want to build a life with you. You couldn't be more wrong. What I thought was that this baby should have his dad in his life at some level. Which is where I was wrong. You've nothing to offer him, David. Don't try to get in touch with me again.'

'But—'

'Oh, and, incidentally, I haven't been talking to Dom. I've been talking to Helen.'

Ending the call, Penny thrust her phone back into her pocket. That last shot was cheap, she thought, but satisfactory. It might even provoke something that makes Helen see through him before she uproots her kids and pins her future to his star. Gathering her things, and feeling uplifted by how she'd dealt with the conversation, she was about to stand up when her work personality suddenly drained away. How could she have been such an ass? she asked herself. To fail to see what he meant that time he called to fix a meeting? To tell myself he must be thinking about the baby's future? How could I lose my judgement so completely that, if Dom hadn't done this deal, I would have established a self-obsessed liar as part of my son's life?

For no reason she could understand, she had a vivid memory of Mark's face when she'd told him she was pregnant, his kindness when he'd handed her the vase of blowsy peonies, and of how he'd reacted whenever she'd spoken about the baby's father. A lump seemed to expand in her chest and she fumbled for a tissue to mop an inexplicable flood of tears. Stop it, she told herself. You're being pathetic. Focus, regroup and prioritise. But for once the mantra failed, and she sat huddled on the hard bench among passing Christmas shoppers, scrubbing her face with her orange scarf and praying no one would stop and ask if she was all right.

She was still there when the bell in the clock tower struck the hour and she realised that Val would soon be arriving at the flat. Pushing herself to her feet, she picked up the box and the bag of watercress, and set off home, skirting the edge of the market. But the tears kept flowing and the lump in her throat refused to be dislodged. We'll be fine, she assured the baby. Honestly, I've got this. We'll be good. Tomorrow I'll practise the nappy thing on Leeann's baby again. It'll be Christmas soon. After that, you'll be born, and this time next year, you and I will be in a whole new place. I don't know what that's going to be, or how I'm going to get there. I don't know how many chances I've lost through being a total idiot, but I promise you, truly, you and me will be fine. But the tears kept flowing and, frantically, Penny started to run. I have to get back to the flat, she thought, and pull myself together. Whatever happens, I can't let Mum see me in bits like this.

Desperately trying to protect her bump from the heaving crowds, she struggled back through the market. As she emerged, a delivery van pulled away from the shopfront and she saw Val, who was standing on her doorstep, push the doorbell and step back to look up at the windows above. Penny froze with one foot in the street and one on the pavement, and an approaching motorbike swerved to avoid her. Hearing its horn, Val turned, ran blindly into the road and grabbed her by the shoulders. There was hardly any traffic and Penny had been in no real danger, but they reached the pavement in a shaken state. Seeing Penny's face, Val gasped aloud. 'Darling! You look terrible. What's the matter? You're crying!'

'Nothing, I'm fine.'

'But you're not. Look at the state of you! Where's your key? Let's go up to the flat and you can tell me what's happened.'

'No!' Mortified, Penny pushed her away. 'I'm fine, really. I don't want to talk about it.' Scrabbling in her pocket, she found her latchkey. 'Look, I'm sorry. I've bought us lunch but I can't sit down and have it now. You take these.' She pushed her shopping into Val's hands and, shaking, managed to fit the key

in the lock. 'It's a pie and some salad. Watercress. The pie's pork.
I didn't get any tomatoes. I'll call you, Mum. I don't want you to
come upstairs. I'm sorry. I'm really sorry. I don't want to talk.'
By now, she'd got the door open and had stumbled through it.
Val put her foot on the threshold. 'Darling, you shouldn't be
alone. Let me come up and make you a cup of tea.'

Penny heard her own voice rise to a childish howl. '*No*, I don't
want any tea. Please, Mum, just go away. I don't want any help.
I don't want you here.'

Chapter Thirty-Six

Marguerite had returned to the keepsake quilt with a deep sense of calm. She'd never know the whole story, or why Ruth had hidden the letter, but finding it and reading the magazine article had seemed to bring her closer to her mother. The following day, having finished removing the central block from Ruth's quilt, she'd sat by the fire piecing her side of the keepsake quilt together, and begun to think about what to pack for her Christmas trip to London.

The tasks of planning her holiday wardrobe and buying presents for Val and Penny were interspersed with homely jobs, like writing cards and tying up gifts to deliver to her neighbours, and taking jars of homemade jam to be sold at a charity fair. There was little to do in the garden. The few vegetables she'd grown had been harvested and made into chutneys, and a sweet-smelling store of apples lay spread out on newspaper in one of Stonehill's cool attic rooms. Now and again as she moved through the house, making preparations, she glanced at her mother's portrait hoping that, if she could know, Ruth would be glad that the pieces she'd cut and quilted were now part of a new patchwork.

The morning before she was due to travel to London, she woke to a bluish light that told her snow had fallen. A few thick flakes still whirled past her bedroom window and, when she looked out, the garden was lost under a shining blanket. She got out of bed blessing the day on which she'd installed central heating, and went downstairs to open the drawing-room curtains.

Pale sunlight gleamed on the wildflower meadow, where the snow was stippled by robins' feet and the broad, heavy pawmarks of a hare. Marguerite remembered standing at the French doors as a child, in slippers and wearing a thick dressing-gown. In those days, a night of snow brought what Mrs Sinnott called 'frost ferns', delicate fernlike patterns made on window glass by frozen condensation. If you heated a thimble at a flame and pressed the metal on the icy glass, you could add circles to the complex fractal patterns, and each dot became a peephole to the garden outside. That particular joy had been lost with the installation of Marguerite's central heating, but the memory of it still made her smile. She was wondering how many years had passed since she'd felt the warmth of the heated thimble on her cold finger, when her phone rang and she saw the call was from Val.

At first, she hardly recognised the agitated voice. 'Mum! I know it's silly to call, because there's nothing you can do, but I'm so worried. It's Penny. I've been texting and phoning, and yesterday I even went over and knocked on her door, but she just won't answer. I don't know what's happened, or what to do next, and Christmas is coming, and you're due tomorrow ...' Close to tears, Val blew her nose, and continued, 'I couldn't believe the state she was in. And I can't understand it. I mean, she'd been in such good form on the phone, and she'd asked me to lunch, and it was all fine, and then, truly, Mum, she slammed the door in my face.'

'Darling, calm down. Begin at the beginning.'

'And with the baby due soon, and Christmas, it's been such a shock.'

'I can hear that. Are you sitting down? Tell me what's happened.'

'That's the point. I don't *know* what's happened. Everything was fine and now it's not.'

It took several minutes for Marguerite to make sense of Val's story. 'And you say you've no idea why Penny was crying?'

'None. She wouldn't talk. I've spent the week getting more and more worried. And tomorrow is Christmas Eve, and I've bought no food and made no preparations ...'

As Val's voice became panicky, Marguerite felt her own sense of calm strengthen. Having come to believe that a wrong word might destroy her fragile mother, her instinct in moments of emotional crisis had always been to retreat. Now she was overcome by a fierce surge of energy. Enough is enough, she thought. Perhaps it's true that one can't help if one doesn't know what's wrong but, this time, I won't tell myself I mustn't interfere. As she cast around for what to do, she saw her finished patchwork and, driven by an impulse she couldn't explain, heard herself bark at Val, like a sergeant major, 'Have you finished your side of the quilt?'

'What?'

'Your side of the keepsake quilt. Have you done it?'

'No.' Val sounded injured. 'Mum, didn't you hear what I said?'

'Of course I heard. Leave Penny to me. I'll go straight to her flat from the airport.'

'But she won't let you in.'

'Yes, she will. I'm going to fix this. I'll call you tomorrow when I've spoken to Penny. Don't argue, Val, and don't try to contact her again. Just make yourself a pot of coffee and get on with your piecing.'

When Marguerite arrived at the street door, Penny was slumped on a sofa. She tried to ignore the sound of the doorbell but Marguerite kept pressing it so, in the end, Penny went and peered cautiously out of the window. Aware of movement above her, Marguerite looked up and made an imperious gesture. With a sigh, Penny trailed across the room and pressed the button to release the street door. Then she went back and slumped again on the sofa, a woebegone figure in a tracksuit with its hood pulled up.

Marguerite came in, noting the sad state of the flat, which matched Penny's bleak appearance. Outside, the market was in full Christmas Eve swing, but here there wasn't so much as a sprig of holly and, downstairs in the lobby, cards lay where they had fallen when pushed through the letterbox. Though her heart went out to Penny, Marguerite was determined to pull no punches. 'Well, at least you opened the door to me, which is more than you did for your mum.' Penny said nothing. Stanley, who'd been stalking around the coffee table, came and jumped on Marguerite's lap.

There was a long pause filled by the sound of a Salvation Army band playing carols in the street below. Then Penny asked if Val was okay. Marguerite eyed her severely. 'There's an easy way to find out. You can pick up the phone and talk to her.'

'I know. I should. But I just can't face her. I wouldn't know what to say.' Penny's lower lip wobbled. 'Oh, Gran, I've made such an absolute mess of everything.'

'Everything?'

'Every damn thing.'

'That seems unlikely.'

'But it's true. I got pregnant, which was totally irresponsible. The man was my employee, and I made all the running, which was so unprofessional that it's practically off the scale. Not just that, but he's married with three kids. I don't know what I was thinking, and I've no excuse whatsoever. I'm supposed to be this big-shot, razor-sharp executive, and I've messed up every step of the way.'

Overwhelmed by the sudden flood of information, Marguerite said the first thing that came into her head. 'What do you mean you're supposed to be a big-shot executive?'

'What I said. It's my job. It's who I am.'

This, at least, was something Marguerite felt she could deal with. 'That's nonsense. A job isn't who you are, it's what you do.'

'And *look* what I've done! Spent months misjudging every situation, thinking I was on top of it all when, in fact, I hadn't a clue.' Penny hunched her shoulders and looked at her miserably. 'Plus I've been a cow to you and Mum.'

'You don't think we bear any blame in this situation?'

'Of course not. Why should you?'

Since she'd found the letter in Ruth's quilt, Marguerite had done a lot of thinking, and her phone conversation with Val had brought those thoughts into focus. With no hesitation, she looked Penny in the eye. 'You're wrong about that. I never interfered in your mum's life, and she took the same approach when she raised you. For different reasons, perhaps, but it's come down to the same thing. This family has always valued reticence too highly. We're part of the same fabric, Penny. Our lives are woven together and we have to accept that. Nothing and no one exists in isolation. That's the nature of life.' Marguerite folded her hands in her lap. 'So, I'm here to interfere.' Automatically, Penny's brain added a hashtag. #HereToInterfere. Marguerite looked at her squarely again. 'It's too late to change the past, but we owe it to your baby to change the future. That means we have to change old, destructive patterns.'

Penny sat forward, pushing back her hood. 'Okay, this is weird. You've pretty much quoted Kit.'

'Who's Kit?'

'Mark's niece. Fifteen going on fifty, and a big climate activist. Mark's the guy with the shop downstairs. He says Kit's educating him.'

Stanley rolled over on Marguerite's knee, and she scratched him under the chin. 'Mark sounds like a sensible man, and any gardener will tell you Kit's right. The trouble is that no one listens to gardeners or grandmothers. I think it's time we made our voices heard.'

Penny gave her a tremulous grin. 'What about great-grandmothers?'

'Us too.' Marguerite was about to expand on this when the doorbell rang. Penny went to look at the screen. 'It's Mark.'

'Let him in.'

'But you're here, and I'm a mess and, Gran, it's really complicated. I need to deal with one thing at a time.'

'It's Christmas Eve and your neighbour is at your door. Let him in.' Unaccustomed to taking instructions, and feeling she needed time to think before facing Mark, Penny bristled. Then, with a shrug, she did as she was told. Moments later, Mark came up, carrying one of Kit and Aaron's painted branches, secured in a large terracotta pot. He manoeuvred it through the door and set it down before realising Penny had company. Penny was doing her best to appear in control of the situation. 'Hi, Mark, this is Marguerite Carson. My gran.'

'Hi, Mrs Carson. Sorry to turn up unannounced, Pen. Charlie had one of these left, so he asked me to give it to you. He's sold the rest, and the kids told him you'd helped out with the pine cones.'

'But I didn't.'

'Well, you cheered me on from the sidelines. That was a help.' Mark lifted the pot and positioned it in a corner. The branch had been painted in two halves, one silver, the other multicoloured. He turned to Penny. 'How's that for an alternative Christmas tree? Silver branches, all urban and cool against your exposed brickwork, stripy ones looking good against your white cupboard doors.' He considered it, then readjusted the placement. 'You want it looking balanced. There you go.'

Marguerite had been watching this scene with interest and, as Mark stepped back, she gave him a warm smile. 'That's really effective.'

'Isn't it? It was supposed to be all the colours of the rainbow, but the paint ran out so the kids improvised. But, look, I'm interrupting you. I'll see myself out, Pen.'

Marguerite stood up decisively, tipping Stanley onto the floor. 'No, don't go. I should be leaving. I've left my case at the station and my daughter's expecting me.' Casting another glance at the tree, she took hold of Penny's shoulders. 'So, here's what we're going to do, Penny. No argument. Your mum and I will come and have Christmas lunch with you tomorrow. Let's say two o'clock. We'll take a cab.'

'But all the restaurants will be booked to the rafters.'

'I meant here at the flat. Is that a problem?'

'No. Well, no, but I've got no food in …'

'Nor has your mum. She wasn't sure whether or not to expect you, and it's not really fair, is it, to expect her to rush about on Christmas Eve? You have the market across the road, so I'm sure you can rustle up something.' Amazed at her own assertiveness, Marguerite turned to Mark who was making himself inconspicuous in the background. 'I dare say Mark might stay and give you a hand. If he's not too busy?'

For a moment Mark looked startled, then he gave her a grateful smile. 'Course I will. No problem.'

'Good. That's settled. I'm glad I came by. Lovely to meet you, Mark. Have a good evening, both of you. Pick up that cat, Penny, or he'll follow me down the stairs.' She swept out and, as the door closed behind her, Mark raised his eyebrows at Penny. 'You never told me you had a formidable gran.'

'I'm not sure I knew myself. She isn't usually quite so forceful.' Penny, who had obediently picked up Stanley, dropped him on the sofa and sat down. 'I can't believe I'm supposed to produce a full Christmas lunch by this time tomorrow.'

'Don't fuss. We can make a list and, like your gran said, the market's just over the road.'

Penny looked at him apologetically. 'I got your texts during the week. Sorry I didn't reply.'

'That's okay. I gathered something heavy was going on.'

'Yeah, well, I should have got back when you'd taken the trouble to text. If it's any consolation, you were treated exactly like family. I was just as inconsiderate to Mum and Gran.'

Mark sat down beside her and tickled Stanley behind the ears. 'I told you ages ago, I'm used to grumpy pregnant women. Do I take it that whatever was wrong is okay now?'

Penny groaned. 'I don't know. I'm not sure of anything these days. And there's going to be so much to get my head around when the baby's born. All I've managed to do this month is buy a pushchair. Thanks for adjusting the hooks in the lobby to take it, by the way.'

'You're welcome. And you'll be fine. You've got this, Penny.'

'That's what I tell myself, but the list of things to panic about keeps getting longer. How to make this place baby-friendly, for starters. And childcare. And, oh, I don't know, gripe water.'

'Gripe water?'

'Don't laugh at me. Gripe water's a thing.' Penny pushed her hand through her hair, which hadn't been brushed that morning. 'Childcare, and gripe water, and health and safety orders being slapped on my open-tread staircase. Plus I've a feeling that soon I'll be unemployed. Jobs at my pay-grade aren't easy to find and, believe me, the fact that you've got a baby is not considered an asset in TV.'

Mark touched her hand. 'Really, you'll be fine.'

'I guess so.' Remembering the conversation she'd just had

with Marguerite, Penny smiled. 'One thing at least is certain. I won't be facing the future alone.'

Mark drew his hand away abruptly. 'I guess it'll all be easier with the baby's dad on board.'

'No, absolutely not! No, he's out of the picture.' Penny's response was so vehement that Stanley hissed in protest. She grabbed Mark's hand. 'I got him completely wrong. I thought he cared about the baby. And it seemed important that he should be part of his son's life.'

'But he doesn't care?'

'He cares about his career, not this baby.'

'Does he care about you?'

'Oh, yeah, he cares about me. Or he did when he thought I was his ticket to new fame and fortune. But he's found a better route, so that's that.'

'Well, he sounds like a shit.' This was so unambivalent, and so unlike Mark, that it almost made Penny giggle. She pushed her hand through her hair again and looked at him ruefully. 'There wasn't an ounce of caring involved on either side, to be honest. Just me wanting something because it was there and I had the power to take it. He's a shit, but the fact is, I'm to blame.'

'Kit says indulgence in guilt and blame is an inexcusable waste of energy.'

Penny stared at the Christmas tree in the corner. 'I think my gran would agree.'

With a deep breath, Mark stood up and looked down at her. 'So. If not now, when?'

'Sorry?'

'That's another of Kit's slogans. Aaron has a plan to print it on T-shirts.'

'They don't waste time, those kids.'

'No one should, Penny. You and I shouldn't. It's later than we think.' Mark waited, telling himself that the next move had to be hers, but Penny appeared so deep in thought that he wondered if she'd heard him, or had understood what he was trying to say. When she made no reply, he held out his hands to haul her off the sofa. 'Come on, we've got Christmas to buy before the market closes. Half the stalls are already sold out so we may have to be creative, but we'll manage. And we can wheel it all across the road in that swish pushchair you've bought.'

THE QUILT

Chapter Thirty-Seven

On Christmas morning, Val woke to find Marguerite by her bedside. Sitting up, she rubbed her eyes and accepted the tea she was offered. 'Gosh, I slept like a log. What time is it?'

'Half ten. I didn't want to wake you sooner. You've had a tiring week, and we were quilting till all hours.'

Marguerite sat on the foot of the bed and Val sighed luxuriously. 'I don't think I've had morning tea in bed since Penny left home – and not often when she was here. Life was far too busy.'

'Well, enjoy your tea, have a bath, and I'll make us breakfast.'

'When are we due at Penny's?'

'There's plenty of time. What are you going to wear?'

Setting down her cup, Val slipped out of bed and went to her wardrobe. 'I was going to splash out on an outfit, but when things went wrong, it felt like there wasn't much point. Will this do?' She took out a hanger and showed Marguerite a dress. 'I love the combination of cerise and navy blue.'

'It's perfect.'

'Did you buy something new?'

'A scarf.'

'Oh, Mum!'

'Wait till you see it. It's paisley-patterned cashmere. Turquoise and orange and emerald green. I adore it.'

'We're going to look like a pair of peacocks.'

'Good for us.' Marguerite felt the fabric of Val's dress. 'I do like challis. It hangs so well, and this bias-cut skirt is lovely. Look, you have your bath. I'm going to make scones for breakfast. I brought you a jar of blackcurrant jam from Stonehill.'

They ate wearing their dressing-gowns, with Christmas music on the radio and the smell of hot scones filling the kitchen. Outside, there was no sign of snow. The day was bright and cold, and Val put crumbs on the windowsill for the birds. Pouring herself a second coffee, she looked across at Marguerite anxiously. 'You're really sure Penny's okay with us having lunch at the flat?'

Mentally crossing her fingers, Marguerite fibbed, 'Of course I am. She invited us.'

'I bet she didn't. I can hardly believe she even let you in.'

'If you want the truth, I simply leaned on the doorbell until she did.'

'I've never got things right with Penny, have I? I hover when I shouldn't, and back off when I ought to take a stance.'

'Oh, for Heaven's sake, Val!' Marguerite set down her coffee cup. 'You may not have been a perfect mother but you're not alone in that. Everyone gets things wrong. There's no shame in it. Whatever mistakes you think you've made, you're going to have to forgive yourself and stop wallowing in the past.'

Val's troubled look turned to amusement. 'If you went for Penny like that, I can see how you got her to snap to attention.' She cut a scone in half and reached for the butter. 'You know, the first time I met Simon, we spent hours discussing forgiveness.' This sounded most unlike the Simon Marguerite had known and, seeing her look of surprise, Val explained, 'I mean we argued about *Cymbeline.*'

'The play? I've never seen it.'

'It was stitched together from bits by other writers as well as Shakespeare.' Automatically, Val switched into her teaching persona. 'It's part tragedy, part comedy, actually kind of a romance. And the plot's got everything bar the kitchen sink. Characters who don't know who they are, cross-dressing, a faithful wife, an anguished husband, and poison that turns out to be just a sleeping-potion. It doesn't get done much, and it's a hell of a text to teach.'

'Why do people bother?'

'I suppose because Shakespeare counts as a finite source. Masses of what he wrote must have been lost over time, so even tags and scraps of him shouldn't be wasted.'

'And is it about forgiveness?'

'It's about how forgiveness reunites troubled families. Simon insisted it wasn't, but he was just showing off.'

Val looked up from the scone onto which she'd been spooning blackcurrant jam. 'You know, I once told Donal I couldn't forgive poor Simon for dying.'

'What did he say?'

'He just sort of cut the conversation off.'

Of course he did, thought Marguerite. No one could have empathised more with that sense of being abandoned, but

Donal wouldn't have known how to say so. I wish things had been different. If he'd shared his feelings, it wouldn't have been a betrayal of Ruth, and it might have done so much to help Val. Still, he gave what he could, and there's no point in demanding more than that from anyone. It's a waste of time.

Standing up, Marguerite began to gather the dishes, thinking that grief and anger were two sides of the same coin. I can't see this family abandoning all our ingrained habits, she thought, but if the future is going to involve a lot more talking, today's lunch is a good starting point. Dumping the dishes in the sink, she turned to Val and smiled. 'Let's leave all this and go and put on our glad rags. I told Penny we'd be there at two.'

Penny opened the door wearing the yellow silk jacket and, between Christmas greetings and exclamations about its embroidery, they avoided the initial awkwardness Marguerite had feared.

'Happy Christmas!'

'Did your cab come on time?'

'Darling, what a wonderful garment! That yellow is practically gold!' The flat looked splendid too. Holly wreaths hung at the windows, and a garland of ivy, apple-rings, and clove-studded tangerines decorated the brushed-steel banister. Penny said the hauri jacket was the only festive thing she had that still fitted her. 'And what do you think of my decorations? When we'd bought food, Mark and I descended on Charlie's flower stall.' There were pots of white cyclamen on the table, candles stuck in saucers filled with walnuts and gilded almonds, and a forest of shortbread Christmas trees dusted with icing sugar. The alternative tree in the corner was hung with star anise and cinnamon sticks, and each of the table settings included a large chocolate reindeer.

Penny grinned. 'It's way over the top, I know. The reindeer were Mark's idea. He says if we don't want them, he'll reclaim them for the kids.' Val and Marguerite studiously avoided each other's eyes and, having heard herself mention Mark twice in well under a minute, Penny clammed up and went to the fridge.

Val sat down on a sofa. 'It's lovely to be here but I'm sorry you had to cater at such short notice.' Penny, who had returned with a bottle of champagne, looked sheepish. 'Well, we both know whose fault that was, don't we?' As she bent to hand Val a glass, Penny gave her a kiss on the cheek. 'Anyway, doing a last-minute shop was fun. Admittedly, we've ended up with an esoteric menu. No sprouts, but then I'm not sure they'd go with the shiitake mushrooms. Stripy ice cream and Turkish delight for pudding. And game pie, because the turkeys were all sold out. It's slightly knocked about, which was why it hadn't gone, but I've added a flourish of watercress.' Handing Marguerite her wine, Penny sat down with a glass of elderflower cordial. 'Your presents are a bit hit and miss too, but I hope you'll like them.'

'I'm sure they'll be super. We have one we've made for you and the baby.' The previous night, holding their breath and sitting at Val's kitchen table, she and Val had laid the two sides of the keepsake quilt together. Despite the emails sent to and fro, and the care they'd taken, there'd always been a chance that they might not produce a perfect match. But the measurements had been accurate. Quilted together with the lightweight batting between them, their work had made a charming cot-cover of multicoloured squares edged with the needlecord Val had found when she'd turned out her ragbag. After midnight, when the last stitch had been set and the final thread snipped, Marguerite had wrapped the quilt in Christmas paper.

Now she sat down and reached into her bag to hand the parcel to Penny but, before she could take it out, the doorbell rang. Val looked disconcerted. 'Are you expecting anyone?'

Penny said she wasn't and went to see who was at the door. 'Oh, it's Mark and the kids.' She let them in, and Mark came upstairs full of apologies.

'I'm sorry, I thought we'd be here and gone before your guests arrived. Aaron and Kit have made you a present, Pen.' Kit held out a parcel. 'We would have come sooner but Gran's having a wobbly about the pudding. This is for you and the baby.'

Penny unwrapped the string of painted pine cones, and took it to the corner to hang on the branch. 'They're really lovely. Thank you. Can you stay for a drink, Mark? Kit, would you like a chocolate reindeer?' Kit sat on the arm of Marguerite's sofa. 'Can Aaron have one too? It'll be ages before anyone feeds us.'

Mark gave her a severe look and smiled at Marguerite. 'My niece and nephew. We don't actually starve them, and their mum would have something to say about their manners.'

Penny laughed. 'Mum, this is Mark from the shop downstairs. This is my mum, Val. Do stay, Mark. Is Sarah okay? How major is the wobbly?'

'Not major at all. Par for the course on Christmas Day. It's far better for us to be here than adding to the drama. As long as you weren't about to sit down and eat?'

Val shook her head. 'Not at all. We've just arrived. I understand you helped Penny rustle up our lunch?'

'I couldn't have done it without him. He fetched and carried.'

'Don't undersell me! I was the one who spotted the slightly knocked-about game pie.'

'I did make you supper after you'd put the wreaths up.' Penny turned to Marguerite. 'Look, now that he's here, I think I should tell you. Last night, Mark and I got talking. We've said we might start an enterprise together.' Avoiding each other's eyes once again, Marguerite and Val registered interest. Penny sat down next to Val. 'I've been thinking I might not go back to work after I have the baby. Back to the show, I mean. Well, actually, I might move on from TV.'

Kit, who was eating a chocolate reindeer, looked at her curiously. 'What would you move to?'

'A different platform. Perhaps a YouTube channel. Maybe something newer than that. Something that's not owned by billionaires and isn't funded by ads selling people stuff they don't want or need.' Penny turned to Marguerite. 'I've had coffee a couple of times with one of the guests I had on my show. She runs a thing called *It Takes a Village*. We talked at my leaving party and, though I didn't see it at the time, she gave me the germ of an idea.'

'Where does Mark come in?'

'He'd be moving on as well. Keeping the shop, of course, but diversifying.'

'Into what?'

Mark exchanged glances with Penny. 'We haven't decided yet. Online sales. Upcycling tutorials. Maybe a restoration and repair service. A format that expands conventional models. That would be Penny's bit. The idea is to dovetail our expertise. She's got production and broadcast knowledge, and I'm the grandson of a rag-and-bone man. It's a match made in Heaven.'

Kit licked chocolate off her fingers. 'So, what's your ethic?

'That's where you come in. We wondered if you'd consider being our consultant.'

'Seriously?'

Penny nodded. 'Absolutely. If you're up for it. In your spare time now, but maybe properly when you leave school.'

'Okay. Cool.' As Kit spoke, her phone bleeped and she fished it out of her pocket. 'Looks like the pudding wobbly's over. Gran has "I Have A Dream" blaring at a million decibels, Dad's arrived with the starters, and the aunties are dishing up. We'd best get back.' Slipping off the sofa, she addressed Val and Marguerite. 'Nice to meet you. Thanks for the reindeer, Penny.'

When Mark and the kids left, the others sat down to eat. Afterwards, when they were back on the sofas eating gilded almonds, Marguerite gave Penny the keepsake quilt. At first, she joined in the conversation as Val explained it to Penny, and all three turned it over and back. Then, as Penny switched on a lamp by the sofa, Marguerite moved to stand at the window and, looking down at the closed market, saw frost sparkle on the iron lace that edged its canopy. In the room, where a pool of light fell on the sofa, reminiscences rose, fell, and mingled. 'That's the chambray I used for your dungarees. Do you remember ...?'

'God, I was foul about them, wasn't I? What's this gingham ...?'

'The cheesecloth's from your gran's wedding dress ...'

'... oh, Mum! That blue terry-towelling! From the summer that Uncle Rory taught me to swim on that stony Wicklow beach! And, look, I love this retro satin bit in the middle of Gran's side. And that piece from my awful Lurex boob tube. And the poplin with the pattern of little cows from the dress Gran made me! And the rose-coloured glazed cotton. And this smoky grey chiffon. Wait, where did the edging come from? Oh, my God, it's the fabric you used for Leo the lion's coat!'

'Do you like the batik elephants? They began life as part of the border of one of your gran's dresses, and she cut them out to sew on the back of a jacket I had in my teens.'

'That's amazing.'

'The centrepiece on your gran's side came from a quilt made by your great-granny Ruth.' Val turned the quilt over. 'And the grey chiffon is part of the dress I was wearing on the night I met your dad.'

'What's the yellow square?'

'That's from a baby-shawl I made when I was pregnant with you.'

'Mum, I love it all.' Penny put her hand on her bump. 'Donal will too.'

'Donal?'

'Donal Paul. Are you okay with that?'

'Darling, it's your decision.'

'I know, but I want you to be pleased.'

'Of course I am.'

you're glad about my plan to leave the show?'

it it's what you want. I'm glad you met Mark.' Val shot an it-sounds-wonderful glance at Marguerite and, smoothing the quilt across her knees, smiled at Penny. 'Darling, I've got news too. I've been trying to make up my mind about a promotion I've been offered.'

'At work?'

'Yes. Well, it's more like an expansion of my role. Anyway, it's going to mean foreign travel.'

'Mum, that's amazing! Have you decided to take it?'

'I hadn't until today. But, yes, I'm going to go for it.'

Standing by the window, Marguerite remembered Val's voice the previous night, half lost in the whirring of her sewing-machine, telling the story of how she'd found and lost Balan. 'It mightn't have worked, of course, but I'll always wonder if it could have. Imagine how different things would have been if I'd swept Penny off to Chennai.'

Life's full of choices, thought Marguerite, her eyes on the two heads bent over the keepsake quilt. If the pieces of Val's life had been arranged differently, Penny might have been raised in Chennai. And each choice implies another. If Ruth's choice had been different, I could have been born in Paris. I wouldn't have met Paul, and had Val and Rory, and Penny wouldn't have been born, let alone have found Mark. As she watched glimmering Christmas lights reflected in ice-rimed iron, Marguerite thought of how, as she packed her suitcase, she'd considered bringing the letter with her to London. But then she'd thought that the incomplete story with all its unanswered questions wasn't really hers to share. So, she'd taken the page and, looking up at Ruth's portrait, dropped Justin's imperious summons into the drawing-room fire. As the flames leaped up, the words *I love the bones of you* had stood out for a few seconds. Then the page had curled and dropped away to blue-black ashes and, in her mind's eye, she'd seen Donal's approving smile.

Val's voice reached Marguerite from the soft pool of lamplight falling on Penny's immaculate white sofa. 'I wasn't sure you'd like the quilt. All this chaotic colour doesn't seem to fit in your flat.'

'I know. But I do like it. Thank you.' Penny's voice quivered. 'Look, Mum, I'm sorry I've been all over the place right through this pregnancy. I've been trying to get my head around the future. Well, the past too, I suppose.'

'You don't need to apologise.'

'I think I do.'

Marguerite smiled, remembering that when Aaron had reached the door, he'd turned back and eyed Mark critically. 'How come you don't have a present for Penny?'

'I have, but it's a chaise longue. Not easy to get up those stairs, so, I thought I should check first that Penny wants it.' His eyes had flicked sideways and met Penny's. 'There's nothing worse than something unwanted cluttering up your life.'

Aaron frowned. 'It sounds kind of cool. Why wouldn't she want it?'

'It won't go with her décor.'

'In that case, it sounds like you made a weird choice.' Aaron's voice had been scathing, but Penny had taken Mark's hand. 'Actually, it sounds wonderful. It's taken far too long

scover that what I've always wanted has been just
stairs.'

'Truly, Penny?' The expression in Mark's eyes had made Val
and Marguerite exchange delighted glances, and Penny had
smiled back at him, more relaxed than Marguerite had ever seen
her. 'Truly, Mark. It's perfect. Edwardian rococo. Rolled back,
claw-and-ball feet, brass pins, and crimson velvet upholstery.
We'll get it up here even if it has to come in through the kitchen
window, like Stanley the cat who knows no borders. I'll recline
on it in my silk jacket, with a muslin square on my shoulder,
and you, me and the baby will make plans to change the world.'

Now, standing by the window, Marguerite heaved a sigh of
contentment. On chilly nights, she thought, or when little Donal
wants a bedtime story, the crimson velvet, yellow silk, and that
practical square of muslin will be perfectly in keeping with the
keepsake quilt.

Acknowledgements

My mother was an accomplished needlewoman and I grew up in a household largely focused on art and design. For much of my childhood, my father was working on a history of flags, so our home was full of images of frayed fabric, tarnished gilt embellishment, and gorgeously painted coats of arms. As the youngest of five siblings, I remember hand-me-downs, dresses revived with ric-rac and embroidery, and a jacket inherited from a stylish aunt. The sister with whom I shared a bedroom taught me art at school before going on to become a textile designer. And the first skirt I made for myself was to a pattern cut by one of my brothers, who was studying architecture at the time, and made his own suits. So, my greatest debt is due to my family – but particularly to my mother, who left me a collection of her needlework, and of table-linen worked by my grandmother's cousins.

Inspiration for *The Keepsake Quilters* came from many sources and memories. I first discovered Hampstead Heath, Borough Market, and Biba in Kensington High Street when I explored London as a student, and Mark's granddad emerged from

355

...ions of a rag-and-bone man who used to work ...nham's streets forty years ago. In some instances, it was ...case of my memory being jogged, for which I'm immensely grateful. Geraldine McGlynn of Golden Ireland introduced me to Cork's Crawford Gallery, where curator Michael Waldron drew me back to the work of pre- and post-Second World War Irish artists, which sparked the idea of Ruth's portrait and offered me her storyline. The book's characters, their homes and workplaces, are imaginary, but I wouldn't have conceived of Penny's story if much of my own career hadn't been in television, where I learned from professionals to whom I'm thankful: you're too many to name, but you know who you are. Unlike Val, I didn't come upon *Cymbeline* at college, but at drama school where, with friends who've since become household names, I spent long hours dissecting Shakespeare. You too know who you are, and which of us thought that, all these years later, so much late-night discussion would be repurposed in a novel?

Huge thanks are due to my brother-in-law, Seán O'Leary, artist and student of genealogy, who produced the family tree that appears at the front of the book, and made many helpful comments while I was writing. Also to Maev, and to Dan and Monica, who provided distraction, encouragement and white wine.

Inspiration also came from people I've never met. Kit and Aaron's characters, and the book's underlying focus on sustainability, owe much to Greta Thunberg and the schoolchildren across the world who have joined her *Skolstrejk* for climate-change mitigation, whose voices came to me via the internet. I'm grateful too for a tweet that provided a link between Simon's drowning and Drake's exciting, exploitative voyages: I wish I could recall who tweeted it, but all I know is that it came from someone at Southwark Cathedral who'd noticed a green shoot from the oak being used to patch the *Golden Hinde* replica, and saw in it an image of hope and rebirth.

Sometimes a point occurs in the writing process when the outside world throws up unexpected resonances with your book. Often it happens in the final stretch when, mentally and physically, you're flagging. As I was reaching the end of *The Keepsake Quilters*, I visited Ireland's National Gallery to see an exhibition of paintings by Jack B. Yeats. I'd already completed the chapter in which Eve says Justin MacMahon had studied with him briefly, indicating that, unlike Ruth's other bohemians, Justin had had the talent to be a world-class painter. On the wall of the exhibition, I found this quotation from Jack B. Yeats. *No one creates. The artist assembles memories*. On another occasion, an exhibition at London's Somerset House, featuring works by Alberta Whittle, Allora & Calzadilla, Carolina Caycedo, Louis Henderson, Malala Andrialavidrazana, Mazenett Quiroga, Otobong Nkanga, Zineb Sedira and Shiraz Bayjoo, chimed equally well with themes I'd been exploring. I left both galleries full of renewed energy, a gift I'd like to acknowledge here.

To return to the practical world of the living, I'm grateful, as always, to Joanna Smyth, Ruth Shern, Elaine Egan, and everyone else on Breda Purdue's brilliant team at Hachette Books Ireland, and to Hazel Orme, my meticulous copy-editor, and wonderful Mark Walsh at Plunkett PR. I'm especially thankful to Ciara Doorley, my editor at Hachette, who responded with such

...ate warmth when I came to her with the idea for *The ...psake Quilters* and always steers my work with assurance and the lightest touch.

Finally, as ever, love and thanks go to my husband, Wilf Judd, for his eagle eye as a reader and his unfailing patience and help; and, at Sheil Land Associates, UK, to Alba Arnau and to my stellar agent, Gaia Banks, whose interest in, and care for, this book in all its stages of development have added greatly to the joy of writing it.